I0563662

THE STREET OF MANY ARCHES

The houses of the women on either side of the street were built between great arches of rock.

THE STREET
OF MANY ARCHES

BY

JOAN CONQUEST

AUTHOR OF "DESERT LOVE," "THE HAWK OF EGYPT"

In collaboration with
GWEN LALLY

NEW YORK
THE MACAULAY COMPANY

COPYRIGHT, 1924, BY
THE MACAULAY COMPANY

PRINTED IN THE UNITED STATES OF AMERICA

TO
THE HAPPY HOURS
WE SPENT IN COLLABORATION

THE STREET OF MANY ARCHES

THE STREET OF
MANY ARCHES

CHAPTER I

"KHA'TSUM! *Kha'tsum!*"

The warning sound blended with the evil atmosphere which seemed to spread from one end to the other of the narrow street. It fell on the foul air like a wisp of the fog which had crept up from the Thames, blurring and grotesquely twisting the outlines of houses and chimneys, drawing a nimbus from the streaks of orange light which struck like knives between the slats of dilapidated blinds and ragged curtains.

The sound came from the shadows, black as pitch, which marked the meeting of two streets, stayed upon the air for a fraction of time, sinister, foreboding, then dropped into the silence.

A child's piercing, agonized scream rent the stillness of the night; came a crash of breaking glass, voices raised in violent anger, a woman's cry, the dull slam of a door.

Silence.

Then, up the evil street the tap-tip-tap of heels, muffled by the mud upon the pavement.

Youth, walking joyfully, buoyantly; heedless, light-hearted; innocence serene, secure in its ignorance of evil; a girl, alone, unafraid in the shadows of a Limehouse street.

An orange streak of light flared from between two curtains, pushed aside for an instant by some unseen hand; in the glare of light the edge of the pitch-black shadows seemed to move, just where the two streets met, and once again a sinister, foreboding whisper fell like a sigh upon the air.

"*U'ip! U'ip!*"

Dull, expressionless, slanting, Oriental eyes watched the fog from the shadows, twisting and writhing under the breath of wind which blew up from the river. Those cunning, inexpressibly evil eyes watched what appeared to be the fog, but what in reality was Fate who stood across the path, somber, grim, in raiment torn to tatters by the clutching of despairing fingers in the passing of Time.

Fate stretched out her withered arm within which she holds the good, the bad, the beginning and the end of every life, and stayed the girl as she stood upon the very edge of the abyss. Stayed her to bend and tighten a shoe-lace, which was the string by which she was hobbled to her destiny, so that, as it shot out from the shadows, the mutilated hand, minus thumb and little finger, with the three, long, middle fingers outstretched like the claws of some great, evil bird to clutch its prey, merely brushed the girl's shoulder as she stooped to readjust her shoe-lace.

Then Limehouse woke as the girl screamed and screamed again as she beat upon the mutilated hand that held her skirt, and, screaming, turned and beat upon another evil, yellow face which pressed so near her own.

"Help! Help! Help!"

She fought desperately, blindly, madly, for more than life, and tearing herself free, rushed screaming down the street, bare feet padding noiselessly in the mud behind her.

Every window crashed wide open to show a head or many heads, each surrounded by a halo of orange, glaring light. Every door opened as men, women, children, white, yellow, half-caste, tumbled into the street to start in blind pursuit of those screams which grew fainter every moment in the distance.

Screams, oaths, brawls, fights, are part and parcel of

Limehouse life; the inhabitants take but little notice of the noise and mix themselves but rarely in their neighbors' quarrels; but this was a night when all souls, white or yellow, honest or dishonest, should have been within four walls, sheltered from the fog which blew up from the Thames. Yet the voice that screamed so horribly was the voice of a girl, and a white girl, and there was but one interpretation to be put upon a white girl screaming in just that one way, in the night, in Chinatown.

"My Gawd! them blasted Chinks er after a white girl!" shouted a woman to a man, making a trumpet of her hands.

"No more a blasted Chink than one of yer dirty English loafers," savagely retorted a huge woman with four half-caste children clinging to her dragging skirt.

Like jungle animals the two women made a sudden, ugly rush, eyes glaring, arms bared.

"Come orf it, mother, it's nuffink to do wiv you!"

A good-tempered-looking man stepped quickly between the women and caught the first speaker by the wrist, just as an immense Chinaman seized the woman with the half-caste children and flung her, without a word, into a doorway and slammed the door.

Tragedy is everyday fare in the slums; it is the dough with which the daily bread of the East End is kneaded.

"Glad she's stopped 'er 'ollerin'. 'Eaven knows we don't want the cops down this way."

*   *   *

The tenement-house towards which the girl ran, pursued by her terrible fear, loomed large and black ahead of her.

A blot upon civilization, a foul spot upon a great city's fair fame, it stood like a prison-house in which must languish and die all that makes life pure and beautiful and holy.

Like a rat warren on a river bank it stood, infested with

vice, windows blinded, doors gaping, courtyard, balconies, rickety wooden stair-rails fluttering with the grimy, half-washed rags of the alien crowd that lived, cheek by jowl, packed together within.

The girl ran blindly, eyes half closed in agony, heart thudding from the pace. The sickening fear of years had suddenly materialized when the mutilated hand clutched her skirt, the yellow face pressed so close, the bare feet padded behind her in the mud.

Fear intensified the sound of those padding feet. Horror kept her face turned to the tenement-house which loomed ahead at the bottom of just one more street, whereas, if she had but looked over her shoulder, she would have seen friendly faces amongst the crowd which ran almost at her heels; heard friendly words shouted to her; felt friendly hands stretched out to help her in her need.

At the top of the tenement-house was refuge, safety, love; up flights of greasy, wooden stairs, past doors which, shut, hid the kennels in which the foreign people lived, or, open, shamelessly exposed the way the human exists when housed like a low-caste dog. Near the roof waited love, radiant, pure; down in the basement lay fidelity, speechless, stricken, but proven through the years. Therefore was the shameless house of vice and horrors unspeakable as a haven of refuge to the girl, a corner of paradise in the midst of the hell of fear which had suddenly sprung upon her from the shadows.

Because she ran, the crowd pursued.

The lure of tragedy, drama, horror, death, drew it through the streets. Big, wide-open, English eyes peered to right and left to find the cause which had drawn those piercing screams from the girl so loved, so respected in the whole of Chinatown; big oaths mingled with the fog; big, brawny hands clenched and unclenched whilst the owners called upon their God to witness what they would do if they could but lay them upon the Chinks.

"Mother of Gawd!" cried Liza Rodd, when the girl tripped over the filthy doorstep and crashed full length upon the ground. "Stop a minit! Ye're nigh dead!—a drop of gin afore them stairs!" She stared after the girl who, choking horribly as she tried to speak, half crawled, half walked, bent double, up the stairs, clinging to the rotting, wooden rail. "What d'yer think yer doin', untin' that there girl through the streets, at this time o' night? Some beastly——"

"It wus a Chink tryin' to get 'er; I saw two of 'em. Two of 'em, damn their yeller skins!" piped an urchin of eight summers with gentian-blue eyes and yellow, curling hair, as he added his quota to the dirt by spitting his disgust upon the step.

"A Chink after 'er——"

"It wus the girl the Chinks 'ave nicknamed the White Rose 'cos of that there scar on 'er arm, weren't it?"

Liza Rodd retired to the den which she called home and reappeared with a bucket containing the water with which she had washed her floor the day before.

"Clear out," she said truculently. "We've enough of them damned furrin vermin already in our 'appy 'ome. I'll slosh the water in them blinkin' yeller faces if they stands in front of my 'ouse another bloomin' minute. Clear out to yer own Chineytown, you 'ear? Clear out, damn yer! I'm goin' to lend an 'and to the White Rose."

Lotah, the girl whom the Chinese had nicknamed the White Rose, lay sobbing upon the heart of the man she loved.

"I didn't know I should be kept so late, beloved. I—I didn't dream that I should be in danger. What are you going to do?"

Rex Power kissed the beautiful, crimson mouth and he crossed to a writing-table, disguising the terror that suddenly held him in its grip. "I'm only going to write to

John Trevor, sweetheart, to ask him to come and see us, just to see the picture."

*   *   *

"She is shamming!"

"Nay, they say she is stricken in limb and speech!"

The two half-caste Tibetans stood looking down at the old woman of their father's race who lay motionless upon the bed in the basement. The night was old and very still; their bare feet had made no sound as they had slipped through the doorway of the tenement-house and down the wooden, rotting stairs.

Chang-ku, the Gray Wolf, drew a heavy clasp-knife from his pocket.

" 'Tis but a tale, Brother! She could speak if she wanted to, and could tell us when to find the girl *alone*."

He drove the point of the knife into the emaciated wrist lying outside the coverlet.

Tsi-tsi, the old Tibetan woman, made no movement; she could not, being paralyzed; she made no sound, being stricken dumb.

She did not open her eyes.

She would not though she could, being faithful unto death where she loved.

Sa-t'ong, the merciless Tiger of Bengal, Chang-ku, the ravening Wolf, paused for a moment before the blackened, broken statue of the dread goddess Paldean-Lha-Mo which stood upon a bracket on the wall.

As a thank-offering for an answer to a prayer made some eighteen years ago Tsi-tsi, the old Tibetan woman, burned a candle, day and night, before the blackened shrine. Her gratitude had burned outwardly in the shape of a candle; inwardly, in the depths of her heart, as a great flame, without having once been extinguished in the passing of the years. It had cost her a small fortune in its material shape; the inward glow of its light had filled her life with a great gladness in the damp, dismal room in the basement she called home.

She raised her eyelids slightly as the brothers paused before the shrine and watched a slender, mutilated hand snuff out the candle-light between the tips of the middle fingers.

A look of understanding and of great fear and of despair shone in her eyes as she lay still in the dark hours of the long night.

She recognized them; by the mutilated hand she recognized the mighty brothers Nyko-Gung.

The secret of Lotah, the White Rose, had been locked forever in her heart since the day she had been knocked down and run over in the Causeway.

Illiterate, she was unable to read or write; paralyzed, unable to speak, to hear, to move, so that the knowledge of the danger which threatened the girl she loved and the girl's husband was shut with the secret in her heart. Terrible danger threatened, and her lips were dumb, her hands useless.

But her heart beat faithfully as she prayed to the blackened and battered image on the wall.

CHAPTER II

"The Yellow Peril in our midst!"

John Trevor shuddered involuntarily as he laid the paper down and looked round the comfortable room with its blazing log fire.

Heavy tapestry curtains shut out the gloom of the November evening; there seemed no disturbing element, no noise nor strife nor danger possible in the vicinity of Cadogan Square, yet John Trevor had shuddered involuntarily.

He sat looking over his shoulder, staring into the shadows, then turned and picked up the paper and glanced again through the paragraph which dealt with cocaine, opium dens, chop-houses, in fact, with the Chinese in general in Limehouse.

"Whatever is the matter with me, solid, stolid, middle-aged, retired architect, as unimaginative as a coping-stone, accustomed to measuring plans, people and problems by the square inch, shivering like a schoolgirl?" He picked up the tongs and moved the logs, then piled them fantastically, to form a sloping roof to whatever he had been trying to build in the fire, and got up. "Ugly-looking beggar," he said aloud to his reflection in the glass as he ran his hand over a shock of brown hair and across a powerful chin. "The eyes are all right, they look thoroughly honest, but *what* an *ensemble*—no wonder that Cecily——" He broke off with an impatient sigh and, with a shrug of the massive shoulders, crossed to a desk and picked up a letter. "I wish I hadn't made my pile quite so easily and so soon. I wish I hadn't retired. I'd give the whole of this house and the

Gables and—oh! everything, to be able to tackle one big, seemingly unsolvable problem and win out." He sat on the edge of the desk staring across at the fire, twisting the letter in his strong hands, then put it in his pocket, rubbed his eyes and stared again at the burning logs. "Good heavens! has a paragraph in an evening paper bewitched me or—— Come in!"

He smiled at the dear old body who stood in the door-way, then crossed to her and arranged the cherry-colored ribbons in the lace cap which almost covered the snow-white hair.

John Trevor turned his old nurse towards the fire and whispered as he pointed.

"What do you see in the fire, Nannie? You with your Celtic blood, what do you see in it?"

Janet Comfort looked for a moment, then backed against the door, a look of fear in her old face.

"Don't, Mr. John, don't! It's just like one of those horrible Chinese temples, and I can't stand anything to do with heathen folk. Ah! there now, the roof has fallen in, and the lay of the logs foretells a long journey and danger for many, and——"

The whole structure which John Trevor had unconsciously built fell in with a crash, sending blue and orange flames flying up the chimney.

"That is just what I am longing for, Nannie, before many more gray hairs show in my thatch. I'm tired of dull respectability. I ache for adventure and hair-breadth escapes——"

"And that's what's coming to you, Mr. John, by the way the flames are flying up the chimney which, by the way, is to be swept to-morrow. I just came in to tidy up a bit."

She rearranged the cushions on the Chesterfield and looked at a picture on the wall as she pretended to straighten it. "I have always felt a kind of pang during all these months, Mr. John, when I look at Mr. Power's chair without him sitting in it, with his long legs stretched out and all the beautiful talk of painting and colors and atmospheres and—and——"

"Temperament," supplied John Trevor.

Nannie nodded. "Where do you think he is, Mr. John? Gone these six months without a word or sign of life."

John Trevor sat forward and stared into the fire, the heavy brows drawn in a frown over the steady gray eyes.

"I feel almost responsible for Mr. Power, Nannie. I'm forty-eight and he's just twenty-seven, without a relation in the world, an artist to his finger-tips, gifted beyond words, impulsive, great-hearted, reckless, optimistic, such a boy, just one of those who will never, *never* grow up."

A little silence fell, broken only by Janet's movements as she walked round the room tidying up innumerable papers.

She stood looking up at the picture she had pretended to straighten on the wall. "Why don't Mr. Power's pictures sell, Mr. John, so that he could move from those two rooms up on the top of the roof?"

"Oh! he loves those rooms, Nannie, and they are so like him."

John Trevor sat silent, thinking of the studio which Rex Power rented in Chelsea. A studio with a view of the sun sinking behind the Thames. A veritable haven of refuge from the fret and turmoil of the world, where he painted pictures in an effort to express the idealism and the beauty of his thoughts, only to stack them in corners and obstinately refuse to sell them.

"I will not paint pot-boilers, and I will not sell my dreams," he would exclaim. "Until I find the girl I am looking for, my Dream Girl, the Lady of my Quest, I will not paint another woman's face."

Janet lifted a brown paper cone and scrutinized a bowl of hyacinth bulbs, then smiled delightedly and carried it across to her master.

"See, Mr. John! a speck of green."

John Trevor followed the point of the steel knitting-needle. "Isn't that just like life, Nannie? A big lump of worry or discomfort buried right in the blackest corner of one's mind, and then one day hope peeps out."

"You're worrying overmuch about Mr. Power's silence, that's what it is, Mr. John. They're writing no end about the pictures of a heathen Chinese just now, whilst Mr. Power's talent seems to be hidden under a bushel."

"Ah! yes, some one called Ling Soo," replied Trevor without a smile at the mixing of the biblical terms. "Lives in Limehouse, paints diminutive pictures of Chinatown, a face, a street, an impression. Awfully clever too they are."

"And Mr. Power was going down that way, to Wapping Old Stairs, when he said good-by six months ago. I can see him and hear him as he stood against the door. He teased me as he always did and said he wanted me to stay and comfort you when the front door banged behind him."

Janet Comfort watched John Trevor as he sat tapping a log gently with the poker, thinking of the last time he had seen the boy he loved so well.

"I have the tastes of an epicure, the purse of a mendicant, and the gift of the old masters, Trevor, old man," Rex Power had said that night, six months before, when he had disappeared for good. "I don't mind selling land-scapes, in fact, I got ten pounds this morning for a corner of Battersea Park, which old Cohen thought represented Japan in springtime; but once more I repeat that until I have found the girl with a soul in her eyes and truth in her smile, who could love, go through hell and worse for that love, fight for that love, endure and suffer and triumph in that love, until then I will not paint any woman's face." He had stood leaning against the door as he had said good-by, handsome, slender, with the eyes of the dreamer and a most unexpected strength somewhere in the mobile, laughing face. "Anyway, I shan't find her to-morrow, because, if the weather holds good, I'm going to Wapping Old Stairs to see if I can catch that amethyst color on the water at noon, which old Browning was raving about, so, so long to you and Mrs. Comfort, and if I don't come back you'll know I've either fallen into the Thames or disrepute."

Janet Comfort touched the ribbons in her cap and sighed as her master laid down the poker. She had sewn them in in the hope that perhaps Rex Power, whom she liked almost as much as she adored her master, might run in at the very last moment, as he had so often done, to fling himself into his favorite armchair and tell them all about his latest adventure.

"Wapping!" she grumbled to herself, standing still to listen to the postman's knock at the far end of the street. "Wapping, which abounds with Chinamen and other awful heathen."

"You're right there, Nannie!" said Trevor who had caught the last remark. "They're not down quite as far as Wapping, but they swarm, simply swarm, quite close, mixed up with our English girls. I don't know what's the matter with me, but ever since this morning, when I got a letter from Miss Cleeve, I've done nothing but read, think and talk of China. If I were the slightest bit psychic I should say that I was going to get news from the East."

"Don't, Mr. John! I can't bear the name even. You must remember that your aunt Beatrice was your mother's favorite sister, and that I was with your dear mother when your aunt was murdered with your uncle Ben and your little cousin Lucy, but a few months old. Murdered by Chinamen and their dead bodies burned in their bungalow, which the yellow rascals set fire to, to hide all trace. And nobody ever found out who did it and why they did it. I can't *stand* those heathen Chinese."

"They weren't exactly Chinese, Nannie," said Trevor as he slowly filled a pipe.

"Well, they couldn't be *worse*, Mr. John."

"You see, uncle Ben and aunt Beatrice lived in Northern India, or rather, in Sikkem, which isn't so very far from Tibet, and it was thought, but never proved, that a certain Tibetan trader, called Nyko-Gung, did or caused the murder to be done. Do you remember that uncle Ben was on the Forestry Department, with headquarters at Kalimpong?"

"I don't remember that, Mr. John, but I remember that he loved trees, just as your father did."

"That's it! Well, three huge forest fires, set ablaze out of pure deviltry, were traced to this man. Uncle Ben fined him to the utmost limit, practically beggared him, so that he lost his position and became a laughing-stock to the whole countryside. My people were murdered shortly after. Punish the Oriental if you like, if he deserves it, but remember it's a damn-fool thing to make a laughing-stock of him."

John Trevor lit a match and absent-mindedly blew it out again.

"I remember aunt Beatrice perfectly. She was almost as pretty as mother, and they murdered her, think of it, murdered her." He looked across at the old woman who was standing staring fiercely down the tragic past. "I'd give all I possess, Nannie, to break that man's neck or his son's neck, if he has a son!"

Janet Comfort looked at him for a moment, unseeingly, then nodded her head.

"And maybe you will, Mr. John, dear, for the logs foretold a long journey and trouble for many—ah! there's the postman."

She bustled from the room, leaving her master to his thoughts.

*   *   *

He looked up when she came in with a letter.

He ripped the envelope open, glanced hurriedly through the contents, laid the letter down, sat quite still for just one second, then forced a smile and looked up.

"He's all right!" There was no need to mention names.
"And I'm going to see him to-morrow night. There's a
great bit of news too; can you guess what it is?"

Janet Comfort beamed all over her dear, homely old face.
"Of course I can, sir! I've been expecting it all along.
Mr. Power is engaged."

"*Married!*" replied Trevor shortly, crushing the letter in
his hand. "Sit down, Nannie, take out your knitting, we've
—we've got to put our heads together over this!"

"Is there anything wrong, Mr. John?"

"It's all wrong, Nannie, as far as I can see!"

"Has he—has he married a chorus girl, is it as bad as
that?"

"Chorus girl! My God! It's a million times worse!
It looks as if he has married a native, a Chinese woman or
half-caste, or something like that in Limehouse, in the
Chinese quarter, in the slums!"

"No! no! no! Mr. John," cried the horror-stricken old
housekeeper. "It's impossible! Mr. Power and a—no, you
haven't read the letter right."

"Just listen, Nannie! Listen to the address first of all.

"25a, Celestial Buildings,
"Eastern Alley,
"East India Dock Road.

"This letter may be a bombshell to you, old man," wrote
Rex Power in his execrable handwriting. "It is to tell you
that my quest is over, that I have achieved my grail; in
other words, that I have found the Lady of my Dreams,
my wife, and that she is sitting on the arm of my chair as
I write. I can't describe her here. Who she is and where
she comes from I don't know any more than she does. The
secret of her birth, her nationality and the reason for her
life being passed on the borders of Chinatown is locked up
in the heart of Tsi-tsi, an old Tibetan woman, who is com-

pletely paralyzed and dying slowly. She may recover her speech before the end or she may not. The doctor says a great fright, a shock of some sort, might bring it back. What matter? I know that Lotah is the most perfect wife a man could ask for, that she is the realization of my dreams and the inspiration of *the* picture which we want you to come and see. Forgive my silence, you'll understand, indeed you will, when I explain, and come soon, old friend, come the evening after you get this to our funny little home on the borders of Chinatown. Come to dinner. Read this to darling old Janet and tell her she is superseded in my heart."

It was signed Rex and Lotah, and over the page had been added a postscript, written under the lash of a great fear, so that in places the nib had stuck and blotted the fair sheet.

"I dared not let Lotah see this," had added Rex Power. "I want your advice, your help. My happiness is almost counterbalanced by the terror I suffer when Lotah is out of my sight for a single moment, in this terrible district. For God's sake, come quickly. Something happened yesterday which has forced me to do, at last, what I have wanted to do and ought to have done long before this, to ask you to come and see us. It was just fear of you trying to force us away from here that kept me silent. You'll understand when I explain——"

John Trevor read the instructions as to the best way to get to Eastern Alley, folded the letter and unfolded it again as he sat looking at Janet Comfort who, horror-stricken, sat looking at him.

"Mr. Power has married her, Nannie. Temperamental and unpractical he has *married* a girl of the slums; has tied himself, irrevocably, either to a native woman or a half-caste, and is living in the squalor of the worst quarter of London. This is the result of his theory that the one woman exists for the one man and vice versa."

"Yes! yes!" said Janet slowly. "What was it he used to say, and so often? 'A rose is a rose even if found in the back yard; a pearl is a pearl even if found in the dustbin.'"

"But he needn't have gone to the gutter for his rose, he needn't have picked up a sham pearl. I wanted to be set a big problem, I clamored for it. I've got it, but there's no answer to it. The boy's ruined, his career ended, it's—it's damnable."

"Wait a bit, dearie, wait a bit!"

Janet got up with a rustling of her black silk skirt and crossed to the master she had mothered and advised and consoled from the first day he had fallen and had cut his knees.

"Do you see a ray of hope, Nannie?"

"Not a ray, Mr. John, nor even a gleam. But there *is* some one who can help us, some one who knows these heathen folk and could advise. I've heard of the fascination these foreign women have for young men; why, it's mentioned ever so many times in the Bible. We'll just find out if, once the glamour, the—the fascination of this person has worn thin, if she couldn't be bought off."

"Who is it you want me to ask advice of?"

"Miss Cleeve, Mr. John. She's up to all their monkey tricks if any one is, wasting her life, her time, her pretty face teaching those heathen children in that heathen town—"

"Darjeeling."

"—in India. She speaks their uncivilized languages too. She's clever and pretty, is Miss Cecily. Just you ask her, sir, what to do about it."

John Trevor took a letter out of his pocket.

"I can't, Nannie, she crossed to Paris this morning, by the early train, before I got her letter."

Janet sat down heavily in a chair.

"And you let her go, Mr. John!"

"I didn't, Nannie," replied Trevor stubbornly, trying to

hide his hurt. "She left without telling me, I couldn't even see her off."

"There shouldn't have been any occasion to see her off. Oh! these men," cried Janet. "They see the beautiful, wild bird they want to keep forever in the cage of their love, they lure it to the tree, but they forget to lime the bough with masterfulness and tenderness and demonstrations of affection. Oh! the feckless lot of them!"

"She doesn't love me, Nannie; why should she? We've known each other for years and years. I knew her in the nursery. I've loved her, always, I shall always love her. I wanted to tell her so, years ago, when she was eighteen, she is twenty-five now, much, much too young for me."

"Yes, and instead of telling her you loved her, Mr John, you let her sit on the bough, all by herself, until she got tired, then let her fly away. She flew away to teach the heathen because you were so slow in the uptak'. She flew away then, she's flown away now. I've no patience with you, Mr. John, none whatsoever."

"She doesn't love me, Nannie," repeated Trevor. "Why should she, a middle-aged, dull, old bachelor, and she such a traveler, so clever, so sweet to look at."

Janet snorted viciously, indignantly.

"Well, Mr. John, all I can say is, if you're going to add humble pie to the rest of the dishes you've been eating, it's a sore indigestion you'll be having. You! a great architect! your name in all the papers! Why should she look askance at you, I should like to know?"

"I don't know, either."

"Miss Cleeve's gone off in a huff, she's been waiting for you to speak, sir."

"Well, she's gone off for three years. She has crossed to see something of France and is catching a mail boat at Marseilles."

Janet rose and tidied the hearth.

"There seems nothing but trouble about China this day.

Mr. Power flinging himself into a heathen marriage, your young lady rushing away to the heathen country the other person came from, and you, Mr. John, sitting there as solemn and unflabbergasted as any Chinese idol."

Trevor smiled at the wrath in the old voice; a wrath roused on account of the hurt done him by Cecily Cleeve, the girl he loved.

"Go and have a peep at the bulbs, Nannie."

She walked across to the table and again lifted the brown paper cone.

"And what about it, sir?"

"There's a bit of green coming through!"

"There is, sir!"

"And that's hope, Nannie, you old curmudgeon."

"So it is, dear! But two love affairs gone wrong in one night will want the whole flower of hope to put them straight. Yet, still we *will* hope."

She bent and kissed his hair as she left the room.

All was quiet and peaceful; there seemed no disturbing element, no other world, no noise nor strife nor danger possible in the vicinity of Cadogan Square.

John Trevor picked up the evening paper mechanically, looked down and shuddered. Across the top blazed the headline:

"The Yellow Peril in our midst."

CHAPTER III

"The Sahib has lost his way? May I be of service to the Sahib?"

John Trevor started at the sound of the gentle voice just behind his shoulder, frowned at the uncontrolled start he had given, and turned to the speaker who stood in a blur of fog under a street lamp.

He glanced at the lascar, from the red fez of the Mohammedan down to the dilapidated, European boots, which, on account of their pulpy, sodden condition had allowed the man to follow him noiselessly through the narrow, ill-favored streets. He noticed the slender hands, purple with cold, folded one upon the other, the splendid teeth stained with the crimson juice of the betel-nut, the home-sickness of the depths of the gentle, brown eyes, and wondered at the power of those dreams of fortune which drag men and women from their lands of sunshine to the horrors of a city's slums in search of gold.

"Sahib!" whispered the lascar, his fine teeth chattering as he spoke. "It is not wise, nor safe for the Sahib in his good raiment to walk alone in the native quarter at night. A few *pice*, a threepenny piece to procure a roof, and I will find the Sahib's way for him. The corners are full of ears, the windows of eyes, see——" A heavy-looking man, with collar turned up to his ears and an old felt hat pulled over his eyes, peered into John Trevor's face as he brushed against him and passed on. "That man one bad Chinaman, he follow the Sahib, perhaps he wait round the next corner."

"Cheerful, I must say!" said John Trevor, his voice

27

sounding loudly in the narrow street in which he had got hopelessly lost. He had carefully followed the directions in the letter received the night before, had turned quickly up a side street to avoid two men who were settling their grievances with their fists and had lost his way.

"Right," he said, a good deal more cheerfully than he felt. "Show me how to get to Celestial Buildings in Eastern Alley and I'll provide you with a whole week of roofs for the night."

"Hist, Sahib! Lower the voice!" The lascar slipped round the angle of the street, but not quick enough to see the figure of the heavy-looking man which seemed to dissolve like a shadow into the fog. He came back quickly, his big eyes shining at the thought of the *baksheesh* which would be given for his service. "This way, Sahib. Follow me closely, with an eye turned over the shoulder."

John Trevor stared in amazement and horror when he stopped at last in front of the tenement-house. "Are you sure this is the right place?" he asked as he felt in his pocket.

"It is the house, Sahib," replied the lascar, his eyes fixed upon the hand which felt for the *baksheesh*. "There is none other, Sahib. Sahib! all that is for me?" He drew himself up and salaamed with the beautiful gesture of the East before he took the two half-crowns. "I will wait here for the Sahib's return, and"—he walked up quite close and whispered—"if there should be danger, if the Sahib shouts, I will fly to his protection."

John Trevor caught the glint of steel in the man's hand as he turned to the doorway which showed black against the discolored walls, and sighed with relief when Liza Rodd's disconcertingly loud voice boomed at him from the doorway of the den she called her home.

"An' what d'yer want? Strike me blind! if it ain't a toff wot's mistaken 'is way to Bucking'am Palace!" Arms akimbo, she stepped in front of John Trevor, barring his way to the stairs. "Wot's yer game? Wot yer after? If yer're come fer the rent what's owin' from the basement to the roof yer'd better sell yer coat an' collect it outer that."

Trevor waited until the storm of abuse, appalling oaths and dreadful adjectives ceased, then smiled across at the woman whose eyes were as honest as her mouth was foul.

"I've come down to visit a friend of mine; he and his wife asked me to."

" 'Ere! come off it. Friend of yours, 'ere, in this cursed rat-'ole. I knows a nob when I sees one. Get out! we don't encourage no followers 'ere, not in our 'appy 'ome."

There was a savage wrath in Liza Rodd's husky voice and tears in her bloodshot eyes as she inveighed against the fate which had driven her to the bottom reaches of the gutter, and John Trevor traced the remains of beauty in her battered, tragic face as he wondered how to overcome her hostility born of the inevitable what-might-have-been.

"My dear Mrs.——" he began, when she broke violently across his words.

"Don't yer 'Mrs.' me, yer've come to the wrong 'ouse, I tells yer!" She flung wide a door on her right. "An' this 'ere is me own particular 'appy 'ome!"

A cloud of steam swept through the doorway, and through it Trevor could see a girl of twelve washing filthy garments in filthy water, whilst five small children played with the soapsuds on the floor.

" 'Alf of 'em, bless 'em. 'S'truth, I wouldn't be wiv'out one of 'em!" She laughed suddenly, and laid a grimy but friendly hand on Trevor's arm. "Yer'll be coming to see the young gent, wot——"

She put her finger to her lips, looked over her shoulder, turned and ran with a surprising lightness and swiftness up the stairs which, built between wooden partitions, twisted steeply and at frequent angles, so that any one mounting the first flight would be hidden from another climbing the second.

She came back, panting from the exertion, a heavy frown upon her face.

"There weren't any one to be seen, but I sees the shadder listenin'. This 'ouse is dangerous, Gawd knows, at any time, but ter Lotah, the White Rose, an' 'er 'usband, an' you in yer glad rags, it's a death-trap, that's wot it is, a death-trap. Them damned yeller men are after 'er, s'welp me if they ain't, an' I've warned the young feller, 'er 'usband, Power's 'is name, an' tho' I'll 'ate to lose them, yet I'll take it kindly if yer persuades them to take their 'ook afore trouble overtakes 'em. Right up to the very top, an' walk near the rails, 'cos the stairs are rotten in the middle. Bloomin' 'ouse comin' down next year. No thank yer kindly! The White Rose's friends are my friends, thank yer all the same. Oh, well, if it's fer the kids——"

Trevor had got half-way up the first flight when he felt her hand upon his arm.

"Mind yer *back*," she whispered. "Walk with yer 'ead over yer shoulder."

The wood cracked like pistol-shots in the otherwise silent house as John Trevor slowly made his way up the stairs, barely lighted by a gas-jet flickering on the landing which divided the house half-way up.

There was no sound nor sign of life as he passed, but, unknown to him, doors opened, bare feet ran noiselessly half-way up the flight of stairs behind, pale faces looked upwards, shining like lemon-colored lamps in the gloom.

"Rex has got to pack his traps and bring his wife away with him to-night, whatever she's like," Trevor said to himself as he rested for a moment in the middle of the flight of stairs which led from the second landing. "He must have been raving mad to have come here, let alone to stay here. Good heavens! what a hash he has made of his life. What a house, what——" he turned to look behind him and stood stock-still, staring. Just round the bend of the wooden partition, which hid one flight of stairs from the other, a mutilated hand lay upon the wooden railing. Thumb and little finger missing, the three middle fingers clutched the rail tight, as though it helped some one round the bend to mount the stairs noiselessly upon tiptoe; the hand slid back, little by little, slowly, more as though it did not move but dissolved in John Trevor's imagination.

And as the slender tip of the middle finger slid almost imperceptibly from the rail, John Trevor sprang and hurled himself round the corner of the stairs.

The landing was empty and silent.

In the deepest shadow of the farthest corner Sa-t'ong Nyko-Gung, known only as the Three-Fingered Tiger, in Limehouse, lay flat upon his face watching the white man until he turned and walked quickly up the rest of the stairs; whilst crouched on the last step of the lower flight of stairs, unknown to him, her saffron-colored hands and face one with her drab garments and the black shadows, Ka-lck, the Tibetan girl, watched Sa-t'ong, the Bengal Tiger, whom she loved with all the fierceness of her passionate, jealous heart.

*   *   *

John Trevor's face brightened as he reached the last flight of stairs and looked up to the top landing. The one and only door, facing the stairs, had been newly painted; it looked like some old lacquer door in a Dulac picture-book; it was Rex's door, painted his favorite blue, deep and friendly, a splash of vivid color in the grim surroundings.

Rex opened it with a shout of joy, standing outlined against the deep orange light thrown from a heavily shaded lamp, whilst a sweet, fragrant perfume, wafted across the squalid landing, seemed to destroy the distressing odors which permeated the horrible building.

"It's me—I—old man, right enough," cried Rex Power, seizing John Trevor's hand and drawing him forcibly across the landing. "By Jove! it's good to see you. Lotah won't be long, she's spoiling her beautiful hands in cooking some special Tibetan dish or something for you. By Jove! it *is* good to see you!

"I've got such tons to tell you," he went on as he turned and bolted the door and drew a heavy curtain across it. "All about Lotah—it is on her account that I take these precautions," he touched the bolt as he spoke. "My picture to show you—painted through her—and your advice to ask." He put his hands on his friend's shoulders. "How are things with you, old man; are you going to follow my example?"

"I haven't been given the chance," replied Trevor, with a wry face, as he turned to enter the studio, and stood still in the doorway.

The Fairy Godmother, Cinderella, the pumpkin, the glass coach flashed into his mind as he looked at the room in front of him.

A corner of the tenement-house turned into a place of beauty!

The room was Eastern in the coloring of its creamy-white walls, the piled-up cushions of orange, blue, saffron, black, its flaming curtains and yellow rush-mats on the stained floor. It was a room with a touch of homeliness somewhere, difficult to define, but there; a room of restful beauty and idealism, as though two souls had met at last in perfect understanding.

"You like my home in the slums? It's better than Chelsea, isn't it? more atmospheric, more—more——"

"Unique, I think is the word," said the elder man quietly, as, in the grip of some strange feeling he could not understand, he put his arm through his friend's and crossed to the farther wall, upon which hung the picture destined, later, to take the world by storm.

"My God!" said Trevor to himself as he looked down the orange lettering of the title painted upon a black background.

"The Yellow Peril in our Midst."

The picture showed the most beautiful girl Trevor had ever seen, walking down a street in Limehouse; a street in which the houses on each side showed dimly through a fog. So cleverly had it been painted that, only after some time did one discover that horrible, leering, Eastern faces, draped in fog, were peering at the girl out of windows, doorways and round street corners. It was a stupendous, terrible picture, and Trevor shuddered as he turned and put his hand on his friend's shoulder.

"You like my Yellow Peril? Better than painting smart ladies in Tite Street, what? I'm going to ask you, as a great favor, to take it home with you to-night. You will? That's splendid of you. Sit down whilst I mix you a cocktail, I won't be a second; that's my wife, you know."

He pointed to the picture as he lifted the vivid curtain which separated the studio from the "pocket-handkerchief" of a kitchen.

"Your *wife!*" Trevor said quickly. "You don't mean to say that there is any one as beautiful as that in the world?"

Rex laughed as he walked back to the picture.

"I used to say that there were no beautiful women left since Helen of Troy took the midnight train to Paris. But you see there is *one*. I found her, literally ran into her in the street. She was coming from the shop where she worked; in fact, she was running for her life, followed by a Chink. I smashed his face for him, made it flatter even than nature intended, and brought her home here to Tsi-tsi, her old Tibetan nurse or foster-mother, and then I married her. The same thing happened two nights ago——" he leant against the picture-frame as he recounted the girl's race for life two nights back, then crossed to the curtain which hid the kitchen.

John Trevor listened to the sound of a girl's voice and laughter, in which Rex's joined, then sat perfectly still with his eyes fixed upon the skylight just behind his head and reflected in the glass which covered the picture.

Fog wrapped the East End in its heavy folds and pressed down upon the uncurtained skylight, but something thicker, heavier than fog, something that looked like a hand clutching at the rough beading of the skylight for support, seemed to be resting on the glass, that and the mere shadow of a face.

It disappeared slowly as Rex entered with two glasses on a tray.

John Trevor forgot all about the reflection in the glass as he got to his feet and openly, unashamedly stared at the beautiful girl who stood just behind Rex Power.

As long as he lived he never forgot the picture Lotah made as she stood against the lacquer-like door. The lines of her face were perfect, with a skin that looked like ivory, tinged with the color of rose petals; her dark hair rippled in heavy waves; her eyes big, wide open, held him spellbound. At first he could have sworn that they were green, until they changed to hazel and then to some color that baffled him completely, just as the colors of the sea baffle even the greatest painters. They were opalescent, if eyes can so be described, fringed with long lashes.

She smiled shyly, showing a glimpse of perfect teeth between the curved, crimson lips which matched the vividness of a bunch of poinzettias, tucked in the belt of the Oriental dress she had put on in honor of the guest.

She was the most naturally beautiful woman John Trevor had ever seen, and made him think of flowers and the sunrise and all the unuttered, indescribably sweet things hidden in a child's thoughts.

She crossed quickly to him with hands outstretched in greeting. "My husband's friend, therefore my friend!" she said.

Rex laughed as Trevor pulled himself up with a jerk, and a look of indescribable astonishment on his face.

"I knew Lotah would bewitch you. She has just come in to say how-d'you-do."

"Supper will not be long, Mr. Trevor. I am making you an especial Eastern dish, the almonds have taken long to peel, see my brown finger-tips! Let Rex show you the outlook from the window, it is very wonderful. And, Mr. Trevor"—she drew her hand away from her husband's and laid it on John Trevor's arm, speaking seriously, smiling sweetly—"you are our friend, and I know that you will not wish us to remain here after to-night. I feel"—she laid her hand upon her heart and looked down at her wedding ring and up at the man she loved with all the passion and intensity and tenderness of her great heart—"I feel that you are going to try and persuade Rex to leave at once. You must not do so, because I have sworn to Tsi-tsi, my old nurse, my foster-mother, that——"

"Yes," interrupted Rex quickly, putting his arm around her and kissing her hair. "She really has sworn to go on living here, so as to look after and nurse the old woman until she dies."

"And death is not far off, Mr. Trevor! He has opened the door, he stands beckoning to her. And she is so very, very happy in the terrible little room to which she came, to which she brought me when I was a baby. She will not come up here, to us, she would die of a broken heart if I left her. You understand, do you not, Mr. Trevor?"

John Trevor looked from one to the other.

"I understand," he said, as, with a little cry, Lotah turned and ran to the kitchen.

"My almonds burn," she laughed; "open the window, Rex!'

*   *   *

The two men leaned out of the window and looked down to the courtyard, lighted only by the rays which streamed through the tenement windows, and across to the East India Dock Road.

"I love it all," said Rex quietly. "But, good God! Trevor, you don't know the hell I live in every minute of the day and night."

His voice sounded startlingly clear as he recounted the mystery of Lotah's birth. How she had been brought from some eastern country, when a few months old, in the care of Tsi-tsi; though from which country, Tibet, Mongolia, Bhutan, no one had ever been able to find out from the old woman, who, evidently in the grip of some great fear, had obstinately refused to give any details as to her own past or to the birthplace or nationality or parentage of the beautiful girl.

"—— She was educated at the L.C.C., then worked for her living in an Oriental shop near Commerical Road, watched over lovingly at home by Tsi-tsi, who filled her mind with a love of beauty and purity, and kept her unspoiled and innocent even in this hellish spot where no girl, white or yellow, beautiful or plain, is safe. Oh, my God! Trevor, if the old woman would only die and release Lotah from her bond. The horror of what might happen to her haunts me. I——"

Lotah's laughing voice called them in to supper. They shut the window without looking up, so that they saw nothing of the evil, oblique eyes a foot or so above them; they laughed and talked happily, light-heartedly as they sat down to the table, so that they heard no sound as the lithe body of Chang-ku, the Gray Wolf, slid, inch by inch, over the roof tiles, until it gained a vantage point from which the evil eyes could see the three through the uncurtained skylight.

"I eat blindly and with great faith when Lotah insists upon an Oriental menu," said Rex, when half-way through the meal. "This may be puppy dog, or white mice, or bird's nest."

"It's awfully good, anyway," interrupted Trevor.

"Darling!" Rex laid his hand persuasively on Lotah's. "Will you, just because you are the most beautiful and talented wife of a miserable, worthless painter, will you sing that weird song and dance that funny little dance?"

"Of course I will."

"You will! Well, I'm—I never know how to take her, Trevor. She almost always refuses."

Lotah turned and looked at the door.

"I only refuse because I am afraid of ears outside the door. They, the Chinese, and they have no right on our landing, are always on the stairs, and this song is a Tibetan song, and the dance also, which——"

Rex stopped his wife's words with a kiss, then lit her cigarette.

"It's a song and dance, so Tsi-tsi says, sung and danced in a certain weird spot outside the British jurisdiction, somewhere near the Indian northwest frontier, by women who are up for sale, or something appalling like that. They have a kind of audition at which they——"

Lotah intervened.

"Enough of horrors, Rex! Do you know he speaks Bhutia quite nicely, Mr. Trevor?"

"Bhutia?"

"Bhutia is a Tibetan dialect spoken in Sikkim," laughed Rex, "and Sikkim, O! ignorant man, lies wedged between Nepal and Bhutan to the west and east, and between Tibet and India to the north and south. In fact, to the south it stops about ten miles short of Darjeeling."

"Thank you for nothing!" said Trevor.

"Oh, of course! Sorry, old man," replied Rex contritely. "I forgot—your people—of course!"

"Oh, that's all right. Tell me, if you are so particular about bolting the door, why don't you curtain the sky-light?"

"Curtain the skylight?" repeated Rex. "Oh! I see what

you mean. I've been up there. Nothing but a cat could negotiate the slopes between the chimney-stacks. That's *quite* safe. And we have such fun on a starry night, don't we, Lotah?"

Lotah turned her head and looked up at the skylight.

"Tsi-tsi, who is Bhutanese, we *think*, taught me to tell fortunes by the stars, Mr. Trevor. I take the hour and the day of the birth of those who are having their fortunes told and prophesy such wonderful things."

"She did it the other night for you, old man, and, by Jove! you're going to be let in for an exciting time."

Lotah laid her hand for an instant on Trevor's arm.

"At the end of which love will come to you."

"May I be as happy as you two! Now tell me, and forgive me the question, Rex, but however do you live?"

Rex shouted with laughter.

"I suppose you think that Lotah takes in washing and that I chalk pictures on the pavement off Oxford Street." He rose as he spoke and crossed to an easel, lifted a small picture and carried it to the table, where he cleared a space and propped it against a cut-glass flower bowl, pointing at the right-hand corner of the picture with a dessert knife.

"Ling-Soo!" read Trevor, then looked at the painting of a corner of Chinatown splashed in in vivid colors. "You don't mean to say—you're not——"

"I am!"

"Yes, he is, Mr. Trevor. And the little pictures sell for very much money, like hot cakes. He is the Ling-Soo who is broadcasting the whole of England with little pictures of the Chinese in Limehouse. Tell him all about it, Rex, whilst I clear away. And then I will sing to you, because I think you are such a nice, good friend, and then you will take away the great picture by a great painter, one Rex Power, to keep until we find a home, in a very little time, in Chelsea."

The light of a lamp struck down on her as, some little

while later, she thrummed on the *Pi-wang*, an instrument like a guitar, which she had taken from the wall. She touched the strings absent-mindedly, then stopped, lost in dreams, and fingered a string of blue beads round her neck; beads that looked like little blue flames on her breast. She evidently loved them; her fingers played with them, caressed them as she sat with her eyes on the face of her beloved.

Then she began to sing softly, in a voice of sweetest purity, whilst a scar, in the exact shape of a wild rose on the outside of her wrist, the scar which had given her her nickname in Limehouse, gleamed in the light of the lamp.

She put the two-stringed instrument down and rose, singing the Tibetan love-song to the accompaniment of little gestures of her hands, and strange, abrupt movements of her arms and shoulders.

The shadows played tricks with the mobile face and masses of black hair; her eyes gleamed, inscrutable, between the long lashes; the eyelids, through the trickery of the shadows, seemed to have been pulled slightly upwards, the whole face flattened through the same cause. It was a girl of the East, alluring, magnetic in some terrible, undefinable way, standing, lost in dreams, under the lamp.

Chang-ku, the Gray Wolf, to stifle his cry of desire, pressed his mouth against the edge of the skylight. Rex suddenly sprang forward, and, seizing Lotah, shook her ever so slightly.

"Stop, Lotah! stop! Don't look like that! It brings the danger nearer, you are too beautiful, too——"

"Danger! What danger?"

The danger of you being stolen from me!"

Lotah laughed gently and put her hands on Rex's shoulder. "Foolish boy! Don't you know that our love will keep me safe?"

Trevor watched the intense, dramatic scene.

"Lotah! Lotah! if anything should ever happen, if danger

should threaten you, remember that I shall be coming to you, that I shall never, *never give you up.*"

"I shall remember," said Lotah softly, and a little later was simple, sweet, and friendly as she held wide the door as the two men passed through to the landing with the picture.

"Come again, Mr. Trevor," she said. "We cannot come to you, because I dare not leave Tsi-tsi now the end is so near, and Rex, the silly boy, won't leave me for longer than he can help."

"Go in now, sweetheart," said Rex as he backed down the first step. "And, for God's sake, don't forget to bolt the door. I'll give our signal, and don't open it on any account, or to any one, until you hear it. Do go in, darling."

"I will, I will, directly I have seen the last of you. I am so happy, oh! Mr. Trevor, I am so very, very happy. Good night, come again soon!"

She stood listening to their slow progress down the many flights of stairs.

"That smell of burned wood," she heard Rex say, "is refreshing and welcome in this black hole of odors, what?"

She stayed for a moment longer, then ran into the room and flung open the window. She leaned far out, listening to the man she loved talking to some one who had appeared out of the shadows. John Trevor's voice came to her distinctly.

"He's the man who showed me the way here, let's find three——"

Then she turned and fought for her life, her lover, her honor.

She had forgotten to bolt the door.

CHAPTER IV

As the telephone bell rent the silence of the night, John Trevor turned and stared across in the dark at the shrieking instrument; cursed it, and, obstinate with the irritation of one aroused from sleep, entreated it to go on ringing till the Day of Judgment if it wanted to, for all the notice he would take of it.

The persistent call stopped suddenly, leaving the night the more peaceful for its previous clamoring.

"I knew it!" said Trevor, sleepily groping for his watch. "Almost half-past two—another wrong number for a certainty—the third this week—as if anybody could possibly want *me* in the middle of the—— Oh, *bother* the thing!"

He switched on the light, flung himself out of bed, and jerked the receiver off the hook.

"Hello! what on earth—yes, of *course* I am—half an hour—indeed you haven't—hello! yes, Trevor speaking—who? what?—my God!—you, Rex—what?—speak slowly and louder—what?—yes!—*what?*"

Sleep, irritation, thought of self disappeared, leaving in their place a feeling of physical sickness, a tautening of the nerves, a desperate longing to be there, then, at once, at the scene of the terrible tragedy which was being enacted in the grim neighborhood of the slums.

Quick and fast came the shocking items of news over the wire, spoken in a hoarse whisper, which he just recognized as Rex Power's voice; a frantic appeal for him to come and help to find Lotah in the hysterical, alien mob which surrounded the blazing tenement building; the click of the receiver slammed down on the hook; silence.

"I'll have hot blankets and bottles all ready, Mr. John,"

cried Janet Comfort a little later from the doorway, where she stood in red flannel dressing-gown and white shawl, muffled against the fog and rawness of the night. "You'll find the young lady all right, and be back with her and Mr. Power in no time."

She watched John Trevor run down the street towards the square, then nodded genially to a policeman who loomed gigantic out of the fog and flashed his bull's-eye into her bonny old face.

"A reckless lot o' loons have set fire to a tenement in the slums, officer. My master knows some one living there."

Constable XX heaved his shoulders under his heavy oil-skin cape and pulled at his chin-strap.

"Well, they'll burn like rats in a trap, mum, that's all I can say. Them streets are a disgrace to a great city like London. No room for fire engines or escapes nor nothin'." He watched Trevor hail a taxi which crawled out of a side street. "He's lucky, your gentleman, if he gets any one to take him down to the East End on a night like this here."

John Trevor's luck was in.

"Not on yer bloomin' loife, guv'nor," bluntly replied the taxi-driver. "I'm on me way 'ome, sir, an' even if there 'adn't been no fog I wouldn't take a perishin' picnic party to warm its 'ands at a fire in the East End at this time o' night, not never so!"

"Five pounds, man! A case of life and death!"

The portly, jolly old fellow, face streaming with the wet of the fog, bundled off the seat and opened the door.

"Make it five-ten an' I'll wait for yer, sir."

"Here's six!" replied Trevor, counting the notes and pushing them into the man's hand. "And drive like the deuce and get as near a public-house called the Three Feathers as you can, with safety." He looked towards the house through the small window in the back of the taxi as the driver accelerated. "How strange!" he said out loud. "How weird! just like a mirage!"

The light fog had lifted from the middle of the street. It draped the walls of the houses in soft folds, obliterating them; it spanned the street in great aches at the level of the windows in the first stories; under the arches the street lay silent, desolate, uncanny, the light of the policeman's lantern shining like a watching eye in the distance.

John Trevor shivered suddenly, uncontrollably, and sat back in the corner of the car as the taxi raced through the empty streets.

Up to the highest heavens roared the raging flames of the fiery furance as, with a thundering crash, the tenement roof fell in just as he managed to fight his way clear of a raving, blaspheming, terrified mob of aliens which had come to grips with a cordon of police stretched across the mouth of the street. A firm hand gripped him by the collar of his coat.

"Now then, out of this! There's two engines coming, can't you hear them? Get out of it."

The dreadful clamor of the fire-engines' bells could just be heard above the roar of the flames, the shrieking of women, the screaming of children.

"Why don't you help, instead of running amuck with a dirty crowd like this?"

Trevor tersely explained his case to the irate sergeant, then turned with him, and, shoulder to shoulder, fought the oncoming mob as it blindly hurled itself up the street down which, with the dreadful clanging of bells, were tearing a fire-engine and escape to join the others which, owing to the narrowness of the streets, could only hope to save the whole quarter by playing their hoses on the adjacent buildings.

Headed by a pack of Chinese the mob ran, screaming, lost to all reason, looking, against the terrible glare, as though it had just been let loose from hell itself.

Men and women and children fought each other in the smother of smoke which followed them up the street;

shrieked and struck and tore at each other as sparks and bits of burning timber fell on their faces, their hair, their clothes; they met the cordon of police and fought and hacked their way right through and fled up the street to meet the engine as it came, as swiftly as it dared, to the rescue of Chinatown. The fire-engine blocked the way, the clanging bell almost drowned the yelling of the maddened mob as it turned back upon itself and fled towards the cordon of police which, strengthened, stretched two deep across the street. Women fainted and fell; children were carried forward, tight-squeezed between their fighting elders, or fell to lie alongside the injured women, whilst the pack of humans, brought by fear to the level of a stampeding herd of panic-stricken cattle, swept over them, trampling them to death or unconsciousness where they lay.

"Keep back there, you——" yelled the sergeant, as he brought his truncheon down upon the head of one who ran, knife in hand. Even as he yelled, with a terrific crash the north wall fell inwards, upon which appalling noise and rain of sparks the mob turned and hurled itself up a side street, where, jammed between the walls, it fought, in some cases, literally to the death.

Then, just as an old hag, white, yellow or half-caste, it would have been difficult to decide, such was her age and filth, flung herself, gibbering, at the sergeant's feet, a stream of water, steel-strong in force, was turned upon the human maelstrom.

It took them unawares, it fell like hammers upon their faces, like whips of wire upon their backs, it bruised, it cut, it beat them, howling like lost dogs, up the side street to safety, excepting for the old hag who clutched the sergeant's knees and begged to be allowed to return to the blazing building to rescue her bed with the counterpane of many colors.

An hour later, grimed with dirt, his coat in ribbons, his mouth bleeding from the blow a buck-nigger had viciously

and successfully aimed at him from the shelter of a doorway, John Trevor fought his way through the yelling, gesticulating, hysterical ring of lascars, yellow men, black men,
and the worst type of white men which haunts the lower
reaches of a great city, to where Rex Power stood.

Grimed with dirt, his hair and clothes singed on one side,
his eyes blazing with the madness of a great despair, Rex
Power sprang at Trevor. Words, wild, whirling, incoherent,
tumbled over each other; in his effort to be lucid his voice
was a mere whisper, raucous, cracked; his face, singed when
he had fought his way into the burning building, distorted,
lived with a horrible fear. His words came thick, like the
words of a drunken man, as he held on to his friend as on
to a rock, while he tried desperately to tell him the ghastly
happenings of the night.

"She's gone! Lotah! gone, I tell you, man, vanished into
the night. Burnt? no, my God, not burnt! I fought my
way up to the room and only just got out in time. No sign
of her—no sign. They've stolen her, I tell you—they've
stolen her." He swayed against Trevor, who caught and
supported the unnerved body.

Rex began to moan suddenly like a hurt child. "My
hands," he whispered, "my hands! Look at them, John.
D'you think I'll be able to paint again? She was so glorious to paint. Oh! the beauty of her face, her soul——!"

He broke away from Trevor, flinging out his blackened
hands, calling upon God to let him find his Dream Girl,
whilst the crowd pressed in on the handsome boy, well
known in the "quarter" as the husband of the White Rose.
The men could not understand the agony he was enduring,
the women crowded round, sympathetic, trying to offer
consolation in their rough and ready fashion.

" 'E's gone clean balmy, this time," said a blousey-looking
young woman to Trevor. She dropped her voice and
whispered behind her hand: "And jes' you mark me words.

Them blasted Chinks 'ave got 'er or me name's not Martha Smith."

She had not whispered low enough. Rex heard the words, and, catching the woman by the arm, almost shook her in the agony of his terror. "You—you can't mean that," he cried, the words coming thickly, unsteadily, barely audible. "My God! not *that*—you don't know what you are saying, you're—you're——"

The woman loosened the boy's hands. "You take me word for it, I'm right," she said, instinctively taking the blackest outlook on the event, as is the way of those who come in daily contact with tragedy, crime and death.

Rex turned in his agony to Trevor, eyes blazing, burned hands clasped upon his heart. "I believe she's right, John. There's something tells me here," he cried wildly, "that Lotah's *alive*. She's been stolen from me, stolen, I tell you."

The men nudged each other, the women stared and nodded their tousled heads. They thought him mad. They judged by what they saw, little knowing that the line between sanity and madness is of the very slightest in those who are blessed or cursed with genius.

They pressed so close that Trevor looked round for a way of escape. He had forgotten the dying Tibetan woman; had but one thought—to get Rex away from the gazing, chattering crowd, to pour brandy down his throat, and then take him home. Lotah had vanished. He was certain she was not burned; he was just as certain that the blousey young woman had spoken the truth, and that the girl had been decoyed, abducted. The thought of Scotland Yard flashed into his mind. Well, let Scotland Yard tackle that part of the problem later, in the meanwhile there was Rex to be looked after. He dragged the boy forcibly through the interested crowd, inside the public-house, and again through a muttering mass of men and women up to the bar.

The mad fury with which Rex had fought the flames, the crowd, even the police to reach his home and his wife had been the fury of one possessed, and his strength had been as the strength of one ten. Reaction set in, suddenly. Like one blind he groped with his burned hands and almost fell across the counter, then straightened himself, laughing wildly, as he staggered and caught at Trevor, clinging to him as might a lost child to its protector.

A huge bully of a man, with gimlet eyes, a flattened nose and the girth of a Samson towered behind the counter, a heavy tankard in each hand.

"Now then, wot's yer game, young feller?"

"A drink," muttered the boy, pointing at Trevor. "A drink of—some sort for my friend, Sjambok Dick, he's—he's been helping the police and firemen."

"I don't care a curse wot he's been doin' or 'elpin', but you're free to whatever yer wants, jes' a-cause yer fought yer way to the top of that there hell-fired building, to save your gal, wot seems to be lost."

He shouted an order to the frowsy Dutchwoman at the end of the counter, pushed a brandy-and-soda towards the two on the other side, then opened the door at the back of the counter and yelled for Liza Rodd. She rushed in, her children clinging to her, wide-eyed, pale even through the dirt on their faces, scared at the thought of losing sight, for a moment, of the one person in the world who stood between them and trouble.

She shook them off as she might have shaken crumbs from her skirt, and ran to the counter.

"For God's sake, come. She's dyin'——"

With a frightful cry, Rex swung himself over the counter and caught the woman by the shoulder.

"In God's name, why didn't you——"

She laughed loudly, harshly, as she patted his back.

"The Chinese woman, Tsi-tsi, I mean. I 'auled 'er out jes' afore the roof fell in, blest if we 'adn't forgot the old lady, and she a-lying there a-praying to her 'eathen idol. Come on, quick!"

They passed through the parlor out to the back, up a narrow street, and then another, and stopped at one of a row of mean houses, showing distinctly against the glare of the building which smoldered some two miles away.

Liza Rodd knocked three times, then stood on one side to let the men pass.

"Your job," she said, pushing them in. "Yer don't want me pokin' into your business. If yer wants me yer'll find me at the Three Feathers."

She ran down the street, eager to get back to the children she loved. She did not pause, she did not look back, else might she have seen the shadow of a man, thrown by the glare in the sky, lying across the doorstep of the mean little house.

*   *   *

Tsi-tsi, the Tibetan woman, lay dying, her eyes, eager, tender, wistful, like a dog's, fixed upon the door; the battered, blackened image of the dread goddess Paldean-Lha-Mo upon her heart.

"They're comin'," whispered the slattern who sat by the bedside. She turned her tousled head with its halo of curl-papers and stared through the rents in the curtains drawn across the window. "Two of 'em! no, three, I 'ears Liza Rodd's voice. Now yer won't be long, old dear, so cheer up. I'll go an' let 'em in."

She flattened herself against the damp wall of the passage and jerked her chin in the direction of the room in which the dying woman lay, then, relieved for the moment of her duties of nurse, closed the door softly behind her and ran as hard as she could to the scene of the fire.

She turned the first corner swiftly, caught hold of a slip of an Oriental girl who had tried to evade her, and shook her fiercely.

"Wot the 'ell are yer doin' up 'ere? This ain't no bit of Chineytown!"

"Ka-lok, wait l'il bit," said the slip of a girl, making a deprecating movement with her slender hands. "Wait l'il piecee or wait much, big, piecee time."

"I'll break yer neck if I finds yer here when I come back, this ain't no place"—the slattern spat back vigorously —"fer yeller women."

She ran on, eager for the warmth, the gossip, the companionship of the Three Feathers; Ka-lok, back to the wall, slipped along in the shadows until she stood where, unseen, she could watch Sa-t'ong Nyko-Gung as he spied through the rents in the curtain upon the two Englishmen who sat talking to the dying woman.

Tsi-tsi lay quite still, her glazed eyes staring up at Rex Power through half-closed lids.

"She's dead, Trevor," whispered the boy. "She died with the secreet!"

"No—dead—one—piecee—time!"

The words came in the faintest whisper, and Trevor gripped the boy's arm hard.

"Steady, old man, steady! Don't frighten her! The shock has brought back her speech, as the doctor said it might. Ask her where Lotah is, she may have her hidden safely somewhere."

Rex sat on the edge of the bed and patted the wrinkled hand.

"Lotah? Lotah no can piecee find, where Lotah, Tsi-tsi?"

A look of horror, of agonizing fear, shot into the faithful, dog-like eyes of the almost dumb woman. Her mouth opened and shut spasmodically, the tips of her fingers twitched as she tried so desperately to speak.

"M'li tell—m'li tell!"—her eyes closed slowly, then opened wide—"s'lecret," she added.

"Oh, my God!"

Trevor drew a chair close up to the bedside and stroked the sleek head on the pillow.

"That's it, Tsi-tsi," he said, speaking clearly and slowly. "What is Lotah's other name?"

"T'levor!"

"Trevor?"

"L'il Loo-loo"—the wistful eyes closed, and Trevor, astounded, incredulous, put his finger to his lips as he looked across at Rex Power.

"——Loo-cie T'levor."

The words hardly broke the silence in the bare room, and neither of the men turned toward the window, else might he have seen some one watching close against the pane.

Trevor shook his head as the boy put out his hand to touch the old woman.

"Pl'apers! Pl'ocket!"

The brown eyes opened wide, the whole shriveled arm twitched as the old woman tried desperately to make the men understand before the death she knew to be so near should overtake her. She wanted to move her hand, to find the packet of documents, wrapped in oilskin, which she had worn on her heart, day and night, for well-nigh twenty years; she wanted to wrest a promise from the two white men before she died.

Trevor touched her gently, just above the failing heart, near which the battered goddess lay.

"Papers in your pocket, Tsi-tsi?"

She smiled with her eyes and flashed a look at Rex Power who had married the girl she loved more than her life; and he looked at Trevor, who nodded, then slipped his long, slender fingers inside the voluminous garment the Tibetan wore, drew out a flat, sealed packet stained a dark brown and tied with tape, and ran a penknife under the silk.

"Aunt Beatrice!" said Trevor quietly, taking the faded photograph from the boy's hand. "Lotah is my cousin."

He put his hand on the boy's shoulder. "You and I are related by marriage, old fellow." He smiled down at the little monkey-like woman, whose fingers twisted without ceasing in the dirty counterpane. "You nurse Mrs. Trevor, in Kalimpong, in Sikkim. You save baby Lucy from bad man—in—big murder—in—big—fire. . . ."

"Save—save——" came the whisper. "Pl'apers—plentee——"

Trevor glanced at the faded packet of frayed papers, all of which had to do with Lotah, Rex Power's wife, the White Rose of Chinatown. A copy of the child's birth certificate; a letter of loving congratulation from his own mother to her sister who, so shortly after reading it, had been so vilely murdered; a paragraph, cut out of the newspaper, recording the sentence passed for incendiarism upon—a smear of brown obliterated the name—a Tibetan trader; a few odds and ends, all tied together with tape.

Sa-t'ong watched Rex take the papers, put them carefully back into the oilskin wrapper, and slip the packet into an inner pocket; watched Trevor uncork a medicine bottle, half full of brandy, standing on a rickety table by the bedside, slide his arm under the dirty pillow and gently force the brandy between the dying woman's strong, discolored teeth.

Very gently Sa-t'ong's long, slender hands felt for and pushed at the window frame as Tsi-tsi began to speak rapidly, almost incoherently, her fingers plucking at the dirty counterpane.

The warped wood of the frame creaked violently, and, like a shadow, Sa-t'ong slid to his knees under the sill when the two men turned quickly.

"I can't understand a word she says," whispered Trevor, as he returned from the window through which he had looked into an utterly deserted street.

"I can just make it out," came Rex's whispered answer

as Tsi-tsi fought to keep the breath which was causing such agony in her sunken breast, until her tale was told.

The tale of the murder committed in Sikkim eighteen years ago; the tale of a fight with a man of her own race, who had slashed at her with the knife with which he had killed the white man who had put up such a splendid fight; of how she had fought the man under the image of the goddess, wounding him in the hand; of how he had missed her, flicking instead the baby's wrist with the point of a knife, making a wound which had healed, leaving a scar in the shape of a wild rose; of how she had seized the image of the goddess; of the mad rush through the night down the mountainside toward Darjeeling; the staining of the white baby a yellow-brown with the juice of a certain root which grew amongst the rocks; the hiding by day; the pursuit, led by the men who had murdered the whites; the escape down through India; the flight to England.

Then the story of that strange, passionate, jealous love which the native woman conceives for the white child in her charge, a love which had forced Tsi-tsi to keep the knowledge of the child's existence from its relations; to hide herself in the basement in Chinatown; to pinch and save and scrape so as to beautify the child's life and surroundings as far as anything can be beautified in the slums.

Then the story of the great fear which had shadowed her all through her life; the fear of the men who, through her, had been foiled in their effort to wipe out the entire family of the man who had heaped insults upon their father.

A revenge which they had only been able to fulfill in part by murdering the white man who had reduced them to poverty, beggared them, holding them up to ridicule in the eyes even of the poorest, meanest, lowest born in the district.

"What —were —they— going— to—do—to—li'l Lotah?"
Rex asked the question slowly, clearly, as a film seemed

to gather over the brown eyes. "Oh, my God! she's almost gone. And we don't know where Lotah is!"

The old woman lay still, the battered idol resting on the faithful heart which had almost ceased to beat. The eyes were half closed, the jaw had dropped ever so little, the small, work-worn, brown hands had ceased their plucking at the dirty counterpane.

Trevor bent down and shouted in her ear:

"Where is l'il Lotah? Where bad man taken her? Where, Tsi-tsi, where?"

The shouted words rang through the room. They passed as a blur of sound to the ear pressed against the window pane.

Rex Power shrank back to the end of the bed as the sleek, brown head turned suddenly, sharply toward John Trevor, with brown eyes blazing, lips drawn back from the strong, discolored teeth in a snarl of hate.

Tsi-tsi's tired feet had stood upon the edge of the world to come; love, duty, eagerness to help had brought her back for an instant to the world of fear from which she had been so peacefully escaping.

"B'lad man! L'il Lotah——"

She glared up into Trevor's face as she tried to break the dumbness which chained her tongue.

"Where? Where is Lotah? Where?"

She turned her head suddenly, sharply toward Rex Power and stared at him without speaking, then slowly, very slowly, raised her withered right arm straight above her head.

She spoke clearly, slowly, as she made signs in the air, whilst her left hand searched for the battered goddess upon her heart.

"Fl'ind Lotah in—in—bl'ad man's—piecee bl'ig—bl'ig—house—in—in—st'leet—of——"

She stopped speaking whilst her finger went on drawing signs upon the air.

"Street of? Street of?"

Trevor shouted the words into her ear."

"——of—m'lany—m'lany—l'Arches!"

"Where is the street, Tsi-tsi, where?" Where?"

She suddenly sat straight in bed.

" *'Lha-sollo, lha'sollo! Lha'gyallo! lha'-gyallo!*"

Tsi-tsi hailed her gods and fell back, dead.

CHAPTER V

"I'm afraid we're beaten, old fellow, and I'm still more afraid that we shall have to go to Scotland Yard for assistance. No, don't go yet, Nannie; your advice is just what we want—now—when we *have* to come to a decision."

"No, don't go yet." Rex Power spoke from the depths of his favorite armchair, in which he lay desperate, hopeless and utterly at a loss. "I don't and won't agree with you about the police. At present I'm just looking for my wife, which is a perfectly natural thing to do, but once the Chinks get the wind up, suspect something, they'll draw right back into the shell of their terrible reserve, their horrible cunning, their appalling patience, then never shall we get out of them the sign, the look, the one word which will give them away. What do *you* say, Janet?"

Janet Comfort patted the boy's arm, then sat staring into the log fire in front of which they had been sitting for over an hour in consultation.

"I think I agree with Mr. Power, Mr. John," she said slowly, hating to contradict her master, but doing it out of sheer duty to the girl who had been lost in the terrible fire and of whom in the last two weeks they had found no trace. "For one thing, I don't think Scotland Yard would handle the case now that we—you gentlmen—have allowed two whole weeks to pass before consulting them. They are mighty touchy about their dignity, I believe; and I think if you just wait a little longer those yellow people will give themselves away."

"I wonder? I shall never forgive myself for not men-

55

tioning the face I saw reflected in the glass of that picture. I must have been mad. Oh! I wish to God something would happen! A girl can't be hidden forever, even in the slums, especially a girl like Lotah. Try how I may, I can't think how she was got away from that house without being seen. She must have screamed and fought and she must have passed Liza Rodd's room, because *I* don't believe any living being could have——"

"She was drugged, man, I tell you, drugged!" cried Rex. "You don't know what goes on down there in Chinatown, and I have only the faintest idea. That's why I'm dead set against calling in Scotland Yard. Heaven only knows what those damned Chinese might not do to Lotah if they got wind of what we are doing. Kill her to hide all trace, perhaps. No, I will *not* give my consent to calling in the police. I'll pit my wits against the brutes who've got her without the aid of the C.I.D., so what's the good of going all over it again?"

Janet Comfort turned her head to listen to the waits singing carols in the square.

"Peace on earth," she said tersely. "How can there be peace anywhere as long as yellow and white mix as badly as do the vinegar and oil in a salad dressing. There's a deal of sense, Mr. John, behind Mr. Power's supposition that some Chinaman got into his apartment somehow, overpowered Miss Lotah and got away with her by the balconies. Peace on earth indeed, when one-half of its population is no more civilized than a lot of chimpanzees."

"And as Graham, of the Foreign Office, said," interrupted Rex, "even with passports and the appalling passport photographs, it's jolly difficult to be perfectly certain of the identity of one out of the thousands of Chinese here in England. Their mothers may be able to identify them, but to us they look almost exactly alike. Besides that, they are so confoundedly tricky and cling together and help each other so, through thick and thin."

"Yes, but," interrupted Trevor, "that yellow devil they called the Three-Fingered Tiger has disappeared."

"But then you forget that Liza Rodd says that he didn't really belong to London, that no one knew his real name, his family name. He had come down from Liverpool on a matter of business he was transacting with the father, or the proprietor, of that girl Ka-lok, who waits in the chop-house."

"Well, we seem to be thoroughly up against it, and——"

"What's that?" Rex Power sat forward with a jerk, his hands pressed down on the arms of the chair, his face, with its haunted eyes, outlined sharply against the brown leather of the chair. "Listen, it's a bell!"

"It's the front-door bell, sir! The waits wishing to be paid for caroling about a peace which does not seem to exist this Christmas for some folk."

"There is five shillings somewhere near the clock, Nannie, if you'll ask White to give it to them. It's a jolly old Christmas custom, like the mistletoe and bran-pies and crackers of our youth."

"They may be peaceful, Mr. John, but they don't seem to be very patient," remarked the old nurse as the bell rang furiously.

Rex Power watched her leave the room, then turned and stared unseeingly into the fire. He had aged ten years during the last two agonizing weeks which he had practically passed in the Chinese quarter.

"I thought some one had come with news!" he said slowly.

Both men turned and looked towards the door from behind which could be heard voices in altercation.

"White trouncing the waits," said John Trevor as he filled his pipe. "What's up, Rex?"

The boy had sprung to his feet, white to the lips. He took a quick step forward as the door was flung open.

"Mrs. Rodd, from Chinatown," announced Janet Comfort clearly, significantly, as she followed the breathless woman into the room and shut the door firmly in the indignant face of the mystified White.

Liza Rodd wasted neither time nor words. She rushed across the room to meet Rex Power, who almost ran to meet her, pushed the battered hat back from her face, gripped his hand in both of hers and spoke quickly and to the point.

"When can yer start?" was what she said.

"You've found her! Mrs. Rodd, you've found her——"

"No, I 'aven't——"

"Oh, my God——!"

John Trevor intervened.

He had seen a great flare of hope leap into the boy's eyes, only to die and give place to a black despair; he could see that the woman was breathless with excitement and with a tale waiting to be told in her own way, and realized that any interruption would only make the tale the longer in the telling.

He pushed her down into a chair, sat down beside her, and motioned to the others to do the same. Liza Rodd leaned forward and tapped Rex on the knee.

"I've got news, a clew, so to speak, wot I follered and wot I'm thinkin' yer'll 'ave to foller roun' the blinkin' world."

"For God's sake, tell me——"

Trevor laid his hand on Rex's arm as he half rose from his chair with an impatient movement of both bandaged hands.

"I told yer so," Liza Rodd continued, flinging back her heavy shawl, unconsciously dramatic in an effort to make the most of the scene in which she was taking the principal part in such unusual surroundings. "Yes. I told yer both so. *They've got 'er.*"

Rex sprang from his chair, white to the lips.

"Who have got her? Who? I shall go mad if——"

"Why! them damned Chinks, of course!"

Trevor stepped quickly between the two and, catching Rex by the shoulders, pushed him down into the chair, whispering the while, whilst Janet Comfort, quivering with excitement, drew out a silk sock which she began to knit with trembling fingers.

"Steady, boy! Don't frighten her! Let me do the talking."

"I can't wait! I can't. It's Lotah. It's——"

"Another ten minutes, more or less, can make no difference. We can do nothing to-night." Trevor spoke quietly, unemotionally, pouring the cold water of reason upon the other's raging fire of impatience. "You'd have heard it all by now, if you hadn't interrupted. Who told you that the Chinese have got Lotah, Mrs. Rodd?"

"It came to me accidental like and through that yeller gal wot waits in 'er father's chop-'ouse, called Ka-lok. Like a blinkin' cat, with its claws out, she was, ravin' fit to kill 'erself with jealousy this very afternoon."

The silk sock dropped to Janet Comfort's lap; the cushion's silken tassel got pulled to pieces between Rex Power's nervous fingers; John Trevor's pipe went out as Liza Rodd, in dramatic, if laborious, words, set them at last upon the track for which they had been hunting for two whole weeks in the labyrinths of Chinatown. Jealousy, a big heart, a fearless spirit and a right arm strong to protect the weak, had helped to elucidate the mystery of the White Rose's disappearance.

Liza Rodd had passed down the street in which lay the chop-house belonging to the father of the girl Ka-lok, at that hour of the afternoon when the Chinese quarter is at its quietest, when gambling is at its height in the quiet back rooms of the mean little houses, and the shopkeeper smokes placidly, awaiting the rush hours of the closing day.

A window had crashed open above her head, through it

had come a girl's muffled screaming and the unmistakable sound of a whip upon bare flesh.

That a Chinaman's house, even in England, is his stronghold and his womenfolk his own to do what he likes with had not entered Liza Rodd's head; in fact, it had been full at that very moment of the mystery of Lotah's disappearance, as it had been for the last two weeks. Acting upon the impulsiveness of her big heart, she had rushed through the empty restaurant, up the stairs, and into the front room from which came the muffled screaming, without giving herself time to think. In the room she had flung herself upon Ka-lok's astounded father, wrenched the strap from his hands, torn the gag out of the mouth of the girl who stood tied to the bed-post, and, baring her arms, had dared the man to touch either of them.

In two minutes it seemed the room had been filled with white and yellow folk who, crushed back upon each other against the walls and round the doorway and out on the landing, had listened to Ka-lok's raving, the menacing replies of her imperturbable father, and the motherly advice, mixed with blasphemous vituperation, of dilapidated Liza Rodd.

For three reasons—all of which came out during the violent scene between father and daughter—was Ka-lok being thrashed with a stout leather strap, the items of which Liza Rodd ticked off with blunt thumb on tip of blunted fingers.

First, the girl had crept in the early hours of that very morning from the chop-house with all her worldly possessions packed in one small basket, and had made her way to Fenchurch Street Station; there her father had caught her just as she was about to enter the boat train taking passengers down to the boat sailing that noon for Calcutta; secondly, she had stolen the money to pay for her steerage passage in the *City of Kulna* from the chop-house till; thirdly, she had stolen the money and booked the steerage passage so as to follow the man she loved with all the fierce, primitive passion of her Oriental blood, back to the frontier of Northern India.

And the man she loved, the man who had looked upon her as a plaything with which to pass the dull hours spent in Limehouse, was the man known as Sa-t'ong, the Three-Fingered Tiger; the man who had shadowed John Trevor through the streets; who had waited with the Oriental's terrible patience and fatalism for his opportunity and then had seized it.

Rex sprang to his feet, and seizing Liza Rodd by the hands, jerked her to her feet.

"What has that got to do with Lotah? What in the world has all that got to do with me and my wife?" He shook her violently as she smiled up at him and patted his shoulder. "If you don't want me to go mad, Mrs Rodd, you'll—you'll——"

"The Three-Fingered Tiger, leastways, so that there girl Ka-lok says, sailed to-day for h'India," she paused and nodded triumphantly at the other two, "with 'is sister.' She reeled back against a table as Rex pushed her away and, turning, leant on the mantelpiece and buried his face on his arms. "And yer can take it from me that that there sister is Lotah, the White Rose." She caught John Trevor by the arm as he crossed to the telephone. "And yer needn't worry about nuffink. See 'ere!"

From somewhere inside her blouse Liza Rodd produced the somewhat grimy, thumb-marked sheet of paper given her by the astounded assistant when, backed by Sjambok Dick, she had made her way to the world-wide touring agency in Ludgate Circus.

Upon this sheet of paper had been written all that concerned the sailing of the slow boat and the mail boat for India.

The *City of Kulna* had started that noon, the mail boat

would start two noons later; they were scheduled to arrive, approximately, on the same day at Port Said.

Rex took the woman's hands in his bandaged ones.

"When we get back, Mrs. Rodd, we'll try to show our gratitude, both of us, Lotah and I."

Liza Rodd, beaming, triumphant, consigned gratitude for the nonce to the nethermost pit. It was a chance! It was a shot in the dark! It was like taking a journey across the world to buy a pig in a poke! It was adventure, risk, peril for life and love! Would they take it? If they did, when would they start?

"By the mail boat the day after to-morrow, bless you, Mrs. Rodd."

"Then will yer take a tip from me, wot knows life inside out?" They gathered round her as she whispered raucously, dramatically, from behind her hand: "Take that yeller cat, Ka-lok, wiv yer. I'll work it if yer gives me ten poun' ter buy 'er wiv. She's got 'er passport and everythink ready, the sly bit o' goods. Set a thief to catch a thief, an' a jealous woman to get 'er man out of the clutches of the other woman. D'yer get me?"

*   *   *

"Ah, there goes the gangway! We're off! At last! I don't think I could have stood another hour of this!"

Rex leaned over the ship's side and stared down at the quay where the relations and friends of those who had caught the mail boat at Marseilles seethed and shouted the customary futile remarks as they spasmodically waved their hands. He looked across at Marseilles town and up to the blue sky, where seagulls sailed on the fresh wind, and over his shoulder to the sea across which, as fast as the mail boat could take them, he and John Trevor were racing to save Lotah, and Ka-lok, the Tibetan girl, to fight for her love.

In the third class she hung over the ship's side, entranced with the noise and seeming confusion, the piercing shrieks of the siren, the raucous cries, the teeming life, the brilliant

sun and the blue sky; a smile lit up her expressionless eyes
as she thought of the fortune under her waistbelt, ten whole
English pounds; of the ease with which she had duped her
implacable father; of the scene there would be when he
discovered the trick played upon him by his only child.
"Some one run velly fast!" she remarked to her neighbor,
who stared in disdain and drew her skirt about her at the
native woman's presumptuous propinquity to the great
white race.

Yells and shouts came from the crowded quay, shouted
orders rang from stern to bows, mixed with the sailors'
sotto voce, but none the less hearty oaths as they obeyed
the shouted orders and once more lowered the gangway.

A girl came running swiftly, light of foot, contrite of
heart, followed by two panting porters laden with the lesser
luggage necessary to a voyage to the East.

Trevor gripped Rex's arm as he watched the girl run
quickly up the gangway.

"The stars fight for us, old man! You may have refused
the aid of the police, you can go on being as mule-headed as
you like about running that scoundrel to earth off your own
bat rather than make use of the wireless to get him held up
at Port Said, but all the same the stars fight for us! Come
on." He pulled Rex towards the head of the gangway, his
face beaming.

"What on earth's the matter? What are the stars fighting about?"

"That's Cecily Cleeve putting dust upon her pretty head
in front of the second officer for keeping the mail boat waiting two minutes—and there's nothing she doesn't know
about Tibet and its people. We'd better fix her up with
Ka-lok as maid as far as Port Said, anyway, and if we four
don't—— Hello! Cecily, that *was* a narrow shave!"

*   *   *

The passengers either openly stared at the gigantic
Tibetan, about whom there had been so much talk on

board, as he passed through the clutter of chairs on his way
to the first officer's cabin, or peeked at him surreptitiously
from behind the books or scraps of needlework with which
they were trying to fill in the time before arriving at Port
Said.

"Very high caste, I hear, and immensely wealthy——"

"I'm told—only, of course, this is a dead secret—that he
is the Grand Lhama himself traveling incognito——"

"Oh! but aren't you getting mixed up with the big, soft-
eyed animal in——"

"He's taking his sister back to Tibet to marry her; that
is why she is so heavily veiled——"

"Very beautiful girl; I caught a glimpse of her. I hear
she's to marry a Maharajah. Of course, very painted, as all
high-caste Oriental women are——"

"He paid an enormous sum to secure absolute
privacy——"

"How fascinating these Easterns are!" whispered Molly
Knowles to her mother.

"Yellow scoundrel, my child, if ever I saw one," replied
Molly's mother.

Sa-t'ong appeared to hear nothing of the whispered remarks which rose, like the buzzing of many flies, as, hands
folded in wide sleeves, he steered a course between the
curiosity-stricken folk. He stood at the rails for a moment
watching a blur of smoke far down the horizon, then turned
and knocked gently on the lintel of the first officer's door,
apologizing with Oriental suavity when the inwardly furious
but outwardly urbane man bade the intruder enter.

"You're the toughest proposition I've ever met three
days out of Shanghai!" thought the Scot as he looked
straight up into the Oriental's eyes, which looked serenely
down. "Oh! that smoke? That's the mail boat, the *Empress Flavia*, bound for Calcutta."

"Will she get into Port Said before us? I have some

merchandise on her which I would go to ask for; a friend brings it!"

The officer watched the placid face in a mirror hung slantwise on the wall, and frowned as the sibilant whispering words seemed to fill the small cabin.

"We shall drop anchor about the same time, I expect, but there'll be no chance of you seeing your friend. We've just had a wireless to say that they've got a case, steerage, suspiciously like plague."

Sa-t'ong Nyko-Gung moved a hand hidden in the wide sleeve.

"Then no one will be allowed to go on board the ship, and no one will be allowed to land from off here?"

The first officer's innocent blue eyes took in every detail of the Tibetan's rich Oriental dress and watched the slight movement inside the sleeve.

"The passengers for Port Said will land, of course, but they'll have the very devil of a time passing the medical authorities. No one will go aboard except the coaling coolies. Owing to the strike at home she is taking on a pinch of coal at Port Said, and their 'Sparks' informed us that, if we watched, we'd get a braw, wee lesson in coaling."

"Tough isn't the correct word!" said the first officer to himself, a little later, as he watched the Tibetan thread a way through the curiosity-stricken folk towards the staterooms he had acquired at such enormous cost. "Wonder if there's any truth in the story that the girl's going back to India to marry a nabob? Tibetan women aren't *purdah*, and high-caste Hindoos don't marry high-caste Tibetans. Wonder if there was anything in that wireless he got off Gib.?" He turned and looked at the mail boat eating up the knots. "Teach *us* a braw, wee lesson in coaling!"

Sa-t'ong stood for a moment at the rail. He did not turn his head, but out of the corner of his eyes he glanced at the first officer and touched a flimsy bit of paper hidden in the wide sleeve.

"They track me across the world." He spoke to himself, perfectly aware, although seemingly unconscious, of the passengers who openly or surreptitiously watched him. "The two white men follow me in that fast boat which is to take a pinch of coal on board at Port Said." In the shadow of the big sleeve he drew out the flimsy bit of paper and smoothed it out with the three slender middle fingers of the mutilated hand, and glanced at the wireless message he had received off Gibraltar.

"The two jars of white ointment numbered seven will follow you. Have been shipped on next mail boat. Ask for them at Port Said."

That was all.

"Only the coolies for the coaling will be allowed on the fast boat." He rolled the flimsy paper into a ball as he spoke to himself and flicked it over the side, stood for a moment staring aft, then turned away and entered the stateroom. There was no look of hate or revenge in his eyes as he stood looking down at Lotah.

"If it were not for my oath to my father!" he whispered.

Love filled his heart, his mind, his life; deep, unreasoning, unconquerable love; love for Lotah, the White Rose, who sat listless, drugged, watching unseeingly the troubled waters over which, in the mail boat, came the man she loved, to fight for her, and with him Ka-lok, to fight for Sa-t'ong.

CHAPTER VI

SA-T'ONG leaned against the jamb watching Lotah as she moved about the cabin which had 'been transformed into a private sitting-room for her especial use. She moved like a doll, an automaton, taking no notice of the Tibetan, nor of the harbor turmoil, nor of the lights of Port Said which gleamed and twinkled in the dusk, nor of the stars which shone above the shipping.

Her reflection looked strangely Eastern, strangely alluring as, ignoring Sa-t'ong, she indifferently studied her face in the mirror. Carmine had been added to the crimson of her mouth, so that it flamed in her face rendered death-white by means of the rice powder so beloved of the Oriental; dextrous fingers had drawn a fine, dark line upwards from the outer corner of the lids and the outer end of the eyebrows, giving a slanting effect to the opalescent eyes, which showed dull and lifeless, with slightly enlarged pupils which neither dilated nor contracted, between the thick, curling lashes. Her finger-tips had been dyed bright scarlet, also the lobes of her ears which showed under the heavy hair plaited round the head, piled high upon the crown and ornamented with two tassels of red silk fastened to a stem of silver wire. A heavy scent hung about the loosely girdled, orange-satin coat which fell to her ankles, covering the knee-high boots of soft leather embroidered in turquoise, coral and silver thread. Jewels glittered on her fingers, upon the hem of her coat, in the plaiting of her hair.

To look at, Rex Power's wife, John Trevor's cousin, was a beautiful Asiatic, a doll, a puppet of fate without will or desire; to the cross-bred Tibetan she was his idea of paradise, and his heart seemed to miss a beat as he took the paint-brush and tilted up her chin with the other hand.

He accentuated the lines at the outer corner of the eye and brow, then suddenly ·swept her up against his heart. She lay with her cheek against the golden embroidery of his satin coat, indifferent, unafraid, in the arms of a man who, for the first time in his life, was learning the meaning of self-denial.

Then she fought, suddenly, violently, to free herself; she beat upon the man's handsome face, then, with both hands pressed against the tremendous width of shoulder, tried to free herself from the arms which held her like a vice, whilst the agony caused by the stirring of her memory showed plainly in her eyes.

Above the turmoil of the harbor she had heard a laugh, the laugh of an Englishman as he negotiated the steep companion-ladder, and she fought to free herself, not only from the arms which held her, but from the effects of the powerful drug which allowed her to remember the events of the past hour but totally obliterated all memory of what had occurred in the hours, days and weeks preceding it.

As the sound of laughter stopped the vacant look crept back to her eyes. She ceased to struggle, and slipped back to her feet, standing unafraid in Sa-t'ong's arms, twisting with scarlet finger-tips the string of world-old, Oriental blue beads Rex had given her.

"What is the matter, White Rose?"

"I thought that was—that was——"

She made a desperate effort to catch the elusive memory tapping its message in her drug-numbed brain, lifted the heavy plaits of dark hair with nervous hands, laughed, shook her head and stood listlessly, plucking at the beads.

"Who did you think that was?"

"I—er—someone—I don't know—someone I met once a long——" She moved restlessly and pressed her forehead between the brows with her finger-tips. "A long time ago—some one I want to meet again—so much—so——"

She crossed to the port-hole and stood, with Sa-t'ong at her shoulder, staring out across the shipping to where the *Empress Flavia* lay flying the black and yellow flag.

"What did you do this morning, whilst I was on shore arranging our sojourn for the night in the house of my friend, the merchant prince?"

Sa-t'ong turned Lotah round towards him and bent and looked into her upturned face, dead-white, infinitely alluring beneath its mask of paint. She looked straight back into the eyes staring down into her own and smiled, showing perfect teeth between carmine lips, unconscious of the passion which caused the man to tremble as he gently touched a curl which escaped from between the heavy plaits.

"I—I watched the people go down the ladder to the boats—I watched the boats take them to the—over there——" She pointed to where the lights of Port Said gleamed and twinkled in the dusk. "I—I——"

"And yesterday?" asked Sa-t'ong in his own language. "Last night, all yesterday, what did you do? What do you remember of yesterday?" The soft vowels sounded like whispering in the cabin as Sa-t'ong repeated the question, insistently, as he endeavored to make certain of the lasting power of the drug he gave Rex Power's wife every night before she went to sleep, every morning when she wakened.

"Yesterday?" she repeated like a schoolgirl. "I do not understand. I—I am here now. What was yesterday? I remember nothing of—yesterday."

At the thought of the girl's helplessness, passion swept the man. He crushed the orange satin of her coat in his hand, then turned quickly away and busied himself with a tray, upon which stood everything necessary to the making of the heady green tea he consumed at every hour of the day, with no detriment to his cast-iron nerves; pulled a silver flask, with jeweled stopper, from his wide sleeve, fingered it with his slender hand, then laid it down beside the tray and crossed to Lotah.

"I love thee," he said gently, taking her hands in his. "I love thee, and would——"

"No, no!" she said quickly, sharply, then stopped.

"Why should I not tell thee that I love thee? I have no wife, no love. I am a rich man. I live in the house of my father, I, the elder, by a few minutes, of my twin brother. We paid back the mortgage upon the house and the land which my father raised to pay the fine to thy father. Bit by bit, *tiruk* by *tiruk*, we bought it back, the old house with the great gambling hall; therefore is the house my house and all therein mine as I am the elder by a few minutes of my brother. My interests are spread throughout all Tibet and over the frontier down into India. Sheep, goats, yak, outside the confines of Ladak; grain upon the borders of the Kiji Chhu River, *ne, dao, tro, katsam;* pottery in Kulna; brassware in Benares—ah! so much, so much, all mine, but thine, for I will buy my brother with many *tiruk*, so that he will give unto me the right to hang my boots upon the wall without thy sleeping chamber." [1]

Lotah looked up into the man's remarkable face, the beauty of which he had inherited partly from his King-po forbears and partly from his beautiful Hindoo mother. She studied the straight nose, the full, curved mouth, the big, languorous eyes, the unusual breadth of the face, the perfect teeth. She looked down to the small feet, shod in high boots of soft leather, and up to the thick black hair, which, owing to his cross breeding, he wore short.

A handsome, intellectual face, with a look of iron will about the jaw which, allied to his colossal stature, boded ill for Rex Power.

She put out her hand and touched the heavy, violet-colored, belted robe with high fur collar and cuffs of white

[1] A custom in Tibet, where polyandry is practiced, to denote a brother's priority.

cloth, and fingered the sleeved waistcoat of green silk with high red collar embroidered in silver thread.

"Yellow man!" she said slowly in English, frowning until her blackened brows met. "Yellow man, bad man! *Ajan! Ajan!*"

"Yellow men love as much as white men, Lotah *chung.*"

"Love? Love?" whispered Lotah, standing quiescent in his arms. "Love?" Her eyes were lit with the agony of awakening memory as she suddenly freed herself and walked quickly to the door through which had come the sound of the Englishman's laughter.

"Love!" she whispered, "and—and——" She leaned against the lintel staring listlessly out to the *Empress Flavia,* where the man she loved sat on the boat-deck, obstinately refusing to risk Lotah's life by calling upon the aid of the British Government to get her out of the Tibetan's power.

"Love!" she repeated when Sa-t'ong crossed to her and stood so close that for a moment her head touched his shoulder. Then she repeated the word and turned and struck him across the face, her mouth opening and shutting as she vainly tried to give utterance to the confused medley of thoughts racing through her mind, and backed away, arms outstretched, fingers spread, across the cabin to the far wall, where she stopped just under a picture of the goddess Paldean-Lha-Mo, before which flickered the light of a wick floating in a saucer filled with liquid butter.

Love, passion, anger died down in Sa-t'ong's heart. He raised his right hand and muttered a prayer on remembering his oath to his dying father, then turned and crossed to the table and dropped ten drops of the colorless, tasteless drug out of the silver flask into the cup of the green tea and carried it to Lotah, who stood, staring at nothing, under the picture of the Splendid Goddess.

"No," she said, pushing the cup away, then took it and drank the amber-colored liquid, and sighed and crossed to a chair, in which she sat for fully half an hour plucking at the blue beads on her breast.

"What did you do this morning?"

She looked vacantly up at Sa-t'ong.

"This morning?—I do not understand—I am here now—there is no this morning." She shrugged her shoulders and spread her hands, palms uppermost.

"What have you been doing, just now?"

"Drinking tea—talking to you—listening——" Her voice trailed off into silence, and she sat still, then got up and wrapped herself in a white silk shawl which muffled her from head to foot, hiding even her face and her eyes, which stared vacantly through the silken fringe.

The whole ship stopped work and watched her as she walked slowly, her hand on the Tibetan's arm, to the top of the companion-ladder, at the foot of which waited the merchant prince's boat with silken awning and curtains, manned by four Nubians as black and glistening as coal.

"Mighty pertickler about their womenfolk be these natives!" remarked one of the crew to his chum.

"May be a case of a face pitted with smallpox," replied the chum, who suffered from a lack of sentiment.

"Well, thank the Lord *this* bloomin' hulk is free of passengers *at* last."

"More than the mail can say. Her passengers are fair mad and ramping, what with the contagious case they've got and the coal they're going to get on board."

They watched Sa-t'ong lift Lotah into his arms and carry her down the ladder, and turned to their duties with a sigh of relief at the ship's emptiness.

*   *   *

"I am going to turn in. A little more of this coal dust in the air and I shall be as black as one of the coolies. Good night! and bolt your door and remove everything from the vicinity of the port-hole. In some ports there is a nice little game played through the port-hole by means

of a short rod with a hook at the end." Cecily Cleeve gave
a hand to each of the men and looked up at John Trevor.
"I still believe Rex is right. We haven't been able to
establish the identity either of the man or the girl with him.
From all accounts she is a native, and he is one of the
Nyko-Gungs, the well-known merchant princes, known all
through Asia."

"Yes," said John Trevor slowly, "and *that* makes it all
the harder. We could have tackled an ordinary native, but
it would mean the very dickens if we interfered with a
high-caste Oriental and his women-folk."

"Yes," said Cecily, "and whoever he is or whatever his
caste, he is innocent until proved guilty, and we haven't
proved that—yet. We can't possibly have him arrested,
and, as Rex says, once we frighten him we are done for,
because he would be perfectly capable of throwing Lotah
overboard or doing away with her on shore, sooner than
give her up or get into serious trouble over her."

"Besides, we know that they are booked through to
Calcutta," added Rex.

Cecily looked towards the third class.

"The way these natives get information is simply
astounding, and without rousing suspicion, too. What
should we have done without my little maid, Ka-lok?"

"And you?"

Cecily smiled up at the two men with whom she had dis-
cussed the problem day after day.

"In the East the lightning intuition of one native is worth
the stolid reasoning of ten honest whites! Good night!
and don't forget your door and port-hole."

John Trevor accompanied her to the head of the companion-ladder, then returned to Rex, who leaned on the
rail, staring across at the funnels of the *City of Kulna,*
lying silent and deserted behind a mass of shipping.

"I'm feeling pretty desperate, old man. Is it Lotah or
not? Are we chasing moonshine or one of the blackest

rogues unhung? Shall we have power, when we intercept her coming down the gangway at Calcutta, to stop her, hold her, keep her, if she is drugged and unable to recognize us, or will the Tibetan be stronger than us and sweep all before him?"

Trevor made no reply as he lit a cigarette.

Hour after hour, day after day he had argued and reasoned, beseeching Rex to employ the days they would have to pass in Calcutta whilst waiting for the *City of Kulna*, in calling the British law to his aid, only to find himself up against his friend's fixed determination, backed by Cecily Cleeve's approval.

John Trevor loved Cecily from her dainty shoes to the top of her russety head, but he could willingly have shaken her for her championship of Rex's mule-headed determination to win out off his own bat.

"I can imagine what it is like waiting to be hanged, waiting to know, waiting, waiting in the dark, hoping even when they come to fetch you to execute you, that the opening of the door means a reprieve. I have to wait for days, for God knows how long, whilst that old paddle-boat chugs down the Canal, over the Red Sea, across the Indian Ocean. Waiting, waiting." Rex lit a cigarette and stood up. "It's late! I'm going to turn in, too. Let's have another look at the coolies. They look like lost souls, laden with their sins, disappearing into the mouth of hell."

They crossed to the port side and watched the natives, coal basket on back, deftly and with the certainty of long custom, run up the narrow plank which connected the coal-lighter with the ship's bunkers.

"They don't distribute the work according to size, do they? Look at that spindle-shanked pigmy staggering under his load, and that hulking great brute carrying just the same weight as though it was a loaf of bread."

The native overseer's voice rang out sharply.

The hulking great brute had stopped in the middle of the

plank to readjust his load. The handsome, sinister face was hidden under a mask of coal grime, as Sa-t'ong flashed a look upwards to where the two white men leaned on the port rail. Then the hulking great brute moved on in obedience to the overseer's cursing.

Two hours later Sa-t'ong took his chance.

He was at the edge of the bunker, the first of a string of coolies following him, sure footed as goats, up the narrow plank. He stumbled, threw his coal basket back against the man behind, then flung himself forward, and, in the shouting and splashing of the string of coolies, who, to a man, had fallen into the water, where they were like to drown, crawled along the narrow edge and disappeared, unnoticed in the confusion, into the shadows of the lower deck. He lay for fully five minutes, then, still upon his face, slid a few yards and rose slowly to his knees, his feet.

Flattened against the ship's side, stopping to listen, running a few yards swiftly, stopping in the shadows to stand stock-still, to run again, he made his way, as only a native could have done, by sheer instinct, across the sleeping ship, along the alleyways, up the companions, past shut doors, to the first class. At the door of the saloon he stopped suddenly and looked back, then, like a shadow, stole behind the door and watched the dim alleyway lighted by one globe; waited to find out the meaning of the sound he had sensed rather than heard. Nothing stirred. He felt for the knife in his grimed loin-cloth, crept out of the saloon like a shadow, and, flattened against the side, slid up the alleyway towards the cabin marked 7. There slept the white men who held the documents concerning the White Rose which could so incriminate him in a Court of Justice, the men who were hunting him across the world.

He crept on, and Jealousy silently followed, running swiftly on bare, slender feet.

Quietly Sa-t'ong fingered and lifted the hook which held the cabin door of No. 7 ajar, and, lying flat on his face, pushed it open inch by inch. Like a great snake he slid in, until he lay full length beside the lower bunk in which Rex Power slept fitfully, turning from side to side, muttering in his sleep.

Outside the door, flat against the wall, her dark hair pulled about her face, a knife hidden in the fold of her dark native dress, stood Ka-lok. She waited for the moment when, by the simple means of driving the dagger home, she would wrest the man she loved and who had loved her for so brief a while in the gloom of Limehouse, from the hands of Lotah, the White Rose.

What wakened Rex? What opened his eyes suddenly, then bade him lie still and listen and peer into the dark through half-closed lids, as he slid his hand inch by inch under the pillow.

God, maybe, who loves lovers!

Came the sudden, crashing, double report of his revolver and Ka-lok's shrill scream as a bullet ripped the top of her shoulder, as she drove the knife down and missed Sa-t'ong. Swiftly, unheard in the shouts and cries which came from every side, he fled like a cat along the alleyway, out on to the deck, and dived over the ship's side, the splash unheard in the uproar made by the terrified passengers as they called for the steward, the first officer, the captain, the life-boat.

Peace eventually restored, they retired to their bunks after duly complimenting the brave native girl who had so valiantly tried to prevent the thief from escaping.

"Tell me, Ka-lok!" said Cecily Cleeve, as she added a fresh strip of plaster to the dressing. "Were you really sitting outside my door, sewing?"

Ka-lok shook her sleek head.

"I take l'il walk. I play l'il idensick."

"Idensick?"

Ka-lok spread her hands before her face, then looked out at one side and said: "Peep-bo."

"Ah! hide-and-seek."

"Ka-lok wait l'il time—kill."

"Kill? Kill who?"

"One, piecee, bad man who t'ly kill M'lister L'ex."

"Who was the bad man? You said he was a thief, one of the coal coolies," whispered Cecily Cleeve in Tibetan.

Ka-lok crossed to the door and looked along the deserted alleyway, then came back to Cecily Cleeve, and, standing on tiptoe, whispered one word.

"Sa-t'ong."

CHAPTER VII

"LET us drink to the happy ending," said Trevor, raising his glass.

"To the quick passing of the next few hours," said Cecily, raising hers.

"To our meeting," whispered Rex. He raised his glass. The slender stem snapped in his steel-strong fingers and the red stain spread across the cloth as the glass fell.

"*Aï! Aï!*" muttered the waiter, as he made the gesture to propitiate the god of ill-luck and endeavored to remove the cloth.

"Leave it," said Rex. "Do you know what that is a sign of?" He looked from Cecily to Trevor as he spoke. "That's not ill-luck or disaster, it's death, and the one to die is Nyko-Gung, or both of them, you mark my words. Spilling wine at the end of a meal always means death, so Janet Comfort said, and she wasn't far out when she predicted this journey, in the fire, was she? Bring me another glass, waiter."

The suspense was at an end; the *City of Kulna* was due to dock in the early hours of the morning, and the three, waiting to be told the exact hour, lingered over their dinner to pass the dragging time.

"To Lotah!" murmured Rex, and drained his glass.

Only the two who knew Rex intimately could have told of the effect the trial of endurance, the horror of the seemingly endless days, the absolute agony of the hour during which the mail boat had sighted, passed, spoken to, and lost the *City of Kulna* to view, had had upon Rex Power.

Obsessed by the fear that the half-caste Tibetan might

78

treat Lotah with physical violence, even cause her death if he suspected that the arm of the law had been stretched across his path to stop his flight with the girl he had abducted, Rex had obstinately refused to listen to Trevor when he had pleaded and urged him to make use of the wireless on board or of Government House in Calcutta. Cecily had sided with him.

In the weeks of agonizing suspense on the boat she had come to look upon Rex Power in much the same way as John Trevor looked upon him. She loved the boy as a sister might love a favorite brother; she admired the reserve which had allowed him to live through the past days without making his agony a burden for others to bear; she loved him for the strength which had enabled him to resist Trevor's constant urging to call in outside aid; she had backed him against the man she loved, and had given Trevor to understand that, until Lotah had been found, until Rex's happiness had been assured, there could only be friendship between themselves.

Cecily Cleeve had realized Trevor's great love for her, yet even she did not guess how that love had grown almost to worship during the days on board when she had, so willingly and cheerfully, shouldered as much of Rex's burden of despair as she had possibly been able to. He admired her unshaken optimism, but even more he loved her for the strength she had shown when, over and over again, she had refused to listen to his pleading.

"Not until Lotah is found," she had said gently, "not until Rex is free of his ghastly suspense can we talk of marriage."

So Rex's desperate need, the shadow of his tragedy, had kept the words of love unspoken on John Trevor's lips, but the knowledge of that love, deep, steadfast, and all-enduring, had run like a thread of gold through the hours.

He would never forget the hour when they had stood at the rail waving their handkerchiefs, hoping against hope

and against all reason, that Lotah might feel their presence, even if she could not recognize them, as the mail boat
thundered past the slow boat in the Red Sea. He would
always treasure the words Cecily had spoken then when
Rex, in an agony of despair, turned and made his way
back—alone—to his cabin.

"Ah!" she said, her eyes alight with the optimism of her
dauntless heart. "Just to think of their meeting!"

"And of their joy!"

"And ours," she replied.

"Ours?"

"Yes, ours! Don't you think we shall have earned the
right to be happy in their happiness?" she answered, shad-
ing her eyes with her hands. "Because, you see, until *they*
are happy we cannot think of our own personal happiness,
can we?"

She had laid her hand for an instant on his arm, and
turned and made her way, with eyes alight with love, to
her cabin.

The waiting was indeed at an end. The manager
approached their table, bringing the news they had been
waiting for.

"The shipping agency has just rung up to inform you,
sir, that owing to an accident in the Kidderpore Docks the
City of Kulna will be berthed in the farthest docks of all,
at five o'clock in the morning."

Cecily Cleeve laid her hand on Rex's arm as she looked
across the dinner-table at Trevor.

"The boat will get in very early, sir, and as our representatives will be aboard almost as soon as she docks"—
the manager bent and picked up a fork which Rex, with a
sudden, uncontrolled movement, had knocked off the table—
"there will really be no actual necessity for the gentlemen,
or madam," he bowed to Cecily, who sat with her hand
on Rex's arm, "to rise at such a most unpleasant hour."

"But——" Trevor stopped speaking as Rex interrupted

quickly, his eyes ablaze, his hands gripping the edge of the table as he half rose from his chair.

"Let us go down to the docks now, at once, to make sure. Perhaps——" He sank back, white to the lips, when Trevor spoke quickly.

"But there won't be any mistake. We'd better——"

"I think we'd better wait, Rex, and it is very kind of you to think about the early hour, Mr. Smith," broke in Cecily Cleeve, smiling at the manager. "But, if you can promise me a taxi or a *gharri*, because I don't want to go down in the hotel omnibus, I would like to be called in plenty of time to get there. You see, we are not quite certain of our friends' movements; they may not be coming to this hotel, they may have made other arrangements."

The diplomatic manager bowed.

There was something out of the ordinary in these three interesting English guests of the Great Eastern Hotel. They did not know that he knew of their pressing inquiries at the shipping agency as to the exact hour of the slow boat's arrival.

Few Europeans in India do know to what extent their movements are known and reported upon.

Until the previous day, when they had learned the approximate hour of the *City of Kulna's* arrival, they had behaved just like ordinary travelers, going here, there and everywhere; since then two only had gone out, and that not for long, leaving one behind in the hotel; they had been in to every meal; had sat in the lounge or stood in the cool marble hall talking together; the younger man had shown a great restlessness, amounting almost to nervousness; the clerk at the shipping agency had been most emphatic that Miss Cleeve should be told at once of the hour of the ship's arrival.

Trevor and Rex did not know that he knew they had fruitlessly searched for a street spanned with many arches, passing hour after hour in the native bazaar, questioning, searching, to no avail.

Why the mystery? What or whom were they looking for, and in such a street?

"Certainly you shall be called, madam, and a conveyance be waiting for you, and if I can be of any help in any way, please rest assured that I am at your service."

Cecily smiled and watched the manager thread his way between the tables, then turned, and, with a sigh of relief, patted Rex on the arm.

"The curtain is up," she said quietly, then looked across at Trevor. "It is up and——"

"Do let's go down to the docks *now*," interrupted Rex, rising from his seat. "Supposing they've made a mistake? Supposing she docks earlier? We might not be there; that yellow devil might land and get away; come on, let's go down now and wait all night."

Cecily looked across at John Trevor, and, unseen by Rex, slightly shook her head. "Let us go upstairs and talk it over first and lay our plans," she said. "We must be awfully careful. Let us go and wait until Ka-lok comes with the flowers; she won't be long. And, oh! Rex, we have to be so careful."

"Men like the Nyko-Gungs are sure to have spies everywhere," added Trevor, as he shut the door of their sitting-room.

"The Nyko-Gungs!" exclaimed Rex impatiently. "How do we know that this particular yellow brute *is* one of the brothers? What have we found out about them—their private family affairs, I mean? This man is supposedly traveling with his sister. Have the Nyko-Gungs got a sister? We know that the father is dead, but have they got a sister or a mother or any living relation? We haven't been able to find out, and our only way of proving that this girl with this Nyko-Gung is *not* his sister, but *my wife*, is by meeting her face to face and accusing him of abduct-

ing her. You are my witnesses. I've got her photograph—
the living image of her—and all the necessary documents."

He flung open the window and stood staring down into
the Chowringhee, whilst Chang-ku stood patiently on the
other side of the famous street, watching the window, the
hotel entrance, the three white people, as he had watched
them ever since they had landed at the Kidderpore Docks.

"I'm not taking another risk," continued Rex. "The
boat may be in at any moment. Remember Port Said,
how we were kept in quarantine because of that case of
wrong medical diagnosis!"

"Rex—dear Rex!"

Rex backed away from Cecily when she put her hand
on his.

He was at breaking-point.

Sympathy was the last thing he needed. He wanted
movement, certainty.

"Can't you see how small a thing can lose me my wife?"
He spoke harshly to Trevor. "Shut up on that boat all
those hours, with Lotah there, almost in my grasp, just
because a case of ptomaine poisoning or something was
diagnosed as plague. We were free to land—free—free!
Do you think I will take the slightest risk now? I'm going
down to the docks, anyway, whatever you two decide
to do."

As Rex abruptly turned away Cecily signaled to Trevor.
He followed him into the adjoining room, and, shutting the
door, faced him as he stood with his back to the window,
looking at his friend with desperate, defiant eyes.

Once more he begged Rex to listen to reason, pointing
out the danger of one false step at this most vital moment;
the likelihood of some of Sa-t'ong's friends being on the
quay to meet him; insisting, above all, upon that secret
bond which spreads from the north to the south, from the
east to the west in the lands of the East, linking, in spite

of the rigor of caste, the rajah with the beggar, the priest with the poisoner.

"Sa-t'ong Nyko-Gung, if that is the man's real name, may know that we have followed him, that we are on his track. His brother is sure to be somewhere near. In these days of wireless——"

"Oh! nonsense," said Rex sharply. Inwardly he acknowledged the wisdom of his friend's words, but outwardly denied it, so desperately anxious was he to put into practice his plans of boldly accusing Sa-t'ong, upon the deck itself, of abducting Lotah. "How can any one know? All this talk of secret brotherhood, or whatever it's called, is all rot. Why, even the manager has no idea that Ka-lok is one of us, when she brings Cecily flowers every morning and evening."

John Trevor jumped at the chance Rex's words gave him.

"Ka-lok will be coming along with the flowers in"—he glanced at his watch—"in fact, she ought to be here now. I'll tell you what we'll do: we'll send her down to the docks to wait all night. No one will notice her Mongolian face; there is a whole street of Japanese and Chinese shoemakers in the city. We'll give her plenty of money, so that if there is any likelihood of the boat getting in before six she can take a *gharri* and come along and tell us."

"*I* am going!"

"You must not be seen anywhere near the docks, and one of us *must* stay here in the hotel. Supposing Ka-lok came back with news and we had started. Cecily must come with me, as interpreter, as we don't know how much English that brute speaks, and you must stay here only until the boat is sighted. Then we will 'phone you, and you'll be down in plenty of time."

"I *will* go instead of Ka-lok," replied Rex stubbornly.

"You *can't* go now by yourself—you wouldn't know your way about down there, old man; you don't speak the language. You must *not* be seen anywhere near the docks until the boat is in, for fear of spies. You've got to stay here, in the hotel, until we 'phone you. Can't you trust us to stop Nyko-Gung from getting away?"

"Yes, of course I can; but, by God! I won't stay behind. I—there's Cecily knocking at the door. I expect Ka-lok has arrived. Come on, let's go in and see what she says. She *is* capable of coping with the brutes and outwitting them, if any one is."

Cecily laid the case before Ka-lok, in her own language, and Ka-lok answered with a deprecating movement of her slender hands.

"She says," interrupted Cecily, "that one of us must wait here in case of accident, and that Rex is not to approach the docks before the boat is in. She says, also, that if I will give her my dressing-case or something to carry she will, if she has to come back here, do the journey in half the time by taking a motor instead of a *gharri* from the docks, pretending to be a lady's ayah going on in advance to the hotel. She says she wouldn't stand a chance otherwise with a native driver."

For half an hour they fought Rex's stubborn resistance, whilst Ka-lok sat motionless, cross-legged, in a corner, her eyes expressionless, her hands still, her heart brimful of love for the man who was coming slowly up the Hoogli towards her.

At the end of half an hour Rex suddenly gave in.

"After five o'clock you have got to ring me every twenty minutes. I still don't see why Trevor should go instead of me."

"Because you'd break the brute's neck as soon as you saw him."

"Of course I should."

"And you would be arrested for assault, and that's not going to help. You've got to break his neck afterwards, when you have got Lotah. Leave it to us. The man can't get off the boat until we let him."

And not one of them heard the laughing of the gods as they crossed their knees.

An hour later, dressing-case in hand, Ka-lok, slipped like a shadow from the servants' entrance, and hailing a rickety *ekka*, drawn by a highly decorated pony with its bones almost through its skin, was driven away to the docks, where, seated on the dressing-case in deepest shadow, she commenced her vigil, sustained by love and hate and a surpassing jealousy.

Chang-ku glanced at the solitary woman as the *ekka* clattered by.

He knew nothing about Ka-lok's desperate effort to follow his brother; Sa-t'ong knew nothing of her passage in the mail boat; those who had sent him the wireless which he had received off Gibraltar, warning him that he was being followed, had known nothing about her, else might they have added to the message that, with the two jars of white ointment, had been shipped a small packet of deadliest poison.

*   *   *

Chang-ku learned many things during the time in which he and Sa-t'ong, to fulfill the oath of revenge they had sworn before their dying father, tried to find the Tibetan woman Tsi-tsi and the white child she had stolen.

By mere chance a rumor about the old woman came to the village hidden in the mountain fastness of India's northern frontier, and without hesitation the two brothers, merchants of renown throughout the world, placed their affairs in the hands of a subordinate and followed the clew.

In their lust to revenge their father's memory they gave barely a thought to the stupendous trade in exports they had built up, the far-reaching tentacles of which touched silks and porcelain in China; leather, sheep, horses in Mongolia; pearls, sugar, spice in Nepal; saffron, salt, silver, rugs, furs in Tibet; and opium-poppy in Yunnan.

They crossed to England accompanied by their sister, who had inherited her Hindoo mother's beauty.

Finding English life greatly to her liking, and with no desire to return to a land where she had been looked down upon for her cross-breeding, she ultimately sold her birthright and passport to Sa-t'ong for many hundreds of pounds and set up on her own in Liverpool's Chinese quarter.

The brothers crossed to England under their own name, as the great merchant princes Nyko-Gung, but, once there, took advantage of the bond which binds all Orientals, the one to the other, in foreign lands, and lost their identity.

Disguised, they passed as Chinese unskilled workmen in the labyrinths of the Chinese quarters of the big seaport towns. There they lost the clew and followed a blind trail to America; picked the clew up and followed it to San Francisco; lost it again and returned to the seaport towns in England, where, for many, many moons, they hunted vainly for little old Tsi-tsi, who lay *perdue* in a Limehouse basement.

The battered image of the goddess Paldean-Lha-Mo, a chance word in Cardiff, put them on the right track at last.

"Behold *amo!*" had jeered a native of Sikkim to another, in Sa-t'ong's hearing. "Behold! art thou almost as fervent in thy worship of the Splendid Goddess as is Tsi-tsi, who keeps a lighted candle day and night before the Dread One in London?"

The words led the brothers to Limehouse, urging them upon the path of crime and tragedy, which had been marked out for them long before false gods had been conceived and blindly worshiped in mortal mind.

Amongst the things Chang-ku learned during his sojourn in the fog-bound seaports of Great Britain was the extraordinary effect fine clothes and a display of wealth have upon the people of those isles.

Dressed as a poverty-stricken, unskilled laborer, he had been kicked and buffeted and despised; wearing the sober but rich garb of a great Eastern merchant, gems gleaming on his fingers, gold glittering on the black satin of his full, heavy robe, deference had been shown him wherever he had gone.

He acted upon this certain knowledge now.

He left his post of spy outside the Great Eastern Hotel, and after giving final instructions to the driver of a ramshackle public motor-car, who would have sold his soul for a golden piece, retired to the house of a friend, situated upon the outskirts of the Bazaar. There he put on his very finest raiment, then made his way to the docks.

The *City of Kulna* had just berthed.

The crowd surged around the great car when it came to a stop, and pressed close upon Chang-Ku, in his picturesque dress, as he got out without glancing to right or left. He made his way to the gangway slowly, imperturbably, fully aware that success or a long spell of imprisonment for himself and his brother, depended entirely upon getting Lotah off the boat before friends or relatives of the passengers or the representatives of the Great Eastern Hotel were allowed on board.

It would be an easy matter for the two white men or the white woman to raise an argument on board the ship about the relationship of the White Rose to his brother, but it would be quite another thing, and most unwise, to raise a doubt and to ask for proof of a native's relationship to the woman traveling with him, once they stood on Indian soil.

He advanced, counting upon his rank, his clothes, jewels and personality to get him past the member of the crew waiting at the foot of the gangway and the officer who stood on deck.

And Ka-lok, watching him, realized that she had to come to a decision.

She had never set eyes on Chang-Ku, he in no way resembled his brother, but, warned by woman's instinct, she intuitively connected him with Sa-t'ong, the man she loved. She watched him slowly descend from the car and follow a servant, who, none too gently, made a way through the crowd of Europeans, Eurasians and natives of every caste, arrayed in flowing garments of every conceivable color.

Something had to be done, and quickly.

Long before the *City of Kulna* had docked, almost to scheduled time, Ka-lok had literally scoured the quay in search of John Trevor and Cecily Cleeve, who, for some unaccountable reason, had failed to appear.

She had passed the night, wrapped in a blanket, hidden in the shadows thrown by a stack of bales; blue with cold and shivering, she had crept out when the sun had risen, had feigned much surprise at the mistake she must have made over the hour of the ship's arrival, and had proclaimed herself as the *ayah* chosen to meet a certain important native lady arriving on the *City of Kulna*.

She had been told that the ship would get in at six, and her heart had lightened; but when her own English people had failed to appear she had been torn with doubt and indecision.

Had they mistaken the dock? Had they forgotten the hour? Had they had some of the wireless, that strange news which came out of the air? Had the gentle Miss Cleeve died suddenly, perhaps of a poison administered by her enemies?

Mr. Trevor had told her to drive back to the hotel at greatest speed if the boat was signaled to arrive earlier.

The boat would arrive at the time appointed. She would wait. Yet would it not be wise to race back to the hotel to see if aught was amiss and to ask for instructions?

Yes, she would do so. And yet again, if she did she would leave the field to the enemy. She would not know if Sa-t'ong and Lotah, the White Rose, were on board or not; she would not see the man she loved, would not be able to find out about his future movements.

She would remain, and yet—and yet——

Anxious to have everything ready if the race back to the hotel should prove necessary, she approached the least rapacious-looking of the taxi-drivers and made a bargain.

She explained her case. She, the *ayah*, awaited her mistress, who returned from a voyage over the Black Waters to Inglistan. She might, at a moment's notice, have to go at lightning speed back to the big hotel on the Chowringhee to fetch her mistress's lady friend, a Mem-Sahib of highest rank. How much?

"Ten rupees!" had said the taxi-driver, who, with his eye on the dressing-case, had not believed a word of the story.

"You one big thief!" had shouted Ka-lok.

"You two big thieves!" had insolently replied the driver, pointing at the item of luggage in the girl's hands.

Dropping it, she had subjected him to a torrent of the choicest vernacular straight from the lowest reaches of the Bazaar, mixed with a certain quality of English she had picked up in Limehouse.

The quarrel had waxed fast and furious until a crowd had collected, urging the combatants to greater verbal effort.

Then Ka-lok had seen an opportunity and had seized it.

She had pointed convulsively at an officer who came their way and had shaken her fist in the driver's face.

"Ha!" she had screamed. "A Sahib, a friend of the Mem-Sahib approaches. I run ask him to have you beaten, you thief, you brother of a family of black pigs."

The driver, who had been cautioned but a week ago for furious driving, had given in. He had winked at Ka-lok and had spread his slender hands.

"I but played with big, beautiful sister. Eight rupees, and in my hand before the start."

"Six!"

"Seven!"

"Six and a half and three in your hand before the start, and the rest at the hotel."

"I take it, you flat-faced daughter of a Bazaar camel. I wait here for you!"

"And I will have your license taken away if you fail to wait for me. I speak the language of the *Sahib-log*, I live with them! I am *of* them! I leave you this, as a guaranty of my most honorable intentions. If you make off with it I call aloud 'thief.' I have your number."

Dropping the dressing-case on the seat beside the driver she had run this way and that searching for her white people; had climbed a bale of goods and had stood on the top looking everywhere, until ordered sharply to come down; had run hither-thither like a lost dog, and had beaten her breast when the great ship had come slowly into view.

But when, a little later, Chang-ku made his stately, unconcerned way through the excited crowds, with one last despairing glance around she literally fought her way towards the gangway which connected the *City of Kulna* with India. She would get there first! She would face Sa-t'ong and denounce him! She would not wait for Miss Cleeve or for Mr. Trevor. No! She would save Lotah and her own love at the same time! Like a streak of lightning she was halfway up the gangway before the astonished sailor caught her.

"Here, you!" he cried, jerking her backwards and planting her firmly on the quay. "None of that! You wait your turn, which'll be last if you don't look out, pushing before your betters, and no orders to go aboard given out yet."

"*Baksheesh*, plenty I give you. I, *ayah*, servant to lady on the ship," she cried desperately, pulling out her purse and trying to force it into his hand. "I pray to be allowed to walk up upon the boat. No! *You* say no!. You *bud-mash!* you . . ."

The sailor fell back before the stream of Limehouse abuse she hurled at him, but spread his arms across the gangway at an order shouted from above.

Then Ka-lok realized that she had made a great mistake.

She had drawn the attention of the crowd upon her, and in less than a minute she would be face to face with Chang-ku.

She did not hesitate.

She dived into the crowd and fought her way back to the waiting car, where the driver salaamed ironically, snatched at the half of his fare, and, once free of the crowd, ripped into top speed. Terrified at the risks he took, Ka-lok crouched back in the corner, her hands before her eyes, praying to her gods to help her, to save her from disaster, to bring her safely to the hotel where Rex Power waited for news. If she had not prayed so fervently, if she had not pressed her hands so tightly upon her eyes, she might have seen two cars lying wrecked at the roadside and a crowd surging outside the shop into which a partly stunned Mem-Sahib and a totally unconscious Sahib had been taken, whilst the native drivers of the wrecked cars, unhurt but violent, stood outside in the hands of the police; neither, farther on, did she see a car rush past, breaking all records in speed through a crowded thoroughfare.

Rex Power did not see her. They crossed. One carrying news, the other lost in a great storm of despair and doubt, which seemed to burst about him when a policeman signaled the driver to stop.

Furious, Rex beckoned the policeman to his side, then flung himself out of the car and forced his way through the crowd to where Cecily stood, a streak of blood upon her cheek, one hand pressed against her forehead, the other holding to the jamb of the door.

"In God's name, Cecily, where's Lotah? Is anything

wrong? Has anything happened? I waited. The manager said the boat was punctual, but you never 'phoned." He shook her slightly by the arm as she looked at him vaguely and frowned. "I couldn't wait any longer. I had to find out. I drove to meet her. Lotah! Where is she? Is she with you? Don't tell me she is hurt, in there—injured in the accident. Cecily! Cecily! speak. Say something! Oh, my God! is—is Lotah—is she dead?"

"Lotah!" repeated Cecily. "Lotah!" Then fear ousted the vagueness from her eyes, and memory came back as she made a valiant effort to recover from the blow which had partly stunned her when she had been flung out of the car against a tree. "Isn't she with you? What is the time? What is it?" She glanced at her watch. "What has happened? My watch has stopped. How long have we been here?"

"The Mem-Sahib has been here a full hour. It is almost the seventh hour of the new-born day," said a soft voice at her elbow, as the owner of the shop salaamed. "Will the Sahib permit that I offer him and the Mem-Sahib a seat and *chotarhasri*, a cup of coffee or a cooling drink? I saw the accident, Sahib. I stood at the door watching the glory of the new day just as the car in which were seated the *Sahib-log* came, of a truth at a great speed, down the street." He pointed at the driver of a ramshackle taxi, lying wrecked at the roadside, who had been bribed by Chung-ku to bring about the accident. "That accursed son of sin, who should verily be driving an *ekka*, crossed the road, and at a great speed flung himself against the other vehicle."

"The other Sahib? Where is he?"

"The Sahib within recovers. He moans. His forehead is covered in sweet ointment. 'Twas a hard blow, but none too grievous a hurt. I return thanks to the great gods. The police wait until the Sahib recovers."

Rex walked quickly into the shop where Trevor lay,

slowly returning to consciousness, satisfied himself as to the nature of the hurt, and returned to Cecily.

In five minutes he had completely changed.

Gone was the impatience, the almost uncontrollable irritability, the desire to do something, anything, as long as something was being done to further Lotah's rescue.

The venerable Hindoo salaamed before the look in the young Sahib's eyes, and Cecily sighed with relief as she noticed the undaunted look in the strong young face.

Rex was a born fighter, and he fought best with his back to the wall.

Rapidly he gave his order, which Cecily translated. A messenger was to be sent to the manager of the Great Eastern Hotel; the Sahib who was hurt was to be informed, when he recovered, that his friends would be with him shortly; the police were not to let the drivers go.

"*Jāldi! Jāldi!*" cried Rex, as hotel omnibuses stacked with luggage and private and public motors filled with passengers from the *City of Kulna* passed them. "As hard as you can go. Tell him, Cecily, I'll give him great *baksheesh* if he'll drive like hell!"

At the head of the gangway Rex met the first officer, who, at his first question, beckoned a sailor.

"Find Jenkins and tell him to come at once." He turned to Cecily. "I'm afraid you're too late. The man and his sister——"

"Sister!"

Cecily put her hand on Rex's arm.

"As such they were down on the list, Mr. Power, and most certainly their passports made them out as brother and sister. He was one of the great brothers Nyko-Gung, the merchant princes."

"I want to speak to him——"

"Wait a minute, Rex."

"Ah! Jenkins. Stateroom-steward, Miss Cleeve! Tell

me, Jenkins, who waited on the sister, the native lady, in your stateroom?"

"The brother, sir. You'll excuse me saying so, miss, but these high-caste natives simply play old Harry when they bring their women-folk aboard. This party had the deck just outside their cabin reserved for them, and, of course, had their meals by themselves, but, excepting for looking after the cabin, the stewardess did nothing for the lady at all. Never saw her close to, never spoke to her."

"Did any one come to meet them?"

"The other brother arrived almost before the gangway was lowered," replied the first officer, "and with the colossal assurance of the high-caste native came on board, even before the medical authorities. Said he would wait, and did wait, just where we are standing, and it was simply impossible to move his high-born Serenity. Directly the medical officer went ashore the two brothers and the sister followed. Jenkins!"

"Sir!"

"Have you any idea where they were going to?"

"Yes, sir. The label on the luggage gave an address at a place called Ballygunge. I took particular notice, sir, because the tips were that lavish, and the mystery lady so closely wrapped up and smothered in veils and shawls and so tottery on her feet."

Rex turned to Cecily.

"Ballygunge! Cecily, that's quite near, it's a suburb!"

"Wait a minute, Rex dear, you don't know the native." She turned to the first officer. "Mr. MacTavish, you will think us very strange, but I promise to tell you the meaning of all this directly we get the matter straightened out. The man may have been one of the Nyko-Gung brothers, but the woman was not his sister. She is a white woman."

"Then, in Heaven's name, why didn't you make use of the wireless, Miss Cleeve?"

"Because success depends on secrecy and on that only!"

replied Rex, in whose eyes once more shone a great flame of hope. "Might I go and look at the staterooms they used? Thank you; do come with us. Cecily, we——"

"I'm going on shore, Rex," replied Cecily, who was staring intently over the ship's side. "You'll find me at the foot of the gangway."

Ten minutes later they met in the middle of the gangway, outwardly calm, inwardly on fire with excitement.

"Look, Cecily, look!" said Rex, as the first officer watched them over the side. "The stewardess found this, *this*, my wedding present to Lotah, stuffed down the side of a couch." He opened his hand a little. In it gleamed the string of wonderful blue beads, Oriental, old, old as the world and its sorrows, the beads which Lotah had worn, loving them, playing with them, fingering them as they had lain like a necklace of little blue flames on her breast.

"The officer gave them to me, against all rules. Come, let us get back to Trevor and start for Ballygunge."

"We're not going to Ballygunge!"

"Not going!"

"Don't look round just now. Two Bhutanese are standing near some crates, I've just been listening to their conversation!"

From the deck Cecily had recognized the typical faces of the people of Bhutan, and, pretending to be waiting for some one, had walked to within earshot, where, with back turned to them, she had listened to their conversation, which they had not for one moment imagined a Mem-Sahib could understand.

"Lotah, whom they imagine is Sa-t'ong's wife, has been taken to Benares, to one of the business houses the two brothers have all over India. The label with Ballygunge was evidently to serve as a red herring across the trail. Come, we must pick up John, if he has recovered, if not we must leave him behind. There is no time to lose. We must find Ka-lok, I expect she's waiting at the hotel, pack the bare necessities, and get to Howrah Station. Come."

They turned and waved to the first officer, who saluted.

"I always said that yellow devil, Nyko-Gung, was about the toughest proposition unhung I'd met three days out of Shanghai," said he to himself.

CHAPTER VIII

"WAKEN her that she may dance before us!"

"Nay!"

The two brothers looked at each other across the *charpoy* on which Lotah lay, lost in a deep, drugged sleep. Eighteen years ago to revenge the insult offered their father, a well-to-do unscrupulous trader on the borders of Sikkim, they had killed the girl's parents and burned their bodies to hide all trace of the crime. Upon their father's death-bed they had sworn before a statue of the goddess Paldean-Lha-Mo to pay back the mortgage on the house and the lands raised to pay the heavy fine; to work until they had reinstated the family name of Nyko-Gung in the list of honorable traders; and to search until they found the baby girl who had been saved from the massacre by Tsi-tsi, the Tibetan nurse.

When found they had sworn to bring her back to their father's home and marry her according to the ethics of polyandry, throwing the dice to decide the question of precedence; to degrade her to the rank of a servant, to force her to the most menial tasks, to make her wait upon other women who might chose them as husbands or whom they might take to wife; to repay the insult offered their father a hundredfold until the girl died, when they would throw her body to the dogs.

Thus they had sworn eighteen years ago, and good fortune having followed them persistently, they had fulfilled part of their oath. They had bought back the house and the lands and had reinstated the name of Nyko-Gung in the list of honorable traders.

Then they traced the girl; found her; abducted her, and stood, one on each side of her, like beasts of the jungle, staring into each other's eyes, watching, waiting warily for a movement, a sign.

Apart, it was difficult to tell the one from the other, owing to their height, their mannerisms, and the exceptional softness of their voices; together, but for their colossal stature, inherited from the Kang-po race of their father, there was but a trace of family resemblance between them.

Sa-t'ong, excepting for a scarcely noticeable uplift to the outer corner of the eyes, had inherited the beauty of his Hindoo mother, her slender hands and feet, the gentleness and grace of her ways; his inborn ferocity lay hidden under the suave bearing of the wealthy Oriental, and he moved with the stealth and noiselessness of the Bengal tiger, after which he had been nicknamed. Chang-ku was nearer the Mongolian, with a greater slant to the outer corner of the eye; a higher cheek-bone; big, well-shaped hands and feet; and the cunning, watchful ways and slinking habits of the black Himalayan wolf, from which he had taken his nickname. Sa-t'ong loved Lotah, and was trying to find a way out of the tangle brought about by his oath to his father and the customs of his country. He wanted her as his only wife, he loved her, and waited for the moment in which to offer even unto the half of his immense wealth as a bribe to his brother to give her up.

He loved her desperately, and would share her with no man, and swore that, in the sweetness and gentleness of his love-making, he would make her forget the boy to whom she had been married for so short a time in the slums of London.

Chang-ku desired Lotah with all the savage instincts of his race. Until he had seen her and realized her beauty he had looked upon woman as a special breed of cattle, good to work in the fields and the house, to bear children whilst young, to cook and to serve when old. But this girl, rose-flushed as the summit of Mount Everest at dawn, straight as a young pine, as fragrant as spikenard, he desired for himself alone. He would share her with no other man. In his mad desire he forgot his oath to his father; he would offer his brother, Sa-t'ong, the handsome Bengal Tiger, even the half of his immense wealth as a bribe with which to buy the right of precedence over the white girl asleep on the *charpoy*. Once he had attained that right, once Lotah was his, he would kill his brother and would see to it that the boy, the husband of so short a time, should die before the year was told.

No, he would not share the girl with his brother, whom, in the secret places of his black heart, he had always hated for the beauty of his face and the suppleness and grace of his movements.

And towards them, as fast as train and car could bring him, came Rex, fearless in his love, a David against two Goliaths endowed with the cunning as well as with the strength of the wild beasts which haunted the mountain fastnesses, in the shadows of which the two men lived.

Lotah stirred, put her hand to her neck, murmured, "My beads—my blue—beads," and was lost again in a sleep induced by drugs, which was near to unconsciousness. She lay upon her side, her head upon her arm; the veils in which she had been muffled on the quick journey from the docks in Calcutta to Benares, the most sacred of all India's great cities, lay in a tumbled heap upon the floor; in the dim light of the shuttered room her hair, in two great plaits, looked like snakes coiled upon the silken cover. Sa-t'ong bent and gently ran his finger through a curl which fell across her cheek, then looked up sharply, understanding in a flash, on his guard, when Chang-ku's hand gripped his wrist.

The two men stood absolutely still, bent down above the girl, their eyes searching, each trying to find out the other's secret; then Chang-ku released his hold; they straightened themselves and looked down at Lotah, then across at each other.

"One half of my fortune, brother. The herd of *yak* without compare, my half, to add to thy half, of our trade in brass, both old and new, here in Benares; what thou wilt for the right of precedence with this white girl, who is as the lotus-bud."

Chang-ku spoke softly, his heart beating heavily under the fine white silk of his robes, his big, well-shaped hands gently folded, his eyes half closed, hiding jealousy, hate and desire in their depths.

There was no sound in the dim, bare room as they faced each other. The light of two lamps, flickering before the statue of a god hidden in the shadows of a corner, shone on two large brass bowls standing on the floor, filled with scented water; a ray of sun filtered through a crack, touched a pile of satin cushions, a brass tray holding teacups of wafer thickness, slid across the matting of the floor, climbed the wooden-paneled wall, and was gone before Sa-t'ong slowly shook his head.

"One half of my fortune, brother, one half and yet a quarter; my half, to add to thy half, of our trade in peltry; the house of our father, which is mine, as, by four minutes, I am thy elder; the necklace of pearls such as no Maharajah can boast of in the whole of Ind; what thou wilt, that this white girl, who is as the most glorious pearl in the necklace of pearls, be mine before she passeth unto thee."

Sa-t'ong spoke quietly, his mutilated hand hidden in the wide sleeve of his fine linen coat, his eyes, fixed upon Lotah's face, hiding the look of surpassing love in their depths which changed to one of terrible wrath and a still more terrible ferocity when Chang-ku slowly shook his head.

They stood quite still, looking at each other, as might two jungle animals about to spring, and bare feet, running swiftly through the house, made no sound, as Fate, hidden in the shadows, opened her gnarled old hands in which lay hidden the love of three men for the girl lying asleep upon the *charpoy.*

"Thou lov'st her?"

"I would have her for my love!" slowly replied Chang-ku.

"Thou lov'st her?"

"I would her for my wife," replied Sa-t'ong.

"Then will we remember our oath, O my brother, to our father upon his death-bed, and will throw the dice for her in the Hall of Gambling, upon the Night of the Full moon."

"Yea, Chang-ku!   And we will go north without tarrying. And let not thy wolfish mind dwell upon tricks of cunning, lest I break thy neck 'twixt thumb and finger."

Chang-ku spread wide his hands, smiling gently, showing all his splendid teeth.

"O my brother, has thou so—— Hist!"

They turned their heads.   A gentle tapping came upon the panel of the wall which showed no door.

Three taps, then two, a pause, and one.

"Rama urgently desires to speak to us!"

"*Nai!*" called Sa-t'ong softly, drawing the silken cover over Lotah's face as a panel slid back in the seemingly solid wall opposite.

"Well?"

Sa-t'ong looked down at the servant who, having shut the panel, ran across the room and knelt and touched the men's insteps.

"Two Sahibs and one Mem-Sahib wait without, masters."

The brothers made no movement, neither did they glance at one another.

"Their business?"

"To make inquiries of their Excellencies Nyko-Gung as to certain porcelain."

"Porcelain!" interrupted Sa-t'ong.   "Why didst thou not inform the *Sahib-log* that, in Benares, the firm of Nyko-Gung deals only in brassware?   Why didst thou not, thou child of little sense?"

"The Mem-Sahib, Excellency, was insistent!"

Chang-ku's eyes were alight with cunning, a little satis-fied smile hovered about his mouth as he raised his hand.

"If my honorable brother, who is by four minutes my elder, permits, his brother of no worth will tell of a plan which has been but this moment conceived in his poor brain."

Sa-t'ong spread his hands with a deprecating smile, upon which sign of brotherly humility Chang-ku told his plan to Rama, the servant, who was as unscrupulous a villain as himself. "—And quickly," he ended. "Keep not waiting the *Sahib-log,* for behold they are not renowned for the virtue of patience. Throw wide all the doors, wide, so that the *Sahib-log* see into the rooms as they pass. Let Makhami and Sohni sit at the entrance, bewailing the death by black fever of their sister. When the gong sounds once, beg the *Sahib-log* to honor me by traversing the corridors, making humble apologies the while that the illustrious head of the firm of Nyko-Gung is even now upon his way to Calcutta, from where he takes the boat to Chittagong, in Burmah. That is all, and for the safety of thy life make no mistake."

Rama salaamed and ran across the matting to the far wall.

"Who sits without the outer gate?" said Sa-t'ong softly, "or stands, or loiters in the shade?"

"But the blind Fatma. When your servant went out to greet the *Sahib-log* he kicked the woman in the back because of her eternal wailing for *baksheesh,* and she, seizing a stone, and seeing naught with her blind eyes through her matted hair, threw it and caught the biggest Sahib between the shoulders."

Rama touched a spring and slid the panel back between slender fingers.

"Rama!" said Chang-ku softly.

"Excellency!"

"Bid Boodna, the Keeper of many cows, to wait upon me."

"Rama!" said Sa-t'ong gently.

"Excellency!"

"For the safety of thy neck and the necks of all those thou holdest dear, add not *dhatura* to the tea when thou bring'st it at the second sounding of the gong."

Rama spread his hands with a deprecatory smile. "I am their Excellencies' humble servant, obedient in all things," he murmured as he slid through the opening and closed the panel behind him.

"And a master-poisoner, railway thief and criminal as well," supplemented Chang-ku with a lenient smile as he opened his hand upon the palm of which lay an ivory square.

"The dice must settle, and in the shortest space of time, O my brother, which one of us accompanies the white dove as far as our house upon the borders of Hilli which lies upon the road to Darjeeling, and which one waits here to deal with the *Sahib-log* who would negotiate for poreclain in Benares. The highest wins!"

Chang-ku flung the dice upon the floor and called five, with exultation in his slanting eyes. Sa-t'ong threw his upon the silken cover and called a six, and, stooping, lifted Lotah into his arms and turned her head and pressed her face against his shoulder as he carried her to the wall.

"I stab thee to the heart, brother, if thou playest false with me."

Sa-t'ong looked back over his shoulder into his brother's blazing eyes and down at Lotah, sleeping upon his heart, and shook his head.

"Fear not, little brother! I would have her for my wife and the mother of my sons. The others can be picked up like dust from the road." He lifted his head and stared at the wall through which, for an instant, he saw down the past, to where a girl of his own race waited for him in the murk of a Limehouse street. "Like the dust from the road," he repeated. "They count for naught. They love not, remember not."

He touched a spring and passed through the opening into the grounds and paused for a second.

"*Baksheesh* for the blind! *Baksheesh!* Pity the blind!"

Ka-lok, who had bribed the blind Fatma with many rupees, gathered dust from the ground and put it upon her head as she peered through the cactus hedge and the tangle of her matted hair.

*   *   *

Cecily Cleeve gripped Rex's arm as, for a moment, she paused on the threshold of the dim room.

At the far end Chang-ku sat upon the pile of cushions in front of the statue of a god which showed dimly in the shadows. He sat staring in front of him, the lamps at his feet, the bowls of scented water at each side. The room was bare, save for the corner where he sat, watching from between half-closed lids; the air was intolerably heavy with the scent of the perfumed water, and the place was as still as it was empty, foreboding. Terribly still.

"Is that the face you saw through the skylight?"

Rex pressed close to Trevor as he barely whispered the words.

"I think so, but I am not sure!" Trevor whispered back, then broke the foreboding silence. He could see the effect the room and the silence were having upon the girl he loved, guessed that it had all been arranged to produce just that effect, and looked round the strange place in which apparently there seemed no doors, as he greeted the still figure at the far end.

"How do you do, Mr. Nyko-Gung?" he said in a matter-of-fact voice from where he stood. "Forgive this intrusion, but we heard, quite by accident——"

"Quite by accident you heard about the porcelain in

Benares. Be welcome!" said Chang-ku, as he rose and stood towering in the shadows, hands folded in his sleeves, imperturbable, indifferent, as he played for the time necessary for his brother to get Lota from the house and the city.

So the Englishmen, having tracked Sa-t'ong, his brother, across the seas, in some unaccountable way had learned of his flight to Benares, and had learned it quickly enough to have been able to follow by the next train.

Fools! he thought. Fools to have followed so hot upon the scent, to have walked into the enemy's camp, relying upon the chance perhaps—in which surmise he was correct —that the White Rose might see them or hear their voices and cry for help.

The work of the handsome boy doubtless, poor fool, who had married Lotah in the London slums and who dared to pit his wits against the most cunning brain to be found in a land of great cunning; a brain into which had already flashed a scheme for the riddance of these blundering white people.

He bent his head to his knees, his hands folded in his wide sleeves as Rex walked across the floor towards him with his two friends close behind.

Handsome boy, he thought, handsome, foolish boy who had come to Benares with his friends in search of his wife, of the girl he, Chang-ku, and his brother loved.

They had entered the Holy City, but, by the great Hindoo god Siva, the god of his mother, they would not find it so easy a thing to leave the City of Temples and labyrinths and narrow streets in which pilgrims and sacred cows and peaceful citizens walked crushed against each other.

Rex crossed the room, his left hand upon the revolver in his pocket. Lotah was in the house. Sa-t'ong, the Three-Fingered Tiger, stood before him, hiding his mutilated hand in his wide sleeve. What easier than to cover him with the revolver and to demand his wife on pain of death!

And yet! In some subconscious way he felt that somewhere there had been a mistake; that he was not quite
certain of the identity of this man; that, of the two brothers,
he was not sure which this one would turn out to be.

"I *think* so, but I am not sure!"

Trevor's words rang in his ears as he walked close up to
the giant half-caste who overtopped his six feet by four
inches. In less than a minute he would know. He had
but to see the mutilated hand to make sure, and there was
no difficulty about that.

"How do you do, Mr. Nyko-Gung? My name is Rex
Power. My friends are Miss Cleeve and Mr. Trevor," he
said, holding out his hand.

Chang-ku bowed until his head was on a level with his
knees and backed a step and sideways so that his foot
struck the brass bowl which boomed like some giant gong.

"His Excellency will pardon his servant's seeming dis-
courtesy, but, as this is the anniversary of the death of the
servant's father, he is not allowed to touch the hand of
living soul within the twenty-four hours."

"You barefaced liar!" thought Trevor, then turned
sharply. On noiseless feet Rama had entered in answer to
the summons of the gong. In one hand he carried three
big cushions, upon the other he balanced a brass tray with
teacups of water-like transparency.

"How nice of you to give us *tea!* Afternoon tea, as we
call it, is quite an English habit," said Cecily Cleeve as
she seated herself on the cushion, so that, sideways, she
could see the doorway, to which there seemed to be no
door, whilst her ears were strained to catch the faintest cry.

"Ah! Mem-Sahib, it is poison, not tea, you drink in
England."

"You have been in England?"

"I have been almost all over the world. Rama!"

"Master!"

"Drink of the *cha* thyself, my son, as an act of courtesy

—it is but a custom to prove to the guest, Mem-Sahib, that the beverage contains no poison—then go tell Makhami to cease her wailing lest she gets herself a beating. She cries for her youngest daughter, Excellencies, who died this noon of the black fever, and is to be carried to the Burning Ghats within the hour."

Who was this man before her, who talked of crime and death with such indifference? Cecily was as much at sea as to his identity as Rex and as determined to make him show the hand hidden in the sleeve. She took the cup filled with green tea, and, when the servant Rama had turned to Trevor, pressed her fingers hard upon it. It broke into small pieces, spilling the tea upon her skirt, and as she sprang up with a little cry she held out her hands to Chang-ku, who leapt to his feet, his hands still hidden in the wide sleeve of his silk robes.

"Rama! A cloth of silk to wipe away the stain, if her Excellency will permit a menial's hand to touch her honorable dress. If it were not the anniversary of his father's death, her Excellency's servant would demand the honor for himself."

Cecily smiled. The man was not to be caught by so simple an expedient.

"It is of no account, Mr. Nyko-Gung. It really does not matter, does it, Rex?" She turned to the men who were watching Chang-ku's every movement. "Does it, John?"

Rex's hand tightened upon the revolver in his pocket as he caught the glance of hatred which flared for a moment in the slanting eyes.

"It's the man right enough," he thought as Rama, having finished wiping the infidel's dress, made his way to the door.

"And as a sign of pardon, Excellency," Chang-ku said suddenly in the Sikkim dialect to Cecily as he stood close to her, looking down, "I will ask you to accept a humble gift of brass, of silk."

But neither was Cecily to be caught unawares. She

smiled again, sweetly, into the inscrutable face and shook
her head. "I do not understand," she lied quickly, quietly,
fighting for the girl who lay in this terrible man's power,
whilst Trevor sighed with relief. "Hindustani, yes, it is not
so bad, I have a friend—from India—who has taught me,
but that language, no! And you speak such good English,
why confuse me, a stranger to the land?"

He repeated his words in English, and she declared herself delighted to walk through the different rooms of the
long, low house and to choose something from amongst the
treasures as a souvenir of her pleasant visit, even if the
porcelain they had come so far to see could not be shown.

"We've been through the whole house, every room and
corner of it," said Trevor to Rex quietly some time later.
"Lotah's not here. I'm as perfectly certain of that as I am
certain that she has been. And I don't think she is far
away."

They had been through the entire house, admiring everything. Cecily accepted a little statue in bronze of the joyful
god Ganesh, holding the pat of butter he stole so many
thousand years ago. They crossed to the servants' quarters
and inspected the scrupulously clean kitchen and staff of
smiling servants, and still Chang-ku kept his hands hidden
in his wide sleeves and Rex his hand upon his revolver,
awaiting his opportunity.

And as they returned from the servants' quarters there
came a great wailing from the gate leading out into the
high road, where Ka-lok sat in the place of Fatma, the
Blind.

Makhami, beating her breast in grief, Sohni, tearing her
raiment in despair for the dead girl who, wrapped from
head to foot in red gauze with silver hem, lay in a hammock
which swung upon two poles from the shoulders of four
men.

"The daughter of Makhami, Excellencies! She died of

the black fever, for which the white people have a great fear."

"*Aï!   Aï!   Aï!*"

The wailing rose to the heavens in which the sun was setting.

"*Aï!   Aï!   Aï!*"

Ka-lok rose and blundered into the procession as it passed, forcing her way as near as possible to the swinging hammock.

Supposing the dead girl was Lotah?

She lay so still.

Was it a dead girl?   Could it be Lotah in a drugged sleep?

She cursed Makhami when the woman pushed her roughly to one side and squatted on her heels in the dust of the road.

She would wait until they had gone some distance on the road, she must wait to slip a note into Cecily's hand as she came through the gate, telling them where to meet her, then she would follow that girl in the swinging hammock and find out who she really was.

"Death!" said Chang-ku indifferently.   "It is but the sleep of the gods, to the young.   What time have they had to have learnt of pain, hate, jealousy—love?   If their Excellencies permit, I will offer refreshment."

He pressed tea, sweetmeats, fruit upon his guests, and when they regretfully refused, owing to pressure of time, he accompanied them to the gate of his honorable dwelling which he placed at their disposal with all that therein was.

"*Baksheesh* for the blind!   Pity the blind, *aï! aï!* Pity the blind!"

By means of his foot Chang-ku forcibly removed Ka-lok from her post beside the gate.   She blundered into Cecily, who pressed a coin into her hand, then moved away cursing volubly, tapping with her staff, in the wake of the procession which had almost disappeared to view down the dusty road leading to the Ganges. Chang-ku bowed until his head almost touched his knees as he proclaimed his pleasure at their Excellencies' visit and his grief at not being able to show them the porcelain they had come so far to see.

"It was worth their Excellencies' while to visit the Burning Ghats after the sun had set. The glow of the fires reddens the holy water. The chant of the faithful rises to the heavens where the great gods dwell. That is the way, Excellencies!"

He withdrew his hands from the wide sleeves of his silk robes. With the left he touched his heart, with the right he pointed down the road.

The hands were big and well shaped, neither was there a finger missing on either hand.

He bowed his head to his knees as his guests made their way to where a motor-car awaited them, thereby hiding the smile in the evil, oblique eyes which had once looked down through a skylight in a Limehouse roof.

CHAPTER IX

On her silvery, placid bosom Holy Mother Ganges reflected the temples which stand straight or lean sideways, splashed in crude colors, festooned with faded flowers; the hundreds of praying rafts moored to poles; the Praying Ghats; the dull crimson of the cinders or the orange and red of the leaping flames which purify the dead by fire on the Burning Ghats.

A slender figure, wrapped in the red gauze which denotes the Hindoo maiden, lay at rest across the pyre of consecrated wood; wailing women knelt, beating the breast; a white-haired man, naked save for the loin-cloth, walked slowly round the funeral pyre with flaming torch in hand.

Thrice he made the circle, then touched the oil-soaked wood, and turned and sang the praises of the Holy River, as the flames shot skyward from the slanting, tilted steps.

Rex sat alone in the shadows of a temple watching the scene, listening to the yelling and laughing of the jackals as they hunted across the plains on the far side of the river, to the murmur of the water against the steps and the soft voices of the wailing women. He looked up to the star-lit sky as though there he might find the answer to his problem, across at his friends who sat so close together on the last step but one of the broad flight, and towards the Burning Ghats where in four places flames danced and flickered in the shadows, marking the spots where four of those who had succumbed that day to the black fever were being purified by fire before entering upon a new life.

They had doubtless found answers to their problems in death.

Where were the answers to *his* problems?   Where would
he find the Street of Many Arches which the dying Tsi-tsi
had described by signs in the air—the street where the
bad men dwelt?   Not in Calcutta, nor in Benares.   They
had found the house where the brothers lived on the outskirts of the Holy City.   They had made inquiries about
a street spanned with arches of the hotel manager and the
hotel guide.   No street approaching their description was
known in Benares.   Where had Lotah been hidden?   How
had she been taken from the house into which, so Ka-lok
had found out, she had been carried?   From Ka-lok's post
at the gate that afternoon she had been able to see the
main entrance and the entrance of the servants.   No one
had gone in, no one had gone out, neither had there been
sign of disturbance in or about the house.

This much they had learned from the note which she
had thrust into Cecily's hand as, propelled by Chang-ku's
none too gentle foot, she had knocked up against her.
Since then they had seen nothing of her, neither upon the
road nor in the hotel, where they returned to talk things
over.   They decided at last to go on to Mughal-Sarai, so
as to allay any suspicions they might have aroused, and to
leave Ka-lok to watch the house of the merchant brothers,
to get into communication, if possible, with the servants,
and to pick up as much information as she could about
them in the city.

Ka-lok, it seemed, had discovered from blind Fatma that
the brothers had returned from a long sojourn abroad with
their sister, who had fallen sick on the voyage.   She had
been carried into the house in Sa-t'ong's arms and had not
been seen since.

Blind Fatma would have sold her one silver earring for
a few *annas* if any one had thought fit to offer her the
sum; for ten rupees she sold her silence, her staff and her
site for the afternoon to Ka-lok, and for ten more she
would be willing to sell any information she could get about

the brothers who, even if they or their servants did kick her at times, saw to it that she never wanted for food or for a few *pice* in her dust-grimed hand.

Rex did not want to leave Benares.

Until they had certain proof that Lotah had left the house and the city he rebelled against moving to Mughal-Sarai.

"Spies!" he had cried at Trevor's very sane suggestion, "of course there are, and will be, spies about us. In every man or woman near us, behind every temple, every door, every tree. They will follow us in the train, wait on us at table, sit outside the *chick* watching us, reporting upon us, so why *move?* Ah! to give those two a little more freedom, to make them relax their vigilance—well, perhaps you are right."

And so he had given in, though rebelling in his heart, and accompanied them to the moon-shaped bend of the mighty river to which pilgrims flock in their millions to find salvation, and where Ka-lok said she would come and find them.

He sat with his chin in his hands, whilst Cecily Cleeve sat with her hands round her knees, watching the dead body of a youth which had been committed to the safe keeping of the Holy Ganges as it floated, face downwards, towards the ocean or the river bank. John Trevor, breaking their compact, had asked her to be his wife.

"But you will marry me some day, Cecily?"

"Oh, yes, John!" she replied with a smile in her steady eyes.

"Then we are engaged, Cecily Cleeve?"

"Nothing of the sort, John Trevor!" she replied with a gentle laugh, and then withdrew her hand and turned her head, staring up-stream.

"What was that? Did you hear a splash?"

"Some pilgrim bathing, I expect," answered Trevor, as he watched her red-gold curls move in the breeze.

A few minutes later she pointed towards a praying raft near the bottom step. It was made of two squares of wood, the bottom one floating on the water, the top one for the pilgrim to kneel upon at dawn. The platforms were connected with four short legs, about a foot long, at each corner, and it swung to the tide, fastened by a bit of rope to a pole.

"Look at those ripples, John." She laid a hand upon his as she pointed. "I wonder what has made them?"

"A rat, I expect!"

"But they say there is no vermin on the banks of the Ghats, and that the water quite near the shore, even with the dead bodies floating in it, is perfectly pure."

"A fish, I expect then, Cecily," replied John Trevor, who, like most men, and unlike all women, could only entertain one thought at a time.

"But look, they are such big ripples." She turned round and looked up to the palaces of the Rajahs which stretched right along the top of the slope upon which the famous steps are built; scanned the thousands of temples and shrines, waved her hand to Rex, and leaned forward and looked at the broad river, seeing nothing of the evil eyes watching her from between the space made by the four short legs which connected the praying raft's upper and lower platforms.

She ran a bracelet up and down her arm as she watched the ripples widen and widen until they faded away, leaving the silvery bosom of the Holy River as placid as before. She and Trevor and Rex seemed to be the only human beings on the steps; the pilgrims waited for the dawn; the beggars had crept away to the crowded streets; even the mad priest, who calls upon the dread Kali from dawn to dusk, to dawn, lay still, lost perhaps in sleep, perhaps in coma brought on through the frenzy of his religion. And yet she peered about her, restless, perturbed, then began to speak, softly, almost below her breath indeed, though every word carried over the waters to the listening ears hidden behind the praying raft.

"I think we might get back now, don't you? Would it be safe to walk back through the streets? I would love to see the pilgrims by night, and the Cow Temple and the Temple with the golden roof. And we ought to get some sleep, because I think we should catch the early train to Mughal-Sarai, don't you?"

She rose as she spoke, her hand in Trevor's, then turned and climbed to where Rex sat, staring into the night, oblivious of everything, lost in his thoughts of his beautiful Dream Girl stolen from him by the man who had played with him, baffled him that afternoon.

They stood, their backs to the river, looking up to the wall of palaces stretched across the top of the high ridge. Had they but turned they would have seen once more the strange ripples breaking the water's smooth surface; had Chang-ku but waited a few more minutes before he slipped beneath the surface and swam some hundred yards to a landing-place hidden by a temple which had tilted to one side, he would have donned his robes and made his way at greatest speed to the station, instead of to the spot where Boodna, the Keeper of many cows, awaited him.

But he slipped like a phantom between the temples and shrines, taking no notice of the dread, flower-festooned gods which peered at him from the shadows, and disappeared long before the figure of a woman suddenly stood upon the top step of the great flight, outlined against the night sky, peering from right to left amongst the temples and shrines and strange gods. And Cecily and the two men were half-way up the steps before, with a little cry, Ka-lok gathered her draperies about her and ran like a deer to meet them. Her robes were filthy, her hair matted and falling about her face, the staff she had purchased from the blind Fatma, together with her silence and her site, fell with a clatter as she caught Cecily with one hand and Rex with the other,

She spoke quickly as she gasped for breath, and Cecily, horror-stricken, translated as quickly as she could, gripping Rex tightly by the arm.

"Rex!   John!" she cried.   "Good heavens!   That funeral procession we saw—the girl who had died of black fever—you remember—that dead girl in red was Lotah."

"They've killed her!   Oh, my God!" cried Rex as he wrenched himself free and turned upon Trevor who had gripped him by the shoulder.

"Be quiet, Rex, old man.   Let her speak.   The quicker she tells the tale the quicker we can act—go on, Cecily."

"No, she's not dead, but she was in the house when we arrived at the door.   Ka-lok followed the funeral procession until it stopped beside a man on the road.   He pretended to be a relation of the dead girl, but it was Sa-t'ong, Ka-lok recognized him by his hand.   She followed the funeral procession at a distance; it went through the streets, turned off into a side street and into a courtyard behind a house, where Lotah was lifted from the hammock and carried indoors.   Wait a minute, Rex, just a minute."

Ka-lok, with all a native woman's expressive gestures, closed her eyes and laid her cheek against her clasped hands.

"Lotah is drugged, she says, heavily drugged, and sleeps all the time.   They waited until a man called Rama, evidently the servant who brought in tea, arrived, then Lotah was put into a palanquin, as though she were a *purdah* woman, and carried to the station.   Sa-t'ong is dressed as an ordinary well-to-do native, the brother is to follow them."

"Where, in God's name, have they gone to?"

"Darjeeling!"

"Darjeeling!"   Trevor's shout brought the pigeons from the crevasses in the walls, the holes in the turrets of the palaces, the windows, the loop-holes, the shadows of the shrines, and of the great Mosque.   They wheeled and flew in thousands, the stir of their wings sounding like the ripping of silk on the night air. "Of course they've gone to Darjeeling, and are going on either to the spot where aunt Beatrice and uncle Ben were murdered or to the house of their fathers. They just came to Benares to put us right off the scent, and now they are doubling on their tracks. And we've got to get there first."

"And we're not so far behind, Rex!" cried Cecily. "Only one train! Come along, let us get to the hotel. We might be able to get a special train at Mughal-Sarai. We must go and find out where we change for Darjeeling. Ka-lok, what shall we not owe you?"

"At the end, Missy Cleeve," said Ka-lok slowly, spreading her fingers against disaster. "At the end! Ka-lok know this yellow man. One cunning fox, jackal, wolf."

Cecily shook her slightly.

"Don't be pessimistic, Ka-lok. We shall be there almost as soon, and perhaps, if we can make use of motor-cars anywhere, sooner."

But she had reckoned without Boodna, the Keeper of many cows, as she ran up the Holy Steps followed by the men.

Ka-lok stayed behind to wash the filth from her hair and her outer robe in the waters of the great river. She washed it out and sat upon the steps, chewing betel-nut until her mouth ran red with the crimson juice. She sat dreaming of Sa-t'ong, the man she loved, until, upon the still night air, came a great clamoring from behind the Rajah's palaces, where the narrow streets stretched in an endless maze.

Shouts of men, screaming of women, bellowing of cattle.

She rose, hair streaming to her knees, mouth running red, half clothed, and fled like a deer up the steps and down the other side to the spot from whence came the dreadful clamoring.

It is an easy thing to find your way to the Praying Ghats

during the day time. Courtesy begets courtesy in the land which was civilized long before the inhabitants of northern climes had progressed even towards the Stone Age. Any one will point the way out to you; a few *annas* will provide a guide who will accompany you; a rupee will cause him to stick closer than a brother until your visit to the Holy City has drawn to a close.

But at night it is infinitely unwise to penetrate the crowded streets without a guide, and even then only with one who is well known throughout the city.

India belongs to her own people—at night—when the Bazaar is packed to suffocation with laughing, singing, happy folk who have—perchance—eaten the one really satisfying meal of the day, shut their shops and left their houses to find their friends in the jostling, merry crowd.

Especially is it unwise in Benares, where at night the streets are almost impassable except at the slowest pace, and crowds collect around the shrines or at the entrances of the temples of the gods, or for no reason at all.

The strong, slow pulse of religion beats in the human stream flowing through the streets of Benares after the sun has set. In the light of lamps, torches carried by Kali's disciples, candles carried by little maids, the strange gods look at you from out their shrines; the sacred cows push you gently, nuzzling in your sleeve as they wander, un-molested, where they will; pilgrims push you, perhaps not so gently, to one side, as they hasten towards the shrine of their intent, be it the Cow Temple, the Golden Temple, or the Temple of Durga, where the sacred monkeys play on the walls and ring the silver bell to announce the advent of a pilgrim to the shrine.

The foreigner with his strange manners, strange clothes, speech and religion is not wanted in the streets after the tourist day is closed, at the setting of the sun. He is tolerated when with a guide, watched hostilely if alone, shown his way to his hotel, and none too gently if his curiosity outstrips his deference to customs different to his own.

No, the foreigner is not wanted in the streets at night, and a little crowd gathered round Cecily Cleeve and the two men, when, without a guide, they walked as quickly as they could through the streets, and stopped, having lost their bearings, within a stone's throw of the Cow Temple.

The ill-lit streets, the shadows, the houses bending towards each other had perplexed them; meaning to turn to the left they had hesitated and had asked the way of a beggar by the roadside, and the beggar, in Chang-ku's pay, had directed them to the right and towards the holiest spot of the Holy City. A little crowd gathered around them, murmuring, whilst across the street, down which they would have to make their way in order to reach their hotel, Boodna stretched the cattle, which he handled as could no other man in India.

"I don't like the look of this," Trevor said quietly to Rex, crossing so that Cecily stood in the middle of them. "Good Lord! What on earth does he want?"

A disciple of Kali, the mark of his religion smeared in red between the brows, a trident in his hand, barefoot, bearded, gaunt, with the glare of the fanatic in his eyes, walked up to Cecily. He raised his trident above his head and shook it as he called down the curses of his god upon the *feringhee*, whilst the crowd murmured and pressed close, the women hiding their children's faces in their skirts so that the eyes of the unbelievers should not rest upon them.

"What does he say?"

"He is cursing us. He tells us to get out of the holy street," said Cecily quietly. "Keep as quiet as you can, I think we are in great danger." She slid her hand into Trevor's, then pulled it gently away when a woman shouted an insult at her and the whole crowd laughed.

"Ask them the way to the hotel, Cecily. Say that we

are lost. Keep your head, Rex. Don't touch one of them as you value your life."

"Please," said Cecily in Hindustani, "we have lost our way to the hotel. Quite by mischance we have walked into this street in which the Sahibs do not walk, I believe, after sunset. If some one would kindly show us, ah! would this little girl?"

A child of six in white muslin robes, bracelets on her arms, anklets clashing above her slender feet, walked slowly forward.

"That way, white woman!" she shrilled at the top of her voice as she pointed down the street where Boodna waited with his cows. "Straight down there, and begone, lest the great gods curse you for defiling the shadow thrown by their temple." She walked closer up to Cecily and spat at her feet, then laughing, ran to the terrible figure with the trident and hid her face confidingly in his long robe, whilst the crowd laughed and shouted: "Begone! Begone!" opening up a way through which the *feringhees* could return to their hotel.

"Don't hurry," said Trevor quietly, "don't, for God's sake, let them think that we are afraid. Make for that grain shop at the corner, once there we're all right."

They passed through the crowd which began to lose its animosity and to turn to affairs which interested them more closely; they arrived at the grain shop, and all might have gone well if Rex, inadvertently, had not caused the storm of hate, roused through religion as it is roused in every country all over the world, to crash upon their heads.

As they neared the grain shop, with Rex next the baskets of grain exposed for sale upon a ledge, a great, sleek cow, soft of eye and gray of coat, walked round the corner, snuffed in a basket of wheat, then took a mouthful and chewed it, placidly content.   ·

Cecily gave a cry of despair as she pulled Rex back, too late. Wishing to prevent the corn-dealer's wares from being purloined, he had struck the cow upon its neck, forgetting that in the Hindoo religion the cow is sacred, held in the highest veneration, and allowed to roam where it wills in Benares and to eat with impunity out of the baskets of wheat exposed for sale.

With yells of rage and screams of hate and abuse the crowd, headed by the disciple of Kali, who shook his trident above his head, rushed the three foreigners who had so grievously insulted the great gods in the shape of the Sacred Cow.

Jerking Cecily by the wrist Trevor pulled her sideways, just in time, as the trident flashed down upon the spot where she had been standing.

"We've got to fight our way through, old man," he shouted above the din to Rex as he caught a youth who had sprung at him, by the wrists and flung him forward upon the crowd, so that for a moment it gave way, leaving a space the width of two men, through which, with Cecily between them, they raced for their lives, using their fists unsparingly upon those who sprang at them from all sides.

Once Cecily crashed to her knees, and, kneeling, turned and beat down upon a woman's hand that held her skirt, then scrambled to her feet, white to the lips, steady as a rock, and, where she could, beat up the hands that struck at Rex, who fought ahead, and at Trevor, who, walking sideways, fought a rear-guard action, in which a knife ripped his sleeve so that blood ran, rousing the crowd to a very lust to kill.

"We're through! We're through!" yelled Rex, "another yard and——"

They were through.

With Cecily in front the two men fought back the people, who, owing to the fact that they fought amongst themselves, had jammed tight between the walls of the narrow streets. Then Cecily screamed suddenly and spread wide her arms to save her men from the danger which threatened ahead.

Up the street, bellowing, heads tossing, maddened with fear, came a herd of cows, terrified by the noise, maddened by the flicking of a long whip, handled dexterously by Boodna, who, in the pay of Chang-ku, hurried the animals from the shadows.

"My God! we're done, we're caught between the two. Lie down, Cecily, lie down, we'll cover you!"

The two men caught her and tried to force her to her knees. She fought them, clung to them, laughed up into their desperate faces.

"Let's die fighting, all of us!" she cried.

"But let's make a damned good effort to live first," yelled Rex, as he hit a man between the eyes and set him crashing backwards, so that those who ran close to him tripped, stumbled, and pushed back upon those behind.

His gray eyes blazed, he yelled, his mouth wide open, a sight for the gods in his youth and his last desperate effort to save his Dream Girl.

"Let's charge the cows!" he cried. "Let's charge them! It's a forlorn hope, but let's charge!"

He stood for a moment, his head flung back, watching the advance guard of the mob scrambling to their knees, fighting amongst themselves—natives, every one, like the men who had stolen Lotah.

Lotah in the hands of Oriental men and women! *His* beautiful wife! What would they do to her? What would they make of her?

Madness fell upon him as he seemed to see a vision of Lotah alone, desperate, fighting for her life and honor. He must save his own life to save hers, he must get to the station if he fought every yard of the way, if he killed every one of the men who failed to reach them because they fought amongst themselves, impeding one another.

He slipped his hand into his revolver pocket and touched the necklace of blue beads.

"Lotah!" he yelled as he turned to fight the humans instead of the cattle. "Lotah! Lotah! Lotah!"

It was a battle-cry, a challenge!

He ran back a yard, then stopped.

Cecily caught him by the arm. Unable to make herself heard above the crowd's screams of agonizing fear and yells of dismay, she pointed backwards up the street.

At the top, half naked, hair to her knees, mouth running red, stood a native woman, calling frenziedly upon the gods to save her from death.

"Pity!" she screamed, beating her breast, tearing her robes. "Pity for one afflicted, pity for one ill of the plague, pity, pity, pity!"

And as she ran the crowd ran before her, fighting each other, screaming their horror of the woman who pursued them smitten with the pestilence.

"Keep Cecily between us! Fight to the wall!" yelled Trevor. "That woman will be our salvation. Fight to the wall before the cows reach us."

A hundred yards, perhaps, separated the frenzied humans from the terrified cattle. The woman stricken with the pestilence ran, throwing her arms in the air, shrieking so as to be heard even above the din; the two men fought desperately and sideways, to the wall, where they stood with their faces to it and Cecily between them, as the crowd fought its way past them, down the street, to the almost certain death awaiting it.

And as the humans and cattle met with a frightful impact, rending the star-lit, tranquil heavens with screams and cries for help and mighty bellowing, Trevor and Rex, with Cecily, pale as death but steady as a rock, between them, turned and ran up the street.

"She won't hurt us, Cecily," shouted Trevor. "Don't be afraid!"

"I'm not," Cecily shouted back. "It's Ka-lok!"

They followed the beckoning figure to the top of the

empty street, slipped after her down a side street, and then
another, and still another, to safety, whilst the night was
rent with dreadful clamoring, and Chang-ku made his way,
at greatest speed, to the station to catch the midnight train.

From the shadows he had witnessed the trapping of the
white people between the mob of humans and the herd of
cattle, and, as certain of their death as he was uncertain
of his brother's loyalty, had left the scene of horror just
before Ka-lok had appeared at the top of the street.

CHAPTER X

CROSS-LEGGED, content, Sa-t'ong sat on the verandah in the full light of noon.

The sun drew a luster from the gold with which his green and white silk garments were embroidered, and a sheen from the necklace of pearls he held in his slender fingers.

A necklace of three strings of pearls, gems such as no Maharajah in the whole of India possessed, clasped with a blazing, blood-red ruby, one of the three priceless, ill-omened gems known throughout the world as *Kali's Tears*. Except for the movement of his hands nothing stirred in the house nor in the compound, and the light of the sun was as the light of the love in his eyes as he looked at Lotah who, motionless, sat on a pile of cushions with her back against the far wall of the room.

The Bengal Tiger was content.

Save for Yi, her woman attendant, the old nurse, Lotah was with him alone in the town of Hilli, which lies upon the direct route to Darjeeling. He sat at the foot of her bed all night, watching her through the white net curtains, lifting one at times to touch her hair, the silk garments she wore, the silk-embroidered sheet which covered her.

So far the gods had been upon his side.

He had thrown the dice and had won against his brother, whom he left behind in Benares to contrive the death of the white people who hunted Lotah across the world. He was convinced that Chang-ku would have met his death with them, crushed, trampled under the feet of an infuriated mob of people and the hoofs of a terrified herd of cattle. With a great peace in his heart he waited for the messenger to arrive from Benares, bringing the welcome news of the death of the white people and of Chang-ku, news which would leave him, Sa-t'ong, free to wed Lotah, the White Rose.

He stretched out his arms to where she sat like a graven image at the far end of the room.

She sat cross-legged, her bare feet with soles turned outward, her slender hands joined, crimson-tipped fingers startlingly vivid against the snow-whiteness of the skin, which showed above the low opening of the long coat of white satin which reached below the knee. There was no trace of paint upon her face, no line of blue beneath the dreamy eyes which stared, unseeingly, between half-closed lids, at the man who loved her even more than he hated his brother and the Englishman who had been her husband for so short a time.

"Lotah *chung!*"

He watched her every movement, loving her; he played upon her half-awakened fear, rather as might a tiger play with a gazelle before breaking its neck between its teeth; to bring her back to a consciousness of his presence, so that the swift crimson might flood her face at his nearness, fear shine in her wondering eyes, and show in the deprecating, furtive movements of her slender hands, he had reduced the drug.

Up till then she had not realized the fact that a man was her constant companion; had not understood the danger of her position, or that love and passion encompassed her. But during the night she wakened, and quietly, furtively, lifted the curtain and slipped out of bed and crouched, watching him from behind the folds of silken sheet, believing herself unseen. Worshiping her he rose quietly, quickly. She sped across the room, clutching the silken garment against her breast, fought him with the other hand and bent and met her teeth in his wrist when he caught her and savagely pulled her to him.

Her fear showed him that she was almost awake to her surroundings, too much awake for safety; he forced her to drink a cup of drugged tea, then lay on the floor all night whilst she slept.

But now, now that the messenger was on his way, due to arrive at any moment with the news of his brother's death which would set him free, now he would keep her on the borderland of consciousness so that when—ah, when——

He looked at the marks of her teeth in his wrist and smiled; he loved her, the gods alone knew how he loved her, but he would break down her resistance a thousand times before he carried her up to the wild fastnesses of his mountains and married her.

"Lotah *chung*, come here!"

But Lotah was very near to consciousness and was afraid. She rose to one knee, her arms stretched out on each side, hands pressed against the wall, and shook her head, an intoxicating picture of Oriental terrified womanhood. She leapt to her feet as he rose, and moved along the wall towards a further door as he crossed the room, then stopped, crouching, her hands before her face as he put out his arms and stayed her.

"Look, Lotah, for you!"

She looked at the shimmering pearls, touched them wonderingly, then put her hand to her throat.

"The blue beads—my—blue beads—where—where are they?"

"These are they, Lotus-Flower; the sun has turned them white." He passed them over her head and caught his breath as they slipped down inside the satin coat, no whiter than the breast upon which they lay.

She touched them, counting in a whisper, then stopped, confused, and began again.

"One, two, three—three—three——"

She pressed the palm of her hand against her forehead, fighting for the memory which, half-awakened, stirred within her brain. The memory of a childish game she had played with Rex in the slums of London, in which she had counted the twenty beads, as old as the world, as blue as the Indian sky, whilst he had—what had he done? When? Why did a memory of laughter, kisses and tender words come to her? Nineteen, twenty! She touched another pearl and stopped confused, then, suddenly, subconsciously aware that she was being tricked, struck Sa-t'ong across the face.

"You liar!"

The English word fell sharply in the lofty, sparsely furnished room, as Lotah, with a little scream, ran to the plaster-covered wall and beat upon it, looking wildly up to the slats near the ceiling through which the reflected sunlight shone.

Sa-t'ong let her be for a while, happily content. He loved to watch the fear in her eyes fighting against the return of memory; he loved the sight of her little hands beating upon the wall, and her bare, slender feet showing so white on the fine mats which covered the marble floor. Another hour, perhaps two, perhaps three, and she would be wide awake, fighting desperately against his all-conquering love. She was almost awake now, dangerously so, considering that he would have to leave her whilst he interviewed the messenger who was due at any moment with the news of the death of those he hated.

He crossed to a small, inlaid table upon which stood everything necessary for making the green tea, a terra-cotta water jug, and a charcoal brazier. He lit the charcoal, then ran across the room and caught Lotah, who, close to the wall, bent double in an unconscious but instinctive desire to hide herself, stole towards the curtain hanging across the doorway. Her hand had just grasped it when he reached her and encircled her with both arms without touching her, a circle of passion within which she fought to regain her freedom as a wild bird tries to break through the bars of its cage.

He narrowed the circle, crushing her until he could feel the thudding of her heart; he whispered to her, holding her gently, firmly, until she stood quite still, desperately afraid, suddenly, desperately tired and sleepy.

"I love you, Lotah, I love you," he whispered in English, delighting in the look of amazement and perplexity which shone in her eyes, in the trick he was playing upon her, in the reward which might be his for his cunning. "Rex loves you, sweetheart, beautiful Lotus-Flower. I, Rex, want your love, your mouth, your sweet surrender. Sweetheart, beloved, I love you, love you, love you."

Gone was all memory of his oath to his father, of his vow to resist the call of love and passion until the girl should be his wife. He shook from head to foot in the room shuttered against the glare of the sun; he held her gently and pressed his lips against her hair when, half asleep, wholly happy in the bemused thought that Rex was with her, had never been away from her, that she had but awakened from a terrible dream in the quiet, dark room, she lifted her arms and touched his face with her slender hands.

Half savage, half civilized, prisoner in the bonds of as mighty a love as ever chained a heart, Sa-t'ong gloried in the hour the gods had flung him.

He intended no harm; the girl was to be his wife, the mother of his sons; neither did he see harm in tricking her so that she should raise her face to his and, if the gods willed, give him the kisses of her crimson mouth. Other women were playthings, servants, cattle, for men to treat as they liked; he thought for a moment of the women of his own country, of the wild cat, called Ka-lok, in the London slums. He smiled.

Playthings! Cattle!

But Lotah, white, slender Lotah, ah, she——

"Love me, Lotah," he whispered, his handsome face

against her scented hair. "Am I not good to look upon? Am I not strong to protect you from harm? Am I not loving you, loving you, loving you!"

She turned in his arms, leaning back against him, her head against his shoulder, her face upturned to his. She could not see him in the dim light, she was too bewildered to understand the strangeness of his clothing; it was all mixed up in her clouded mind with the teeming streets of Limehouse and the crowded ports and cities of her journey.

"Rex! Beloved! Rex!"

She put up her arms and pulled his head down and laughed softly when he kissed her on her crimson mouth, her eyes, her throat and shifted her a little, holding her on one arm, and kissed her shoulders, her bare arms and finger-tips and the white skin gleaming under the shimmering pearls, and knelt and kissed her bare, slender feet standing tiptoe upon the fine matting on the marble floor.

His hour which had fallen from the lap of the gods when, laughing, they had crossed their knees.

One short hour of love which passed, which died, almost at its birth, yet which stayed with him, a flower of wonder and fragrance, rooted in his savage heart until the hour of his death.

He bowed his head and touched her instep with his forehead, then sprang up and back as she suddenly wrenched herself free and ran screaming across the room towards the verandah. He reached the doors just in time and slammed them to and bolted them, and, lifting her, carried her back to the pile of cushions and threw her down upon it.

"Lie there! Do you understand? You are to lie there until tea is brought you!" He held her down by the shoulders until she ceased struggling and lay quite still, terror-stricken.

"Rex," she said piteously. "Rex, he was here, where has he gone? You, who are you?"

"I am your servant," he said slowly.

"Ah!"

He sat on the floor beside her, pulled the table laid with tea-cups closer, and slowly, hands still trembling from the flood of passion which had almost engulfed him, drew out the silver flask containing the drug. With a swift glance at Lotah he dropped two instead of ten drops into a tea-cup full of tea, then placed the flask upon the floor behind the cushions and rose and knelt at her side, watching the smile on her mouth and the look of indescribable love in her sleepy eyes.

"Rex," she said. "Rex, I—I can't see you very well. I—I love you, Rex, beloved."

He lifted her into his arms, holding her across his knees and reached for the tea-cup.

"Drink it, sweetheart, all of it." His words lost their foreign accent, so softly did he speak.

"Why?"

"Because *I* want you to, because I love you, love you, love you, and—and——"

She laughed softly and made a face and laughed again as she drank the contents of the cup, then pushed it away and sighed and smiled and leaned her cheek against his.

"Rex! Rex! Hold me tightly, beloved. The ground seems to be slipping, slipping from—lay me down, dear heart—hold me in your—arms—I—I love you—don't let me—me—go."

She closed her eyes and yawned a little and opened them and smiled.

"You must sleep, beloved."

Sa-t'ong rose to his feet and stood with her in his arms, looking across the room to the smaller one in which, under the white net curtains, she had slept the night before whilst he had kept guard at her feet.

At her feet!

He lifted her high above his head upon his upstretched

hands and laughed, laughed in the joy of his hour which
had struck at last. Then he crushed her to his heart and
carried her to the curtained doorway of the smaller room
and stopped.

"Excellency! Excellency!"

The Hindoo servant's soft voice outside the further doorway broke the stillness and shattered Sa-t'ong's hour of
love to fragments.

"Yes?" he said softly. "What is it? What do you need?
What is the meaning of this interruption?"

"Your Excellency's brother, his Excellency Chang-ku
waits without!"

*   *   *

Dal-Singh watched his masters from the shadows. He
was intrigued, mystified, had been so since the advent of
the veiled, mysterious woman who, so rumor said, was
destined to be the wife of one or the other of the wealthy
merchant princes, or of both, in accordance to the custom
which ruled on the other side of India's northwest frontier.

If either the one or the other, which one?

If both, why had the two mighty men sat for the passing
of one hour, without movement, without speech, watching
each other from under half-closed lids, like two great jungle
cats?

And who was the girl? If so rigorously *purdah* upon
the journey, so closely veiled, so strictly hidden, why had
she come alone, unprotected? Why had his master passed
the night near her, in the big room outside the sleeping
chamber?

The intrigues of love are as the breath of life to the
Oriental.

Dal-Singh was mystified, at a loss and full of a seething
curiosity which had to be appeased if his peace of mind
was to be restored.

He watched them from his hiding-place behind the *chick*,

watched them warily, apprehensively. He stood in awe of his Excellency Chang-ku's violent temper which flamed upon the merest pretext and died out as quickly, but he simply dreaded his Excellency Sa-t'ong's gentleness, his imperturbable manner, the slow, deliberate movements which hid the indomitable will and utter relentlessness of purpose underneath.

But the servant's curiosity was stronger even than his dread. See the veiled woman he must, even if by the foolhardy and disloyal act he risked his well-paid and assured position of body-servant to their Excellencies; the comfort of his family, which lived at great ease in the servants' quarters; his life, which his Excellency Sa-t'ong was quite capable of extinguishing by the simple method of breaking his servant's neck 'twixt thumb and finger.

Just a glimpse! A fleet glance so as to determine the coloring of the veiled woman's hair and eyes, her age, her caste. That was all! Only a glimpse to appease his raging curiosity and that of his wife. Little enough, if he could but be sure of their Excellencies' movements for ten minutes.

But could he?

If he could just count on ten minutes! Then he smiled, and, after allowing enough time to elapse, lifted the *chick* and salaamed before the brothers, as though he had run from the back of the house in answer to the clapping of hands.

"Tea! And see that for the space of one half-hour we are not disturbed."

Noiselessly Dal-Singh returned, barefoot, balancing a brass tray with the wherewithal to make the heady green tea, drunk night and day by the brothers Nyko-Gung. From behind the *chick* he watched them for a moment as they sat, cross-legged, upon the cushions, motionless, their faces expressionless masks, their eyes full of undying hatred; listened to their soft voices, understanding nothing

of what they said, then lifted the *chick,* salaamed, and
placed the tray between them on the floor of the verandah.

He waited for orders, salaamed when dismissed, lifted
the *chick,* watched the brothers for a moment from behind
it as they offered each other the tea, with gestures of
brotherly affection and hate in their eyes, then, like a
shadow, stole back through the house. For a full minute he
stood hidden behind the curtain which hung across the
doorway of Lotah's dim, scented room. He stood and
stared across at the doorway on the farther side, the opening to the other smaller, luxurious, scented room, in which
the veiled, mysterious woman lay asleep under white net
curtains.

He could see them from where he stood.

White net curtains meant that the woman was foreign
to the insect-ridden Land of the Peacock; that she feared
that which crawled; had to be protected from the gnat
which flies by night and leaves its sting.

Neither did she seemingly require a retinue of servants
to wait upon her. Only the old woman, Yi, who had been
nurse to their Excellencies. She filled the bath every hour
and swept and put the rooms in order and placed the trays
of delicate food upon a certain table, and doubtlessly
brushed the mysterious woman's hair, tinted her finger-tips,
drew the alluring blue line beneath her eyes.

Was her hair black? Did it curl? Her eyes, were they
as the gazelle's? Her mouth like the pomegranate? Her
teeth like pearls?

A swift run across the marble floor, a glimpse, a swift
run back with curiosity appeased, and Fate would not have
reached for her shears; but, with his back to the wall and
his head turned towards the doorway through which he had
entered, he needs must make half the circuit of the room,
feeling protection in the solid substance at his back whilst
perpetrating his disloyal act.

He moved quickly, stealthily, then stopped with a

smothered exclamation of dismay, and lifted his bare feet wet with the contents of the flask he had not noticed on the floor behind the cushions and had overturned.

Colorless, the liquid lay in a little pool upon the close webbing of the fine mat over which it had been spilt; he knelt and scooped some up in the palms of his slender hands, and, forgetful in his dismay of his countrymen's notorious skill in the fine art of poisoning, put his lips to it.

Tasteless! Colorless!

He did not pause to think, time was passing, and his curiosity raged unappeased. He carried the empty flask to the small inlaid table and refilled it with water from the terra-cotta jug and carried it back, and, pulling a pile of cushions a little to one side, so that the mark on the matting where the liquid had been absorbed was hidden, placed it upon the floor.

He stood a little away from the spot and examined it carefully, and was content. There was no trace whatever of the accident; the flask was three-quarters full of colorless, tasteless liquid, the pile of cushions covered the wet mark, he had but to finish the circuit of the wall or, as time pressed, to run across the middle of the room, glance into the sleeping chamber and run back, and all would be well.

If he had but finished the circuit of the wall all might have been well. But time pressed. He ran across the room. True, half-way across, with fear in his heart, he turned and looked back towards the doorway by which he had entered. He was safe. The brothers partook of tea upon the verandah, whilst discoursing in the sibilant language of their own wild country.

The house was still.

If he had but turned again, a few seconds later, he would have seen Sa-t'ong, the Bengal Tiger, approaching noiselessly, unsuspectingly towards the doorway. But he did not look backwards, he stood entranced, looking down at the most beautiful woman he had seen in his life, heedless of the huge man who stole, without sound, across the room and stood close behind him.

Lotah lay fast asleep, smiling in her sleep, her teeth gleaming between her lips like the pearls which shimmered on her breast. She murmured and threw her arm above her head and laughed softly, opened her eyes, stared unseeingly, and went to sleep again.

"*Kya khub! Kya khub!*" whispered the Hindoo, then twisted sideways and pulled at the hands which gripped his neck.

A wisp, a feather in Sa-t'ong's merciless grasp, he stared up at the mask-like handsome face in which eyes, as cold as stone, stared back into his.

"*Doha 'i,*" he whispered, though no sound came from his lips. "*Doha 'i,*" he whispered again, as, holding the man's knees between his own in a vice-like grip, Sa-t'ong the Bengal Tiger, bent his servant slowly backwards by the neck.

Fate opened her shears and cut the string which held Dal-Singh to his destiny, and Sa-t'ong, lifting the limp figure with broken back and neck, carried it to the far door and flung it out into the compound.

"Mine!" he whispered as he stood looking down at the girl he loved. "Mine, by the gods!" Then crossed to the pile of cushions, picked up the flask, screwed tight the jeweled stopper, and hid it in his silken garments.

"She sleeps," he said gently to Chang-ku as he sank cross-legged upon the floor of the verandah. "Let us wait until the moon shines above yon banyan tree, then, as thou dost so insist, let us go and look upon this girl who is to be thy wife, or perchance mine, before two moons have passed."

There was no sound in the house. A snatch of song, a laugh, a jingle of bracelets, of anklets, from the servants' quarters on the far side of the compound; the moon rose slowly; the brothers talked softly in their own tongue, as Lotah, wide-eyed, almost freed from the drug, awake at last, awake to the horror of her surroundings, stole, wrapped in silken garments, through the house.

This way she looked and that, searching for some one who would explain. Voices on the far side of a room, voices speaking in Tsi-tsi's language, therefore friendly voices. Two men sitting in the moonlight, friends of Tsi-tsi's, therefore her friends and Rex's. She moved slowly across the floor, barefoot, making no sound, stretched out her hand to lift the *chick*, then stopped and crept back and to one side.

"Tell me, Sa-t'ong, O my Brother, of this drug with which thou has bound the will of Lotah, the white girl, leaving her the use of her limbs which are as slender as yon moon-bathed pine. I love her, O my Brother! I would have her, and quickly, for my love!"

"I love her," said Sa-t'ong quietly as he drew out the flask. "I love her, and will have her for my wife." He spoke gently, indifferently, yet with a deadly purpose beneath his quiet words, glanced at Chang-ku, unscrewed the jeweled stopper with the three middle fingers of his mutilated hand, emptied the dregs out of a teacup, poured into it a little of the liquid, which he thought to be the drug, and passed it to his brother.

"Dost remember the old hag, Mo-li, who, pretending to gain her living by concocting love-philtres and charms against disease and death, traded cunningly with the big poisoners? Not a herb that she had not plucked, distilled and tried upon animals or, when the gods smiled upon her, her enemies. Dost remember her in the days of our father?"

Chang-ku nodded.

"Verily! and she died a violent death of her own poison dropped into her broth by one who loved her not. She gave this unto thee?"

"Nay, nay, unto our father! As thou knowest, he desired to kill the white man Trevor but to spare his wife, even the mother of Lotah, whom I love and thou lovest, and to make of her a servant to our mother. Fate ruled otherwise. Thy knife was too quick, too sharp. Not content with the death of the man, thou didst also kill the woman, the mother of Lotah, the White Rose." Sa-t'ong looked up at the sky and at the slender pine, bathed in the light of the moon that was slowly rising. "The blind moves in the breeze, yet yon tree is still."

" 'Tis the ghost of Dal-Singh blowing death-curses upon thee through the blind." Chang-ku rose as he spoke lifted the *chick* and stared around the room. Divided only by the thickness and hidden by the fine rush blind, held back by the man who desired her, Lotah stood, flattened against the wall, sick to her heart with terror, determined, if she should escape detection, to make a desperate bid for liberty before the dawn.

" 'Tis the ghost. There is naught else," Chang-ku said indifferently as he sat down with his back to the rush blind. "And so this is the drug the hag Mo-li gave to our father. Dost know with what roots the old witch concocted it?"

"*Mazum,* which, O my Brother, is a fine mixture of opium and *ganja,* stupefying without endangering life, makes one part of it. The name of the root added to take away the color and taste I know not; but 'twas whispered that, upon the banks of the Kin-sha, the River of Golden Sand, Mo-li gathered a weed named the Ya-ti, which, simmered in dew, restores the use of the limbs to the one drugged, whilst leaving the senses numbed. 'Tis a concoction of the black one, the secret of which passed with her. This," he held up the flask, "is all that is left. 'Tis enough for our use, Chang-ku, enough to keep the white girl quiet until——"

Love stopped him, he could not, would not utter the words. Not so Chang-ku.

"Until we place her upon the dais upon the Night of the

Full Moon, O Tiger! and gamble for the privilege of calling her wife before the dawn."

Like jungle animals the two men sat, bitter hatred in their eyes, whilst the girl they were fighting for stood behind the blind, petrified with horror, her hands over her mouth.

"And thou gav'st her first drink the night when, to further thy escape with her, having soaked the fine shavings of the wood in oil, I set light to them. The night I made a fiery furnace of the house of vice in the evil heart of Limehouse, wherein dwelt this fair flower called Lotah with the boy, the yearling, she called Rex, her husband."

Longing in his hatred to fling himself upon his brother, Sa-t'ong hid his hand in his wide sleeve. Naught would be gained by haste. There were more drugs than the one which the flask contained, poisons swift and sure and of a surpassing deadliness, and did not his brother drink the heady green tea through the hours both of the day and of the night?

"Yea!" he answered slowly, "that night, when, in the screaming and fighting of the rats trapped in the burning building, I swung from balcony to balcony with the white maid, Lotah, tied to me by the girdle which once had wrapped his dressing-gown about her husband. Thou wilt of a surety break in pieces the blind if thou leanest thy great bulk against it, O Brother."

Chang-ku turned his head and looked at the *chick*, behind which Lotah stood as though carved out of stone.

"I touch not the blind. 'Tis the spirit of Dal-Singh blowing death-curses upon thee through it. Remember my words, O my Brother, if, before the waning of next moon, death smites thee."

Sa-t'ong smiled and spread his hands with a gesture of resignation.

"He blows also upon thy neck, my Brother! The same mother bore us, close the one upon the other, the same spirit of tyranny links us, love—of a different kind—but love of the same woman binds us. 'Tis likely, if death strikes one, it strikes the other." He held the flask up to the moon and screwed the jeweled stopper tight. "I swung from balcony to balcony. I carried her in my arms—in my arms—asleep under the narcotic I had placed upon the silken scarf with which—from behind—I covered her beautiful mouth. I made her drink, I forced her to drink the drug under threat of torture, death to her husband."

He sat quite still, staring through the purple, silvery, Indian night, back along the past to the room in Limehouse where, whilst the tenement fired by Chang-ku blazed to high heaven, he had held Lotah, fighting like a tiger-cat, in his arms and had forced the drugged milk down her throat.

"Five drops then, then ten, and twenty upon the boat which brought her to India, and five now, so that she may not waken, and, with her screaming, bring the servants, agog with the curiosity which smote Dal-Singh in death, flocking to the doors. Ah! I held her in my arms—my arms!"

Sa-t'ong watched his brother out of half-closed eyes.

He could not kill him—at least, not yet awhile—but he could hurt him—torture him—through the passion which consumed him.

"Be she thy wife or my wife, O Chang-ku, my marriage dower shines upon her breast. Even the triple necklace of pearls, clasped with a ruby as red as her soft lips."

Chang-ku leaned forward, his splendid teeth showing in a snarl of hate; suspicion flaring in his slanting eyes; uncontrollable rage causing his hand to shake as he pointed at the handsome man, his brother, linked to him with the same chain of inherent cruelty, bound to him by the same love of Lotah, the White Rose.

"Her breast, her lips, thou speakest as master of her lips, thou——"

"As master—to—be, O Brother!" indifferently replied

Sa-t'ong as he inwardly exulted over the pain he was causing. "And of her slender feet like unto bridges which span
the stream, and of her hair like unto the shadows upon the
high mountains before," he paused and sighed softly, then
added more softly still "——the dawn."

"Thou traitor! thou accursed traitor! I go even now to
see, to discover if thou hast left thy mark upon her. If
thou hast, before the dread goddess, I will make thee pay
for it in death!"

Sa-t'ong spread his hands in a deprecating movement as
he looked up at the pine tree, over the top of which the rim
of the moon showed.

"Yet a little while, Brother, even until the full moon
balances upon the top of yon tree. Sleep she not the *full*
hour after the drinking of the liquid, it will but serve to
rouse Lotah to a fury of anger when she wakens."

"Nay, now, upon this moment!"

Chang-ku sprang to his feet, and Lotah ran, ran without
waiting, so that she did not see Sa-t'ong spring and grip
his brother by the shoulder, urging him to patience until
the moon should balance upon the tip of the pine.

She ran for her life through the silent house, into rooms
lit by slats high up in the lofty walls, across to doors barred,
bolted, padlocked, out of the rooms and along the passage,
searching wildly, in a frenzy of terror, for a way of escape.

There was none.

The only way out of the house was through the room
she had just left, past the men, across the verandah, and
out through the compound to the dusty, broad, tree-lined
road leading to the town.

She did not know. She did not understand.

She had wakened slowly, so slowly to consciousness under
the white net curtains in the dim, scented room; stared
about her looking for the familiar objects of her home in
Limehouse; called Rex, called softly, persistently, and,
terror-stricken, fought her way out of the strange net cur-

tains, and crept like a phantom through the silent house in which there was no sign or sound of life.

Voices, the soft, sibilant words of Tsi-tsi's tongue, had drawn her to the room at the far end of the broad passage, and there, hidden, she had overheard the explanation of the house, her clothes, the strange dizziness in her head.

Drugged, drugged after the fight—ah, yes!—she had forgotten to bolt the door, and the man, the man with the mutilated hand, had overpowered her.

Then where was Rex? Dear Heaven! Where was Rex? The man had threatened to torture him, kill him.

Like some wild animal in a cage she ran from room to room and back to where she had started, and on and on.

Curtains before a door.

She pulled them to one side and stopped, crept back into the passage and listened. There was no sound. Then where was Rex? She knew the room, surely Rex had been with her in it. She would call to him, call so that he should know that she was there, she would scream until the servants of the strange big house would run to her.

She crept back into the room, opened wide her mouth and stopped.

Like a whisper from the past came advice, given by Tsi-tsi before dumbness had stricken her:

" 'Lotah *chung*, remember if ever thou hast dealings with those who live in the shadows of the Himalayas, meet their cunning with cunning, their deceit with deceit, their patience with patience. Violence, tears, threats will avail thee naught, meet their cunning with thy cunning, if thou wouldst be victorious in thy dealings with them!' "

Lotah pressed her hands to her forehead as she tried to think coherently, then stared across the room to where white net curtains showed through a curtained doorway.

The white net curtain above her bed, the bed from which she had crept, upon which she was supposed to be lying asleep—drugged.

" 'Meet their cunning with thy cunning, if thou wouldst be victorious.' "

She was alone, separated from Rex, fighting for her love, her life and her honor. The two men thought she lay asleep, then asleep they should find her. They thought her drugged, then, with the help of God, sustained by her love, she would pretend to be drugged, would act a part, would match their deceit with deceit, would wait and watch, pitting her patience against their patience.

What did she do? What did her eyes look like when drugged? She did not know, but the God of Mercy would help her in her need.

And when she was offered tea, drugged tea, what then? What would she do?

"God of Mercy, have pity upon me! Have pity upon me! Show me the way out, let me escape, show me the way. God of Mercy, have pity upon me!"

Her clasped hands touched the necklace at her throat. She smiled. The blue beads, old as the world, a necklace of little blue flames which she had counted, one by one, whilst Rex had kissed her fingers one by one.

She smiled and lifted the string of pearls, milk-white, glorious pearls, two rows, no, three, of glimmering gems, and looked down with a little stifled cry.

"Be she thy wife or my wife, O Brother! my marriage dower shines upon her breast!"

She shivered, staring down at the jewels, then reached for the clasp and stopped.

The two men knew that the pearls hung about her throat. She must wear them, wear them in the place of the blue beads she had so loved.

She lifted the curtain and laid herself down on the bed, pulled the silken sheet to her chin and turned her head so that her face was half hidden in the bend of her arm.

Through half-closed lids she watched the two brothers

standing in the far doorway, side by side, towering like giants in the shadows, the silken curtains in their hands.

Side by side they stood, then walked slowly, noiselessly across the floor. They paused at the doorway of her room. She lay quite still, her heart beating madly in terror, watching them from half-closed lids.

They entered; stood one on each side of the bed; lifted the curtains.

CHAPTER XI

"LET her rise and dance before us!"

"Nay, Chang-ku! let her sleep until she wakens."

" 'Tis always nay with thee, O Brother. What fearest thou? Why is thy heart soft towards this girl whose father beggared our father? When she passeth to me she will not sleep. Nay! she shall dance before me and before my good friends, and the whip shall speed her feet."

The two men glared at each other across the bed upon which Lotah lay, her eyes closed, her heart racing, her ears open to catch every word that might help her to know how she behaved when, drugged, she obeyed Sa-t'ong, the handsomer, more gentle of the two terrible men.

"Yea! Chang-ku, when she 'is thy wife, *then* mayst thou do what thou wilt with her. But if fear strikes her drug-chained brain, then is madness like to fall upon her, and behold a mad wife is of no avail to thee nor me, nor would the whip help thee against her.

"Behold, she is gentle, coming when called, going when bidden, eating and drinking like a little child. She smiles not, neither does she laugh, nor speak o'ermuch, likewise are her lids, like unto the petals of a closed lily, cast down, so that the eyes, which shine like moonstones underneath, are not seen. She is obedient in all things, but let her sleep until awakening comes."

For answer Chang-ku ripped the silken cover off the bed, then caught his breath and stood quite still looking down at Lotah, who lay with her face buried in the bend of her arm.

His hands trembled to touch her, then he sighed and rubbed his hands across his eyes, and shifted on his feet.

"From the waxing unto the waning of the moon is she to belong to thee, Sa-t'ong, or to me, according as to how the gods cause the dice to fall." He looked up and across at Sa-t'ong, who stood with his hands hidden in his sleeves, his face a mask, his eyes a blank, his heart ridden with a lust to murder his brother. "I will play thee for her now. I will not wait. The sooner she passes unto thee, if so she must, the sooner comes she to me; if she comes to me first —then—then—— Wilt play?"

Sa-t'ong shook his head.

Why should he risk the victory falling to his brother when death might fall upon that brother before the waning of the moon.

"Dost forget, Chang-ku? Dost forget our oath to gamble for her in the Great Hall, with all men as witness? Hast forgotten that, in our territory, upon which the white man hardly dares place foot, the great Ceremony of Inspection with feasting and dancing must take place before the gambling—the gambling for women—not wives—for servants, dancers and singers?"

"Nay, I have not forgotten! But I will not wait! *I will not wait*. Wilt play for her?"

Sa-t'ong spread his hands with a deprecating smile and shook his head.

"Then waken and dance before me!"

Mad with rage, in a frenzy of thwarted desire, Chang-ku seized Lotah by the wrist and jerked her off the bed.

Moaning, she staggered back against the wall, praying to God to help her in this great moment. Would she have strength to act a part, to act as though drugged whilst wide awake; to dance, to sing, to answer when spoken to; to sit submissively whilst longing to scream for help, to run through the curtained doorway out of the road, to the town? Should she sink to the ground and remain there, motionless, or should she feign the madness the more gentle of the terrible brothers prophesied would fall upon her, should she be wakened suddenly from her drugged sleep?

She had no knife, no weapon of defense. She shrank back against the wall and moaned and tore at her raiment and fell to her knees, her face turned to the wall.

"Thou fool!" said Sa-t'ong softly as he walked round the bed, caught his brother by the shoulder and flung him through the doorway, then backed as Chang-ku hurled himself upon him.

Like two magnificent animals they stood close pressed, great chests touching, eyes glaring. Then they backed the one from the other.

What avail to fight?

Had they not tried from boyhood for victory? Trained every muscle in their gigantic bodies for the hour which must surely come and in which one would be the victor.

"Thou fool!" repeated Sa-t'ong contemptuously. "Seat thyself in yon room and I will bring Lotah unto thee. She knows me, my voice, obeys; go thou, thou man of girth and little sense."

"Lotah *chung!*" he said gently as Chang-ku strode out of the bedchamber, looking back so as to keep an eye upon his brother. "Lotah, beloved, come thou with me, fearing no hurt, and dance awhile before my brother who has heard of thy skill and of the sweetness of thy voice. He shall not hurt thee, White Rose, he cannot hurt thee when I am with thee. Come!"

He touched her upon her shoulder, then took her hand and raised her to her feet and led her through the doorway into the room, where, upon the pile of cushions, Chang-ku sat, a pipe between his lips, a look of peace, set there by the fumes of the blue poppy, in his eyes.

One oil lamp, hanging from the ceiling, threw a circle of flickering light in the center of the dark room; in a corner a wisp of blue smoke floated above an incense bowl, filling the air with heavy perfume; there was no movement as Lotah stood quite still in the circle of light, her eyes cast down, her hands crossed, before the brothers Nyko-Gung; no sound until Chung-ku spoke softly to himself. "A dower of pearls about thy neck, thou white girl, yea! a dower of pearls from the Tiger unto thee, but a gift of rubies from thy crimson lips unto the Wolf. Dance, white girl, dance so that my dreams be of thee—my dreams— my——"

His voice trailed into silence, then he softly hummed the music of the song Lotah had sung for Rex and John Trevor under the skylight in Limehouse.

Lotah had her clue. She was to sing the little song Tsi-tsi had taught her. The song Rex loved to hear her sing, which she had sung the last time, the very last time, in their home under the roof of the tenement-house the song sung by women in a certain village, in a certain street spanned with many arches, a street of ill-fame near the frontier of Tibet. She had sung it last for her husband, the man to whom she had given her heart and her love; the man for whom she must pretend, act, fight, if she would win her way back to him.

Chang-ku laughed softly.

"If the White Rose but knew, Sa-t'ong, that her husband had been in the same house with her in Benares, but a few days ago. If she—but—knew that he hunts the world for her. If she—but—knew!"

He laughed and began to clap his hands as weird, barbaric accompaniment to her song, too bemused with the fumes of the blue poppy, as Sa-t'ong was intoxicated with the fumes of love, to notice that Lotah had driven her teeth into her underlip to stop the cry which had almost burst from her, and that her hands were clenched in the folds of her long coat.

She could have shouted for joy, laughed aloud at the thought that Rex was near her; instead she stood with her eyes cast down, singing softly, beneath her breath, singing a prayer into her song.

"If she sings not better in the Great Ceremony there will be but poor prices offered," said Chang-ku drowsily. He swayed slightly, a look of ineffable peace upon his evil face, then frowned and rose to his feet and crossed to Lotah, whilst Sa-t'ong sat, his hands upon the ground, ready to spring.

"Get thee to thy bed, I have had enough of thee," said the Wolf, touching her cheek with his finger. "Get thee gone to bed, to rest, let us all rest."

And Lotah turned and walked slowly to her bedchamber and crept, fully dressed, between the silken sheets of her bed as Chang-ku left the outer room, the opium pipe between his lips, and Sa-t'ong, unknown to her, crossed into the shadows and sat down against the wall, hidden from her by the silken curtains which hung to one side of her doorway.

An hour, two perhaps, passed, and Lotah sat up in bed and stared through the doorway to where the lamp threw a circle of flickering light upon the floor. She crept from the bed and stood peering into the shadows, listening for a sound in the house in which she was a prisoner. She was filled with a desperate longing to escape, to get out of the house in which all the doors were locked, to get out to the road, to the town where perhaps Rex was still looking for her, must be looking for her if he had been in the same house with her but a few days ago.

She stood in the doorway for a moment, her eyes cast down, her hands outstretched as though to feel her way, then turned to the right, walking slowly, swaying a little as she moved, the hem of her long coat touching Sa-t'ong where he sat hidden in the shadows and the folds of the silken curtains.

She crossed to the pile of cushions and sat down, cross-legged, hands joined, her crimson finger-tips touching the dowry of pearls.

"She walks in her sleep," said Sa-t'ong to himself as he sat without movement. "Where will her dreams take her? Where does my brother, born without a heart and without bowels of compassion, hide himself? Does he, too, watch, or does he sleep, lost in dreams of the White Rose in a field of blue poppies?"

Lotah sat still, listening, straining her ears to catch the faintest sound, then rose and stole noiselessly, followed as noiselessly by Sa-t'ong, through the far doorway into the house.

Only a passage, a room, the compound to cross and she would be free, free to fight for her life, to cry, to beg for help. Such a little way to freedom and Rex and love. Where were the two terrible men? Where did they sleep? Why, if she was a prisoner, was the way to escape made so easy?

She lifted the *chick* and shivered at the slight rustling sound it made, then stole out on to the empty verandah and looked swiftly round and anxiously across the bare, moon-lit stretch of ground which lay between herself and the water-tank at the edge of a belt of trees.

Supposing some servant saw her? Supposing one or perhaps both the brothers were watching her?

Chang-ku, who, like the animal he was, had been lying on the floor half asleep in a corner of the room and had wakened at the rustling of the *chick*, stood behind the blind watching her, waiting for her to move. Sa-t'ong stood hidden just outside the farther doorway of the room, watching his brother, waiting for him to move.

They thought she walked in her sleep.

Chang-ku, merciless in all things, waited to spring; Sa-t'ong, merciless where he hated, waited to strike his brother down so as to protect the girl he loved.

And Lotah, standing upon the brink of disaster, stretched

out her hands towards the full moon sinking to her rest, uttered a prayer and walked out into the moonlight. She stopped in the middle of the moon-lit square and stood still, listening. She longed to turn round; she dared not, for fear that she was being watched; yet something urged her to look round and back towards the house lying so still and seemingly deserted in the moonlight.

Instead, she walked slowly on, towards the tank which marked the beginning of the path leading through the trees to the broad road. Then her heart missed a beat as she almost screamed with fear.

For a second, not more, the huge shadow of one of the terrible men had crept like a spreading patch of ink before her. She had distinctly seen the shadow of the head and colossal shoulders, thrown by the moon from some one who followed her on to the silvery ground; then it had disappeared suddenly, as though the one who followed had stepped swiftly back.

She trembled from head to foot, but made no sign; indeed, she walked straight on, up to the tank and sat upon the edge and stirred the slime-covered water with a stick, then rose, and, singing under her breath, retraced her steps, making a circle of the moon-lit patch in an endeavor to find out who followed her.

But when, as she mounted the verandah steps, two arms encircled and lifted her, she fought like a tiger-cat, beating down upon the evil face with clenched fist until blood streamed from where she cut her hand against Chang-ku's splendid teeth. And as she fought she screamed and caught the man's throat and hammered with her fist between his eyes, and screamed until the servants ran to the boundary of their quarters. Sa-t'ong smiled as he quietly lifted the *chick,* and, catching his brother by the elbow from behind, twisted it so that he let Lotah drop to the ground, where she lay shuddering at their feet.

"Thou fool!" said Sa-t'ong gently as he lifted her up

against his heart and pushed the curls back from her face. "Thou thrice accursed fool! Not content with bringing her to the verge of madness by waking her from her sleep, yet must thou waken her when she walks in her dreams, to carry her to thy couch. Behold, art thou as a jackal in thy love-making, and as melted fat in thy power of resistance."

Chang-ku's hand crept towards his belt where the jeweled handle of a knife glittered against the satin of his coat.

"Put up thy toy, little Brother," laughed Sa-t'ong. "We will settle our dispute 'neath the shadows of the great mountains, and to-morrow, even before the noon, we will start upon our journey, thou and I and the White Rose, who is to be thine or mine."

" 'Twere wise to give her of the white medicine, perchance, O Brother." Chang-ku bent and scrutinized the beautiful face, white in the moonlight with great black rings beneath the closed eyes.

"Yea! and twice as much, so that she wakens not upon her travels. We will give it her upon her bed, so that she sleeps without stress. And I break thy neck, little Wolf, if thou dost approach her bed-chamber once we have left her to her sleep."

"And I thine, for the same good purpose and in brotherly solicitude, little Tiger."

Lotah prayed desperately as she was carried to her room. Prayed that death might strike the men, that the flask might slip from Sa-t'ong's fingers and spill its contents. She prayed in an agony of horror, when, upon the bed, the two men loosened her belt and smoothed her hair and exclaimed at the beauty of her bare, beautiful feet and the slimness of her ankles.

"Drink, Lotah *chung*. Drink the good medicine. Drink, White Rose, and sleep—sleep till noon—sleep until he who loves thee brings thee to eat and drink and silken raiment for thy travels."

Chang-ku laughed softly, brutally.

"Thou wilt see silken raiment a-plenty and jewels of great rarity and price, White Rose, in the Street of Many Arches, when thou sittest upon the dais. Yet wilt thou, in thy flower-like beauty, outshine those who deck themselves in silks and jewels to"—he laughed again—"to lure the brothers Nyko-Gung to their hidden rooms, perfumed with musk and shuttered against the light."

There was nothing to do but drink out of the cup half-filled with tasteless, colorless liquid. She must drink, this once, for God had not answered her agonized prayer, and, after, she must find some means of circumventing the terrible men who were fighting for her.

"Rex, beloved!" she whispered as she sighed and pushed away the cup, and sighed again as Sa-t'ong held it to her lips until she drank the last drop, his cheek against her hair.

She lay quite still as the men stood looking down at her.

"If she but knew how close her husband has been to her. If she but knew that the gods have willed for him to remain in the Holy City, whilst we take his girl-wife up, up to the great snow mountains." Chang-ku laughed and carelessly flicked her cheek. "Come, Sa-t'ong, beloved Brother, let *us* sleep side by side so that we watch over each other in brotherly affection."

She lay still long after they had gone, lay waiting for sleep to overtake her, longing for it to come so that she might wake the sooner to the great fight ahead. A fight to the death in the snowy fastnesses of the Himalayas for the man she loved and whom the gods, the terrible, heathen gods, had willed to stay in India's Holy City.

She waited, but sleep did not come; instead, her brain grew clearer and clearer as her hunger increased and the hours passed until the crows chattered and croaked and fought at the coming of the dawn.

And then she knew that her prayer had been answered. How, she did not understand, she did not try to under-

stand. She had taken the drug and it had had no effect.
She was awake, mistress of her thoughts and her movements, capable of defending herself if need be, capable of
killing herself if the need for such drastic measures should
arise.

"Pit thy cunning against their cunning, thy patience
against their patience."

The words rang in her ears as she turned and buried her
face in her arms and fell into a sleep of exhaustion.

If she had but known, Rex, with John Trevor, was speed-
ing on his way to deliver her out of the hands of the
ungodly, whilst Cecily Cleeve fought for her life in a small
room in a native house in Mughal-Sarai, to which she had
been taken by Rama, the servant of the brothers Nyko-
Gung.

CHAPTER XII

"I WONDER where Cecily can have got to? I'd better get out and look for her."

Rex got up from the seat and crossed to John Trevor, who stood at the carriage door, anxiously looking up and down the platform of Mughal-Sarai for Cecily Cleeve.

"We still have ten minutes." Rex looked at his watch as he spoke. "Cecily won't be left behind, you may be sure. I expect she slipped off to buy up the bookstall, as she always does, when we went to buy her that brass stuff."

Trevor looked at the figure of Kali, the Hindoo Goddess of Destruction. It stood upon the floor, hideous, about a foot high, showing the goddess squatting upon a heap of skulls, with slanting, fish-shaped eyes of mother-o'-pearl, her huge mouth wide open, exposing a crimson tongue.

Trevor scowled at it.

"I've a mind to chuck it out of the window, Rex. I don't like the idea of Cecily having it in her room."

Rex turned and glanced at it.

"No," he said indifferently, his mind on other things. "Don't do that, it's a fine piece of work, and only a bit of this accursed country. Ah! There's Cecily down there. I'll go and fetch her."

Trevor caught him by the arm as he jumped from the carriage steps and pulled him back.

"Don't get out. She's all right, and these trains think nothing of starting before time. Mustn't risk you getting left behind, you know, old man. What a crowd there always is on India's platforms." He clutched the hand-rail and swung out to arm's length and waved to Cecily as she

156

pushed her way towards him through the seething, chattering, gesticulating crowd of natives.

"Don't these *purdah* women covered in the *baku* make you feel the mystery of the East," said Rex, flinging himself on the long seat which stretched down the entire side of the carriage. "And I understand the custom too. I'd love to hide my Lotah from the eyes of all men, cover her from head to foot in a great white circular sheet, with two slits for her lovely eyes, and the slits, too, covered in gauze. I wish Cecily would be quick, what's she doing?"

"She's coming. It's all right." Once more Trevor waved his hand and smiled as Cecily waved hers, as best she could for the pile of books she carried.

"Did one ever imagine such coloring?" said Rex as he got up restlessly and crossed to the door, talking solely with the object of keeping his mind from the thought of the terrible danger hanging over Lotah and the unknown power which threatened to prevent them from reaching her in time. "The splashes of color in the men's robes, the fruit, the fly-blown sweetmeats, the clashing of anklets, the painted eyes and betel-red lips. Look at that fat, jolly-looking fellow, in a saffron-colored garment, with staff and rice-bowl. Cecily says they're Buddhists. Oh! look, that kind of thing always gives me the horrors."

Trevor glanced at the beggar, who made his way through the crowd which opened before him.

The man was mad, therefore an object of solicitude to all who met him, shouting unintelligible words, contorting his emaciated, ochre-daubed body until his one tattered garment seemed likely to fall from off him.

"He's coming on this train, poor devil, and because of his madness will be offered the best seat and as much food as he can eat."

In which surmise John Trevor was hopelessly at fault.

The seeming madman was Rama—servant to the brothers Nyko-Gung—as sane as his masters and as cunning and unscrupulous. Learning from Boodna of the *Sahib-logs'* escape from death in Benares he had promptly used his wits, disguised himself as a beggar, and had made his way to the station. There, feigning madness, he had, through his seeming affliction, boarded the train just as it had moved out, helped there by the willing hand of the superstitious guard.

"Yes," said Trevor. "He's as mad as they—— Oh, heavens! He's had a fit right at Cecily's feet. Look out, Rex. We're off——"

Rex sprang and caught Trevor by the arm, and pulled him forcibly back into the carriage just as the Eurasian guard slammed the door to. He kept Trevor back with one hand as he flung out of the window and pointed to where, with much shouting and yelling, like flies round a honey-pot, the men pushed their wives, who pulled their children, goats or poultry, into the native compartments, impeding his view of Cecily.

"A Mem-Sahib down there, guard, left behind. Get her in, ten rupees at next stop."

The Eurasian guard smiled and saluted, not having heard a word.

"All right, sir! all right, sir!"

"That's all right," said Rex with a sigh of relief. "Cecily's in, and will come along at the next stop."

It was anything but right.

With ten minutes to spare, Cecily had gone to buy up the bookstall, which stood facing the native compartments of the long train. Purchases made, she began a slow passage towards her own carriage; turned back at the sound of the book-vendor's voice, who held the pair of gloves she had forgotten above the heads of the throngs of natives, and then, once more on her way to her own carriage, found the passage blocked by the man afflicted with madness.

She glanced at her watch and waved to Trevor, who was frantically signaling to her; then, as the clanging of iron on iron announced the train's immediate departure, made a great effort to push her way through the crowd which swarmed around the madman.

Desperately she cleared a way, and started to run just as the man afflicted with madness crossed her path with a loud shout and, throwing up his arms, fell at her feet in a fit, during which he clutched convulsively at her skirts. No one paid attention to her. Half the crowd pushed and fought its way into the moving train, and the other half fought and leaped on to each other's shoulders, the better to see the man stricken by the gods.

And well was it for Cecily Cleeve and all connected with her that Ka-lok, crushed in a herd of her own kind in the last carriage of all, leaned from the door to help a woman, who, impeded by the *baku*, tried to scramble on to the step of the moving train. Ka-lok leaned down and snatched the bundle the woman carried as best she could through the voluminous folds of the *baku*, hauled the woman up, glanced back to where the man lay in convulsions on the ground, recognized Cecily standing alone, and swung like a cat to the platform just as her carriage jolted out of the station.

She fell in a heap, clutching the bundle of the woman who cursed her volubly for a thief from the doorway of the carriage, and lay still for a moment, stunned; then gathered herself up and sat cross-legged for a space, trying to collect her senses scattered by the sharp rap her head had received from the stone.

Followed a still sharper altercation between herself and a furious official, who took her by the shoulder, shook her, and summarily ejected her through the left-luggage office into the high road.

By the time she had been refused admittance to the platform until she had procured a ticket, had bought one to the next station and had forced her way through the gyrating, screaming throngs of her own kind on to the platform, there was no trace of Cecily.

"A Mem-Sahib? Does not the station teem with Mem-Sahibs and their ayahs, their bearers and their pale-faced children, and do not the Mem-Sahibs look alike, even as two berries on one stalk?" So replied an indifferent official to Ka-lok's frantic questioning. "The man afflicted by the gods? Ah, he disappeared into the town, and the Mem-Sahib, at whose feet he fell and who gave silver coins for the benefit of the sick man, went to an hotel to await the evening train. Which hotel? The gods alone know, but certainly not the big and *pukka* European hotel near the station, as that is full and overflowing with Sahibs and their Mems, their ayahs, bearers and many pale-faced children."

Ka-lok spent the afternoon, the unintentionally purloined bundle in her hand, in searching for the hotel which sheltered Cecily Cleeve. The town of Mughal-Sarai containing nothing of interest to the *Sahib-log*, she concluded that Cecily would pass the afternoon in the siesta, rousing herself in time to catch the train from which they would change to catch yet another train, which would take them as far as Siliguri, where the mountain railway starts to climb the steep heights to Darjeeling. She passed a fruitless afternoon. No trace of Cecily Cleeve could she find anywhere.

With fear in her heart Ka-lok tramped the dusty streets of Mughal-Sarai.

Into the Bazaar she penetrated, searching and questioning. Hiring an *ekka*, she was jolted from one native hotel to another hotel, only to receive the same answer, with threats of blows in some places, offers of refreshment in others, remarks upon her handsome features in all.

Weary she was, thirsty and hungry, but even more fearful than she was weary. With all the native's intuition she had summed up the three white people with and for whom she was working. The men stood for determination, power and a slow but sure victory at the end, once they had overtaken Lotah, the White Rose; but Miss Cleeve stood for subtlety and quick decision, also she spoke the languages of the country and understood the people.

If Lotah, the White Rose, was to be wrested from Sa-t'ong, thereby allowing her, Ka-lok, to regain the hold she had once had upon Sa-t'ong's affections, it would come about through Miss Cleeve; therefore must she be found and restored to the two men.

Ka-lok's keen power of observation, Rama's incredible carelessness, put her upon the track of the girl she was looking for, at last.

Dispirited, beaten, she returned to the station.

She returned by a different route, one leading from the Bazaar, westward, through a labyrinth of mean streets, a tangle of *neem* trees and undergrowth, and along a native track which gave upon the high road leading to the station.

A few emaciated hens roused her to the fact that a house of some kind was hidden in the tangle of *neem* trees and undergrowth; the acrid smell of smoke to the presence of a man somewhere in her immediate vicinity.

What caused her to stop dead and to draw behind the trunk of the biggest *neem* tree and to peer about her uneasily? She was a native, walking in a public part of the town; she was accustomed to the crowded streets of foreign cities and perfectly capable of looking after herself. But she peered about her uneasily and sighed for the sharp dagger she had worn in its sheath, run through her masses of black hair as an ornament, and which she had left behind in her squalid bedroom in Limehouse.

And then she held her garments close about her and flattened herself against the tree trunk as a man passed slowly, stopping, as Fate stretched her withered arm across his path, for one brief moment.

Rama in turban and loin-cloth walked slowly, content. His emaciated body had been washed clean of the red ochre which had besmeared it when he had fallen at Cecily Cleeve's feet in a seeming fit; he no longer frothed at the mouth or shouted mad and unintelligible words, but he had forgotten to cover his feet. He walked barefoot, and the imprint of his left foot, which turned slightly inward so that the big toe made a deep impression in the dust, was the imprint of the foot of the man who had followed the funeral procession which had carried Lotah, the White Rose, out of the house in Benares, passing Ka-lok as she had sat, impersonating Fatma the Blind, by the roadside.

He passed on, his emaciated body glistening with the oil with which it had been covered, his thoughts on the great reward the brothers Nyko-Gung would give him when he delivered the white woman, with an unpronounceable name, into their hands.

Ka-lok watched him go, then stole back upon the path by which she had come from the Bazaar. It was too early yet, too light for her to approach the house in which she felt certain Cecily Cleeve lay, likewise was it too early and too light for the servant of the Nyko-Gungs to carry out whatever plan he had in his evil mind towards the white girl.

Kill her he would not dare after the punishment but lately meted out to the criminals who had set upon and almost murdered a white woman in Northern India.

She stole back upon the path and, once sure of being enough in the public eye to disarm suspicion, sat in the dust and counted her money in the folds of her petticoat.

A dagger she must buy, one long enough and sharp enough to reach a man's heart; also a disguise for the white girl and a cotton *sari* for herself.

She shook her sleek head in despair.

She had asked Cecily to keep her savings for her, hidden in the secret pocket she wore somewhere about her person. One rupee and a few *annas* was all she counted. She flung a prayer for help to the Goddess Paldean-Lha-Mo and opened the bundle she had unintentionally purloined from the woman in the train.

Then she got to her feet and made signs of thanksgiving

to the dread goddess. The bundle contained two *bakus* with gauze over the eye-holes, shoes and under-robes. She had evidently acquired the woman's entire wardrobe, and returned thanks for the abundance of the gifts from the gods.

A little while later she stood in a shop in the Street of the Silversmiths, haggling over the price of a tawdry bracelet as she worked her way to a corner where knives of various lengths and price, but all of the same sharpness, were spread.

She stood with hands clasped behind and just above the spot where a knife, the length she desired, lay; she shook her head and threw it back in a fine show of indignation, feeling for the weapon with slender fingers.

"Thou art an usurer and the son of an usurer," she stormed, as she lifted the dagger carefully and spread her elbows on each side as she ran the sharp blade through the cloth of her garment about the waist. She moved sideways and backwards down the shop, gibing at the irate shopkeeper who had been roused from contemplation by this slip of an impudent thing. Once outside the shop and certain that the dagger held firm and was hidden in her robe, she smiled and searched for her money.

"Three *annas* thou asketh for the bracelet! Behold, thou robber of the fatherless, I will give thee one!"

"One and a half, thou beautiful child of ungodly parents, who essays to cheat the poor and needy."

She coveted the trash, bought it, slipped it on her arm and disappeared into the night.

Some hours later, like a great white moth, she stole between the *neem* trees and the undergrowth, enveloped in the *baku* which guaranteed her protection; like a ghost she crept to the verandah and along it, and slid down into a corner outside a *chick*, through which a faint light shone. And once more she returned thanks to her gods.

Through the *chick* she saw Cecily Cleeve, bound and

gagged, upon a *charpoy;* with his back against the wall and a look of content in his eyes sat Rama, the servant of the brothers Nyko-Gung, unaware that Fate's crooked finger touched his shoulder.

*   *   *

Bound hand and foot, gagged and almost crazed with thirst, Cecily Cleeve had lain on the *charpoy* throughout the seemingly endless day.

She had tried desperately to reach the train as it moved out of the station, endeavored frantically to wrench her skirt from the madman's grasp, and shouted to the guard to inform the Sahib Trevor that she would catch the night train and follow them on to their destination.

The Eurasian guard, not having heard one word of what she said, nodded his head, smiled and saluted, so that she, believing that her message would be taken to John Trevor at the next stop, resigned herself, after an interview with the station-master, to an afternoon spent in the siesta in some hotel, and did so with none too heavy a heart.

She felt utterly tired out, having had but a few hours' sleep—and those disturbed by frightful dreams—after the terrible escape from death in Benares. Led by Ka-lok, who had run ever before them, they had got back at last to their hotel and had caught the first train to Mughal-Sarai, little knowing that Rama, the servant of the brothers, disguised, acting the part of a madman, traveled on the same train.

Having interviewed the stationmaster at Mughal-Sarai, who had informed her that the *pukka* European hotel was full, but that the annex, which was some little distance away, had always one or two rooms empty on account of its distance, she walked straight into the trap laid for her.

Europeans—citizens of well-policed towns, inhabitants of normal, conventional countries—smile incredulously at the tales they hear of the thread which binds the rich and the poor, the mighty and the humble, of India in one vast web of conspiracy. Cecily Cleeve knew of the vast web and did not deride it, but gave it never a thought as she walked out of the station and into the *gharri* waiting exactly opposite the steps.

Europeans were all around her; at the big junction many rushed up to her to offer assistance; some one asked to be allowed to send a telegram to her friends for her, which, for fear of spies, she had decided not to do; another, a distracted-looking woman with an ayah and two peevish children, invited her to tiffin; but Cecily Cleeve, so accustomed to fending for herself, so thankful for the hours of sleep awaiting her, declined and walked out of the station and into the snare.

"To the annex of the big hotel," she said, giving a coin to a beggar who had wiped the dust from her shoe with a corner of his long sleeve, little recking that he and the driver of the *gharri* and the madman were all in the pay of the brothers Nyko-Gung.

Arrived in the center of a tangle of *neem* trees and undergrowth, the driver stopped the pony and turned in his seat to ask a question about the Mem-Sahib's luggage, to which she replied without turning her head. Then she fought like a tiger to free herself from the cloth saturated with some powerful drug with which he covered her face; fought until her senses left her. She woke in agony to find herself bound with leather thongs, which cut her wrists and ankles; crazed with thirst; her mouth gagged with a filthy bit of cloth; alone in a miserable room with a native, naked save for a turban and loin-cloth, seated, cross-legged, at the head of the bed.

The hours passed, the sweat of agony stole down her face. It stained the rough, hempen bands which criss-cross the *charpoy* and form its mattress, and dripped to the floor. Three times she fainted, waking to consciousness, moaning and tossing to and fro, which only served to intensify the pain of her lacerated wrists and ankles. She felt that she must die of agony, or thirst, yet she lived throughout the day, watching the shadows fall from eyes deep-sunken in their orbits. Awake, she forced her body to lie still, and kept her eyes closed, so that when the native turned and peered at her he should not guess at the agony she endured. There was no sound in the house, no one came near them, Rama sat throughout the day, placid, content, dreaming under the influence of the fumes he inhaled from the gourd-pipe he held in his slender hands. Once he moved to light an oil lamp, then sat still, dreaming, placid, content.

What the man intended to do with her or who he was she could not tell, but she intuitively knew that he was in the pay of Sa-t'ong, the Tiger, and that therefore she could count on no mercy from him.

And well for her was it that Ka-lok crouched down in the shadows just as Rama, placing his pipe upon the floor, rose and stood over Cecily, looking down at her face which seemed to have shrunk to half its size.

She looked up fearlessly into the eyes glaring with hate into hers, and made no sound when he bent, and with deft fingers felt for the end of the gag knotted behind her head and pulled the filthy bit of cloth out of her mouth.

"Let not the white woman pretend that she speaks naught of my tongue, for behold, in Benares, have I heard her speaking even as I speak, likewise did I hear her speak when, feigning madness, I held her raiment, so that she caught not the train in which were seated the white men, who," he spat in derision as he spoke, "essay vainly to save Lotah, the White Rose, before she is put up for sale in the Street of Many Arches, where, behold, are many women gambled for and sold, and," he spread wide his arms, "sent to every corner of Asia."

He stood with his back to the reed blind so that he saw nothing of the movement in the shadows, which had fallen suddenly, as Ka-lok slipped from under the *baku*, and out of her under-robes, standing in a saffron-colored bit of linen which reached her knees, knife in hand, a dusky slip of a thing, barely distinguishable from the undergrowth.

Silently, swiftly, she pushed the white garments into a corner and stole close to the blind, making signs to Cecily to let her know that help was at hand.

But Cecily did not understand. Her eyes were ablaze with fever, her mind distorted by pain, so that, mistaking the slender figure for an accomplice of the man who stood at the side, she closed her eyes in horror.

"Open thine eyes, white woman, and tell me whereunto travel the white men? Even he who looks upon thee with eyes of favor and the stripling who, for a space, was husband of the White Rose."

Cecily could not speak, her swollen tongue cleaved to the roof of her mouth, her swollen lips were black and pulled back from her beautiful teeth.

But she would not have spoken even if she had been capable of uttering one syllable.

"Speak!"

She shook her head, though the movement intensified the agony of her racked body a hundredfold.

"Thou *feringhee*," muttered Rama as he lifted the brass bowl of water with which he had replenished his pipe. "Behold, the reward will be great when I place thee in the hands of the Wolf, Chang-ku, but for the hate I bear thy people, against whom my father's father fought even in Cawnpore, losing his life near the Great Well, for that hate and for his death would I torture thee awhile." He placed his hand under Cecily's head and tried to force some water into her swollen mouth, and laughed when she coughed and moaned uncontrollably, then let her head fall back with a jerk.

"I will make thee speak, even if I keep thee here for a moon, even if death comes to claim thee when thou hast spoken." He emptied the contents of the bowl over the leather thongs which bound her wrists and ankles. "Lie thou here until the rising of the sun, whilst the leather of thy thongs shrinks under the moisture, shrinks until the thongs cut down, even to the bone, then see if thou wilt shake thy head when I bid thee speak, thou *feringhee*."

The hate in the old mutiny word was terrible to hear, and filled Cecily's cup of terror to the brim.

She screamed, screamed until the night rang with her awful cries, and jerked her body sideways when Rama bent over her with the gag, and screamed again and again until Ka-lok stuffed her fingers into her ears as she watched, knife in hand.

Brutally Rama gagged Cecily, deftly tied the narrow strip of linen across her mouth, knotting the ends behind her head, and, after searching in a corner of the room, returned with hempen rope and lashed her through the thongs which bound her wrists and ankles, sideways, to the bed.

"Now scream, white woman, now dance upon the bed to thy heart's content. There is no one nigh, and of a surety thou dost know that a woman's screams are of no account in the land of the Hindoo gods."

Ka-lok stood flattened against the wall as Rama crossed the miserable room and lifted the corner of the reed blind farthest from her.

"Dance!" he mocked, as he spat towards the *charpoy*. "Sing, sing sweetly until I return from the Bazaar where I go to eat. No one will hear thee, no one passes this way—sing—dance!"

He laughed softly and let the blind fall, stood for a moment and looked through at the white woman he was torturing out of revenge, then turned away.

Like a shadow Ka-lok, but a pace behind, crept after him along the verandah; for an instant he stopped upon the edge and looked up at the stars showing above the *neem* trees, then, with a cough, crumpled up into a heap and died, when Ka-lok, with the knife in both upraised hands and a prayer on her lips, drove it down to the hilt between the shoulder-blades.

"May the jackals feast upon thy body and the great gods crush thy soul under their heel," she muttered as she unconcernedly cleansed the knife upon the dead man's turban, then turned and ran to Cecily and cut the bonds and held her to her breast, rocking her gently, soothing, as best she could, the terrible sobs which shook her from head to foot. She tore an under-robe into strips, soaked the lengths in the oil of the lamp, and bound up the terrible wounds, and undressed Cecily as she lay on the bed. Then she covered her in the all-enveloping *baku*, which disguised her completely, and ran out to the verandah and dressed herself.

"Behold, must thou look upon me as thy sister for a space, lady," she said when she returned, speaking in her own tongue. "Beneath the *purdah* we are safe, thrice safe, forever safe. Stay here we may not, so that I will carry thee to the station where we will enter the train. This is the working of the dog Chang-ku, for behold is Sa-t'ong gentle with women. Yea! is he very gentle with women." She sighed as she thought of the hours she has passed with him, then laughed softly, gathered Cecily's clothes into a bundle and took them out and pushed them far down into a tangle of undergrowth and returned. "I will carry thee, sister, for catch the train we must, though of a truth, we have much time ahead, the great Night of Festival, of which the white rulers know nothing, or if they perchance know of it, dare say nothing, falls one moon hence. At the station I will buy thee food and the juice of fruit, for, behold, there is much money of thine own and of mine in the secret pocket which yon dog did overlook." She gathered Cecily up into her strong young arms and rocked her gently as she moaned. "In the train will I say that thou art afflicted by the gods, therefore wilt thou be given the soft seat and much food and kindness, being sacred beneath the *purdah*."

Cecily fainted from agony during the journey to the station, and, unnoticed in a corner of the platform, sat huddled in an unconscious heap, whilst Ka-lok went in search of information and food and milk of goats.

She learned that they would have an hour to wait, and that the train would be as full as the Holy River in the monsoon, owing to a detachment of soldiers who were entraining, and who had been waiting, with much impatience and words of cursing, for many hours. Yea! even the mighty soldiers of the Rajput regiment, with whom were two officer-Sahibs of much courtesy and good humor.

Ka-lok, out of pure curiosity, sidled up to the two officer-Sahibs of much courtesy and good humor; she stood quite close to them and looked at them through the gauze-covered slits of the *baku*, her eyes glinting with a sheer delight in theft as they rested on something which shone in the captain-Sahib's hand.

"Best little friend ever, Jones, clip emptied out and t'other shoved in, in the twinkling of an eye. Don't like yours half so much," said the captain-Sahib as he slipped his automatic back into an outside pocket in his tunic.

"Don't think much of it myself, to tell you the truth, but it's not worth worrying over. Another six weeks and I'll be on my way home on leave. *Home.* Think of it! Stand back a bit, that's a leper coming along, I think, or something of the kind. Wonder what sort of face there is under that *baku*. She may be a pearl of fifteen or a hag of ninety, you never know." The two men stepped back as the crowd also stepped back hurriedly to allow a beggar, stricken with some terrible complaint, to pass. The crowd thronged about the two officers, pressing upon them. No one saw Ka-lok lift her covering for an instant as she slipped her hand into the captain-Sahib's pocket, and it was some hours before he discovered that his revolver was missing.

"M'liss Cecily will smile," said Ka-lok delightedly as she

hid the stolen revolver somewhere about her person. "She is one big fool to love and trust everybody and not to carry a weapon upon her. She will smile at Ka-lok."

But Cecily did not smile. She muttered in delirium in the corner of the station, and for an instant Ka-lok's gallant heart sank, then she stooped and gathered Cecily once more into her strong arms.

"For two days, perhaps three, will we abide in the Bazaar," she said, carrying Cecily out of the station and hailing an *ekka*. "With herbs and much tending and much oil upon the wounds she will recover, and then I will go and find the man I love." She held Cecily in her arms all the way to the Bazaar and whilst she bargained for a room in a house at the back of the Street of the Silversmiths.

"In two or three days we shall be gone," she said to herself as she sat beside Cecily all through the night. "In two or three days."

But the days were to pass into weeks before she and Cecily traveled up to India's northwest frontier.

*   *   *

At the next stop out of Mughal-Sarai, John Trevor jumped from the train almost before it had stopped and ran down the platform to find Cecily.

Save for a knot of natives the platform was empty. No one got out of the train, no one got in, neither was there sign of Cecily.

"Guard!" shouted Trevor, whereupon the stout, smiling Eurasian ran up and saluted. "The Mem-Sahib at Benares, with lots of books in her arms, where on earth is she? You said she was in the train."

"I, sir, never! I merely gave the customary signal to inform the engine-driver that the train was complete."

"Then, my friend, the lady——"

"The lady, sir, was most unfortunately and distinctly left behind. I think, sir, you should not be unduly disturbed," he continued. "Doubtlessly a telgram awaits you, sir."

"Don't you let the train go without me," cried Trevor as he turned and ran down the platform.

"Very well, sir," answered the guard.

He swaggered past the carriages, blandly ignoring the irate questions as to the train's want of punctuality in starting which were hurled at him by irate passengers, and saluted Rex.

"Your gentleman friend, sir, has traversed the bridge to inquire as to the arrival of a telegram from your lady friend, sir."

"You don't mean to say she's not on the train?"

"There is no sign, sir."

Rex jumped from the train and ran to meet Trevor.

"Anything?"

"Nothing! But I have sent her a wire, care of the stationmaster at the junction, telling her to go straight on up to—er——"

"The guard says she made him understand that she was following on, and that she was smiling and did not seem at all disturbed, so that's all right."

The guard beamed all over his face and saluted at the munificence of the tip thrust into his waiting hand.

As the train moved out of the station Rex flung himself on the seat, stretched his long legs across the dusty floor, and knocked over the brass image of the goddess Kali.

"And Cecily was going to make tea for us all. Shall I have a shot?" he said as he leaned forward and picked up the fallen bit of brassware, pushing it back against the wall with his foot without noticing a streak of mottled green and brown which slid into the shadow of the lower bunk with a little hissing sound.

"Yes! let's have a try, it'll keep us from thinking."

An hour or so later they decided to turn in.

"I wish you'd get up to the top bunk," Trevor called

out. "All sorts of things happen to travelers in India, and always to those who occupy the lower bunk."

Rex yawned and stretched his bare arms above his head.

He had fallen into a light sleep when Trevor switched off the light; he turned on his bunk and muttered in his sleep, then turned almost on his face, his arm hanging down, his fingers nearly touching the floor, across which crawled one of the most poisonous snakes in India.

Unknown to the vendor, it had crawled through the wide-open mouth of the brass statue representing Kali, the Goddess of Destruction, and there had lain *perdu* until Rex accidentally overturned the statue, when it crawled out, unseen by either of the men, and disappeared under the bunk.

Still lying almost upon his chest, Rex wakened some time later and lay wondering, sleepily, at the strange cold feeling of his arm, which felt as though a bracelet encircled it.

"Cramp!" he muttered to himself, and closed his eyes and opened them, uneasily, as the cold feeling seemed to creep up towards his elbow and the bracelet to feel as though it were made of elastic, which tightened and loosened as he breathed.

He frowned, and, but half awake, lifted his head and looked at his arm, then wakened completely with a terrible suddenness and lay still, petrified with fear, cut off from all means of getting help through the snake, which, coiling and uncoiling, slowly crawled up his arm. Without moving his head he looked up at Trevor, who lay asleep, his back towards him, then at the communication cord above the door at the far end of the carriage, and down again at the reptile which lay still, coiled about his forearm.

Move he dare not, although his whole body jolted gently from side to side and his arm swung as gently to the rhythm of the wheels. Was the snake poisonous or of the harmless water variety? He knew nothing about the snakes of India. Was it angry, or did it flicker its thread-like tongue from habit? Was it watching him with those infinitesimal eyes, or was it asleep? God! how his arm ached, and how he longed, craved to move his fingers, if only to curl them inwards, then to straighten them out. His finger-tips throbbed, all the blood of his body had been driven by his thudding heart down to the tips of those five fingers. His other hand, his arm, bent under his face, was dead, quite dead and cold, but the arm, the right arm, round which was coiled the snake, throbbed like a hammer, although it, too, was cold. The snake's head was moving from side to side. Was it angry? Had something disturbed or attracted it? Suppose it crept upwards and twined about his neck or hid in the bedclothes, well content in the warmth, waiting, watching, out of those hideously evil eyes.

It moved downwards, down to his wrist and across his hand. It half slipped; it hung, swinging from his hand. Go on, go on! Drop! That's nothing but the shadow of the blind swinging to the rhythm of the wheel. Drop! There's only an inch, drop, in God's name *drop*, and——!

Ah, ah! Something has frightened it! It hissed, ever so slightly. What if the train jolted violently or Trevor turned and spoke to him? He had already let his book drop. What if the pillow dropped? It rested upon the very edge. Snakes always struck when frightened! And then what happened? Snake-bite! A frightful death! Agony, a swelling, blackened body, and death in convulsions. God in Heaven, have mercy!

It was creeping slowly upwards again, frightened perhaps by the moving shadow, attracted perhaps by the heat of the bed. If only Trevor would turn! But could he turn without dislodging the pillow?

How slowly it moved! Just as though it liked the warmth of the arm, although the arm was quite cold, and only the finger-tips throbbed and hammered with the blood which had been pumped down to them by the racing heart.

Then reason fought with fear, and between the two Rex lay, waiting for the outcome of the hour.

The snake, the lithe, ringed band, lay between him and Lotah, but it only needed some moments of courage, perhaps an hour, perhaps a little more, and he would be free again. Death stood on the near side of the snake, hand outstretched, within an inch of his arm, that cold, hot arm which swung to the rhythm of the wheels.

He lay quite still, watching the snake from between his half-closed eyes. He had not known, until now, that love and life meant exactly the same thing.

To save his love, not the spirit of love, for that was eternal, but the outward, beautiful form of his love, he must live, yet death held his wrist, death which hissed faintly as Trevor spoke in his sleep and hunched his broad shoulders under the sheet.

Then Rex screamed as the pillow fell, and something sharp pricked his arm.

He sprang straight out of his bunk, his arm upraised.

"Snake-bite! Old man! Snake-bite! Help!"

Trevor leapt to the ground and flung the boy upon the bunk with one word.

"Where?"

A little red patch showing clearly just above the elbow in the gray light, and a faint sound as Trevor sucked the poison, whilst his brain worked clearly and steadily. Rex lay upon his face, his head turned, his eyes upon his friend's dark head as he knelt by the bunk, without a thought to the snake which hid somewhere in the shadows.

Not a word did he say, not for a moment did he cease sucking the wound. He lifted Rex's arm and stood upright and pushed him across to the door and pointed up to the communication cord.

For an eternity of time, which was in reality but a few seconds, Rex pulled at the cord, then staggered back to the bunk as the brakes were put on and the train jolted and stopped. Cries and screams came from every part of it, with sounds of doors and windows being flung open, and irate, anxious, and terrified voices asking questions.

"Doctor! Snake-bite! Snake on the floor!" said Rex clearly, as the door swung back and the guard looked in, swinging a lantern in his hand.

The guard turned and ran down the train, shouting at the top of his voice. "Doctor! Doctor! Doctor! Quick! Snake-bite! A Sahib bitten by a snake, doctor!"

In an instant the train was empty and the passengers running to offer assistance to the victim of the dread snake-bite, regardless of their night attire, snakes on the line or passing trains.

Out from the next carriage jumped a thin figure, clad in pajamas, carrying a black bag.

"Come on with a stick, guard! Try and kill the snake whilst I kill its bite. I'm Dr. Cromwell, of Calcutta. Is there a nurse amongst you ladies? I shall want help."

He swung up into the carriage as he spoke, regardless of the snake, and, seizing the lantern, held it close to Rex's face.

"No time to lose," he said shortly as he lifted Rex's lid and touched the eyeball, then glanced at a capable-looking woman who stood at his elbow. "Nurse? That's fine. Go on sucking, sir, whilst we lift him on to the floor."

A shout of triumph came from the guard as Rex was swiftly lowered, face downwards, to the floor.

"The snake has been killed, sir!"

"Needle, nurse! Here you, sir." A passenger scrambled into the carriage at his call. "Help turn him over and get every drop of that brandy down his throat, every drop, then massage his heart with—more—go on sucking, you—going to fill him with antitoxin—swab, nurse—that's right. Now, sir—don't stop—when nurse says ready—pull your friend's arm right across your knee—going to cut the bite out—fleshy bit, thank God—no veins!"

"Iodine and nitrate here, doctor," said the nurse quietly. "Now—*ready.*"

A flash of steel, a scream—echoed by the people thronging at the door—and Rex opened his eyes.

"Any hope, doctor?"

Dr. Cromwell glanced up at John Trevor.

"I think you've saved his life! I won't swear to it, but I think you've saved his life. Wash your mouth out, iodine and water, weak, swallow some. Nurse! some boiling water. We're off, thank God; the sooner we're there the better."

"Where—the sooner where?"

"My clinic at Calcutta. More brandy, nurse."

"Calcutta? My *God!*"

CHAPTER XIII

Rex fighting his way back to strength in Calcutta, Cecily winning out against delirium, fever and agonizing pain in the native Bazaar of Mughal-Sarai, and Lotah, wide awake to her danger, hopeless, defenceless, weaponless, on her way to the notorious House of Nyko-Gung.

The brothers traveled as great merchant princes, with a retinue of servants in the adjoining compartment, whom they summoned by knocking on the door of the further end of the carriage.

The whole town of Hilli had turned out to watch the procession to the station, many of the passengers of the waiting train and those of a train going south had got out on to the platform, and had gathered, as near as possible, to the steps of the private compartment in which the merchant princes traveled.

The native spectators sighed in envy at the display of wealth, the Europeans thrilled at the sight of the shut litter in which reclined the *purdah* woman, doubtlessly some slip of a girl of ten or eleven, destined as bride to one of the gigantic, magnificently attired men who walked one on either side of her.

"The richest men in Asia——"

"The Nyko-Gungs——"

"Of evil repute—living outside our jurisdiction—can't be got at or touched——"

"Don't look at them, Molly, my dear, don't attract their attention—what? Yes, I know they were on our boat, but don't stare at them, this is India——"

Lotah, covered from head to foot in a *baku* of white silk,

watched the proceedings from behind the lattice of her litter. For one moment, at the sight of Molly Knowles's homely, kindly face, she had nearly screamed for help, then remembered the ring of protection which encircles the high-caste Oriental where his women are concerned, and realized the futility of such a proceeding.

Her one chance lay in acting her terrible part to the bitter end; in tricking the brothers by leading them to believe that she was drugged; in waiting patiently until she found a way of escape or a weapon with which either to kill them or herself.

She was helped out of the litter and stood on the platform between the two huge men. For a full minute she stood staring through the gauze-covered eye-slits at the people of her own race, then, with Sa-t'ong on her right and Chang-xu on her left, mounted the steps and entered the carriage.

"How strange meeting that girl again!" said Molly. "The mystery girl who came out with us. I'd love to get a chance of speaking to her."

"Do remember you are in India, Molly!" replied Mrs. Knowles. "Well, if you really want to, there's your chance, dear, but *don't* speak to the men with her, and *don't* let our train go without you."

Molly Knowles took the chance and pushed her way up to the open window near which Lotah sat, covered in the *baku*.

"I don't know if you speak English, but I hope you'll be awfully happy," said Molly, standing with her hands behind her back, smiling up at the mysterious Eastern figure.

Lotah bent slowly forward, her resolutions swept away in a flood of hope. If she could but whisper a message, one or two words, just—"Help me"—to this confident-looking English girl, it might, it surely would, serve to create a scene, in which, perhaps, she could rush to the door and fling herself into the arms of the people of her own race. Her fighting instincts were roused at last! Help was so near, but a few feet separated her from Molly Knowles and safety.

But who stood behind her in the carriage?

She dared not turn round.

She was acting the rôle of a doll, a puppet, in which she sat for hours, long, endless hours, doing nothing, so that she dared not suddenly show an interest in her surroundings, dared not turn round to see if the brothers were behind her. She swayed slightly in her seat, as though overcome by sleep. Lower she bent her head, lower still, until just within whispering distance, then, as the first word hovered on her lips, stopped and leaned her head against the side of the window with a little sigh. Molly was staring, wide-eyed, over her head, staring up into the handsomest face she had ever seen, into eyes which slanted ever so little, but which smiled at her. Molly, unperturbed, unaware of the tragedy in which Fate had assigned her a part, smiled back.

"*Chho nai kambe ong mo?*" said Sa-t'ong, leaning forward and pulling Lotah towards him so that her head rested against his heart. "Why have you come here?" he repeated in English, seeing that Molly did not understand.

"To wish your bride every happiness, that's all," replied Molly. "We came out on the boat with you, so we're kind of acquainted. You don't mind, do you? It's just a sort of friendly feeling for another girl, you know, in the great moment of her life."

"I do not mind," said Sa-t'ong, "not in the least, but——"

He fell back as Chang-ku, with a savage movement, swept him on one side, lifted Lotah into his arms, and shouted for a servant to raise the wire dust-blinds.

Through the eye-holes Lotah watched Molly Knowles run swiftly back through the crowd and enter the train just on the point of starting for Calcutta, then, trembling, lay like a frightened bird in Chang-ku's arms.

"Put her down!"

"If thou canst rest her head against thy heart, Sa-t'ong, I can hold her to my breast."

"Thou fool! I drew her from the sun. Hast forgotten she is of a northern clime and like to be seized with sickness from the heat?"

Chang-ku laughed mockingly.

"And like to be seized with love of thy handsome face, O Brother. From the heat of thy love, thy passion, I withdrew her."

Lotah watched Sa-t'ong. She smiled faintly and sighed. Just such a look had she seen in Rex's eyes, just such a set to his mouth, when she had stumbled up the stairs and had fallen at his feet, that night when these two men, who were fighting for her, had pursued her through the Limehouse street.

Sa-t'ong smiled, and turned and knocked upon the communicating door, blocking the servant's view into the compartment. "Tea, sweetmeats, and hasten!" He shut the door and stood with his back to it. "Put her down!"

Chang-ku shook his head, and, lifting Lotah, pulled the silken *baku* from about her and flung it on the floor.

"Dost think that she is one of those who are to be won upon the Night of Gambling, Chang-ku? Hast forgotten that she is to be my wife and thy wife, and that we do not hold our *wives* upon our breasts before our servants?"

"Thou didst hold her head against thy heart in the face of all people. What is good for the Tiger is also good for the Wolf, O my Brother!"

"Then shalt thou hold her *dead!*"

Flinging Lotah upon the bunk, Chang-ku caught his brother by the wrist, holding it, a knife in the three fingers of the mutilated hand.

For a moment they stood, their eyes afire in their mask-like faces, then stepped back and sat down, side by side, cross-legged, upon the bunk, just as the train moved out of the station and the servant entered with tea and sweetmeats. Lotah, with a sigh, stretched herself on the pile of red cushions and closed her eyes against the glare of the sun, the crimson of the embroidered satin and the watchful eyes of the two brothers.

They thought her drugged, deaf to their conversation, blind to their movements, a puppet in their hands; they watched her, feasting their eyes upon her beauty, which they thought enhanced by the smear of *kohl* upon the upper lid, the carmine on her mouth, the barbaric jewels in her hair, her ears, and upon her fingers, wrists and knee-high boots.

They watched her, but more closely did they watch each other's hands from out the corner of their slanting eyes, ready to spring, ready to kill upon the slightest provocation.

Each longed for the provocation, prayed for some chance which would allow him to slay the other, thereby rendering their father's dying wish null and void and their oath a thing of no account.

When the old woman Yi, who tended Lotah, came with food, ready to watch over her for the night, they withdrew to a far corner and gambled to pass away the time. They watched her and each other throughout the night and the hours until they reached Siliguri, where waited the mountain train. There they threw dice to decide which of them should carry her first, wrapped in a great fur cloak, to the box-like compartment of the little train. They held her in turn as the train chugged its way up through the driving clouds which blotted out the villages, the tea gardens, and Darjeeling, surrounded by the overpowering wall of the Himalayas.

Save for Gerald Banks, tea-planter, and a few women porters, stocky or gigantic, but all of Herculean strength, the station of Darjeeling was empty; the hill station wrapped in a fine blanket of snow and veiled in mist; the sky heavy with still more snow to come. The people of the country were indoors, there was nothing to bring them out; more than a month stretched between this stormy, bitter afternoon and the day which would see the arrival of the first visitors from the plains.

Truly, the notorious brothers Nyko-Gung were due to arrive by the late train. An army of servants and snow sweepers, and grooms with the ponies of the famous stud, waited outside the station.

Let them wait! Let their masters come!

The merchant princes required no help from outside; indeed, did they not reward any offer of assistance with harsh words or the lash of the whip?

The women porters stood sullenly by and watched the brothers get out of the box-like compartment of the diminutive train, and nudged each other when Gerald Banks called out to Sa-t'ong.

"Hallo! Nyko-Gung," he said. "Got back at last? Had a good time, and the hand, is it all right?"

Sa-t'ong turned.

"Thank you! We had a very good time traveling in foreign lands. And the hand is always ugly, but useful." Did danger threaten in this Englishman? Did he know, guess anything? "And when are you coming again to see us?"

"I'll blow in some day," said Gerald Banks. "I haven't forgotten the sign." He made certain movements with both hands.

"Come for the hunting! Come soon," said Sa-t'ong as he followed Chang-ku out of the station. He liked Gerald Banks, liked him immensely, but he loved Lotah, and danger in the shape of this Englishman threatened that love.

He decided to change the sign and to order the sentry to shoot Gerald Banks on sight.

"The gods of chance favor me, O Brother!" said Chang-ku as he mounted his pony with Lotah on his arm.

"Yea! but they *are* but the gods of chance, O Chang-ku," replied Sa-t'ong, fingering his knife as he turned to mount, and gave the word to start. "Perchance at the last fall of the dice shall I throw the highest number."

"Perchance! Perchance not!" said Chang-ku mockingly as he pulled the cloak over Lotah's face. "Behold, thrice in one day have I thrown the winning number."

Gerald Banks turned and watched them with their retinue of servants disappear into the mist.

"I wonder who the girl is they've got hold of? Some little Hindoo or Cashmiran, poor little thing!"

"Yet another lamb for the Wolf!" Dzo, the Herculean woman-porter, spat as she spoke to her neighbor. "Yea! and a feast for the Tiger!"

Up and down the zigzag paths, swept clear of snow by an army of servants, went the ponies; across a valley strewn with bowlders; along the bottom of a deep gorge and up again, and up to a great cleft in the mountain above where the Rangeet and the Rungmo Rivers meet.

They took it in turn to carry Lotah, well wrapped about in furs; the servants, enforced by the scores who had come to meet the dread brothers upon their return, running behind, to the monotonous chanting of a song.

The furs enveloped Lotah from head to foot, she could scarcely breathe, she could not see at all as she lay in Sa-t'ong's arms, which pressed her close.

The ponies' hoofs clattered sharply upon the pavement of the street near which was built the House of Nyko-Gung. Sounds of laughter, women's laughter, catches of song, the ringing of thousands of tiny silver and golden bells came to Lotah through her furs as she passed down the Street of Many Arches; and the thud-thud and the perfume of heavily scented flowers, thrown at the brothers as they passed, riding side by side, through the village in which, except by invitation, no European dare set foot.

Snow fell throughout the night, obliterating the marks of the brothers' passage over the mountain paths; it piled softly upon the roof of the Great House and the arches

which spanned the terrible street; it seemed to build a wall
of terror about Lotah as she lay wide awake through the
night, face down upon a great divan beside a blazing log
fire, praying desperately for escape or for a weapon which
would enable her to open the door of death through which
she would pass to freedom.

*   *   *

Lotah was a prisoner.

The Himalayas crowned with eternal snow; Chang-ku's
fitful, blazing passion; Sa-t'ong's unfathomable ocean of
love surrounded her and shut her off from freedom; the
spirit of the dead man, the father of the two brothers who
were fighting for her, the man who had slain her mother
and her father, and had cursed her as he had died, seemed
to walk with her by day and to watch by her bed at night;
the very air seemed filled with revenge, hate and evil
indescribable; fear to grin at her from the shadows; absolute terror to be waiting for her in every corner of the
terrible dwelling.

One stupendous picture kept her sane during the days of
her captivity.

From one window of her room, high up in the house of
stone, she could see Mount Everest, the highest mountain
in the world, where God dwelt, above the strife and turmoil of the plains. So at least Rex had said when he had
woven tales of fantasy and poetry out of the shadows in
the studio under the tenement roof in Limehouse.

At sunrise and at noon, at sunset and in the middle of
the night she would cross to the window and stand looking
out at the snow-white peak, sometimes crowned with clouds,
at others draped in mist; sometimes bathed in color, from
sheer crimson to the softest rose, at others gleaming white
or dove-gray or cream, like the first primrose of an English
spring.

The far-away peak, so clear, so pure, uplifted her, filling her with hope; the great wall of mountains, high up on the side of which she lived, a prisoner, with its thousand thousand peaks and myriad precipices, its grim fastnesses and unbroken tracks of eternal snow, oppressed her, crushed her weary spirit, weighed upon her aching heart.

A mountain range, capped with the eternal snows, uplifts the heart filled with love and laughter, urging it onwards, upwards, but if the heart is heavy, then the range seems to stand as a grim and mighty barrier across the road to happiness.

Generations back the house of Nyko-Gung had been built at the end of the great ledge which stretches, some six thousand feet up, along the entire length of the ravine called, by the natives, "The Valley of Fair Women." The ledge, some two miles wide, some three in length, ends in a towering peak, and is reached by one tortuous path alone, a bridle path, zigzagging from the ravine up the mountainside. The path is steep, precipitous in places, strewn with bowlders of all sizes, and can only be safely negotiated by the Tibetan pony. The original house had been built flush with the base of the great peak, the north wall of the caves, in which had been stored the goods with which the founder of the family had traded, being formed of the rock itself. A humble home of a peaceful trader, whose descendants, waxing arrogant with prosperity, had extended their trade and enlarged the humble house, adding three sides, until it stood a solid square with a massive arch as entrance.

Servants of the Great House lived outside the walls. They were the descendants of those who had come with the first Nyko-Gung, and had married and brought forth children, who had married and intermarried, until an entire village, almost a town, spread over the great ledge, inhabited only by those in the service of the Nyko-Gungs.

A fierce, warlike, perfectly contented community, which mixed Buddhism with demonology, and, amongst other gods, worshiped the spirit of the peak, christening it "The Little Finger of the Great Spirit." The inhabitants lived in daily dread of its menace of death; prayed to it; placated it with votive offerings and candles; burned incense before it, and decorated it with flower garlands when the spring sun melted the snows and the thunder of the avalanche could be heard upon every side.

To this lair had come women, attracted by the tales of wealth. They had drifted in on the flimsiest of pretexts. The plainer ones had either been summarily sent packing, secured as servants or taken to wife; the others, more generously endowed by nature, had settled in their own quarter, appropriating a street, spanned by natural arches, which had been built against the mountain rock on the far side of the ledge, and which led to the Great House by a circuitous route. The houses on either side of the street, appropriated by the beautiful women, were built between great natural arches of rock, while the street itself was connected with the village by a web of smaller streets, given over to vendors of jewels and other luxuries coveted by women.

When the father of the brothers Sa-t'ong and Chang-ku had been almost beggared by the fine imposed upon him by the British Forestry Department, and had been forced to live as best he could, penniless, servantless, in the Great House, which he had ultimately mortgaged, the women had fled the place, as is the way of these human birds of passage. When the father died and the two unscrupulous brothers, having paid off the mortgage, took up the reins of government and brought back prosperity to the village, they returned, painted the arches white and hung a red lamp from the middle of each, so that the street shone like a necklace of rubies in the shadows of the night.

Beautiful Hindoo women, lovely women from Cashmir, women from the borders of Russia and Turkestan, attracted by the tales of wealth, made their way to the village on the ledge.

Such dancing and singing, such slender fingers thrumming musical instruments, such melting eyes could not be seen elsewhere in the whole of Asia. From Tibet and China, India, Egypt and Russia flocked men. Without demur they paid the enormous sum imposed as price for the password which allowed them to ascend the mountain path, and which was demanded from them by the two brothers who lived remote, contemptuous, in the house under the great snow peak.

Some of the beautiful women, as long as they were beautiful, made their home in the street; others, as beautiful, came, stayed until the Great Ceremony of Inspection, which fell in the early spring, and passed on to wherever Fate beckoned them.

Beyond the Hall of Ceremony in the Great House no woman had ever gone; of marriage it seemed the two brothers would have none, so that a great murmuring arose in the Street of Many Arches when it heard that a girl, a beautiful foreigner, had come to live in the Great House, and that over her, so gossip said, the two brothers fought in love.

In the rooms allotted to her at the top of the Great House lived Lotah, tended only by old Yi. The old woman had been foster-mother to the two brothers, and from the days of their youth had learned to worship Sa-t'ong for his gentleness and to hate Chang-ku for his fits of rage and brutality.

"Night and day, old Mother, every hour of the night and day must thou be near her," had said Sa-t'ong. "I fear my brother—yea! and my hate for him is as great as thine—and it is not good to leave the lamb in the path of the wolf, old Mother, for fear that harm befalls it in the darkness of the night."

"Night and day, little Son, night and day will I keep her safe for thee from the fangs of the Wild Dog," had replied the old nurse, who delighted in her task, and who, in superstitious fear that it would bring a pack of wolves down upon the village, would not have pronounced the word "wolf" for a fortune. "If thou shouldst summon me, little Son, to give thee news of her, what then?"

"I shall summon thee when the Wolf, my brother, is far from the house, old Mother. Come to me then and not at any other hour."

The rooms allotted to Lotah were huge and luxurious. Night and day fires burned at either end of each; curtains of fleecy wool, worked in colors, draped the doorways and windows; great fur rugs covered the floors, the chairs, the couches. Her bed was spread with an ermine quilt and hung with curtains of Chinese blue satin, patterned at the hem in jewels and held back with gold cords ending in huge golden tassels. Chests of cedar wood, of worked metal inlaid with precious stones, filled with satin and silk garments, gossamer fabric and jewels, stood against the walls; boots of every kind of skin, plain or decorated with jewels or wool patterning, stood in rows; fur-lined coats and cloaks and indoor wraps hung in cupboards of cedar wood. Musical instruments hung on the wall, a great mirror in an ebony frame, patterned in gold, stood in a corner of her bedroom.

In the early morn and at sunset the brothers came together to watch her drink the water they supposed to be a drug; each day, each night she drank it obediently, praying for strength to continue in the terrible rôle she had to play, to the bitter end.

In her acting lay her safety.

Quiet and seemingly barely conscious of their presence, the two brothers, knowing her to be completely in their power, were content to wait until the Night of Festival to decide to whom she should belong; were it otherwise, were she to let them discover, by word or gesture, that she was wide awake to her danger, might they not throw the dice upon the instant to decide her fate, and then——!

The strength and purity of the great mountain in the distance and a musical instrument she had found hanging on the wall, the *pi-wang*, a replica of the one she had played in Limehouse, served to keep her sane in the dreary, endless hours of the day and night.

For hours she would sit near the huge log fires playing softly on the strings, her thoughts in the past when she had sat with her head against Rex's shoulder and had sung to him in the firelight.

One night, wrapped in a cloak of satin lined with sable, her bare feet in fur-lined shoes, her hair reaching to the floor, she sat on a stool in front of the mirror thrumming softly on the strings.

She made no sign when, in the mirror, she saw the two brothers standing in the shadows outside the doorway listening to her, watching her; she went on playing softly, her heart racing, then stopped and yawned, and, stretching her arms, rose and left the room; neither did she make any sign when, some hours later, she heard a faint rustling by her bed, and out of half-closed eyes saw the two brothers standing, side by side, looking down at her.

Later in the night when the house seemed strangely still and the old woman, Yi, slept soundly beside the fire, Lotah rose from her bed, tiptoed across the floor, and stole out of her room upon a voyage of discovery.

Pools of silver, flung by the moon, lay upon the skins which covered the long corridors from end to end; like a ghost she slipped across the moonlight into pitch-black shadow, and on, and down a broad flight of stairs hewn out of the rock and lighted by means of flaring torches stuck into niches in the rock wall.

If she could but find the front door of this house, the front door giving on to the great courtyard with its mas-

sive arch, leading to civilization, freedom; if only, amongst
the weapons, hung upon the wall in divers patterns, she
could find a knife small enough to hide in the gossamer
under-robes or the fur-lined outer garments she wore.

The house was huge and silent, with curtains of the skins
of wild beasts hanging over the doorways of the rooms into
which she dare not peep. She stole down the broad flight
of stairs and turned to the left and ran along another
corridor, and sighed and pressed her hand upon her heart
and turned to retrace her steps, then stopped quite still,
standing like a statue in the moonlight.

She was lost, and from behind a curtain came the sound
of men's voices. Should she go back? Should she hide
behind the curtain? She dared not run for fear of watching eyes, she dared not go forward, she dared not go back.
Terrified, she crept to the curtain and peered through it into
a great hall.

The hall was full of men clad from head to foot in furs,
the snow still heaped upon their shoulders and fur caps.
Guests and their servants, with Chang-ku in their midst,
welcoming them with all the hospitality of the East.

Why was the house full of men? What did they want?
What had they come for? Hunting was the only thing that
would have brought them so far out and the snow was too
thick on the ground and mountainsides for hunting; besides,
they were not in hunting dress.

Terror gripped her.

She turned and ran back along the corridor and half-way
up the stairs to where, under a torch, a star formed with
hunting knives, glittered on the wall. She could stand no
more, her heart was breaking, a great pulse hammered in
her brain.

"Let me out!" it throbbed. "Let me out! Let me out!"

She could not find the door of the house, the terrible
house filled with men and nothing but men. She could not

find her way back to her rooms, but she could, she would, find a way out, through death.

She fell against the wall, leaned against it, her heart almost bursting, her reason nigh to snapping as her brain throbbed and throbbed and throbbed.

The knives were big, unwieldy, with razor-edge and needle-point; they were high up above her head, placed there by one of the gigantic servants who waited upon their gigantic masters.

Her fingers touched the lowest, she pulled it partly from the sheath, then stopped suddenly and stood quite still and looked down as something touched her foot.

She did not scream, she could not, being stricken dumb with horror; she stood stock-still, staring down at the Himalayan bear which snuffed at her robes, then, as it raised itself on its hind feet and snuffed at her bare neck, fled, pursued by the brown beast, up the stairs, along a corridor, straight into Sa-t'ong's arms.

"Lotah *chung!*" he whispered as he lifted her up against his heart, then bent and hit the bear between the eyes, upon which the beast rolled playfully upon her back, then got up and rubbed herself against the master she so dearly loved.

Very gently Sa-t'ong held Lotah in his arms, rocking her to and fro, stroking her hair, whispering all the while.

"My little wife to be! I would not hurt thee, frighten thee, nay, *I* would not cause thee pain!" He held her like a feather on one arm, her cheek against his, his heart thudding in the ecstasy of the moment and called to the bear who sat rocking herself to and fro. "Behold, Lotah, Sona is but a friend, a she-bear whom I saved from death as a cub. Tender and faithful, bearing me a great love. Put out thy hand and touch her, so that she shall know, in future, that thou, too, art her friend. Give me thy hand, Lotah, thy little hand with the scar of the rose upon the wrist with which I marked thee when I essayed to kill thee as a babe." He knelt on one knee as he spoke, and taking Lotah's hand in his, held it out to the bear who snuffed it, grunting, then lay down at her master's feet. "She is not like all women, Lotah mine, she is not jealous as I am jealous of thee. I love thee, little White Rose, I love thee, I love thee." He held her for a moment, then pressed her hand to his forehead. "I am thy servant! Ah! If thou couldst but understand, if I could but stop the accursed drug and kill my brother, so that thou couldst understand how I love thee." He rose and walked slowly down the corridor through the pitch-black shadows, through the silvery pools of moonlight to her bedroom, the bear padding noiselessly behind.

"To-morrow night, beloved, when my accursed brother entertains our guests who have come for the great Night of Festival, I shall come to thy room, and there, whilst he eats and drinks, I shall clothe thee in thy bridal garments, just to look upon thee, alone, to pull the boots over thy slender feet, to fasten the knotted girdle about thy waist, to crown thee with the marriage crown. Oh! Lotah! Lotah! my woman out of all the world."

He turned and carried her to the old woman who stood terrified in the doorway.

"Be careful of her, old Mother! A knife through thy heart will be thy reward next time for thy sleeping."

Yi knelt and kissed the hem of his fur coat.

He laughed and called the bear softly, and laughed again.

Sona lay stretched out beside Lotah's bed and did not stir.

He turned and walked away and stopped and looked back at the girl he loved, then laughed softly as the bear rose and ran, at an incredible speed, to him, and standing on her hind-legs put her paws on his shoulders.

"Thou lov'st me, Sona, indeed thou lov'st me. Faithful

has thou been whilst I have been far from thee, searching for the girl I love. Wouldst be faithful to me in death, little brown love? Wouldst?"

The thunder of a distant avalanche answered him as he walked down the corridor with the bear at his side.

CHAPTER XIV

LOTAH walked from window to window looking out at the storm raging high above her head, thousands of feet above. The wind howled over the house and tore the clouds to shreds, then pulled the remnants together and dashed them against the grim barrier of the Himalayas; Everest was blotted out; the Three Sisters were hidden in the driving snow lifted from the lower peaks by the wind; the topmost peaks of Kinchinjunga's mighty mass showed like great giants, then disappeared behind a curtain of snow and driving cloud, whilst the wind howled like a pack of ghost-hounds far above the Great House, built in the shadow of the "Little Finger of the Great Spirit."

The moon drove a silvery spear through a rift in the clouds and touched the top of the Little Finger which soared serenely above the wrack; drew a myriad sparkles from the fine snow whirling in clouds where the wind whipped it, and shone through the window for a moment upon Lotah's white face and white robes.

The ravine echoed and re-echoed to the avalanches which crashed on every side, until it seemed that gigantic guns bombarded the mighty range, whilst the gods thundered their disapproval of the disturbance of their eternal peace.

Lotah looked up involuntarily at the Little Finger when, somewhere behind the curtain of cloud, the snow which had wrapped some peak about for centuries, broke loose and, with an appalling roar, hurled itself with masses of ice and rock to the valley beneath.

But the Little Finger soared majestically, as it had soared throughout the ages, whilst the womenfolk who served the

Nyko-Gungs crept to the base of the mighty mountain, lighted candle in hand, and prayed and stuck the candles in niches, and prayed again to the Great Spirit to keep the snow tight-held. Not a flame flickered, not a shawl fluttered. The wind howled above, the avalanches crashed on every side, but the ravine was as calm as a lake and dark with shadow. Lotah moved restlessly from window to window, then turned and sat down on a pile of cushions near the fire which roared up the chimney.

Had she done right in not calling for help, in not trying to escape, or had she done wrong?

Day after day, night after night, she had thrashed the question out, to arrive, invariably, at the same conclusion.

Caste and the seclusion of women in the East had wrought against her. In any other country she could have, would have made some desperate effort to obtain help. In India she was helpless through the unbreakable customs of the country.

Had she done right or not in pretending to be drugged, in drinking what was supposed to be the drug, night and morning? What effect would the real drug she had taken have upon her later? What had been the liquid which apparently had allowed her to live and to move like an ordinary human being for weeks, whilst wiping out her memory completely?

India she knew to be famous for its subtle poisons, but it scarcely seemed possible that any drug could be taken, day after day, without ending in coma or death.

How could the brothers and Yi, the old nurse, be so blind? How was it possible that they did not discover their mistake? She answered so naturally to their questions, obeyed them so implicitly, so docilely. Her eyes? Surely the pupils of her eyes were different—either bigger or smaller? She did not know—oh! she knew nothing and feared everything, as she sat in front of the fire, her face buried in her hands. Rex would not have been deceived by her acting. Rex, who noticed every turn of her head, every expression on her face, in her eyes.

Ah! dear God! how she loved him, and longed and wearied for him. How desperately she hung on to life, how she would hang on, until the very last, through her conviction that their love would triumph in the end. She stretched out her arms towards the face she saw in the smoke curling up the broad chimney; a face full of charm, of poetry, of hidden strength. Where in the name of the All Merciful One was Rex? What was he doing? Where was he looking for her? He was in India, she knew that, the brothers Nyko-Gung had said so.

She turned and looked over her shoulder towards her bedroom. It blazed with light. Why? What for? What was the old woman, Yi, who worshiped Sa-t'ong, doing? What was she holding up to the light? Something that glittered and which she stroked with her wrinkled old hand.

Lotah sat quite still, the light of hope, lit by an idea which had just flashed into her mind, flaming in her eyes.

"I wonder," she said softly to herself as she fingered the triple necklace of pearls at her throat. "I wonder if, through her love for Sa-t'ong, the older brother, she could be bribed. If I pretended to be terrified of the other, if I begged her to take me away and hide me for a time, making her believe that, as I do, I go in fear of my life morning, noon and night, because of Chang-ku whom she hates. If I offer her my pearls to hide me, if I cry and plead, if I——"

She turned round once more and looked into the fire, in which she had seen the face of the man she loved; then looked out through the window to the storm raging over the Himalayas. "It's that or death!" she whispered. "And if I can find no weapon, a leap from the window down into the courtyard. Smashed to pieces on the stones, safe, anyway, from this house full of men. Safe before the night when I shall be gambled for—I, Rex's wife."

She touched the necklace, then started and smiled.

By her side, sitting upright, small eyes twinkling, long tongue curling over the formidable teeth, sat Sona in most friendly fashion.

The bear, having felt her master's love for Lotah, had seen fit to adopt the girl who sat so close to the fire and who seemed so plenteously provided with sweetmeats, not to speak of a pot of honey which stood on the tray, with sugar and milk, when she ambled in, in the early hours, and stood on her hind-legs beside Lotah's bed, grunting a good morning.

Being a big-hearted bear and totally unlike her biped human sisters, Sona knew naught of jealousy where she loved.

When, during the day, she had been able to tear herself away from Sa-t'ong, she ambled down the corridors and climbed the stairs to Lotah.

She had sat, this night, behind her master's chair during the feasting in the Great Hall, and then, for some reason best known to herself and perhaps not totally unconnected with the pot of honey, ambled out of the room and once more climbed the stairs to Lotah.

She sat well back upon her haunches, her paws together, asking as plainly as could be for the luscious honey-pot, then grunted and rose to her four feet and lurched, with more gruntings, across to the doorway in which stood the master she loved.

The light of hope in Lotah's eyes was extinguished, suddenly, forever. She made no movement, gave no sign of her horror; she sat looking straight into the fire in which she had seen Rex's face, her hands locked on her knees, her heart racing madly under her fur-lined robe.

She was far more afraid of the quiet, dominating love of Sa-t'ong, the Bengal Tiger, than she was of the violent passion of Chang-ku, the Gray Wolf.

Passion is the thing of a moment; a scorching flame,

leaping from flower to flower; laying waste as it goes; dying down as suddenly as it arises.

Love is enduring—unshakable—eternal.

Chang-ku's passion might die down at any moment, leaving her free; the love of Sa-t'ong, who towered behind her in the dimly-lighted room, would make her a prisoner for life.

He bent suddenly and lifted her into his arms.

"What didst thou do this afternoon, Lotah *chung*, whilst I entertained my guests?"

Lotah closed her eyes and turned her face against the white satin coat.

"Verily! shall I rejoice when there is no more need for thee to take the medicine without color or taste. Of a truth was the old hag, Mo-li, a hag of great cunning, to take away thy memory and yet to let thee live as other women. Lotah! White Rose! When wilt thou smile, laugh—when?" He lifted her like a feather, high above his head, then held her close against his heart. "Ho! old Mother, thou gnarled oak, hither!"

The old woman ran as swiftly as her years would let her and knelt and clasped his knees.

"Get thee gone, old nurse! and wait without again."

The old woman rose, her eyes alight with love, and pointed through the doorway to where Lotah's bed showed, piled high with satins and silks and furs; then she nodded, kissed her master's instep and ran out of the room, Sona snapping playfully at her heels.

Sa-t'ong stood Lotah on her feet.

"Am I so ugly, Lotah *chung?*"

He knew he was the handsomest man in all Asia, he knew that he had but to beckon for any woman to come running to him, yet his heart was forever in the keeping of this wisp of a girl who looked at him gravely and stood with her hands clasped on her breast.

"Dost like my raiment, little Statue of Ice? 'Twas

made to find favor in thine eyes. Of white silk, lined with the blue of the silk gown thou didst wear the night I carried thee over the balconies of the burning house." Lotah shivered suddenly. Rex seemed so near. The lining of the coat was of his favorite blue, the blue of the studio door, the blue of the dress she had worn on her wedding day. She glanced at Sa-t'ong as, in sheer vanity, he took off the coat and flung it on the floor, standing in white silk shirt and breeches so voluminous that they hung almost like a skirt to the high boots of undressed leather, patterned in sapphires. He was the East personified, barbaric, overpowering, and he trembled for love of the girl beside him.

He put his arm about her shoulders and gently led her across the room.

"Whilst my brother ravens upon the viands like a starving wolf and drinks his fill of the fermented *murwa*, I will show thee the raiment I have had prepared for thee, Lily of the Plains. 'Twas woven by the spiders at dawn, threaded with the rays of the sun at noon, laced by the bulbul's golden notes in the moon, studded with the diamonds of the night sky."

They stood side by side, looking down at the sheen of satins and silks, furs, laces and jewels heaped upon the bed, then Sa-t'ong looked up and round the room and down at the girl he loved, and sighed and bent and kissed her hair.

Had he but looked over his shoulder he might have seen Chang-ku, the ravening Wolf, sated with the feast, aflame with the fermented *murwa*, standing in the pitch-black shadows outside the far doorway, watching them.

But he did not look over his shoulder, so that he did not see, and, laughing, took the bridal crown from out the pile of jewels and placed it gently on Lotah's head, then with dexterous fingers slipped her fur-lined satin coat from about her.

"I know naught of the tangle of silks and satins women call clothes, Lotah *chung*," he said as he lifted a heavy white satin coat embroidered in pearls. "This has no ribbons nor clasps, yet is it worn by brides beyond the borders of Tibet, where dwells the race of my fathers. An opening for thy head which is like unto the cedar tree, and openings for thy arms which are as ivory." He laughed softly as he slipped the bridal garment over her head and pulled her hands through on either side, and stood back and stared and stared at her, his face drawn, his mouth like a trap of steel.

The golden, diamond-studded crown pressed close upon her forehead, the bridal gown fell straight to her ankles; she was Eastern, beautiful beyond words and helpless in his hands. He ran to her and knelt and bowed his handsome head and kissed her feet, her knees, her hands, then leapt to his feet, and roughly, blindly, without looking at her, lifted the crown and the bridal robe and wrapped her in her fur-lined cloak.

Silks, satins, furs, laces, jewels he snatched from the bed and flung into a far corner, and crossed to her and gripped her by the shoulders, whilst she stood shaking like a young tree in the storm.

"I can no more, Lotah *chung!* I can no more! I have sworn upon the deathbed of my father, and the oath I must keep, and I love thee too well, too well to call thee aught but wife."

He picked her up and laid her on the bed and pulled the ermine quilt over her, high about her neck. "Rest thee— sleep—Sona will guard thee for me, she sleeps beneath thy bed." He stood looking down at her. "Lotah! Little Rose Tree as high as my heart, have pity on me! One word, Lotah, one little word, a smile! I starve, little Cold Mountain Peak, I thirst, little Snow Hare." Lotah lay still, her eyes closed. "No word? No little word? No smile? Ah! Lotah, 'tis well for thee that I love thee, else———"

He turned and strode from the room, looking neither to right nor left. He went straight on and into the room in which his mother had died, the mother who had loved him so dearly.

Sounds of shouting and revelry came from the banqueting hall, where the guests had supped too well to notice the absence of their hosts.

An hour passed. Lotah slept, guarded by Sona, who dreamed under the bed, and the old woman who, wrapped in a sheepskin, slept near the fire.

But Yi, the old nurse, was wide awake on the instant, alert, apprehensive, when a squat figure, unrecognizable in a sheepskin coat, tapped her on the shoulder.

"Our master, Sa-t'ong, calls thee! He lies ill, stricken with great pains. He orders thee to the kitchen, there to brew him thy cordial, thy charm against poison," the man lowered his voice, "administered perchance in wine. He bids thee to hasten, leaving me to sit without the door of this chamber. The pains grip him fiercely, causing the sweat to break upon his face, which is as death."

"Who art thou?"

Chang-ku's servant, Dong, indistinguishable in the dusk and the cumbersome coat, whispered the name of a servant trusted by Sa-t'ong. "And says our master, hasten, so that all is well before the return of the wild dog, Chang-ku, who, with some of those who have drunk o'er much, have gone to visit the street where a necklace of rubies hangs athwart the arches."

The old woman did not pause to think. Her well-beloved, her little Son was ill, perhaps dying. The cordial was not brewed in an instant. Time pressed. Never a thought did she give to Lotah. Her little Son lay ill, perhaps a-dying—time pressed.

She ran from the room, and Chang-ku, the ravening

Wolf, crept from the shadows which hid him outside Lotah's doorway, and stole into her bedroom.

He smothered her screams in the ermine quilt and wrapped her tight, binding her with the silk robes he picked up from the floor.

The shouting of the guests drowned his almost noiseless tread as he stole out of the house to the stables; the thunder of the avalanches, the howling of the wind, drowned the sound of the pony's hoofs on the snow.

With Lotah, strapped to the high-peaked saddle in front of him, he took the pony slowly down the deserted high road towards the zigzag path leading to Darjeeling.

He turned and shook his fist in the direction of the house built in the shadow of the "Little Finger of the Great Spirit."

"Thy Rose Tree will bear no flowers, thy Snow Hare will be marked with the trap, O Brother," he shouted. "Thy little Cold Mountain Peak will have melted away, thou fool, thou great, love-besotted fool."

*   *   *

The half of an hour passed, the snow fell steadily, the wind howled like a pack of ghost-hounds round the house, when Sona awoke.

She stood on her hind-legs and snuffed at the bed to find the girl whom her master loved, and who, somewhere, hid the luscious honey-pot.

Then she grunted dismally and dropped to her fore-feet and ambled off to find Sa-t'ong, her master, whom she found, sitting with his head in his hands, in the room of his mother.

*   *   *

Big snowflakes, like feathers escaped from a pillow, fell heavily, covering the roofs of the village houses, the arches, the trees, the rocks, and the road down which Sa-t'ong rode the short-legged, stocky, thick-necked horse.

Far above, the snow-clouds were hurled against and across the Himalayas, and the flakes whipped into eddies; in the ravine the flakes fell straight, monotonously, obliterating every mark upon the ledge, softening the rugged outline of the rocks, smothering the bare branches of the trees.

Sa-t'ong could not see a foot ahead. He sat in the saddle, knees slack, reins just held in his fur-gloved hands, urging the horse with words as it cantered through the storm, following the road by instinct to where the precipitous zigzag path began, leading down to the bottom of the ravine.

Once Sa-t'ong looked back.

A dull orange glow showed where the light gleamed out across the ravine from the west window of the banqueting hall; higher up a fainter glow showed where the light shone through the window from which Lotah could see Mount Everest, the Three Sisters, and chains of mountain peaks.

But Lotah was not there!

His suspicions aroused when Sona had come in, grunting dismally, Sa-t'ong had run through the house and up the great stairway to Lotah's room.

She was not there, the bed was still warm, but neither she nor the old nurse was there, nor was the ermine quilt to be seen, and the house echoed to the sound of many voices as servants, from all sides, hastened up the stairs to answer their master's summons.

The old nurse came hurrying, shaking with fear.

She flung herself at her master's feet, beating her breast, screaming abuse on the spy who had tricked her.

She had seen marks of a pony's hoofs and a man's boots in the snow lying between the stables and the high road; she had seen them as she had returned from the kitchen to answer the summons of the gong; from the kitchen where she had gone to prepare the cordial against poison for her little Son, whom the thrice-accursed spy had said lay sick unto death.

Marks of hoofs and boots in the snow, but never a sign of the wild dog Chang-ku, when, her suspicions aroused, she had peeped into the banqueting hall, where the guests slept drunkenly under or upon the table.

She knelt at Sa-t'ong's feet as he shouted for his furs, and touched his foot with her forehead when he ordered the black horse, with the white star between its eyes, to be saddled on the instant, the surest-footed, hardiest, most resisting and gentle in all the famous stud.

Then she got to her feet, helping him with the furs, tying the ear-flaps, belting the huge coat, pulling on the gloves, whispering the while.

"Little Son," she had whispered, "little Son, ride to overtake the wild dog, thy brother, ere he reaches the bottom of the Valley of Fair Women, lest perchance, when there, he hides behind a boulder laughing at thee as thou passeth on. Lay first thy hand upon the White Rose, holding her, lest perchance also he flings her out into the storm so that, if she belongs not to him, she belongs not to thee. Then little Son, ride thou down upon him. The horse, White Star, will outweigh the wild dog's pony. The path is narrow, the precipice upon thy right hand or thy left hand, and the night is dark, and love waits thee in the shadow of the Little Finger of the Great Spirit."

He could see nothing but the curtain of snow, hear nothing but the raging of the storm in the mountain peaks, nor made he any sound when the horse stopped short at the beginning of the zigzag path leading down to the valley.

For fear of brigands attracted from Mongolia by the tales of wealth, for fear of attack, the path had never been cleared of the boulders, of all sizes, which strewed it. A path between the boulders there was, wide enough to allow cattle to pass in single file, easily defended and easily discerned in the daylight. On a night of storm it had never been negotiated in all the annals of the Nyko-Gungs.

Uncertain, uneasy, Sa-t'ong sat staring down into the ravine. Instinct alone had led him to believe that Lotah was being taken to Darjeeling and from there to the plains, to one of the big trading houses scattered all over India. But supposing Chang-ku had hidden in the village for the night, waiting for the storm to pass? There was many a house which would shelter him, many a hand ready to help him. The Wolf's friends were few, but there existed a crowd eager to fawn upon him, to win his money, to drink his wine, to curry favor.

Then giving the horse its head he touched the flanks with his heel and urged it down the first few steps of the zigzag path.

His uncertainty was at an end. From some spot farther down, how far down it was impossible to say on account of the snow, had come the neighing of a horse. The wild ponies did not come as far down as the ravine, neither were the Mongolian-bred horses of the famous stud allowed to stray, so that Sa-t'ong urged his horse down the first few yards of the steep path. He could have slipped from the saddle and followed the path by himself, but that the snow was already deep and the going heavy. If he led the horse it might cover the ground more quickly but would try to push him along or off the path; if he remained in the saddle it would scramble and slither round and over the boulders like a goat, and, once Chang-ku killed, would turn and as easily scramble up again, carrying the double burden of its master and the White Rose.

Cold!

Sa-t'ong's frozen breath covered his face in a thin coating of ice, icicles hung from his furs and the horse's rough coat, the snow froze into chunks of ice on his shoulders and the animal's haunches, but Sa-t'ong was warm enough. A lust to kill fired his blood, a hatred inconceivable raged like a furnace in his heart. Lotah, whom just a few hours ago he had crowned with the bridal crown, was down there, in the dark, in the hands of a man who knew no mercy where women were concerned; who was as the beasts of the field, and as careless of the life of others as he was of his own honor.

Twice the white-starred horse blundered into a boulder and stopped, whinnying with pain, then plodded on and down, walking close against the mountainside or upon the very edge of the precipice which, at every turn of the path, yawned on either one side or the other.

The snow deadened all sound. Sa-t'ong could hear nothing of the pony ahead. Chang-ku smiled as he rode slowly, unconcernedly, down the path, unaware of the hate hard upon his heels. Snow lay thick upon Lotah, wrapped in the ermine quilt, stretched, unconscious, across the high-peaked saddle. He felt nothing of the cold that turned the snow to ice as it piled upon his shoulders and the pony's haunches. Truly, the girl might be dead, frozen indeed to death long before they reached Darjeeling. What then? It would not break his heart if she died, she was too thin, too dull for his taste. True, she was a woman, and bound to him by the oath he had sworn upon his father's death-bed, but his passion had wellnigh died out, and only flared spasmodically, kindled by the love he had seen in the eyes of his hated brother.

Out of hatred, revenge, he was stealing her, taking her to the plains. Not for love, nay! nor even passion. If she died there were many precipices along the road in which to hide what was left of her, and many other women waiting to parade to the sound of drums and pipes upon the Night of Festival.

They were half-way down, he knew it, because his boots had scraped the sides of two boulders which faced the one the other just about half-way down the path. From there on the going would be easier, but more dangerous; fewer boulders, but the path at a steeper incline, with a precipice at either one side or the other all the way down. He drew out a flask of *murwa* and almost drained it as an avalanche, somewhere in the distance, tore down the mountainside, then turned and fought like the demon he was, as Sa-t'ong, falling upon him unawares and with but a foot or so between his horse's hoofs and the precipice, pressed the white-starred beast close to the pony, gripped his brother by the back of his sheepskin coat, and, using every ounce of his incredible strength, jerked him backward out of the saddle and flung him on the path.

It all happened in a moment.

They could not see each other, so dark was the night, so thick the curtain of falling snow; they could hear nothing above the raging of the storm.

The horses, so trained, stood stock-still where they had stopped, the white-starred beast a pace behind the other; the brothers scarcely breathed as they, too, stood stock-still, divided by two yards or so of mountain path, carpeted in snow.

They waited as they had waited for days, for months, for years for an opening, a pretext, the chance of fighting to the death.

Chang-ku, risen to his feet, barred the path to Lotah, and until he was either killed or stunned Sa-t'ong could do nothing. The Gray Wolf felt over the path with his foot and smiled as he bent and picked up a heavy boulder in both hands.

Heavy it was, but he raised it above his head as easily as he might have raised a loaf of bread, and waited for a puff of wind or Fate to blow the snow-curtain aside for just the fleeting second which would allow him to measure the distance separating him from the pony with Lotah strapped across its saddle.

He smiled at the thought of the revenge he was about to

take upon the brother he had always hated for his great good looks.

Either the boulder would fall on Lotah and kill her outright, or it would startle the horse and send it tearing along the path and over the side down to its death, and the girl's death, at the bottom of the ravine.

Just for a second the snow-curtain was blown aside. He swung back his arms and flung the great piece of rock.

There came a scream of agony from the pony as the boulder fell to one side of it, ripping the flesh from the haunch, a clatter of hoofs as it tore down the path, a shout of terror from Chang-ku.

In the fleeting second in which he had seen the pony, in the same second Sa-t'ong saw Chang-ku, and, bending double, reached forward, and, catching him by the knees, with a mighty swing flung him to his death, far out over the side of the precipice.

Sure-footed as a goat, the pony, with Lotah strapped to the saddle, raced down the path with the white-starred beast, ridden mercilessly by Sa-t'ong, hunting knife in hand, close upon its heels. He had no fixed plan, he could not have, the path was scarce wide enough to allow two horses to walk side by side, let alone two who raced madly to their death.

The shaggy head of the white-starred beast reached the other's tail, passed it, drew level with the saddle. Sa-t'ong, reaching forward, felt for Lotah in the dark, touched her, pulled at her.

He cursed aloud.

Lotah was bound to the girth by her wrists on one side and her ankles on the other.

He did not hesitate. At the terrific speed the horses were tearing down the path and taking the sharp corners there could be but death ahead.

The knife between his teeth, he bent and reached for the girth under Lotah's hands and, gripping it, loosened his knees and slid from the saddle. His own horse, still tearing at top speed, fell behind a pace, the other, stocky, enduring, lurched to one side for an instant, then, terrified at the thing that clung to its side, righted and hurled itself down the path to certain death.

Running by its side, clutching the flying mane with his mutilated hand, Sa-t'ong suddenly let go of the girth, gripped the off-side of the saddle, and flung himself into it. The pony staggered as he slashed at the thongs which bound Lotah, stumbled to its knees and scrambled to its feet, giving Sa-t'ong the necessary time to fall, dragging Lotah, unconscious, stiff as marble, with him to the ground, just as the horses, on the top of each other, blinded with snow, maddened with fear, collided, and, trying to turn in the narrow space, sprang straight over the side down to their death at the bottom of the ravine.

*   *   *

The log fires blazed, the sun poured in through the windows as Sa-t'ong sat without movement beside the bed on which Lotah lay.

"Old nurse!" he whispered. "What thinkest thou? Will she live? 'Tis hours, many hours since——"

"Since thou didst carry her here in thine arms, little Son."

"Will she live, old Mother? Tell me, will she live?"

The old nurse smiled and nodded her head as she pointed at Lotah, who had opened her eyes and lay looking at them.

"Yea! little Son, she lives, thy maid in thy house, for behold, art thou at *last*, through the death of thy brother, the master of the home of thy fathers. The only master, the——"

She stopped speaking and looked up.

"*A-tsi-ma!*" she whispered, as Sona growled softly.

Chang-ku stood in the doorway, looking at them, a mocking smile on his evil face.

"The bed upon which my wife or thy wife rests, O Sa-t'ong, is wellnigh as soft as the bed of snow, some score of feet below the ledge, into which thou didst, in all brotherly affection, hurl me in last night of storm. Behold! do the gods fight for me, O my Brother?"

Without speaking Sa-t'ong looked at the man, risen from the dead, then smiled and bent his head and kissed the scar of the rose on Lotah's arm just as she opened her eyes.

"Rex!" she whispered.

And fell asleep.

CHAPTER XV

Rex was still in Calcutta.

He rebelled in vain against the orders of Dr. Cromwell, who had forbidden him to start for Darjeeling until he had completely recovered from the snake poison which, combined with fear and the agony of uncertainty, had brought him so near to death. He was installed in the doctor's own bungalow, with the best nurses to be found in Calcutta to bring him back to health at the quickest possible speed and in the best possible way.

"The slowest recovery I've ever known," grumbled Dr. Cromwell, after a week had passed, whereupon Trevor told him as much as he felt his loyalty to Rex would allow him, pointing out that anxiety and fear were keeping his friend back as much as the effects of the snake-bite.

Dr. Cromwell shook his very wise, gray head.

"Right!" he said. "Now I understand! Pity you didn't tell me before. I'll get him along as fast as I can, but I'm not going to have his death on *my* conscience by sending him from the plains, chock-full of poison, to the below-zero altitudes of the Himalayas." He looked at Trevor keenly out of his shrewd, kindly, all-observing eyes. "You don't look *exactly* at the top of form yourself. Worrying about your friend, eh?"

Whereupon, solid, stolid, unemotional John Trevor suddenly and uncontrollably poured out his heart-load of misgivings and fear.

We're both in this, doctor, up to our necks in it, and it seems as if we must smother, go down in it. Power's wife has been stolen—out of loyalty to him I can't tell you who by—nor where she is—in fact, we don't *know* where she is really—it's pure guesswork going up to Darjeeling, and Power is so *sure* the devils who have got her would kill her if they thought there was any chance of their being caught, that he has taken an oath to win out off his own bat, and nothing will shake him."

The doctor lit a pipe before answering.

"He's right, absolutely right!" he answered slowly. "A snake in her bed, a drop of poison in her cup, a knife, a cord, they'd just think nothing of it. He's wise, as well as damned good-looking and interesting. And you—just you get off to Mughal-Sarai and try to find out what has happened and get on the track of your friend Miss Cleeve. She isn't in Darjeeling, that's certain."

"No, she's not there!"

"I know the manager of the Mount Everest well, and he'd not be likely to make any mistake about visitors in Darjeeling so early in the year, and he knows every one of the residents. There's nobody of her description, he wrote, you say, up there; she hasn't written to you, either to the Great Eastern here——"

"I wonder if she left a message with the station-master at the junction? It's a faint hope, but it's hope."

"God bless my soul!" had heartily replied Dr. Cromwell —who thought things looked as black as they possibly could for the men and their women-folk—as he looked up the trains, "if you'd lived as long as I have in this country of mystery and misery you'd expect an answer to your letters, telegrams, and special messengers when you got it, and then you'd look twice to see if it was correct and not meant for your neighbor. You get along up to the Junction and see if she ever had your telegram."

Trevor's own telegram to Cecily was handed to him at Mughal-Sarai. Of her there was no trace whatever. The station-master, who spoke to scores of English ladies in the month, could not remember her.

The hotel manager could not recall her, had no trace of her in their books; it was useless to question the native servants, who see all Mem-Sahibs exactly alike and rarely know which way up a photograph should stand.

Trevor passed hours in the Bazaar with a native clerk from the *pukka* European hotel, questioning here, there and everywhere, but no one had seen or heard of a Mem-Sahib in difficulties.

Women of the *purdah* drew their veils as the Sahib approached, or ran into their houses, or turned their backs, their fingers spread before their faces. Cecily and Ka-lok, two supposedly *purdah* women, knew nothing of Trevor's visit until long after he had started back again to Calcutta.

During his visit Cecily, fever gone, wounds almost healed, had lain asleep with Ka-lok sitting by her side, fanning her; it was long after sunset, upon Ka-lok's return with the wherewithal for the evening meal, that she heard of Trevor's visit.

"Something has gone wrong, Ka-lok! Something has gone wrong! They should have been in Darjeeling, they should have found Lotah and have had her safe by now, if something had not gone wrong. What has brought Mr. Trevor back here? What has given him the *time* to get back here? Where is Mr. Power?" Cecily sat up in bed. "We must start at once for Darjeeling. I am quite strong again. Something has gone wrong, terribly wrong!"

"Verily, something has gone wrong!" Ka-lok replied cheerily, as she drew the knife she had stolen from its sheath and ran her finger along the edge, which she sharpened from point to hilt upon a whetstone every morning. "But not so wrong as it has gone with me! Behold, are there six of us tied, knotted, bound in love, and I, because I have given most, the most bound of all. I know not in what way the white people will cut their bonds. I shall——" She looked at the knife lovingly and hid it in her robes, then urged Cecily to eat and sleep and to leave the matter in the hands of the gods until three more days had passed. " 'Tis by good food and much sleep that the strength will come back for the journey and the health will return for the big fight," she whispered. "Feign sleep whilst I go to find out what is to be found out at the station, so that our neighbors, if they peep in upon you, disturb you not."

At the station she drew a blank. As a woman behind the *purdah* she found it impossible to make inquiries about the movements of a Sahib or any other man; when, taking the big risk, she slipped behind a pile of luggage and out of the baku, rolled it into a bundle, tucked it under her arm, and proceeded to question the station-master, she was asked for her ticket.

"Ticket? I wait for news of the Sahib before I purchase a ticket," she replied, cursing herself for her lack of foresight, whereupon she was likened unto a hussy in the choicest vernacular and summarily ejected from the station.

"Nay! weary not, weary not," she urged, when Cecily wrung her hands upon the news. " 'Twould be of no wisdom to start to-night! There is yet time for all of us, yet time to save the honor of the White Rose. I know of the customs of the accursed House in the shadow of the Little Finger. The whole of India, yea, and of Asia, knows of it. The Night of Festival falls upon the eve of next full moon, which is within the week. As I have recounted, with music and song the women pass before the men gathered from all parts to buy——"

"A slave market! A slave market upon the very borders of civilization! It does not seem possible!"

"Nay, no slave market, because nothing is sold or bought. Money upon the night is not seen, nor upon the next night."

"The next night?"

"Upon the night of the *full* moon, as I have also already recounted, the women for whom there are more than one bidder are gambled for with the *cho*——"

"Ah! yes, the dice!"

"Therefore have we the time, three days before we start, for it would be without wisdom to be seen *before* the Night of Gambling. For that night I have a plan by which we shall be able to penetrate the fastnesses of this town of ill-fame, built upon the ledge of disrepute." Ka-lok spread wide her fingers, then snapped them contemptuously. "There is no difficulty in a *woman* gaining admission to the House of Nyko-Gung."

"And then?"

Ka-lok laughed as she stirred the broth.

"Then the gods will be either propitious or unpropitious. Drink to bring back the strength, sleep and wait until the moon waxeth and weary not."

And Cecily waited with a great wearying, waited for three more days until the evening of the day when Rex, in Calcutta, took the reins into his own hands. Upon that evening she started, with Ka-lok, for Darjeeling.

While she was still waiting, John Trevor returned from his fruitless journey to Mughal-Sarai.

"Well, the doctor will be back to-morrow," exclaimed Rex. "And I'm just going to tell him that I'm out of leading strings, as fit as a fiddle, and off at once. I'm not going to stand another day of this."

Trevor glanced at his friend sitting on the edge of the bed.

"Wait another few days, for heaven's sake. It's a beastly journey, and how would you feel if you crocked up at the end and were able to do nothing?"

Rex turned on him savagely.

"If you had your wife, the woman you loved, in the hands of two devils, don't you think *you'd* be at breaking-point? I suppose you think it's fever, poison, snake-bite that has reduced me to skin and bone? It isn't; it's worry, uncertainty, absolute horror. I couldn't go before, because

I couldn't stand steady, but I can now, and nothing will stop me."

Trevor crossed to him and sat down on the bed, and as he looked at Rex his thoughts flashed back to the hulking Chinaman, or what he had mistaken for a Chinaman, who had brushed against him in the Limehouse street.

"David and Goliath!" he thought as he lit a pipe. "With revenge behind the giant and love in the boy's sling."

"A crowd!" muttered Rex irritably next day as they crossed the room to where Dr. Cromwell stood talking to two guests.

"Three make a crowd, there are only two."

"Yes, but——"

"Let me make you all known to each other," said Dr. Cromwell. "Mrs. Knowles, this is Mr. Power, the snake victim, and this is Mr. Trevor, the snake hero. Molly," he introduced the men as he spoke, "you tell that young sawbones you're engaged to, to be sure to carry antitoxin about with him wherever he goes. Mr. Power would most certainly be dead if I hadn't happened to have had it with me on the train."

Molly smiled up at her old friend as they entered the dining-room. "You old story-teller! Mr. Trevor had sucked *all* the poison out long before you got a look in, hadn't you, Mr. Trevor?"

"I had a good shot, Miss Knowles."

"Were you frightened of being poisoned yourself?"

Trevor turned to the woman at his side who so uncomplainingly followed the drum, and, as is so rare in India, had managed to retain some of her good looks during the process.

"I never gave it a thought, Mrs. Knowles, and—at least, that's my theory—where you don't fear you don't suffer."

"There now, Molly!" cried Dr. Cromwell. "What do I keep on repeating?"

"That theory has nothing to do with freckles," laughed Molly. "I look in the glass to see if I have enough powder on my nose, not freckles. And if fear has anything to do with the propagation of freckles, mother's the culprit. She's forever dinning them into my ears, although they only show on my nose." She smiled across at her mother. "Aren't you, darling? you know you are. Even in public, even upon the station at Hilli she said that she must consult you about them, you horrid old man, and they're my freckles and my nose, and I'm engaged—oh!" she turned to Rex as she spoke and then to Trevor. "Such an interesting thing happened at Hilli."

"Really!" said Rex disinterestedly.

"We're not long out from home, you know; we came on the *City of Kulna*, and——"

Molly Knowles stopped short as Rex dropped his spoon on to the dish with a clatter and stared up into his face, which had gone dead white. Mrs. Knowles stared at Trevor, who leaned across the table and whispered to the doctor:

"Can the servants leave the room?"

The doctor gave an order to the barefooted servants, who placed different dishes on the table and disappeared.

"Did you see——?"

John Trevor interrupted Rex quickly.

"This may have nothing whatever to do with us, Power, let Miss Knowles speak, and when she has done we will explain."

Molly Knowles looked from one to the other in perplexity.

"Fire away, Molly," said the doctor, who had been watching Rex. "You may be able to help Mr. Power tremendously."

"Oh! but," said Molly, helping herself to rice, "what can the mystery girl on the boat have to do with Mr. Power?"

"For God's sake, Miss Knowles!" Rex gripped her by

the arm, and a good deal tighter than he knew. "Did you
—did you get a chance of speaking to her?"

"Come along, Molly," quickly said Mrs. Knowles, who
had seen the look in Rex's eyes. "Tell Mr. Power all about
the girl." She turned to Dr. Cromwell, rapping the table
with a spoon. "I knew, I was perfectly *sure* that those
devils were up to no good."

"What devils?"

"The Nyko-Gungs!"

Dr. Cromwell leaned right across the table, sweeping
glass and cutlery on one side as he stretched and touched
Trevor on the arm.

"Have the Nyko-Gungs got her? Are *they* the brutes
you spoke about?"

Trevor nodded.

"My God! How awful! If I had known, if only I had
known I would have gone myself." He turned to Molly.
"Quick, dear, everything you know of the mystery girl,
every incident, every word, tell it just as quickly as you
can. Every minute is precious."

Molly told them, looking from one to the other, prompted
by her mother. She told them how she used to long to
speak to the mystery girl on board and how she used to
hang about near the part of the deck just outside the girl's
cabin. "But she was *purdah,* closely veiled. No one ever
saw her face, no one ever spoke to her. She used to sit
hour after hour looking out to sea, without moving."

"The stewardess swore that she was drugged," interrupted Mrs. Knowles, and laid her hand on Rex's arm as the
stem of a wine-glass snapped between his fingers. "Go on,
Molly, tell Mr. Power about our meeting them at Hilli.
She went right up to the carriage window, Mr. Power, and
spoke to the girl."

"Did she say anything, or make any sign?"

Molly told them about the meeting, her face white with
excitement, her hand on Rex's arm.

"And she leant right forward; I thought she was going to speak to me—and, of course, she was—then one of the men pulled her back, and I had to run because our train was starting."

Trevor leaned forward.

"Did you notice anything about the man who pulled the girl back?"

"Yes. One, that he was the handsomest man I had ever seen, and the other——" She shuddered and held up her right hand, unconsciously bending the thumb and little finger over the palm. "He had no thumb or little finger on his right hand."

Rex gave a little sigh, then raised his head and looked across at Trevor.

"May we know who the girl is?"

Rex looked for a moment at Mrs. Knowles without speaking, then looked at the doctor.

"She is my—*wife.*"

Molly gave a little cry as the doctor called.

"*Kitmudgar!*"

"Sahib!"

"I want the time-table, the almanac in the red leather cover, and the big book in—— No, I'll get that. Don't stir, any of you." He crossed the room as he spoke and turned at the doorway. "I may be wrong, but I'm positive I'm right, and if I'm right and the almanac is right, you two will only *just* be in time."

He came back in a few minutes carrying a heavy leather-bound book fastened with three, big, steel clasps. The *kitmudgar* followed him, carrying the time-table and almanac.

The servant disappeared on a sign, and the doctor waited until he was out of the room, then searched in an inner pocket until he found a small key.

In dead silence the others watched him as he turned the leaves of the book until he came to a certain page which, frowning, he read from top to bottom, then turned the leaves of the almanac and ran his fingers up it and frowned again.

He looked at Rex.

"Your wife is in the most appalling danger."

He spoke quite quietly, then lifted his hand and looked at Molly as Rex sprang to his feet.

"It won't hurt Molly, Mrs. Knowles, to learn of what goes on in India as she is going to live in India. Come here, my boy, just a few minutes more and you'll be on the move. This," he held his hand on the open book as he spoke, "this is my hobby, my Book of Secrets. Every province of India has its headline, under those headlines are written down the mysterious happenings—and God knows they abound in this land—of each province. Mysterious deaths, mysterious disappearances, the habits, good and bad, of the big men of each province. See!" he pointed to a red cross half-way down the page. "The bad sign that, and, on this page, against the House of Nyko-Gung." He looked up at Rex, who leaned over his shoulder. "On the eve of the full moon every year in *this* month women from all parts of Asia are paraded in that house for inspection——"

"Doctor!"

He took no notice of Mrs. Knowles's interruption.

"It has never been proved for what purpose. One or two men who have been to this ceremony have been bribed, heavily bribed, to speak. They have sworn that it is a night of feasting and dancing, and that no money, not an *anna*, has ever passed from one man to another. The women go there of their own accord, there has never been a complaint made."

Rex's hand clenched as he read what the doctor had left untold of the written page.

"On the *night* of the full moon gambling takes place in the Hall of Gambling!"

"Gambling!" Molly whispered.

"For the women for whom there has been more than one bidder!"

A shudder went round the table, and Molly leaned forward.

"*Both* the brothers are"—her voice sank to the merest whisper—"in love with Mr. Power's wife; they walked on each side of her, watching each other, *hating* each other. I—I could see it in their eyes."

"When is the night of the *full* moon?"

Dr. Cromwell looked at Trevor, a world of meaning hidden from Rex in his eyes.

"In three days' time!"

The little party sat quite still, quite silent.

"You can *just* do it."

"The house—is it far—very far away?"

The doctor looked at Molly.

"It is twenty miles—about—from Darjeeling—an impregnable fastness in the Valley of Fair Women."

They rose to their feet. The tension snapped.

"A train starts for Darjeeling this afternoon, Mr. Power," said Mrs. Knowles briskly as she walked round the table to him, and shook him, quite unconsciously, by the hand. "When you *all* get back, which will be in quite a short time"—in her innermost heart she thought, with the doctor, that everything looked just as black as it possibly could—"you will bring your wife to *me*. The room will be waiting for her."

"Can I help?"

Rex smiled down at Molly.

"You have helped already, Miss Knowles. You have saved my wife. It may be an impregnable fortress, and a locked door, and a barred approach, but I'll break through, I'll get in somehow. If only we hadn't got separated from Cecily Cleeve!"

"Cecily Cleeve?"

Trevor explained Cecily Cleeve, whereupon Mrs. Knowles quietly said:

"There will be *two* rooms ready. You will bring your fiancée to me. You will be sure to find her up there." In her heart of hearts she was positive that Cecily Cleeve had been murdered. "Come along, Molly, we shall only be in the way. We shall be at the station to see you off."

Molly turned at the doorway.

"Got a good gun, Mr. Power? You have, that's fine. But I think you had better have two. What is your wife's favorite color? Chinese blue! Right! Mine's green, matches the freckles—what, doctor?" To reassure the men she laughed cheerily as she waved her hand, convinced deep down that Lotah would never be seen alive again.

"You'll want lakhs of rupees to buy your way," cried Mrs. Knowles.

"I'm banker," said Dr. Cromwell.

"Can we come up with you? Couldn't we help? The language, oh! in a dozen different ways!"

"Let 'em go alone," said Dr. Cromwell. "Mr. Power speaks Bhutanese. They'll be less conspicuous by themselves. Friends of tea planters, waiting for the planters at the Mount Everest Hotel. It's a near thing, with but a hair's-breadth to spare, but the gods are fighting on their side."

"God is," said Rex quietly.

He turned to Trevor.

"Mount Everest will be twenty miles nearer still," he said.

The two men traveled openly, as passengers en route to Darjeeling.

Cecily Cleeve and Ka-lok, wedged in the compartment for native women, traveled one train behind them. They sat, side by side, silent, in the deafening clamor of shrill-voiced women and shrieking children, whilst poultry crowed and clucked and perched upon their knees, and goats were milked or wandered, as best they could, amongst the passengers sitting on the floor.

The two *purdah* women, supposedly under a vow of silence and solitude, were treated with the greatest kindness, the sweetest courtesy.

No one tried to make them speak, no one tried to pry behind the veils; food was offered them and milk, warm from the goats, which they ate and drank under the *baku*.

They slept as best they could, gallantly enduring the manifold discomforts of the journey.

They were out to fight, those two silent, mysterious women, one for her love, the other for another woman's honor and life, ignorant of the fact that the two men preceded them by just a train.

Happily the *baku* is voluminous and heavy and not to be easily lifted or blown aside, else might the women's fellow-passengers have been surprised and doubtlessly scared.

In Ka-lok's belt glittered the knife she had stolen and had sharpened each morning upon a whetstone; in Cecily's belt was safely tucked the fully loaded revolver which Ka-lok had stolen from the officer on the station of Mughal-Sarai.

CHAPTER XVI

THE eve of the full moon.

The "Little Finger of the Great Spirit" pointed straight at the blazing disc which wrapped the Himalayas in a silvery sheet; huge birds of prey, eagles, vultures, flew, screaming, terrified, in flocks, this way and that way, round the peak and up towards the peace of the Everlasting Snows and downwards to the orange, red and dun of the roaring bonfires and up again, and round and away to the great chain; shadows, black as ink, thrown by the leaping flames, danced across the snow-covered high road leading to the House of Nyko-Gung, over the snow-laden roofs of the village dwellings and up the base of the Little Finger, climbing like goblins, dancing like wraiths, retreating and meeting and parting, round and over the snow-bound ledge.

The night was still. A breath of wind soughed against the highest peaks, lifted a veil of snow, twined it about the mountains' face and passed on; a girdle of fire cut the ravine in two, dividing the depths which showed, a pool of blackness, below the ledge, from the heights above where bonfires leaped; lanterns twinkled as they swung in the hands of the servants of the House and in the trees; candles, lit to propitiate the spirit of the mountain, whose outer robe of snow melted in the heat of the flames, flickered in thousands and went out.

To those who lived upon the ledge, to those who visited it for the Great Ceremony and to those who hurried towards it through the ravine and, led by a servant of the Nyko-Gungs, scrambled up the tortuous path on horseback, the thunder of the avalanches, loosened by the spring sun, was lost in the roar of falling water.

Excepting for the one spot where the zizgag path began, bonfires flared at every few yards upon the edge of the ledge. An army of servants had dug great holes through the snow and ice, and into them had lowered weighted tripods of steel which had been screwed into sockets in the rock and covered with bars of iron fastened together to form a square; upon the bars had been placed, well above the snow, branches of trees soaked in oil; the roof of each rock-built village house, swept of snow, had its weighted tripod and bars of iron and pile of oil-soaked wood; upon the rock-roof of the House itself towered the biggest tripod of all.

A bonfire upon the roof of the House; bonfires upon the roof of every village house; bonfires right along the outer edge and the inner wall of the high road, set alight as the rim of the full moon tipped the shoulder of the far mountain. Then the snow melted, as it was intended to melt, to add still more merriment to this night of festival.

Tons of it melted—in trickles, in streams, in rivers—until it poured over the side, down to the bottom of the ravine, in a thundering cataract.

Terrified, Lotah ran to the west window and stared out at the great curtain of water which fell sheer from the overhanging roof down to the shadows, then ran to the inner room and stared down into the courtyard. There men fought for their lives, with shouts of dismay and laughter, and horses for a foothold, before they were swept back, through the arch, out on to the High Road, over which poured the cataract and along which other men fought for life in what had been christened the Hour of Fishing and Good Courage.

In a moment of sheer devilry Sa-t'ong had planned the flooding of the ledge.

"Behold, O Brother!" had he said, the year after their

father had passed to his account, and when from far and near and in great numbers men had flocked for the Night of Festival at the Full Moon. "Behold they are not guests, these men who hasten like beasts of prey from all corners, to fatten upon our viands, to drink our wines, to turn the home of our fathers into a travelers' rest. We will not ask payment of them, but those who come late to the feasting— and there are many—we will make fight for what they desire. We will melt the snow and ice so that they shall fight through great waters, whilst we sit within waiting to greet them. We will station servants in the boughs of the great trees, and arm them with hooks with which to catch man and beast as they sweep over the edge. Those that are swept over will find the haven of death; those who are saved will pay one thousand *takals* for man and beast, which sum we will set aside as dowry for the unwed daughters of our servants. Unto those who win through we will give raiment and food and wine of the best, a soft couch, and a good welcome; to those who do not——" He had indifferently shrugged his great shoulders as he had set himself to draw a design for the weighted tripods. "To those who fail to win through we will place candles before the great goddess."

"And the women? What of the women who are late?" had inquired Chang-ku, as he had written down the names of the servants to be entrusted with the different tasks of collecting wood, cutting through the ice and hewing runnels in the rock, slanting towards the edge of the ledge.

"Women? Oh, the women who are late for the Great Ceremony will be women of small account, so let them go over the edge. Besides, why distress thyself about them? The world is full, well-nigh to bursting, with women; it can spare a few."

The village had come to look upon the Hour of Fishing and Good Courage as the best hour in the whole year. The roofs of two big houses, running parallel with the high road, were cleared of snow and reserved for the women and children, from which point of vantage they could witness the sport of men and horses being swept to their death in ice-cold water, or being pulled back from the very edge of death itself by the men's grappling hooks.

The house to the east was reserved for the women of the village and their children, hideously plain most of them, worn with work, and of temperament rendered submissive through verbal and corporal punishment.

The mothers, for the most part Mongolian of feature or of the withered Hindoo type, clumsily shod, clothed in cumbersome outer garments over ankle-length skirts, and covered with an unwieldy sheep-skin coat, would look at their plain, ungainly daughters squatting beside them and, making trumpets of their work-worn hands, would shout to their men to push as well as pull with the grappling hooks fastened to stout wooden poles.

The house-top to the west was reserved for the permanent residents—divided into two classes—of the Street of Many Arches, at either end of which street flamed a huge bonfire, while down its length flickered the necklace of ruby-red lamps. The women—beautiful or ugly, but possessed of the fascination which far outrivals mere beauty, sat upon fur rugs, piled to the height of couches, and as close as they could get to the great braziers. Upon the braziers simmered the water for the never-ending cups of *cha* they drank, whilst they watched the sport out of *kohl*-blackened eyes, and smiled with carmined lips and clapped their pretty, useless, beringed hands in fur-lined gloves.

Fastidious creatures known as the Birds of Paradise, with gentle, doe-like eyes and speech as soft and caressing as their languorous movement; the hearts of savages and merciless, greedy hands ever stretched to grasp yet more money, jewels, furs, silks and satins to add to the fortunes piled high against old age, in the upper chambers of their houses set between the arches of the evil street.

Aristocrats, who had nothing to do with their sisters of lower rank—known as the Laughing Thrushes—who, living for the day, gave never a thought to old age, and, by order of the dread brothers, lived, each one alone, behind the barred windows of the lower rooms in the houses occupied by their higher caste sisters.

The Birds of Paradise flocked to the roof in the hope of seeing men and cattle swept to their deaths; the Thrushes to the Ceremony of Inspection for the joy of the music, the dance and the sight of the brothers Nyko-Gung banqueting with their guests, each one attended by his own retinue of servants.

"U'ip! U'up! Rikogyim! Audi dik-e! U'ip! U'ip!" shouted the village women, this eve of the full moon, as they squatted in their wet garments, oblivious of the cold. Intense was their desire to see their men piling up the dowries for their plain, ungainly daughters who, hardy as the mountain pony, weather-beaten, weather-proof, squatted near their hardy mothers who would succumb in the end to hard work and that only.

The lovely women's laughter sounded like silver bells above the rushing of the waters. They crowded to the edge, wrapped in their furs, when the great fight for life began at the top of the zigzag path which leads down, some three thousand feet, to the bed of the ravine.

'Twas indeed a night of festival!

The winter snow lay thicker than it had lain within the memory of the oldest inhabitant in the town of Nyko-Gung, therefore the rivers of water were deeper and stronger than they had ever been; likewise had men, from every part of Asia, flocked in numbers greater than ever known since the Night of Festival had been instituted by the two dread brothers.

A whisper had gone abroad that the girl, beautiful as a dream, pure as the virgin snow, who lived in the Great House and over whom the brothers fought in love, would be present at the Great Ceremony. Of a type unknown was she, and of a nationality kept secret, but of a beauty beyond compare!

'Twas surely enough to empty the world of men and to bring them hurrying to the Valley of Fair Women, even if she were destined for either one or the other of the brothers Nyko-Gung.

"Thy necklace of pearls," whispered one Bird of Paradise to her neighbor, as they watched the first of the stocky, patient, mountain horses, knee-deep in the swirling waters, fighting its way, urged by whip and voice, towards the House. "Yea! my necklace against thy necklace that La-wa, the Musk Deer, who, for the first time and out of love for Sa-t'ong, the Bengal Tiger, is to appear with her Red Mastiffs of Lhasa, knifes this girl about whom the brothers have become besotted in love."

Her neighbor laughed.

"Verily, I will lay my necklace against thy necklace and more, will lay my sheets of silk embroidered in seed pearls against thy bed-curtains of amber satin patterned in turquoise, that it will be Py'a, who yet again essays to win the love of Chang-ku, the Gray Wolf, in the dance, who will slay this girl who falls from the snow-clouds on to the ledge, yet passeth the Street of Many Arches with downcast eyes."

The two beautiful creatures laughed good-humoredly, then leapt to their feet and clapped their hands.

Lighted by the bonfires and the lanterns hanging in the trees, in which the men sat, the scene beneath was as clear as day.

The first victim of the swirling waters had been swept off its feet. All-enduring, patient, stubborn, gentle, the horse had fought its way valiantly against the tide, urged by cries and prayers and the whip across its dripping haunches.

"Aï! Aï! little one," cried the Indian prince who rode it and who, with many others, had been waylaid at the commencement of the ravine by the inhabitants of the village on the ledge. Waylaid purposely, so that they should arrive at the foot of the zigzag path after the appearance of the first star in the sky, after the first bonfire had been lit and the first trickle of melted snow had begun to run.

Upon the visitors' own heads rested the outcome of the climb up the rock-strewn path down which foamed a stream of ice-cold water; and the struggle along the high road to the House, on the roof of which flared the highest bonfire of all, bringing the melted snow and ice down in cataracts which poured over the sides of the projecting roof, down to the ravine or into the courtyard.

Nobody had invited them to come, nobody in the House of Nyko-Gung seemed particularly interested in their advent or in their forced departure at dawn.

They were at liberty to turn back.

The bonfires would be quenched at the very moment the rim of the moon tipped the peak of a far mountain, behind which she sank to her rest, and the high road, within the hour, would be transformed into a sheet of ice, unnegotiable in its glassy smoothness.

"Aï! Aï! little one," cried the Indian prince as his horse stumbled to its knees, flung him over its head, and floated, kicking and screaming, to the edge.

"Ah—ah——" softly exclaimed a Bird of Paradise in an ecstasy of excitement as she turned and beckoned a gigantic Mongolian.

"Lift me, thou yellow dog," she said sweetly. "I cannot see, and the first horse is down and a prince of blood fighting for his life."

The eunuch, who, by order of his dread masters, kept peace amongst the women, lifted the Bird of Paradise like a feather into his arms, then bent and lifted another who, as summarily, had ordered him so to do.

"Thy sables against my ermine, Flower of Dawn," cried one woman to the other, "that they both go to their death."

"Taken, Night of Stars," cried the other, her arm about the Mongolian's neck. "*Aï!* a pest upon those women who cackle like unto a flock of peahens in the spring. The cries of the drowning are lost in their clamor. Go thou, thou yellow dog, and bid them cease their noise lest they, too, be pushed over the side into the waters."

The Mongolian dropped the beautiful women wrapped in furs, and stood still, looking at them out of scornful, indifferent eyes.

"*They* hold the higher place! Death is not for honorable women, wives and mothers and wives and mothers to be," he replied contemptuously, and, when they sprang at him and beat at him with useless, fur-clad hands, caught and twisted their arms and flung them, screaming with pain and rage, amongst their tittering sisters.

The hideously plain, though honorable, wives and daughters stood perilously near the edge of their roof, shouting encouragement and advice to their men at the top of their shrill voices.

"Hooked! Hooked!" they screamed as the prince of blood was hooked through his cummerbund just as he disappeared over the edge. "And the horse hooked likewise, making a prize of two thousand rupees."

A cross-bred woman, the sister of Dzo, the giant woman-porter of Darjeeling, huge of girth and limb, struck herself vaingloriously upon the chest.

" 'Twas my man," she shouted, "perched in the fourth tree near the brink, who hooked the prince."

"Thou liest," screamed her rotund Hindoo neighbor. " 'Twas my eldest son, thou woman of many women-children."

Whereupon the other struck her rotund neighbor with a hand like a flail and laid her fairly upon her back.

"Push him! Push him towards the edge——"

"Now hook him—*Ts'ol nya!* Hook! Hook!"

"Thrust—thrust——"

"Ah—ah—ah—he slips! *Gu a'tsichi!* He dangles! Ah
—ah—ah——!"

"Caught! Caught! A fish of size——!"

"One, nay two, three—ah—the horse too——!"

"Five thousand *takals* to be divided——!"

The women and their daughters caught each other by
the hand and danced round and round in groups, shouting
their joy as the horses and men slipped, slid, and were
drawn, dexterously and with great shouting, to safety.

"Ha! thou ape of size," quoth the rotund Hindoo who
had risen to dance and shout with the best. "Thou hast a
chance, at last, to palm off a few of thy ape-like daughters
upon men who care not of what shape or intelligence are
their wives as long as their ugliness and imbecility are
covered by a dowry."

She snapped her fingers in the huge woman's face and
stamped in derision with both feet, then turned and fought
one of the Mongolian daughters who had caught her knob
of hair.

"Thou Indian crow!" shrieked the infuriated daughter,
who outdid her hideous mother in ugliness. "Thou jackal
of the plains! with thy three sons who steal thy grain and
spend thy money upon those——" She spat towards the
neighboring house, where perched the Birds of Paradise
upon the roof.

"Thou twelfth female baboon, born of a female baboon!"
shrieked the rotund Hindoo, held by her knob of hair, then
fell fairly on her face as the twelfth female baboon let go
her hold upon the knob and rushed to the edge of the roof.

"A death! A death!" shrilled the Birds of Paradise,
clapping their little, fur-gloved hands and laughing sweetly
until the place rang with the silvery sound.

"*A-tsi-ma! A-tsi-ma!*" wailed the village mothers and
daughters as they watched a rider, with foot entangled in
the stirrup, swept by the swirling waters towards the brink.

"Alas! one thousand, nay, two thousand *takals*—for behold, the horse goes with him—lost——"

"By the clumsiness of him who percheth in the fourth tree."

The cross-bred woman paid no attention to the gibe. Fear had seized her, the shadow of the coming tragedy had fallen upon her; she stood silent, big hands crossed on mighty breast, slanting eyes half shut, watching her man, her rightful mate, father of her twelve daughters. He leaned dangerously far forward over the branch on which he perched, and, not realizing that the man's foot was entangled in the stirrup, swung his hook to catch the last guest of all as he swept to his death.

"Hooked! Hooked!" cried the women of the village, clapping their hands as the hook caught in the man's garments.

"A death! A death!" shrilled the Birds of Paradise.

The triple tragedy happened in the passing of a few moments.

In a last desperate effort to save himself, the man, foot entangled in the stirrup, the hook firmly embedded in his clothes, gripped the pole above the hook and hung on with all his might.

"Let go!" shouted the cross-bred woman to her mate, her voice lost in the rush of the waters and the screaming of the women. "Let go! Let go!"

He did not let go. He had twelve plain daughters who would find husbands through their dowries.

He twisted his hand in the looped end of the pole and put forth all his strength just as the horse swept over the side, and, with the tremendous force of the fall, jerked him from the bough.

They were gone in a flash!

The sister of Dzo flung her arms up to the heavens and wailed in mourning, as her twelfth daughter, seizing the

Hindoo mother of three sons by the throat, called down the curses of the gods upon her.

"May the gods curse thee for bringing death upon him! May they blast thy crops for speaking his name! May they strike thee *dead*, even as thou hast caused him to be stricken dead through the evilness of thine eye!"

The wailing of her mother mounted to high heaven as she tore her hair and beat her mighty breast. The women, the mothers and daughters of the village, made no movement to intervene between the other two who, their hands clutching each other's garments, stood close to the roof's edge.

Each family settled its own difference in the village of Nyko-Gung, and in the manner it thought best. Knives were used almost as frequently as finger-nails, death following or not as willed the gods.

Let these two settle their own quarrel, and speedily, and return to their houses to prepare food for their men when they returned, primed with news and wet to the skin.

"My father it is who——"

"Yea! the father of twelve women-children!" interrupted the Hindoo woman derisively, reeling back as the other smote her across the mouth; reeled to the very edge of the roof and over, pulling the twelfth daughter with her down into the swirling waters and between the trees where no men waited with hooks, and over the brink and down to the bottom of the ravine where death waited.

The booming of a deep gong announced the beginning of the banquet, during which the women from all parts of Asia would parade. With little cries and much laughter the Birds of Paradise were carried back to their houses built between the rocks, whilst the village wives and daughters fled homeward to prepare the food for their lords.

Only the cross-bred woman remained kneeling at the edge

of the roof, staring down into the waters which had swept those she held most dear from her.

To and fro, to and fro she rocked, moaning like some wild animal in pain.

'Twas indeed a night of festival!

CHAPTER XVII

THE original House of Nyko-Gung had been built, generations back, against the base of the "Little Finger of the
Great Spirit"; built two-storied, flat-roofed, with walls of
immense thickness to withstand the snows and tempests of
the Himalayas; to it had been added the wings, and then
the fourth side divided in two by a great arch, closed with
iron gates topped with razor-edged spikes.

The east wing accommodated the guests, who, throughout
the year, came for the hunting, and the traders who came
in spring and autumn with merchandise.

In the west wing lived the two brothers.

Sa-t'ong in four huge rooms, surrounded with the barbaric
luxury which served as a fitting frame to his savage beauty
and his stupendous personality; waited on by a score or
more of servants who worshiped him for his gentleness and
wit and good-humor, almost as much as they feared him
for his uncontrollable outbursts of rage and fits of ungovern-
able and appalling cruelty.

Chang-ku, like the wolf after which he had been named,
lived in two huge, bare rooms, a fitting setting for his giant
body and cunning brain.

All feared and hated him for his colossal strength and
his sullen, constant ill-humor, his daily deeds of brutality,
his personal indifference to pain and his callousness to
suffering in others.

All except Dong, his huntsman, who followed him like a
dog, worshiped him, fought for him, and waited upon him
night and day.

Above the two brothers Lotah lived, in a suite of rooms

which stretched the entire length of the wing. In the top story of the fourth, the south side of the square divided by the arch with iron gates, was stored the most precious and most costly of the merchandise: jewels, ivories, rare manuscripts, rarer porcelains, laces and satins, silks and peltry; the lower rooms of this side were reserved for the women who came for the great festival; their pets, dogs, half-grown lions or tigers, snakes or bears being accommodated in a certain section of the famous stables.

When the brothers had come into power, upon the death of their father, they had built the wings and south side and had made one vast banqueting hall of the original house, which stood on the north side, built against the mountain base. They had pulled down the rough staircase and the small rooms of the upper story, leaving but the four bare rock walls standing, upon which, in decoration, they had spent time, patience, and unlimited wealth.

In the southwest corner of the huge room, high up against the roof, had been built a three-cornered balcony. On ordinary occasions throughout the year, when guests dined with or without their hosts, musicians squatted behind the grill, playing the monotonous, intoxicating airs of Tibet on rough instruments.

Upon the Night of Festival, the Laughing Thrushes from the Street of Many Arches, perched there on little stools, pressing their painted, doll-like faces to the grill, whilst the musicians squatted on the ground beneath them in the corner.

In the center of the west and east walls were enormous windows representing hunting pictures in colored glass, protected by fine wire netting from the storm; on either side of the windows the flames of huge log fires roared up great chimneys; at the south end of the side walls doorways led to the east and west wings.

Bronze chains, in the form of snakes, hung every two yards from the ceiling; red, purple and amber-colored lamps, filled with perfumed oil, swinging from the reptiles' mouths. Colossal brackets of bronze, carved to represent a man's arm with hand outstretched, holding alternately amber, red and purple-colored lamps of glass and bowls of burning incense, thrust through the curtains half-way up the walls and right round the hall.

Bearskins covered the floor and the rock dais, which, stretching across the north wall, was divided in the center by steps hewn out of the rock. Upon the dais stood the banqueting table of solid ebony, divided into two, clamped and hinged with gold. Behind it stood the chairs of the guests, and, at the ends nearest the steps, those of the two brothers.

Sa-t'ong's, of ivory, with arms formed of two great, curving tusks, to the right, he being by a few minutes the elder of Chang-ku.

Chang-ku's, of hide, with arms formed by two great horns, to the left.

Between the two brothers, set far back upon the platform made by the top steps, stood the chair reserved for Lotah.

Patterned in silver, it was painted a shade deeper than Chinese blue, the blue of the door in the tenement-house in Limehouse, the blue of the dress she had worn when Sa-t'ong had caught her, at last, alone. It stood raised upon a step, a golden stool in front, a lamp of amber-colored glass swinging just above.

Exactly behind that chair, at the back of the small platform, sinister, undecorated, lay the *Cella,* the "Cupboard of the Gods," the grotto of the Goddess Paldean-Lha-Mo, lit by hundreds of candles that were stuck, haphazard, on the natural ledges of the rock.

In that small place the head of the Nyko-Gungs for generations had died, until, throughout Sikkim and farther up, even into Tibet, had spread the superstition that disaster to the family would most surely follow if he elected to die elsewhere.

Upon the bare rock ledge, beneath the image of the goddess, had died the father of the twin brothers, cursing Lotah as he had died; before the goddess the twin brothers had taken oath to find her, to marry her, degrade her and throw her to the dogs.

Beautiful, gentle, English Lotah, who crouched in front of her fire, terrified at the roaring of the waters and the shouting and laughing of men, longing desperately for Rex.

From ceiling to floor curtains covered the walls and the windows of the hall.

How many thousands of deer had been shot to provide the skins, soft as velvet, to make the inner curtains covering the rock walls, only the head huntsman could have told; how many pack-horses had come to the house laden with the orange and purple silk for the curtains to cover those of deerskin, no one had ever found the time to count; how many months it had taken to ransack China for the Chinese blue, magenta, old rose, cream and jade satins of the outer curtains only the Nyko-Gung travelers knew, and only the hundreds of Chinese girls with breaking backs, pricked fingers, and smarting eyes had counted the weary, ill-paid hours passed in stiffening those satin outer curtains with gold thread and embroidering them in uncut precious stones.

Heavy gold chains looped back the curtains of silver brocade from the doorway leading to the east wing, through which the women would come, ranked by the giant Mongolian eunuch according to their beauty and nothing else.

The most beautiful in mere looks would come last, and the final choice of beauty was left, indifferently, by the brothers to the eunuch, and to him alone.

There had been a fierce fight, brought about through jealousy, that very evening between beautiful La-wa, of the Red Mastiffs of Lhasa, and exquisite Py'a, of the wonderful limbs.

The fight had ended in the women making use of their daggers, which brutal method of settling their difference the eunuch had stopped with a method but a little less brutal, after which, and just because he hated dogs, he had given the place of honor at the bottom of the list to Py'a, the dancer, who, in her own way, loved Chang-ku.

Heavy silver chains looped back the curtains of gold brocade from the doorway leading to the west wing, through which the guests had come. They had entered as they had liked, each with a minimum of five servants to wait upon him. Well pleased, the servants carried gold plate to the kitchen adjoining the stables; brought back highly spiced viands, bottles of rare wine, or the ordinary wine of the country, or fermented *murwa;* bowls of rice or of scented water; golden goblets with jeweled stems; spices or sweet-meats in small ivory plates; tobacco of every description and in every form; opium pipes; overpowering perfumes in jeweled sprays, and garlands of scented flowers.

Two servants stood behind each guest's heavily carved, cushioned chair, the rest stood in rows at the opposite side of the room, ready, at a signal from those who stood behind their chairs, to leap to do their master's bidding.

The self-invited guests sat in the order in which they entered the hall, the brothers Nyko-Gung being too power-ful, too utterly indifferent, to study precedence. Tibetans, Mongolians, Chinese, Japanese, the Indian prince who had been hooked beneath the cummerbund, an Egyptian, an Assyrian, fierce of beard and eye, two Russians, and other Orientals sat in a great, if temporary, fraternity. Differ-ences of nationality, opinions, customs and caste were, for the moment, forgotten, the village on the ledge being, for one evening, a no-man's-land where pleasure ruled. They had feasted; drinking would not cease until the second booming of the great gong announced that the sky had lightened away down in the east; shouts of laughter and the clatter of huge pewter mugs, drinking horns, or golden goblets upon the ebony table greeted each belated guest as he appeared, fresh from the fight in the icy water, garbed in fine, if borrowed, raiment.

Chang-ku, the heaviest drinker in the whole of Asia, shouted and laughed and banged upon the table with the rest, being only slightly exhilarated by the amount of wine he had already consumed, but which would have caused any other man to fall fast asleep in his chair or under the table.

The guests were resplendent.

Gold thread and silks of vivid coloring gleamed on satin of purple, orange and magenta and every imaginable color; jewels glittered around throats and fingers, and high above the turban of the Indian prince in a huge aigrette of diamonds set in finest platinum wire; white cloth and cloth of deep Assyrian purple, silks of rose and blue and of every color of the sunset; jeweled sheaths and scabbards, empty of weapon, it being the rule that hosts and guests and servants should come to the banquet unarmed. High boots of softest leather patterned in jewels, silks, wools; shoes of leather or satin; sandals of white doeskin with thick felt soles sewn with gold thread; huge cloaks of sable, ermine, astrakan, wolf, bear, lined with violent-colored satins or brocades, fastened with barbaric clasps of gold or silver set in jewels, lay across the back of the chairs or at the side or under the table.

Chang-ku made the one inharmonious blot in the gorgeous scene.

He sat, elbows on the table, face slightly flushed, a shock of coarse black hair tumbled over his slanting eyes, which watched the doorway through which would come the first of the women. He had not changed from the hunting kit he had worn all day; purposely he had not changed, hoping to annoy his guests thereby, and to anger his hated brother, Sa-t'ong, by his intentional insult to Lotah, for whom they had been fighting for so long.

His heavy leather jerkin was worn and stained with blood and mud, his boots heavy and thick-soled, nailed and tied below the knee with cord; he wore a massive steel belt, a necklace of solid gold plaques with signs of good omen roughly hacked out upon them, and his favorite whip, short-handled and with twenty feet of thong, hanging from the belt.

The whip he refused to count as a weapon or to be parted from, and vowed to lash over the ledge the first who should complain about it.

His servant Dong stood behind him. By order he had not changed from the clothes in which he had hunted all day with his master.

Sa-t'ong sat back in his ivory chair, silent, indifferent, hating the noise, loathing the twittering and excited squeaks of the Laughing Thrushes in their cage, the twanging of the instruments, the thought of the parade of women, at the end of which was to appear Lotah, the girl he loved.

He wore a high-collared, full-skirted, knee-length coat of Lotah-blue satin, as he had come to call it, lined with sable. It was embroidered at the edge in a pattern of the letter L, picked out in seed-pearls and entwined in roses of small uncut rubies, with leaves of emeralds and butterflies with wings of golden thread and small precious stones of every color; high boots of buckskin laced with gold, a cap of sable, and a belt of buckskin embroidered with the pattern on the coat.

The Indian prince sat on his right hand, but he took no notice of him; others amongst the guests leaned forward and called to him; he took no notice of them; he barely touched the foods or wines, so stricken was he with love.

He longed for the moment when Lotah, followed by his old nurse, Yi, should appear; he longed still more to have the right to prevent her from appearing, unveiled or even veiled, before a multitude of men.

He wanted to look into her great opalescent eyes, to

watch them, to see if in their depths there showed any signs of interest in himself; he had, unknown to his hated brother, thrown away half of what he thought to be the drug and had added water, so that, or so he thought, Lotah should be on the verge of consciousness when he and Chang-ku gambled for her the following night.

He grasped at every chance, left no smallest stone unturned to gain his end.   Even supposing Chang-ku won, yet might Lotah refuse to go to him, and cling instead, in terror, to Sa-t'ong, who loved her.

By the gods! how he loved this slip of a girl who belonged to another man and one as handsome as himself.

He leaned back in his chair uninterested, unconscious of the eyes that peered at him through the grill, and of the whispers of men who, in high fettle through overmuch food and an abundance of wine, whispered amongst themselves as they strained forward to look at him.

Then he stiffened suddenly and sat up straight, scowling at Chang-ku, who had shouted some lewd remark to the Thrushes in the cage; he spoke sharply under his breath, at which Chang-ku roared with laughter, then rose slowly to his feet, white to the lips with rage.

He towered behind the table, a giant in height and girth, a god in Oriental looks, and looked up to the cage and down at his brother and along each side of the table at the self-invited guests.

"I am master here," he said slowly.   "Truly by a few moments only am I the elder, but the elder I am, and therefore the master.   The woman who is to be my wife," he stopped and looked up at the cage, from which had come the insufferable tittering and giggling of the Oriental women, and waited ominously until silence fell—"this woman of beauty inconceivable, this girl, brought here through the oath we swore before our dying father, is to appear before you this night, so that you may see what beauty means in a land where women are like apes or empty water-skins or overripe fruit." He spoke bitterly, contemptuously, in the agony he felt at Lotah being inspected by the horde of men and women. "This beautiful woman is to be my wife——"

"Or mine!" shouted Chang-ku, springing to his feet.

"Wilt hold thy tongue?" whispered Sa-t'ong, almost speechless with rage. "Or shall I tear it out?"

Chang-ku leapt down on to the steps and up beside his brother. They stood, two giants, close to one another, waiting for provocation.

"Couldst?" sneered Chang-ku, holding out his hand with thumb and little finger crossed. "With but three fingers, O my Brother?"

The Indian prince caught Sa-t'ong's arm before he struck Chang-ku across the face; the Assyrian leaped down and up again beside the brothers and pulled Chang-ku back with him just as the Thrushes giggled insufferably.

"Peace!" thundered Sa-t'ong. "Peace, you bedraggled gutter birds, lest I give orders for you to be flung through yon window down to the rocks beneath. The common, ordinary Laughing Thrush," he said contemptuously to the guests. "Low-caste birds, fit for the lowest of your servants. One word, one glance towards them and the hall shall be emptied. I will have no netting of thrushes in the hall in which the woman, who is to be my wife, is to set foot."

Complete silence reigned as he looked about the hall; then he leaned forward and picked up a metal rod.

Three times he struck the great gong hanging on a chain held by two servants. The ominous booming sound reached Lotah. She sank to the ground and covered her ears with her hands, just as Sa-t'ong sank back into his chair and made a sign to the Mongolian eunuch.

The guests leaned forward, the servants filled the drinking horns and golden goblets as the eunuch pulled back the curtains leading to the east wing; then came a shouting, a twanging of stringed instruments and shrilling of reed pipes as a troupe of Mongolian dancers, as hideous as sin, as nimble on their feet as goats, rushed into the hall.

*   *   *

The Mongolian dancers were followed by a Hindoo snake-charmer, an ordinary profession, therefore second on the list.

But no second-rate snake-charmer was beautiful Tatia as she placed her baskets in the center of the Hall and sat, swaying on her heels, piping her cobras out of the baskets and round her slender limbs and waist and neck.

An ordinary trick that; but all except Sa-t'ong leaned right forward, when, having played the cobras back into the baskets, she walked to the curtained doorway, piping a plaintive tune on her reed as she went.

The musicians fled to the opposite side of the room, where the servants huddled back against the wall; the guests looked furtively at each other and nervously fingered their drinking horns or golden goblets.

"Come, my little one, come, my beloved!" sang the Hindoo girl monotonously. "Come to me! Come to me! Come to me!"

A deep sigh sounded in the quiet Hall, when slowly, then swiftly, a python slid through the doorway and twined itself around Tatia, its head flat upon her head. Tatia laughed softly, surrounded in the glistening, ever-moving folds, then, inch by inch, swaying with the tremendous weight, moved forward until she stood well inside the room. Some woman in the balcony screamed, when, under the reptile's weight, the Hindoo girl fell suddenly forward, and the python, enraged at the pressure of her knees upon its body, unwound itself from about her and shot across the floor, the servants shrieking as they fled before it.

Tatia laughed softly, loving the great reptile, and ran after it and stood before it, singing the plaintive song as it reared, enraged at the noise and light.

"Come with me, little one," she sang. "Come after me, come after me."

And Chang-ku suddenly sat straight, his hand upon his whip, as she ran towards the steps, the snake at her heels.

"I drive a knife into thy side, Tatia," he cried, leaning far back, "if yon vile beast comes nigh unto me."

She looked at him, a little mocking smile in her soft brown eyes.

"Think'st, O coward Wolf, whelp of a jackal breed, that I bring my love to thee?" She turned her back upon him and looked at Sa-t'ong, who leaned back in his chair, smiling at her, unafraid. "He shall not touch the hem of your Excellency's garment," she said as she leaped up beside him and moved her hands in circles over the table in front of him. "The King of Snakes, my beloved, would but salaam before your Excellency. Come, little one, come, come." The python coiled itself about her until she stood lost in a pillar of gray-green glistening skin, then swung its head down over the table and coiled itself upon it and reared, swinging its head, following the motion of her hand, and bowed and swayed in salutation to the man.

She ran away from it, reed pipe to lips, ran down along the outer edge of the dais, calling it as it followed upon the table, a glistening, evil menace, taking no notice of the objects it encountered in its path or of the guests who shrank far back as it passed.

She fled like a doe out of the doorway; it followed; and when she laughed softly in the distance Sa-t'ong beckoned a servant, who ran to him with a canvas bag full of golden pieces in his hands. Sa-t'ong took it and flung it into the middle of the floor, upon which the eunuch ordered a greatly fearing slave to pick it up and to run with it to the Hindoo snake-charmer, who had so pleased their dread master.

Followed dancers from Burmah, jugglers from China, and an exquisite little troupe of Geishas who, with their fluttering fans and gorgeous coloring, looked like butterflies in a den of lions.

Questions by lifting the eyebrows and flicking the fingers and answers by the same method passed between the guests; notes were taken down in hieroglyphics, unintelligible to all but the writer; drinking horns and golden goblets were filled and emptied and filled again, whilst the women, all talented in some way and some of rare beauty, performed, or made their trained animals perform, to the best of their ability, in order to secure engagements in the great cities of Asia, throughout the coming year.

The Hall echoed to shouts of laughter when a troupe of bears gamboled and frolicked all over the place; the Thrushes twittered and squeaked in horror when Sa-t'ong rose and walked down the steps to speak to a slip of a child, when she entered with one hand on the mane of a full-grown lion and the other on the lioness' neck.

"Behold! and where is thy sister, little One?" Sa-t'ong inquired gently, whilst the huge beasts snuffed at his boots.

"She is dead!" the child of ten answered quietly, her eyes on the lion, which reared behind Sa-t'ong and dropped to its feet, then trotted round the room snuffing the ground, stopping, and growling, and trotting round and round. "Leo killed her. Come, Leo! Come to me. He killed her in play, with a stroke of his paw upon her neck. I take her place. I love the great beasts. Come, Leo! Come to me!" She kept her hand on the lioness' neck and stopped speaking to watch the mightly lion. "Leo is not dangerous, Excellency," she continued, frowning. "He is as gentle as a kitten, yet is he at this moment nervous, angered. He scents an enemy, he feels some black heart amongst those gathered together. Is his Excellency not afraid? Not that his heart is black, but even kittens sometimes bite and scratch."

"Nay! little One, I know no fear, and——"

He stopped short when the Hindoo maid gripped his arm as the huge lion, with an appalling roar and with one mighty spring, landed on the table in front of Chang-ku.

The Thrushes shrieked and shrieked, the men shouted,

the servants fled to the doorway, where they met the
eunuch, who crashed his fist into their terrified faces and
drove them back.

Chang-ku, the mighty hunter, without heart or bowels of
compassion, who slew wild beasts indiscriminately, and
trapped them in divers and cunning ways, sat far back in
his chair, silent, terrified before the King of Beasts who had
scented and had hunted out the enemy, the black heart, in
the room.

Dong, unarmed, stood ready to throw himself between
the lion and the master he adored, as the great creature
crouched on the table, front paws, claws spread, half over
the edge, great fangs showing, growling softly and barking
the short, choking bark of the enraged lion.

"Excellency, your hand upon his mate. Hold her! This
wise! There is no time to lose. Leo will spring." Sa-t'ong
stood in the center of the room gently rubbing the lioness
behind the ear as she stood, tail lashing, eyes ablaze, watching her mate who stood erect upon the table, roaring until
the Hall re-echoed with the sound.

Across the floor and up the steps ran the Hindoo child,
and only just in time. She flung herself over the arm of
the chair, ripping her robes on the point of the horn, and
fought to her feet, standing perilously on Chang-ku's knees.

"Back, Leo! Back!" she cried, holding wide her arms
so that Chang-ku and his servant were hidden. "Back! 'tis
one who loves thee. Back to thy mate who calls thee,
back!" The lion made a dab at her with his paw, twisting
his head sideways, snarling softly, then backed, dominated
by the child who knew no fear; backed to the far edge of
the table and crouched and snarled when the girl jumped
up upon it and drove him back and over the edge and across
the floor to where Sa-t'ong stood watching the scene.

Sa-t'ong beckoned the servant and waited until he
returned with ten canvas bags which, greatly fearing, he
carried out behind the Hindoo child as, with the great cats

gamboling at each side, she ran out of the room to the thundering applause of the guests who, one and all, put a mark of disapproval against her name.

Followed six Cashmirans, veiled from head to foot, shepherded by an old hag who spoke to them like dogs and made servile obeisance to the assembled company.

Veiled in white, they carried water jars upon their graceful heads, and raised their veils as they walked before the dais and looked from out their languorous eyes and sighed as the men sighed at the vision of such wondrous beauty, and dropped the veil again and walked on and out of the room as La-wa the Red ran in with six great mastiffs held on leash, three in either hand. Each year she came, each year she seemed to grow in beauty, dark and wild, black-eyed, crimson-lipped, slender and deep-breasted, strong as the mountains from which she sprang, weak as water in her hopeless love for Sa-t'ong, the Bengal Tiger, who would have none of her.

As a hunter of the wilds she stood before the dais, the huge dogs at her feet, a bow across her shoulders, her hand upon the arrows in the quiver, her great eyes flashing round the room in search of the girl for whom, so rumor said, the two brothers fought in love. A leopard skin wrapped her about, open at one side from neck to knee to show the beauty of her slender, sun-bronzed limbs; her feet were bare, soft hide leggings, strapped with wild-cat gut, covered her from ankle to knee, a red flower gleamed in her red hair. She looked infinitely dangerous as she watched Sa-t'ong from under half-closed lids.

With a word, two words, little gestures, she posed the great dogs in one picture after the other, until the guests murmured their approval, and a faint clapping came from the balcony.

The six dogs lay, nose on paws, still as statues, in a ring about her as she posed the last picture; then Chang-ku rapped upon the table with his drinking horn and shouted at her as she loosed the bow and fitted an arrow to it.

"Put up thy bow, woman! Methought 'twas one of make-believe. The order is that none may enter armed upon the Night of Festival."

"Nay, let her be!" said Sa-t'ong indifferently; " 'tis but a game she plays, she designs not to strike thee dead. A wolf would be but poor quarry for such a hunter."

Chang-ku laughed loudly, mockingly.

"Yet shows she but little skill, O my Brother, in the trapping of the Tiger of Bengal."

Came an insufferable burst of giggling from the balcony, followed by a scream and a beating of hands upon the grille.

Enraged at the insufferable giggling, La-wa had swung upon her heels, and, with unerring aim, had shot the arrow she had intended for Sa-t'ong's heart through an opening in the grille and through the shoulder of one of those who mocked her.

Sa-t'ong sat quite still watching La-wa, as, back turned to him, she fitted another arrow to her bow. Would she turn and send it through his heart? Or his brother's heart? Or would she try to kill, as well as injure, yet another of the Thrushes in their nest?

A curse upon all women with their loves and hates and jealousies and ever-varying moods; soft as kittens at noon, wild as the tigress bereft of her cubs at the setting of the sun. He frowned as the thought of Ka-lok, the girl who had loved him so passionately in the evil Limehouse street, flashed across his mind, and turned quickly when somebody tapped him on the shoulder.

Who had touched him on the shouder? Which of the servants had dared? They stood some feet from him, their eyes fixed on La-wa, who stood waiting to turn and speed the arrow through the heart of the man she had loved since the day they had met on the mountain pass.

As superstitious as his Occidental brothers, Sa-t'ong

touched his left shoulder, hoping thereby to propitiate Fate who had tapped him with her gnarled finger, then turned at a shout from the guests and sprang to his feet.

Chang-ku, on the very verge of intoxication and in a playful mood, had loosened the whip hanging at his belt, and, standing as steady as a rock in spite of the amount of *murwa* and wine consumed, had sent the long leather thong whistling through the air and round La-wa's slender waist.

With shouts of laughter and ribald jest he pulled her savagely towards him, just as Sa-t'ong sprang across the steps and hit up his wrist, and the eunuch, picking up La-wa the Red, flung her through the doorway.

"Thou drunken dog," said Sa-t'ong quietly and none too diplomatically. "Dost think this Hall is a traveling booth, and the women to be treated like the beasts of the circus? I will have no more of this." He looked down and across at the guests who were breathing heavily, their eyes afire, their hands pulling at their robes, fingering their jewels, plucking at their beards. "We have had enough of these women and their scenes. The Ceremony is at an end." He spoke quietly, his heart racing as he made a last effort to save Lotah from the degradation of appearing before these men. "Ha! listen." The booming of a gong came clearly through the silence of intense disappointment which had fallen in the Hall. "Dawn has broken, the fires are quenched, the way is clear for you, and the women and the beasts."

Chang-ku, in reply, lifted his drinking horn and called for *murwa*. He was mad with hate, with wine, with the desire to humiliate his brother before the guests and servants.

"Nay, not so!" he shouted. "The day is but a puling babe, and of the two fairest of all women have we seen naught. Go thou to thy couch an thou wilt, O my Brother, for 'tis not until the moon has arisen yet again that we gamble for the fairest of all fair women to wife." He drained his drinking horn to the dregs and hurled it across the Hall, then pointed and laughed, shouting at the top of his stentorian voice.

"Depart not, friends," he shouted. "The gods are on our side. Not for a space will the Ceremony be ended. Come, beautiful bird, come!" He held out his arms. In the doorway stood Py'a, the most beautiful woman and most perfect dancer in all Asia.

*   *   *

Thunders of applause greeted beautiful Py'a as she walked in slowly, lifting her lovely feet knee-high, strutting in her walk in imitation of the peacock she represented.

A head-dress of the bird's feathers towered above her. The feathers sprang from the diamond cap which covered her golden curls and ended in a peak of rubies far down between her brows. Breastplates she wore, of jewels fashioned as the eye of the peacock feather, and a flying petticoat of emeralds set in finest platinum chains, which fell to her ankles and swung to every movement of her slender, snow-white body. On her fingers were jewels, and in her ears and behind her trailed an enormous fan of peacocks' feathers, against which vivid background she stood outlined as an ivory pillar. She walked with her hennaed finger-tips upon the fine platinum girdle and minced and strutted in the walk and posed and stood to preen her feathers with strange, bird-like movements until the men shouted and crashed their drinking horns and golden goblets upon the table.

She walked the length of the dais, pausing for just one second in front of Chang-ku, who looked at her with eyes of desire, yet, just because he knew that she was his for the lifting of a finger, would have none of her. She trailed away to the middle of the Hall and stood scratching the bearskin with one slender foot, shaking her shoulders after the manner of the Oriental dancer until her jewels sparkled and flashed like raindrops in the sun; then turned and took little steps to the right and to the left, and twisted round and round, then stood still and preened her feathers with little clucking sounds which drove the men to a veritable pitch of frenzy.

"Cairo! Bagdad! Bombay! Tokio! Pekin! Calcutta! Lhasa! Damascus! Singapore! Jhari-Yong! Shanghai!"

From every side the names of great Oriental cities rang, as the guests held up their hands or rose in their seats to attract the attention of the self-willed, spoilt beauty who had more money than she knew what to do with and lived one long life of ease and pleasure.

No, she would have none of them.

She turned once more and trailed indifferently away towards the door, lifting her feet knee-high, strutting in her walk, and at the doorway looked back over her shoulder at Chang-ku, who held out his arms, so that she suddenly clasped her hands upon her heart and stood quite still, oblivious of the Mongolian eunuch who motioned her to move on.

And when he lifted her bodily out of the way she turned upon him and smote him across the mouth, cutting it with her rings; then stood quite still and covered her own mouth with her hand to suppress a cry of astonishment, and, shrinking back into a curtained alcove, pulled out the ornamental dagger which secured the head-dress of peacocks' feathers to the diamond cap and flung the feathers to the ground; then twisted round and cut the feathers of the great tail through and stamped on them, and crept, a slender, beautiful thing, mad with jealousy and ripe for mischief, to the curtains.

Preceded by Sona, the Himalayan bear, followed by the old nurse, Yi, Lotah approached slowly up the long corridor.

So beautiful was she, so remote, so sad, with slender hands crossed upon her heart, and big, opalescent eyes looking steadily ahead, that even the eunuch, who hated women more than he hated dogs, bowed to the ground as she passed.

The old nurse had deftly wound yard upon yard of white, soft satin, lined with Chinese blue, about her, *sari*-wise, and in such manner that her right arm and shoulder showed bare, like ivory, against the masses of her hair, which rippled and tumbled in a great scented mantle to her knees. The *sari* trailed in shimmering yards behind her, and pulling upon her ankles forced her to walk slowly and with short steps, which made her swing a little in her gait, as does the beautiful Oriental in her walk. There were no jewels on her hands or arms or upon her slender, sandaled feet, nor paint upon her face; no guile in her eyes; no invitation in her hands or mouth or slender body.

She was as a dove compared to beautiful Py'a, the peacock; as a snow-hare against La-wa of Lhasa; as a necklace of pearls thrown on a heap of tawdry jewelry of the Bazaar in contrast to the other women.

She did not know what to do, nor where to go, nor what was about to happen to her. She cared less. A weapon she had not found; the old nurse had prevented that. She had always stood beside her at her toilette, behind her at meals; of knives or scissors or anything with an edge or point there had been no sign in her apartments.

If it had not been for the old woman she would have been dead by now, asleep in the snow at the bottom of the ravine, at peace, but, as though she read her thoughts, the old woman had shadowed her the whole day long, crooning a fantastic tale in which Sa-t'ong had figured as a king amongst men and his twin-brother as the abomination of all wickedness; had followed her about, squatting on her heels behind her, watching her furtively.

Lotah had been desperately afraid at the shouting of the men, the booming of the gong. When the Mongolian eunuch had appeared in the doorway of her room to inform the old nurse that the masters and their friends waited for her charge in the great Hall, she shrank back and fled behind the bed, working her way to the window. But the old nurse ran to her and held her close, cursing the monster of a man, bidding him shrilly to be gone, as she would conduct the wife-to-be of their masters to the Hall.

Lotah had been afraid then, but she was absolutely terrified now, when the men rose to their feet and shouted their admiration as she stood in the doorway.

She stood quite still, incapable of movement, staring first at Sa-t'ong, who stood looking at her, then at Chang-ku, who lay back in his chair, and back again to Sa-t'ong. She clutched at the curtains when the old nurse pushed her gently forward, and threw out her hands and pressed back when Sa-t'ong ran down the steps and across the floor towards her.

He laughed aloud in sheer joy as he ran to meet her and knelt and kissed her foot, whilst Chang-ku waved his drinking-horn and the guests stood silent, wondering at such subjection in a man, and the women in the balcony fought each other for a place near the bars.

Lotah pulled her garment from Sa-t'ong's hand and turned to run back through the doorway. The Monoglian, arms folded, his eyes upon his master, stood in front of it, blocking the way to escape, ignorant of the fact that Py'a, flattened against the wall, hid behind the satin curtain.

Then Lotah turned again and looked at Sa-t'ong slowly from head to foot, and put her hand upon her heart when she realized that the color of his coat was that of Rex's blue, the blue of the studio door, of her wedding dress, of the beads she had lost. She touched the necklace of pearls on her breast, the pearls the man in front of her had given her for a marriage dowry, and looked up into his eyes alight with love, and shuddered, terribly afraid.

There was no escape there. Love her he did; she had seen just the same look in Rex's eyes, wistful, infinitely tender; and if he loved her as Rex loved her, then he would never give her up.

She pressed her hands against her eyes as she flung a

prayer for help across space to Rex, wherever he should be. *"And—remember—I will never, never give you up!"*

Wherever he was, Rex had answered the prayer for help.

Clearly, and as though spoken close to her ear, she heard the words he had spoken the night John Trevor had dined with them in Limehouse; the night of the fire; the night when the handsome Oriental in front of her, one of the mighty brothers Nyko-Gung, disguised as a coolie, had stolen her.

She turned once more and looked at the Mongolian who barred the way to escape, and at the old nurse, and round the great Hall, as though to find the man she loved with all her heart.

Rex!

He was so near, so close beside her, bidding her to hope and to stand fast. She pressed her hands again over her eyes to hide the dazzling lights swinging from the ceiling, gleaming from the walls and shining in the "Cupboard of the Gods" behind Chang-ku, who sat moodily, chin on breast, watching her stealthily from out of half-shut eyes.

Just for a moment she saw Rex as clearly as though he stood before her; saw his great height, his blue eyes and splendid teeth, paint-brush in hand, head thrown back, laughing as he had so often laughed whilst painting his big picture.

No, he would never give her up, and until the very last minute she would not give up hope, and at the last moment, if she but had a weapon, she would fight desperately to revenge the hurt done to the man she loved before she killed herself. She walked straight forward and across the Hall.

In front of the *Cella*, ablaze with candles, she could see a chair, unoccupied. She would occupy it; she would see if, through sheer personality, she could not win her way through the tangle brought about by the desire two men had for her and the great love she had for the one man, Rex, her own.

She moved forward, with Sa-t'ong at her side; the old nurse trotted to where the other servants stood, whilst the Mongolian walked some distance behind his master, ready to do his bidding, leaving Py'a free to move as love and a surpassing jealousy dictated.

The guests stood as Lotah passed, and turned and stared openly, and commented freely upon her great beauty.

"The mark of the white rose upon her arm, didst see——?"

"Her eyes like pools of silver and gold in the moonlight——"

"As the rose of Sharon 'neath the cedars of Lebanon is she, yea, and as the gazelle in her walk——"

"And the virgin snow in her color, with lips as a curved bow of rubies set with pearls——"

Lotah sat down in the chair, her slender hands upon the arms. She looked from Chang-ku to Sa-t'ong and down the line of men who leaned far forward to gaze at her, and up to the balcony where a score of little hands fluttered in salutation through the interstices of the grille.

Sa-t'ong frowned at the presumption of the Laughing Thrushes, then smiled. Lotah sat looking up at them, interested, perplexed. He was content. She was nigh to consciousness, her fear had told him so, likewise her anger when he had touched her robe; her interest in the Thrushes confirmed it. He rose and crossed to her and spoke to her softly, so that no other ear than hers should hear his words, then sat at her feet and leaned his head against the side of her chair, and looked up at her as she sat looking down.

"Hast no word—no little word? No sign? The color," he lifted the edge of the sable-lined coat of blue satin as he spoke. " 'Tis thy color. Hast no pleasure, no little pleasure in the color?" He tried so hard to wring a word of appreciation from her, lifting the edge higher, pointing out the letter "L" entwined in roses, over which had been embroidered butterflies in precious stones. "L—dost know for

what the letter stands? No? Thou makest no sign. 'Tis
for one who is as the cup of water to him who dies of thirst;
as the acacia tree which, in the heat of the day, throws its
shade upon the parched ground; as the breeze of the dawn
which——"

He sighed and rose and returned to his chair of ivory at
Lotah's right hand. She had not smiled nor said one little
word, nor shown one little sign of appreciation. Indeed, a
frown, like a small cloud in a summer sky, had shown for
an instant on her face as she had leaned, alas! away from
him.

Then she leaned towards him, or rather away from
Chang-ku, who turned in his chair and laughed at her
evilly, mockingly, his shock of coarse, black hair falling
over his slanting eyes and flushed face.

He raised his drinking-horn.

"My wife," he shouted, "or thine, O Brother!"

He stopped suddenly and rubbed his eyes and leaned
forward across the table and stared again as a thunder of
applause burst from the guests.

Like a bird's feather on the wind came Py'a, on the tips
of her beautiful, bare feet, hovering like a humming-bird
above a flower, running like a hare in the moonlight, leaping
like a frightened deer high into the air, arms upraised,
slender feet twinkling ere they touched the ground.

She looked like a child, yet in her eyes flared a flame of
hate as she danced lightly this way and that way, but ever
nearer the beautiful girl who, so she thought, had won the
Gray Wolf's love. She looked like an arrow so slight was
she, her jeweled skirt swirling as she moved, the ornamental
dagger, needle-pointed, razor-edged, hidden in the platinum
girdle.

Sa-t'ong beckoned the Mongolian, then motioned him
back, seeing that Lotah sat forward, interested in the exquisite creature who danced before her. He was off his
guard, Chang-ku hazily content; neither of them made an

effort to stop Py'a as she approached nearer and nearer to the steps, at the top of which Lotah sat, in all her beauty, looking down.

She stood for a moment poised upon her hennaed toes, quivering from head to foot like some sweet honeybird above a flower, then, like a flash of lightning, dagger in hand, was up the steps.

Up to the third step, the dagger raised to strike, when Sa-t'ong, in one desperate movement, caught her by her jeweled skirt and pulled her back, then gripped her by the elbow and jerked the dagger from her hand and beckoned the Mongolian, who came running swiftly.

There was no mercy in the Tiger's eyes.

He gave a sharp order and turned, and, lifting Lotah in his arms, carried her into the alcove and covered her head with the end of the soft white satin lined with Chinese blue.

Lotah saw nothing of the flames as they flickered in the sudden draught of the open window; felt nothing of the icy blast of air which swept the hall; heard nothing of the Laughing Thrushes' screams, quickly suppressed, or the oaths of the men, or Py'a's little moan, when, flung through the window, she sped like a humming-bird with broken wing, through the light of the coming day down to her death in the snow so far beneath. The Mongolian eunuch had shut the window, the flames burned steadily, when Sa-t'ong unwound the soft white satin from about Lotah and stood her on her feet. She swayed for a moment, then stood still, staring up at the statue of the Goddess Paldean-Lha-Mo, who looked down at her from her seat upon the mule she rode with a bridle of snakes, holding an umbrella of peacock's feathers above her head.

Lotah knew nothing of the oath the brothers had sworn before this image and before their father upon his deathbed, but she shook from head to foot and threw out her hands and backed out of the grotto as far as the chair, against which she stood for an instant, her hand upon her heart; turned and looked desperately about the great Hall, then ran to the top of the steps and stood staring down.

Near the bottom step, almost hidden in the thickness of the bearskin rug, lay the dagger Sa-t'ong had jerked from the dancer's hand.

Chang-ku lay half-asleep in his chair, Sa-t'ong stood just behind, looking at her; the guests could not see the silver blade shining in the fur, but the Mongolian approached, crossing the floor towards her. If she was to get the dagger, unseen, there was no time to lose. She dared not hasten, she dared not wait. Escape from worse than death was within her reach; an easy way out; a little pricking of the needle-point, and sleep, sleep, in which she would wait until Rex should come to her, and waken her and take her with him farther on the path of love which has no end.

She stood erect on the top step, trusting to her beauty and her dignity to stop the Mongolian in the middle of the floor. Slowly she descended, the white satin of her robe trailing far behind her as she moved. Her foot touched the dagger. She stopped. Supposing she acted clumsily and grasped the fur as well as the dagger when she bent to gather up the trailing yards of satin, supposing she let the dagger fall? The Mongolian moved forward, there was no time to lose.

"Rex! Beloved!"

The words were a prayer as she bent slowly down and swept the satin round her feet and gathered it up, and with it the jeweled dagger. Slowly she walked across the floor, the Mongolian backing before her, Sa-t'ong following, Soma, the bear, at his heels.

As slowly, preceded by the old nurse, who threw a sable cloak about her, she traversed the interminable corridors and mounted the stairs to her own rooms, where, as she fell across the bed, she pushed the dagger far back under the pillows and lay still.

CHAPTER XVIII

A MIGHTY amphitheater, range upon range of towering peaks and slopes, glistening white and satin smooth, of virgin snow; remote, enduring, thrusting their pinnacles through and above the clouds, the rain, the storms which press and beat down upon the earth; silent, wrapped in mystery, the Everlasting Hills.

A fold of white cloud, and above, a spire, snow-crowned, pointing ever upwards, a slender finger, towards the sun; a sign of hope; of the ending of the bitter road marked by the faltering feet of those who fall and rise and fall to rise again. Spire upon spire, height upon height, rose-tipped or white, amethyst or emerald, golden, sapphire, gray; slashed with the glaciers' green and blue and purple; the precipice's inky black; girt with icy battlement, wrapped about in the passing of the centuries and the sighs and prayers of those who have lived, who live, uplifted, downcast, in the shadow of the Himalayas.

Rex stood speechless before the stupendous picture, a dawning look of battle in his eyes. He realized, at last, the might, the grim power, of this inconceivable range of mountains, which stretches to the east and to the west of Darjeeling, the Place of the Sacred Thunderbolt. As a picture it almost stunned him, as a prison in which the woman he loved was held captive, it filled him with a desire to fling himself upon it, to tear and hack and hew his way across the slope and down the precipice and up to the point of the snow-crowned spire, which marked the end of the bitter road.

Twenty miles, perhaps more, perhaps less, lay between him and life, for life was Lotah, and without her he had no desire to live; twenty miles and the noonday sun shining from a sky as blue, as radiant as the necklace of beads, which, old perhaps as the Everlasting Hills and as mysterious, he carried above his heart.

Lotah, his wife, a prisoner in the Himalayas!

Yet why was he so sure that Lotah lived?

Love told him that she lived! The love that binds two hearts so close that distance is as naught when, counting by weary, dusty miles of earthly road, they are separated the one from the other. Had he not heard her calling him in the night just passed? Had he not flung out a message across the plains of India and up to the mountain snows, whispering close, quite close to her ear: "Remember—I will never, never give you up!"

She was alive, and she had passed this way but a little while ago, a prisoner, but he was close upon her track. And Tsi-tsi, the little old woman who lay asleep, faithful unto death, under the cold English sky, she, too, had carried Lotah here, all those years ago; had hurried with her down the mountainside, hunted by the men who, with the terrible patience of the East, had waited throughout the years until they had caught the girl at last, and brought her back to the country to fulfill their oath.

He turned to John Trevor who, after one glance at the Hills, had watched the tragedy and the strength of the face at his side.

Rex pointed at the overpowering chain of ice and snow.

"She's there somewhere, and we're in time! We *are* in time," he repeated—insistently—doggedly.

"Yes, thank God! we are in time," replied Trevor, fighting the insidious fear which was knocking at his heart, for Rex as well as for himself. "I shan't be a moment. I want to ask the stationmaster if——"

"I can't wait, I can't stand still," Rex answered quickly. "I'll walk on slowly. Shall we go to the east or the west, do you think, when we start? God! how little we know. What a blind trail we are following! Yet somebody, some native could tell us if we dared to ask——" He turned again and looked at the great frozen, awe-inspiring barrier.

"If we weren't afraid of spies," said Trevor. "I'll follow you. I won't be long."

Lost in his thoughts Rex started up the narrow path and stopped to let a troupe of Mongolian dancers pass. With much laughing and singing and clashing of bracelets, as ugly as sin, clothed in *tug* dyed yellow, blue and red and other violent colors, they made their way on foot to Siliguri, where the night before they had been booked to perform by one of the self-invited guests to the House of Nyko-Gung.

Four coolies, snake-baskets swinging from the rods they carried on their shoulders, passed him at a trot, and when Tatia, carried in a *dandi* shoulder-high, passed him also and turned to look at him with interest in her smiling eyes and saluted him, he saluted her mechanically, totally oblivious of a woman's presence, little knowing that she could have given him all the information he required about the House of Nyko-Gung.

He stood staring at the Hills, lost in thought, then turned to John Trevor, who came towards him, followed by a gigantic woman-porter who smiled and touched her forehead and her broad shoulders, entreating in torrents of the vernacular, interspersed with fervent ejaculations of "Good! Good!" to be allowed to carry the Sahibs' luggage up the hillside.

"I can't make her understand that we haven't any luggage, old man!"

Slowly, haltingly, Rex translated Trevor's words to the woman who, on hearing the tongue of her adopted country spoken by a Sahib, however badly, bent and touched his instep, then laughed and clapped her hands.

Rex waited for a moment to allow her child-like merriment to cease, took in, in a lightning glance, the utter poverty of her garments and the driven, pleading look in the eyes which belied the laughter, then spoke, confidently, fearlessly, looking straight into those slanting, honest eyes on a level with his own.

"Where is the House of Nyko-Gung?" he asked, almost beneath his breath.

The woman, clutching her *sung-bu*, the charm against evil, about her neck, jumped back as though she had been struck and turned away from him, spreading her hands before her face smeared with *tuiga*, with first and second fingers crossed to ward off bad luck.

Rex watched her, gave her time to think, turned to Trevor and gripped him by the arm in his agony of suspense.

"What is your name?" he asked at last.

The woman turned slowly, hands before her face, looking through her fingers first at one, then at the other of the Sahibs who questioned her so strangely.

Animal in her birth, her upbringing, her instincts, as strong and honest as she was primitive, she summed the men up as a dog would have summed them up—and trusted them.

"Dzo!" she answered, twining her fingers in her *kya-blonwa*, the long, thin plaits of hair which reached below her waist and almost to the hem of her long, heavy, blue robe.

"With a good husband and many children?" Rex asked slowly, thanking God in his heart for the happy hours he had spent in Limehouse learning the language spoken in Sikkim.

"*N'ga,*" replied the woman, showing her strong, discolored teeth in a broad smile as she made movements with her work-worn hand to show that five small children clamored daily for bread and milk around her meager table. "And my man is dead, asleep, yonder!" She pointed to the Himalayas and rocked herself to and fro, assailed by a great temptation, then clapped her hands and beat upon the ground with one foot and moved round and round as on a pivot.

Poor she was, desperately poor, but not for an *anna* would she beg from these rich folk who looked at her with kindly eyes and questioned her so strangely.

Had she not the strength of the cross-bred yak, after which she had been nicknamed? Could she not, did she not, earn her living in the fat months, even if she came well-nigh to starving in the lean, by carrying the trunks of the *Sahib-log* upon her back fastened by a strap about her fore-head? Could she not carry the heavy Sahib, with the big jaw and gray eyes, upon her back up to the Mount Everest Hotel with scarce a quickening of her heart? True, the great weights she carried were causing her neck to swell until sometimes she came nigh to suffocating on the road, but even if one copper piece could not be saved out of the money earned by carrying heavy loads, still children clam-ored once and twice and thrice a day for food, so there was naught else to do but to toil up the mountainside with staggering burdens, thereby earning the wherewithal to bring the milk and bread.

"*N'ga!*" she repeated, and smiled, making gestures with her hand, whilst Rex watched the great, savage love for her babes shining in her eyes.

"If you will tell me how to find the House of Nyko-Gung," he said slowly, "and how long it will take to get there, I will give you a hundred rupees."

Dzo spread wide her arms, stricken dumb, then looked from one man to the other, and touched a shell, her *t'ung-kha*, fastened, for luck, by a string about her wrist.

"Rupees?" she said at last, with a look in her eyes like that of a starving dog with a bone just out of reach. "*Rupees?*"

Rex drew a hundred-rupee note from the note-case and offered it. She touched it, took it, smelled it, as is the custom of her mother's people, laid it against her cheek, held it to her heart, and gave it back.

"Question, Sahib!" she said. "I will earn the thrice-

blessed money and will pray the *Kyung* bird to alight upon
your roof-tree, bringing happiness and plenty 'neath its
twisted wings." She pointed up the hill. "Sahib, the spies
of the Tiger and the Black Dog are on every side. 'Twere
wise to walk upwards, and I will follow in the Sahibs'
footsteps."

They started to walk up the narrow path, then stopped
and drew on one side.

Down the path, holding three huge red mastiffs of Lhasa
on leash in either hand, came La-wa, running lightly.
Abreast with the men she stopped suddenly, and jerked the
great dogs back so that they surrounded her, leaping and
barking, eager to be gone.

She stared at Rex, her red-brown eyes full of questioning,
and smiled as the dogs tried to pull her down the road.

"Behold," she said, "are you of a great beauty, almost of
as great a beauty as the man I love, and who will have
none of me. Also are you known to me, although 'tis for
the first time my eyes have rested upon you."

Dzo, almost hidden behind Rex, whispered in his ear.

"Nyko-Gung," she said softly. "The House of Nyko-
Gung."

Rex smiled. Lotah was near, so very near; at every step
upon this last mile of the bitter road he had news of her;
perhaps this woman, in the whirl of great red dogs, had seen
her, spoken with her; yet must he go warily for fear of
spies, for fear of a pitfall, a snare at the end of the bitter
road.

"Perhaps in the good company of the brothers Nyko-
Gung have you seen me?"

La-wa shook her head.

"Nay! not there. Yet somehow are you connected with
them in my mind. Of a truth, 'tis a pity you were not at
the Night of Festival."

"We were delayed."

" 'Twas a night of laughter and tragedy and love." She

laughed harshly, her eyes dull with pain. "Love has come to the House of Nyko-Gung—at last—at last. Behold, is the Tiger of Bengal like to die of love for her whom they call the White Rose, and like to kill the Gray Wolf, Changku, his brother, this night when they gamble for her to wife. Love——!" She laughed until the place rang with the ugly sound, and turned, and, calling to the dogs, ran down the narrow path to the train by which she and Tatia would start for Bombay.

Dzo, finger on lip, ran up the hill as far as the turn in the path and down the hill and returned.

"The road is clear, Sahib," she said. "The Sahibs and the Mems use the farther path; the luggage is taken by yet another road. Let us take counsel here, in the shadow of the trees. Sahib," she moved close to Rex's side. "You may trust me. I am one half Kyung-Kar, the white tribe, by my mother. I swear that you may trust me, by the god of my mother, the *Kyung* bird with twisted wings. The Sahibs have spoken gently to the cross-bred yak, Dzo, she would show her gratitude, yea! and would earn the good money offered for her help."

John Trevor took out his note-case and offered her yet another note of a hundred rupees.

"Help us, Dzo, all you can and this is yours."

Stunned with the weight of the gifts of her god, she bowed to the ground as Rex translated the words.

She stayed on her knees, a strange Oriental picture in a shaft of sunlight shining through the trees; she could not move; she would not from gratitude; dared not for fear of the shattering of her dream; she spoke at last when Rex had finished, her eyes fixed on his.

"A woman in the House of Nyko-Gung, Sahib," she said slowly. "*A-tsi-ma! A-tsi-ma!*" she beat her breast as she spoke, and picking up a pinch of dust threw it behind her. " 'Tis not well for women, beautiful women, upon the ledge to the west of Dorling-lo. Behold, my sister is upon the

ledge, the mother of twelve daughters. 'Tis well with her
and hers, for are they not like the Manu, the monkey of
the hills, but for a woman of beauty, lo! is it evil that will
befall her."

She sat back on her heels and wrung her hands.

"Ask her why the brothers are allowed to live as they
do? Why we, the white race, haven't been able to step in
and stop it, turn them out of their house, off the ledge, out
of the Valley of Fair Women?"

Dzo only repeated Dr. Cromwell's history of the brothers
Nyko-Gung.

It seemed that they were traders of great renown and did
no wrong; that the Night of Festival, just past, was but to
amuse the guests of the House, as were amused the guests
in the palaces of the Indian princes; that gambling was a
national pastime, almost as commonplace and harmless as
the game of knuckle-bones, and could not be suppressed,
and that if a Sahib *could* find his way up the narrow path
to the top of the ledge he would be welcome to gamble
with the rest.

"Nay, Sahibs! The Tiger and the Dog are too cunning,
they cannot be trapped. There is naught against them, yet
do we, mothers with daughters, live in great fear."

She sat on her heel rocking herself to and fro, then
accepted the cigarette Rex offered as he translated what she
said, and sat still, blissfully inhaling, working her cunning
brain.

"How do the other guests, the traders, find their way to
the ledge?" Rex spoke gently as he leaned against the tree,
smoking, only the knuckles, white through his clenched fist,
showing the agony of impatience he was suffering.

"The servants of the House conduct them, lead them,
either from here, the town of Dorling-lo, or farther along
the path, at the beginning of the Valley of Fair Women."

"Could no one show us the way?" Trevor offered the
woman his cigar-case as he spoke.

Her hands trembled with delight, her eyes sparkled as she took one, rolled it between her fingers, smelt it, and hid it in the upper part of her *chuba,* bunched to make a gigantic pocket.

"If the Sahibs were women," she looked from one to the other when Rex put his hand on Trevor's shoulder, " 'twould be easy, for behold, Dzo has been there upon a visit to her sister. 'Tis easy for a *woman* to gain admittance. Ha!" She sprang to her feet suddenly and laughed, turning round and round to the clapping of her hands. "My brother! my brother! He knows each bowlder, each turn, each crack upon the road. He will lead the Sahibs to the foot of the path which leads upward to the ledge, and he shall not, must not, be paid until the Sahibs return, for behold, even as the sun melts the snows, so does a cup of *arak* warm the heart, and, for a moment, lift the cloud of poverty from the roof-tree. He will pass upon this path as the sun strikes mid-heaven. Let the Sahibs walk up the hill and wait at the hotel, and I will speak with him."

"Wait!" Rex broke in quickly, then turned desperately to Trevor, translating the woman's words. "I can't wait much longer. There is a limit to my endurance!" He turned to the woman. "Why must we wait? Why not start at once?"

Dzo turned and pointed to the west.

"When the sun sinks, *then,* Sahib, my brother, yet another cross-bred yak, will await you with ponies, to lead you through the town, past the great houses of the great white race, out on to the road leading to the ravine, and on, on into the snows for the love of a woman. 'Twere folly to be seen in the light of the sun!"

"All these hours!" said Rex to Trevor. "Another interminable day!"

"By the light of the moon," went on Dzo, feeling for the cigar, her eyes sparkling; "yea! by the light of the moon the men will be in the Hall of Gambling, all but him who stands as guard upon the edge of the path——"

She broke into a torrent of prayer and beseeching at the top of her strident voice as two men came running down the path, swarthy, laughing, smoking as they ran, then clapped her hands and turned round and round.

"Ha! Brother," she cried, and ran to meet him and smote him a blow upon the chest which might well have felled an ox. "The Sahibs would hire ponies of thee, and have commanded me to have speech with thee thereon." She raised her voice for the benefit of her brother's friend, who waited farther down the path. "The Sahibs ride to Kalimpong." She drew the cigar from her capacious pocket and stuck it in the corner of her mouth, whereupon the brother smote her upon the back with a blow that might well have felled a horse, and pounced upon the cigar as it fell to the ground.

"A few rupees, Sahibs, and one cigar like unto this one for each pony, and I am the Sahibs' servant." He ran off laughing with his prize to rejoin his friend, who eyed the cigar covetously. "I will find thee, O gentle yak," he called back as he saluted, "later, here."

Dzo touched Trevor's sleeve in sign of servitude and took another cigar with sparkling eyes.

"He will take the Sahibs to the *end* of the path, but to the great God must the opening of the way to the House be left. A sharp knife between the shoulders of the guard is one way, but maybe he will give the alarm before he dies." She frowned and shook her mighty fist towards the west. "No, Sahib, no white man has set foot in yon town of evilness"—in which statement she was much mistaken—"would that the Sahibs were women that I, even I, might aid them in their need."

Rex put a hand on the woman's shoulder as he translated her words to Trevor, who turned and looked down towards the station to hide the look which had sprung to his eyes at the thought of Cecily Cleeve.

"Tell her about them, about Cecily and Ka-lok, she might be able to—to suggest—er—something if the *should* arrive."

Dzo clapped her hands and touched the shell upon her wrist. At last she could help, she herself, as well as her brother. Let the Sahibs leave the Mem-Sahib in her care. She would meet every train until the Sahibs returned; if the Mem and the other woman of her own race did not arrive, then were they safe in the plains; if they arrived she would lead them to the big hotel and give them news of the Sahibs.

"Tell her I will give her two hundred rupees more if she brings Cecily to me at the House of Nyko-Gung. Having sworn to Cecily to take her with me, wherever Fate led us, I've got to keep my oath, however dangerous it may be. Tell her if we return I will buy a plot of ground and hens and grain for her, and *then* give her five hundred rupees, and that if we do not return the manager of the Mount Everest will give her the notes."

Dzo dropped to her knees and touched the men's insteps with her forehead.

*　　　*　　　*

The lounge of the hotel was empty, but, with the herding instinct so common in mankind, and especially to be noticed in an almost empty lounge or restaurant, Gerald Banks and his friend sat down at a table but two removed from where the others sat.

"To Lotah," said Rex softly, and put down his empty glass and sat forward, his arms upon his knees, lost in thought; sat quite still, then, unconsciously, began to listen to Gerald Banks talking to his friend.

"Yes," he was saying, "Darjeeling *is* dull at this time of the year; you see, the whole flock of swallows hasn't arrived yet, only a few of the advance guard, eager to get the best nests and worms," he laughed. "I mean, the best of the unbooked bedrooms and the best seats to be secured, by an unlimited distribution of *baksheesh* in the dining-room. In a month's time you'll be so fed up with festivities that you'll be only too glad to get to the seclusion and quiet of the tea-gardens."

The youngster with him laughed and stretched his long legs. "Right," he said, "I'll believe you when I am fed up with festivities, but all the same I'm frightfully disappointed with my first experience of the great mysterious East. The trip out was homely to deadliness. All old stagers with new frocks that were old-fashioned by the time we landed; Calcutta the last thing in second-rateness, with its various cliques, little tin special gods in their own eyes and much-of-a-muchness in the eyes of others, all staring at each other icily, like shrimps in aspic; and now this, one's backbone frozen by the Himalayas and the rest of the day and night stretching in front of one, a vacuum to be filled with nothing to do."

"Well, Nature ordains that every vacuum shall be filled, and dinner's not far off."

"Yes, but I've got the whole family at home, from the mater downwards, sitting on the edge of the nest like a lot of hungry sparrows, waiting for me to drop lurid and Eastern tit-bits of news into their widespread, ravenous beaks—bless 'em."

Gerald Banks beckoned the *kitmudgar* and gave an order, then lowered his voice, but not so low that every word did not carry to the men at the other table.

"Well, young feller-me-lad, there's such a tit-bit waiting for you, so lurid and Eastern——"

"What!"

"Well, don't shout! That's why I didn't tell you before. Nobody must know about this jaunt, because I am going to take you to a place where no white man, except myself, has ever been."

Ian Gascoigne hunched himself with excitement. "I've

got a top-hole gun," he said, fishing in his pocket, "and haven't had a chance of using it yet."

"No; it's not an every day custom, even in India, and you won't use it to-night either, that is, unless you want a knife in your back. We're going as friends to watch some gambling . . ."

Gerald Banks looked round as Rex scraped back his chair, but saw nothing but two men interested in their own affairs.

"Gambling!"

The boy's face was blank with disappointment.

"Yes, but with *women* for the stakes!"

"*What!*"

"It's true."

The elder man gave the boy a brief resumé of the events which happened in the Valley of Fair Women on the Eve and the Night of the Full Moon.

"Well, I'm damned!" said Ian Gascoigne at the end, whilst Trevor got up quietly and moved to a chair next to Rex and sat with his hand on his arm.

"You'll feel every bit like that when you've seen it. The gambling starts at midnight. The place is twenty miles hard going to the west, and you may come back and you may not, depends on the temper of the two extraordinary men who live there. I've got Tanga ponies waiting for us after dinner."

"They'll never get there by midnight!"

"Won't they! They're Sikkim ponies with a touch of goat and cat in their composition. They jump and climb and slide . . ."

"Boy!" shouted the lad.

"You go steady on that, we're going up a bit, and the air'll be like champagne to start with."

"We are only going to drink to the home-birds sitting on the edge of the nest waiting for lurid worms of news." He gave his order and turned excitedly to Banks. "I'd just love

to be in a first-class, thundering, unholy row.   Any likelihood of there being one?"

"Not the slightest, unless you gamble and win the fair
maiden, and by Jove! I've only been there once, and then
some of them were as ugly as sin, multiplied by ten."

"Yes, but how on earth did you get invited to the show?"

Gerald Banks lit an evil-looking and overpowering cheroot
and slid down in his chair, his eyes half closed as he looked
back down the years to the night when Fate had picked his
thread of life from out the tangle she holds in her shaking
hand, and had knotted it with those of Rex and Lotah and
John Trevor.

"One night, seventeen, no, eighteen years ago," he said
slowly; "I think it was eighteen—a man came running to
my house at Kalimpong. A young fellow, native, handsome
as a god. He'd had a scrap with his brother, in which the
thumb and little finger of his right hand had been hacked
off, and the other three fingers left hanging more or less by
threads. I had taken my M.B.—oh! years before that, long
before I discovered that tea is far more lucrative than pills
and scalpels. I had, beside my *pukka* practice, a non-pay-
ing, but very extensive, interesting and entertaining one
amongst the natives. I operated on that man's hand, sewed
on the other fingers, stitched up the wounds, gave him a
whole bottle of iodine and lint and boracic, with copious
instructions how to poultice it if trouble set in."

"Good Lord! Go on! Couldn't he have called again—
kind of out-patient?"

"I was leaving for Assam the next day, chucking drugs
for tea. I should have forgotten the incident altogether if
it hadn't happened on that one particular night, my last in
Sikkim for some time and the night of the appalling
murder."

"Murder?" the boy questioned. "What murder?"

"The murder of Graham Trevor and his wife and their
baby. Trevor was a wee bit too much the *burra-sahib*,

treated the natives as natives and not as human beings.
Oh! it happens, you know, in India, though off the beaten
track, as a rule. Sahib found with a broken neck under an
overhanging branch, bitten by a snake and so on."

"Did you meet the man again, the man with no thumb
or little finger?"

Rex and John Trevor sat still, smoking mechanically,
pretending for the benefit of the servants who, in India,
are always watching, listening, spying, to be talking together.

Gerald Banks had met Sa-t'ong Nyko-Gung many years
later in Delhi. Their cars had collided outside the Cecil
Hotel. The Englishman had been slightly bruised; the Merchant Prince had insisted upon helping him to the hotel;
had followed courteous regrets, recognition and a warm
invitation to Gerald Banks to go to the House of Nyko-
Gung for hunting and for as long as he cared to stay.

"My house, my wealth, my horses, cattle, women," had
said the Oriental, "are all yours. Behold, you saved my
hand, there is nothing I would not do for you, nothing.
Bring your friends with you, but not more than one at
a time. My people are distrustful. A certain sign shall be
yours, and come when you will, and for as long as you will."

"You went?" The boy sat rubbing his forehead with
the point of his cigarette-case, a puzzled look in his eyes.

"Yes, some many years ago, alone. By Jove! it took my
breath away. You couldn't, if you tried, imagine such
luxury. Of course, there are some pretty stiff stories going
around about 'em, but I swear that not an *anna* passed
between any of the men the night I was there." He rose as
he spoke. "You watch out to-night and see if you can see
anything. Besides, they are natives and we can't interfere
amongst them or disturb their customs without stepping
right into a hornets' nest."

The boy rose and looked out of the window, the puzzled
look still in his eyes.

"Did it ever strike you that the man might have murdered the Trevors?"

Banks looked at him and nodded his head.

"It did. I didn't connect the two incidents for a long time, and then it was too late, but it's been in my head ever since." He told the boy of how the old trader Nyko-Gung had been suspected and had cleared himself and his sons; had proven alibis; had, himself, employed the police to track the culprit down, but all to no purpose. "But would the son, do you think, if he had been guilty, have invited me to stay with him, where a chance word, a look, anything might have given me a clew?"

"I don't know!" the boy replied slowly. "I don't know." Then added as he tapped his pocket, "Anyway, I'm dying for a first-class row."

"Well, just in case we get separated before we get there, as we're going without a guide, this is the sign that gives admittance to me and my friend. Look," he held up his right hand, his thumb and little finger crossed. Oblivious of Rex and Trevor watching him from the corner of their eyes, he touched the crossed thumb of his right hand three times with the middle finger of the left hand.

"Right-ho! And when we get there where do we go, just in case we arrive separately?"

"We go to the House of Gambling"; he pronounced the words in the vernacular, and laughed as the boy stuttered and stumbled over them. "That's it! And we get there through the most appallingly evil street in the whole of Asia."

"Phew!" whistled the boy. "This *is* going to be a tit-bit for the hungry sparrows in the home nest, and no mistake! What's its name?"

"The Street of Many Arches! Let's go and dress for dinner."

John Trevor sat quite still when they had gone. This was Rex Power's hour, the one in which everything had to be decided, once and for all, for good or bad; the hour in which the slightest mistake, too great haste, too little, might result in death for them, and in far, far worse for Lotah, a prisoner in the House of Nyko-Gung.

Would Rex call upon the aid of the two men who had just left the lounge? Would he stick to his determination to win out off his own bat?

Rex looked up suddenly and Trevor leant back. In the depths of the blue-gray eyes flamed a light which boded but little good to those who might pit themselves against him before the sun rose behind the Everlasting Hills.

His hands were steady as he lit a cigarette and rose to his feet, and he smiled as he touched the blue beads above his heart.

"I'll leave a note, to be given after dinner to those two," he said quietly. "It would be a pity, a thousand pities, to let the boy miss the thundering, unholy row there's going to be—up there—to-night, but I—I must get in first."

He stood quite still looking out at the night.

"Into my hands, O Lord," he said beneath his breath, "into *my* hands deliver them," then laughed, shortly, savagely, as he walked across the room.

"A spark, a touch," said Trevor to himself, following him, "and he's mad, berserk mad."

*   *   *

Dzo squatted in a corner of the station blissfully smoking her tenth cigar.

"Hast broken one of thy slender ankles, O gentle *djiran*," laughed a stocky little woman as she stopped to readjust the enormous load upon her shoulders, "that thou sittest here throughout the day, earning nothing, passing hours of sloth, smoking tobacco which, of a surety, thou hast not come by through thy purse?"

"Gazelle thyself!" laughed Dzo, shifting the cigar from one corner of her mouth to the other. "Behold, I await one from India, old or young I know not, as she is veiled from head to foot."

"Would it not be wise if thou wert to veil thy face, O cross-bred yak?"

"And thou of the monkey face?"

They laughed right heartily, kicking each other as Dzo offered her coveted cigar.

"A puff for each finger and not more, Monkey-Face," she said, "whilst I tell thee of this woman with her maid who rides to Kalimpong, *if* they arrive, this night!"

Monkey-Face let the cigar drop out of her broad mouth in astonishment.

"To Kalimpong, i' the night!"

"Verily! and for the journey have I brought cloaks of sheepskin and boots and gloves. 'Tis for a birth, or marriage, or death, I know not which, they ride thus hastily, what matter which? All three must end in disaster," said Dzo, retrieving the cigar from the dust and offering it once more.

"Well, 'tis the last train this day," said the other, swinging a little to her load, "and if they come not by it the disaster will have happened before they reach the house door." She handed back the cigar and walked out of the station, leaving Dzo squatting in the corner dreaming of a house and a field of grain.

The woman, veiled from head to foot, had been sheer invention on her part, she had no idea what the two women would look like—if they arrived, but when the train puffed into the station at last and let loose its passengers, she stalked straight up to a woman, apparently strictly *purdah*, hidden underneath the all-enveloping *baku* and touched her attendant, a woman of her own race, upon the shoulder.

Ka-lok swung round like a cat.

"*Riko-gyim!*" she snapped. "Hast no care for one who walks veiled amongst men?" then put her hand on Cecily as Dzo put her finger to her lips.

"The Wild Dog barks i' the moon," said Dzo slowly.

"The Tiger of Bengal prowls in its light," said Ka-lok.

Began a vociferous and prolonged bargaining between the two at top pitch of their strident voices, during which Cecily Cleeve stood mute listening to the appalling insults they flung at each other.

A little crowd collected, urging the two combatants to greater vocal efforts, the station rang to the cries, the stamping of feet and the clapping of hands.

A Mem-Sahib, advanced in years, and with sense of humor lost under India's grilling sun, beckoned the station-master with bony finger, pointed with another bony finger, and bade him summarily to stop the nuisance.

Ka-lok flung herself in front of Cecily as the man, with deference, approached her.

"Nay! speak not to her, defile her not with words, she is under a vow of silence until the birth of her great-grand-child. She is old, very old, and this lumbering yak of no breed keeps her standing whilst she clamors for ten," her voice rose to a shriek of rage, "ten rupees to conduct her, I, her servant, us, to Kalimpong."

"Ten rupees less one-half of a rupee," said Dzo.

"Nine," snapped Ka-lok.

"So be it," said Dzo. "Thou parrot-voiced daughter of a she-camel!" she added pleasantly, at which Ka-lok let rip a shriek which would have put any similar effort on the part of the engine to shame, then subsided into silence when the station-master shook his fist.

Cecily Cleeve had stood patiently, understanding the reason for the by-play.

Strictly *purdah* women are not too common in Darjeeling. If she and Ka-lok had slipped out of the station without any explanation they would most surely have been followed; having satisfied the curiosity of the general public as to their reason for being there, their destination, and the status of the veiled woman, the public took no further interest in them.

Dzo picked up the heavy sheepskin cloaks, and, grumbling, led the way. Once outside she turned to the right and led them by a circuitous route to where the Tanga ponies stood under the trees, and as she led them whispered the whole wonderful story to Ka-lok, who whispered it to Cecily.

"Ask her if we shall be in time, Ka-lok."

Dzo looked up at the moon.

"For the end, perchance, sister, not for the beginning."

"Where is her pony, Ka-lok?"

"She runs at your pony's head, lady. Twenty miles? It is nothing for one of her build or race."

"Four ponies, Ka-lok," Cecily said suddenly. "Why? Who rides with us?"

"Two Sahibs will follow the two first Sahibs whom we pursue," replied Dzo. "One from the hotel came running with a message. Four Tangas instead of two was all the message said, but Dzo, the cross-bred yak, even I, understood, and lo! procured yet two more ponies and took them to stand where the two for the Mem-Sahib waited. They have not yet started, but they will; they will follow the Mem-Sahib and her servant—drawn by love."

"Love," said Ka-lok as she touched the knife in her girdle.

"Yea! 'tis love that draws us all, even thou, perchance, little sister. Love for the man, love for the woman, for the man again, and yet again for the woman, love for the sport——"

"And thou? What love draws thee?"

"Love of five calves of the cross-bred yak," said Dzo slowly as she plodded through the snow towards a field of grain ripening, in her vision, on the mountainside.

CHAPTER XIX

THE night was as clear as day under the light of the full moon hanging in the heavens like a silver, polished, dented shield. There was no sound, nothing moved, until, with a mighty roar, an avalanche thundered in the distance.

Then the snow scrunched under the ponies' hoofs as they threw up their heads and backed, long tails and manes streaming like flags on the light breeze, flanks heaving, big soft eyes rolling in distrust at the sound.

One whinnied softly and backed against the other.

" 'Twere wise, masters, to dismount, for here, some hundreds of feet above the bottom of the ravine, begins the true path of the ledge," whispered Zo-p'o, the brother of Dzo, who showed no sign whatever on his swarthy, smoke-browned face of the twenty miles he had done on foot, loping beside the younger Sahib's pony. "Let the masters make the ascent on foot, quietly, to fall upon the sentry unawares, so that the knife slips in between his shoulders as he sleeps, or smokes, or gazes at the wonder of the moon. My sister says that the masters fight the Tiger and the Wild Dog for a woman. Ah—ah! 'tis a goodly cause." He clapped his hands softly, after the manner of his mother's race, and rocked from side to side. "Yea! my cross-bred sister, who has a sister who is also mine, here, upon the ledge, told me the reason of the Sahibs' visit to the House of Nyko-Gung. I had a woman—ah—ah!—once—comely as the first bloom of the rhododendron in the spring. She disappeared! She, too, disappeared! If the gods be good I will slip this knife to the hilt between one pair of shoulders, or two pairs, or—perchance—three pairs, before the dawn. Ah! ah!—ah-ah-ah!"

He sighed in anticipation of the glorious moment as he

drew his hunting knife and rubbed an imaginary speck from the needle-pointed, razor-edged blade; then, barely touching the stout string which fastened the parcel of sandwiches John Trevor had taken from his pocket, cut it clean in two.

"Get something down, man! Push it down, you'll want it before the night is over."

Rex refused the proffered sandwich with a shake of the head, and, taking his revolver from his pocket, released the safety catch.

"Couldn't! I'd choke and give the alarm. Pretty good going, wasn't it? Jolly good; and she's up there, Trevor. Lotah! She's just above my head, within reach of my arm—almost—yes, good going, but nothing compared to what it's going to be a little later—up there." He looked at Zo-p'o, who held out a second knife, short, sharp, with nicks in the horn handle. "For me? No, thank you all the same."

"Beseech him, master, beseech the young Sahib!"

Rex held out his revolver.

"For the man who stands far away, Zo-p'o, I use *this;* for the man or the men I am after, I shall use my bare hands. Come on! Let's get up." He looked about him at the wall of rock and everlasting snow that hedged them in, down to the black well of the ravine, up to the moon climbing the heavens. "I'll give the sign when we reach the guard."

Unseen, Dzo's brother took an amulet for good luck from about his own neck and slipped it into the young Sahib's pocket.

"That, with the light of madness in his eyes and the protection of the gods, will keep him safe. That and his love for his woman."

"The ponies? What about them?"

"Safe, master, safe and still." Zo-p'o backed the animals between two rocks and tethered them by the reins to a stunted tree. " 'Tis good to have courage and a stout heart at the beginning of a fight, Sahib; 'tis twice as good to have speed and a means of escape at the end. I will lead the way."

He turned and stopped dead.

Just a little above, watching them from the shadows, stood the sentry, rifle in hand.

"Ah! ah!" sighed the brother of Dzo softly, as he stood stock-still, then moved as Rex pushed him on one side and passed him, slowly walking up to where the sentry stood.

"The password? The password, or I fire!"

Rex took no notice.

He walked slowly and as one totally unafraid; he was "caste," and the sentry stood staring, dominated by the courage and the personality of this man who feared not death, and whose eyes shone with a strange fire under the fur cap.

Rex walked up until the muzzle of the rifle touched his chest, and stood quite still in the middle of the path, which ended abruptly to the left in a sheer drop down to the bottom of the ravine.

There was no courage in what he did.

He did not realize the foolhardiness of his action; he had encountered the first obstacle on the last lap of the bitter road that led to Lotah, and that obstacle, with as little noise as possible, had to be removed.

That was all!

He looked up, the sentry looked down.

Who were these white men, these unannounced, unexpected visitors to the ledge?

A light of understanding shone suddenly in the place of that of perplexity in the sentry's slanting eyes.

Rex had made the sign.

He crossed the thumb and little finger of his right hand and touched the thumb three times with the middle finger of the left hand.

Ah! this was the man his master, Sa-t'ong, the Bengal Tiger, had warned him of. The man who would give the wrong sign and who was to be shot on sight.

Yet surely this man was a Sahib.

" 'Tis not the sign!" he said at last, after a long moment of deliberation, too intent on Rex's face to notice the movement of his hands.

"You *dog!*" replied Rex as, with a single lightning movement, he gripped the rifle with both hands, and with knees bent and a tremendous swing of the shoulders slung the man, who clung for dear life to the rifle, far out over the precipice.

Then Zo-p'o's arm, gnarled with muscle, browned by the sun and smoke and storm, shot out and caught Rex by the hem of his sheepskin coat when, reeling under the impetus of the movement with which he had slung the sentry to his death, he staggered towards the edge of the path.

"My God!" said Trevor. "That was a near thing!"

"Ah! ah!" sighed the brother of Dzo.

"First blood to us!" said Rex indifferently as he turned to mount the path. "Come on!"

"Nay, *I* will go first, masters!" said the guide, and disappeared like a snake between the boulders.

They found him at the top squatting on his haunches behind a boulder peering to right and left; he signaled them to kneel behind a rock, and crept to them on his hands and knees.

"All is well, masters! There is no sign of living thing, and the Great Road, lined with trees, leading to the House, being as a lake of glass, we must follow the Street of All Evil, the Sahibs walking through it as lords and I behind, their servant. For behold! danger cometh from *behind* where dwell the Nyko-Gung, and the Street of Evil has shadows a-plenty thrown by the arches lit by ruby lamps."

Rex looked at Trevor, and Trevor at him, without a word.

The Street of Many Arches!

The street of which Tsi-tsi had tried so hard to tell them before she died; the Street of Many Arches where the bad men dwelt; the street they had found at last with but a few minutes left, an hour at the most perhaps, in which to save Lotah from worse than death.

They had arrived truly at the journey's end, the journey by sea, by land, by rail, by road, but what of the end of the quest itself?

Death to them? If so, worse than death to Lotah, the White Rose, unless she found a way out herself in death. Would she be able to kill herself? Had she killed herself?

Rex's splendid optimism crumbled suddenly into dust. Up to that very moment he had been fighting, fighting the great odds of distance, the unknown, illness, and the hidden power of those who wrought against him. He had fought to get to this village, this town in the Himalayas. He had fought to arrive in time, and now, when in a few moments he would make sure if Lotah lived or not, a great cloud of horror descended on him.

He looked along to the far end of the ledge to where the House of Nyko-Gung loomed, dark, desolate, under a towering peak crowned with snow, and round at the village which seemed to him a town built against and up the base of the mountains which stood, like sentinels, at the back of the ledge.

A few lights twinkled; one went out; it was like the shutting of an eye. There was no sound, the place seemed dead, deserted, buried, pressed down by death and sin.

Rex shivered suddenly, violently, made a quick gesture with both hands as though to press back something which advanced towards him, and moved forward.

"This way, masters. To the right. Let the Sahibs follow me, and walk like lords, brooking no affront."

They walked some two hundred yards and stopped.

The Street of Many Arches stretched before them.

"You stay here, hidden, we will go forward alone!"

"Master!" Zo-p'o clasped his hands. He wanted to help the Sahibs, truly, but even more did he want to use his knife to revenge the girl like unto the first rhododendron bud of spring, who, too, had disappeared. "Master!"

"I fight for my own woman, Zo-p'o, I must go alone." Zo-p'o glanced at Trevor towering beside him in the shadows. "The Sahib is of my woman's people, Zo-p'o, he has a right."

Zo-p'o touched the boot of the young Sahib.

"I will stay here hidden, master. Perchance the Sahibs will fight their way to where the ponies stand, then will Zo-p'o pick off the enemy from the shadows. Straight on, master, to the end, neither to the right nor to the left of the street, *let the Sahibs bear that in mind*. Straight beneath the necklace of ruby lamps to the end, then to the east, and the gods guide your footsteps through the Street of Many Arches."

Dear God! What a street!

There were arches all down it; spanning it at every thirty feet or less, giving it the look of some fantastic arcade. There were houses each side of it; houses in which were windows, long windows reaching to within three feet of the ground. Windows? No, not real windows; they had no panes, no glass, just casements with curtains drawn aside and barred with slender bars of iron.

In the center of these windows, these casements, sat women, outlined against the red glow of fires burning in the inner rooms; the Laughing Thrushes, silent, inert, hardly breathing, like garish, gigantic, horrible dolls, dressed for some sacrifice. Their faces terrified; masks of paint, blue and carmine, white; their eyes moved, following the two men down the Street of the Arches.

One woman sat in a window in each house, and down one side of the street these women were adorned with garish-colored ribbons—red ribbons—flaming—they all wore the terrible color. On the other side the color was in violent contrast—orange ribbons—flaming—but the same kind of ribbon.

The women wore white, white with violent flaming ribbons, and their eyes, their *kohl*-smeared eyes, beckoned, threatened, followed the strangers down the street.

Between the arches, some of the arches, were faces, faces of men, watching from the shadows; men who crept to the edge of the arches, peering stealthily at these strangers whose footsteps wakened the echoes at this untoward hour of the night, and disappeared.

Ahead the street showed silent, deserted, divided by the necklace of ruby lamps swinging in the night breeze; behind them the street was alive, silent but alive with figures that showed for a moment and were gone; with watching eyes and hands that touched the hilt of the knife stuck in the belt; with fingers that touched the lips, but above all, with eyes that watched in the shadows thrown by the many arches.

Came the sound of opening windows; of women's subdued voices; of the tinkling of a thousand silver and golden bells. The Birds of Paradise had caught the sound of heavy footsteps at the unusual hour of the night. Little, useless, be-ringed hands fluttered at the open windows above the casements where the garish, gigantic, horrible dolls sat; joy bells, thousands of them, hanging from ceiling and curtain, tinkled in the breeze of the open windows; soft laughter, whispered words, flowers flung upon the stones; the *pi-wang* thrummed in the shadows, some woman singing Lotah's song, but ever underneath, behind the bars, those ghastly eyes staring, threatening the men as they quickened their pace, looking straight ahead to the end of the terrible street.

"I saw it," whispered John Trevor. "I saw it in the fog the night of the fire."

"I painted it," whispered Rex. "I painted it with those eyes watching Lotah, who is there—my God!—at the end."

Then the street was full of sound.

Like the under-tow on a beach of pebbles, like wind whistling through the crack in the wall, it whispered and rustled from casement to casement, from end to end, swinging the lamps, filling the upper windows with beautiful heads tired to the undoing of weak men.

The Thrushes laughed.

Without movement, without merriment in the *kohl*-smeared eyes, they laughed beneath their breath, horribly, in a deadly monotone which swelled like the notes of a great organ and dwindled to the whispering of the wind in the trees.

The hateful, hypnotic sound surrounded the two men, pressed upon them, pushed at them, pulled them back and sideways.

Witchcraft?

The power of minds many, on unprotected thought?

Who knows!

Rex walked forward slowly, his head bent as though against a hurricane of wind, then stopped and looked up and put out his hand, gripping Trevor's arm above the elbow.

The necklace of ruby lamps no longer hung above him, it was to his right; and to his left, close to him, behind the iron bars of the lower casement, a Thrush laughed, looking down at him from evil, *kohl*-smeared eyes.

Thought had swept him out of the middle of the street towards the door of the evil house, the thought of those garish, gigantic, motionless dolls; and thought saved him.

He put his hand up quickly and felt the necklace of blue beads above his heart which thudded sickeningly, heavily; he pressed back against the casement, staring down to the end of the street where Lotah, Lotah in distress, in fear of death and worse, waited for him, called to him. His face was wet, his hands were cold as ice as he tried to pull himself away from the casement, where, unknown to him, a woman's finger-tip touched the center of his neck.

"Help me!" he whispered to John Trevor, who stood quite still staring at him, frowning, a victim—almost—to the hypnotic evil of the street.

"Lotah!" whispered Rex. "Lotah! Help!" then suddenly lurched forward, free, his mind filled with the wonder of his love; lurched forward, staggered, gripped John Trevor's hand and ran with him, ran down the evil street; away from the painted puppets sitting motionless; away from a nameless fear; pursued by a nameless dread. From the laughing of the Thrushes, the mocking of the Birds of Paradise, they ran and turned to the east and into a narrow street and stopped dead, flattened against a wall in pitch-black shadow.

*   *   *

A narrow street spanned by two narrow arches, one at either end; a dark and short and silent street; a lantern or two flickering over strange shops.

Here were no painted women's ruby lights, nor sound or sight of human being.

To the left, between the narrow arches, stood a house, raised upon a platform, with roof built in three tiers, tapering to a point. The Hall of Justice, the Hall of Gambling, the open Mart, unlighted, forbidding, secretive, with a great gong hanging high in the tapering roof, and gods, in brass, squatting at the four corners, peering down at those who entered, who came out, who tarried, hastened, laughed or wept.

An orange streak of light tore the shadows into shreds as both sides of the shuttered door were suddenly flung wide. Then came the sound of voices, laughter, singing; a glimpse of a huge hall packed with men; the odor of the East, pungent, indescribable, then the door closed and the shadows settled down.

Rex gripped John Trevor above the elbow as two men stopped for an instant on the steps, talking softly, laughing as they talked.

"Let us hasten, O Brother! 'Twere folly to miss the fight between the brothers Nyko-Gung over a woman from a strange land."

"Verily! Let us run at speed and back to witness the Tiger's claws in the Gray Wolf's side, the Gray Wolf's fangs at the Tiger's throat. Yet will they enter, in some small space of time, as twain lambs of meekness and brotherly affection."

Rex watched the two men as they ran down the street, making no sound in their native felt-soled shoes.

"It's here!" he whispered. "My God! Trevor, she is in there—Lotah—come."

Like shadows they crept up the steps and stood listening, ready for flight, their ears against the door, safe in the pitch-darkness caused by the first overhanging tier of the roof which jutted like a verandah.

The door opened suddenly and they ran, each one way, ran sideways, flattened against the wall and round the corners of the house, where John Trevor stood peering at Chang-ku's servant, Dong, who ran hastily to meet his master. Rex, reconnoitering, slipped like a cat along the edge of the platform upon which the house was built.

They crept back as the door closed and stood, taking council, whispering, ready for flight.

"There's a smaller kind of hall built on to the end of this one," whispered Rex, "and a door near the end of the side wall, in this, the big hall. The door's a quarter open and covered with heavy woolen curtains. Come on round to your side, it may be the same."

They crept round the east side of the house, their heavy boots making no noise on the thick matting covering the platform. There was a door near the end of this wall, also a quarter open, with a heavy woolen curtain hanging in front.

"Is it one curtain or a pair, d'you think?"

Slowly, inch by inch, Rex pulled one side of the door

back, and, as slowly, felt the curtains with the tips of his fingers.

"A pair," he whispered. "Thank God!"

He opened the edges of the curtains by half an inch and stood staring, the light of battle flaring in his eyes, then beckoned Trevor and bade him look.

"My God!" was all John Trevor said, then whispered to Rex, gave him the signal for attack and turned and ran to the opposite side.

Across the upper end, the north end of the hall, stretched a platform of oak, plain and covered on the top with white skins. An iron barrier divided the platform from the body of the hall, packed to suffocation with men; on the ground, inside the barrier, were two cushions, one at each side of a faded Persian carpet patterned in old rose and blue and worked in tarnished golden thread; a tray for coffee at the right of the cushions, a tray for the *narghileh* or whatever form of smoking the gambler preferred, at the left, and nothing else.

Nothing but rows of Oriental faces, laughing, serene, excepting for the eyes which burned in every face like red-hot coals; faces pressed to the barrier, against the wall, against each other on either side of a narrow strip of matting which stretched from the rail to the great door.

They sat in rows or in circles or huddled one against each other, these men who were a law unto themselves, and the willing, devoted servants, children, subjects, what you will, of the brothers Nyko-Gung; stubborn, Herculean for the most part, a tendency to the Mongolian in the high cheek-bone and slanting eyes, with here and there a slender Hindoo figure with face of great beauty, immobile, artistic, eyes wide and full of dreams.

They had been drinking steadily throughout the evening; *murwa, arak, vodka,* drinking enough to have left any ordinary man senseless on the floor, but only just enough to incite them, hardy, steel-strong, to a spirit of mischief, which needed but the necessary match to flame into a lust to kill.

Merry they were as they waited for their dread, but greatly beloved, lords to appear; played knuckle-bones, threw dice, ate, drank and sang in chorus, so many against so many, and rose and moved in circles, pivoting on one foot, clapping their hands.

And outside, peering through the curtains, stood the two white men, who, against such appalling, overwhelming odds had come to save the woman for whom the dread brothers were to gamble, and for whose appearance, in great patience and content, the hundreds of men waited.

A shout went up as Yi, the old nurse, parted the curtains at the back of the platform and beckoned to some one on the other side.

"Ha! old one, so the Great Ones gamble for thee——!"

"What is thy dowry? three score and more of years hung about thy withered neck——?"

"Behold, her beauty! Does she not put to shame the maids as heavy as a fall of snow, as sweet as *chura,* as graceful as the bulky yak, for whom we have thrown the dice this night——!"

"Ha! Ha! old one. Go fetch the White Rose! *Gyop— gyop!* Ha! ha!——"

"*Gyop—gyop!*" came from every side of the hall, "*Gyop —gyop,*" to the clapping of hands.

The old nurse faced the ribald crowd and shook her fist.

"*Kha'tsum!* thou sons of mules, *kha'tsum.*"

"Be silent, thou sayest, old one! *Lok-te lap!*"

"Aye, so will I say it again, thou mule-headed son of sin. *Kha'tsum!*"

The mule-headed son of sin brayed like the four-footed beast which had been included in his ancestry, then leapt to his feet and shouted.

Two women staggered through the curtains at the back of the platform, carrying a chair. A chair painted a shade deeper than Chinese blue, patterned in silver, the chair in which Lotah had sat the previous night in the House of Nyko-Gung.

The uproar was terrific. The moment was nigh; the girl about whom there had been so much talk was coming. Where were their lords? The men shouted at each other, laying wagers as to the outcome of the throwing of the dice. Where were the dread brothers, Sa-t'ong, the Tiger, Chang-ku, the Wolf, where?

Silence fell like the sudden falling of the night.

There was not a sound nor movement as the great doors opened wide, then, with one tremendous shout the men, every one of them, sprang to their feet.

In the doorway stood the brothers Nyko-Gung.

Magnificent, fully armed, side by side, two giants, they stood for a moment, then walked slowly forward.

Unattended, Sa-t'ong walked, his eyes fixed ahead upon the chair, his thoughts on the girl he loved, clothed from head to foot in white. A full-skirted, high-necked coat he wore, of buckskin, worked as fine and as soft as satin, white as snow. White breeches, white knee-high boots, and heavy silver belt, an ermine cloak hanging to his heels, a cap of ermine and one great string of pearls. He was as a god in beauty, save for the mutilated hand he held hidden in his breast.

Black as night beside him, in hunting jerkin, breeches, boots of leather, Chang-ku looked contemptuously about the room. A cloak of panther skin hung to his heels, a heavy golden girdle about his waist, a cap of panther skin upon his blacker hair.

And outside stood Rex Power, a sapling beside the oak, with madness in his eyes; madness in his eyes and the lust to kill and kill and kill woven with his great love in his heart.

He stood quite still, blood dripping from his lip where he had bitten it right through.

He waited to see upon which cushion each brother would sit; he waited to be sure that Lotah would sit above them in the blue and silver chair; Lotah who hated and dreaded the Oriental; Lotah the cynosure of all those hundred slanting eyes.

Hundreds of eyes, hundreds of men, hundreds of them against him.

What matter!

He would kill the one in white, the one of gentle, evil beauty, and would kill the other, ha! the one who had fooled him in Benares. Then Lotah! Yes, he would kill Lotah, too, and over her dead body would die himself, with John Trevor fighting to the death at his side.

The madness of the gods had fallen upon Rex Power; he threw back his head and laughed, laughed savagely and long, the terrible sound lost in the shouting of the men.

Then he stopped—suddenly—and stood quite still.

Who was that standing between the curtains at the back of the dais, that girl, wonderful, glorious, beautiful, clothed in white, with a crown of diamonds flashing on her small head? A marriage crown! God! the Tibetan marriage crown.

Lotah? Yes! Lotah, his wife!

She stood looking down, her hair in two great plaits hanging to her knees, one hand on her breast, one on the golden girdle at her waist. Then she moved slowly forward and sat down, one hand on the arm of the chair, one still on the girdle at her waist.

She bent her head lower, lower still at the thunder of the shouting, and put her hand before her eyes to hide them from the eyes of Sa-t'ong, who sat still, silent, looking up at her from his seat below the platform.

She raised her right hand and covered her eyes, and the men behind the barrier shouted and pointed at the scar on her arm in the shape of a white rose, which showed plainly in the light of the lamps swinging above her head.

Then she looked up and across the hall, and to one side and then the other, and sighed.

She was not afraid. Her hand rested on a dagger in her belt, the dagger she had picked up but the night before and had hidden under the pillow of her bed.

Death? What was death but a closing of the eyes in sleep?

She did not want to die. Life stretched before her, life and love, with Rex. Rex who seemed so near, close to her side, whispering in her ear.

"I will never give you up. Remember, I will never, never give you up!"

So close, so far away, dear God! She would wait, wait until the last second of the eleventh hour had struck, until either the one or the other of those two men looked up at her with possession in his eyes, until one rose to claim her before all men, to come to her, to lift her in his arms and to carry her hence.

She touched the satin garment above her heart. There was naught but the satin between her and death.

The moments were slipping, the eleventh hour was passing, and she was alone.

Yi, the old nurse, had left her, had gone from the platform, had closed the door behind the curtains, locking it. She had heard the key turn. Even Sona, the bear, had left her, early in the day, had moaned and moaned, running this way and that, and had disappeared out of the house, up to the snows of the Everlasting Hills.

The curtain on her left moved. Did the wind blow or was Sona there, watching, waiting to come in? Why should she think so much of the bear—or the wind? Why did the curtain move? It moved so slightly, no one noticed it; three times it moved. Yes, again and again, three times. One, two, three.

She covered her eyes with her hand, her eyes ablaze with

a great hope; the eyes which might betray her, or whoever it was who stood behind the curtain, to the men.

There, again! One, two, three! One, two, three! What could it mean? Ah! yes—yes—one, two, three—three letters—three letters of one short word.

Love translated the movement of the curtain, love swept the curtain of doubt and dread and mist from before her eyes.

She knew.

Rex was behind the curtain. Rex. Death might be waiting for her, but death with Rex fighting at her side would be life.

And the madness of the gods fell upon Lotah, the White Rose. She sprang to her feet, glorious in her madness, and flung wide her arms.

She pointed down at Sa-t'ong.

He flung the dice and then Chang-ku, and Sa-t'ong once again.

She laughed, pointing at him, laughed until the place rang with the splendid, maddest sound.

The men shouted, springing to their feet.

"Throw! Throw!" they shouted. "She chooseth the Tiger. Throw! Throw!"

The place rang with their cries, the barrier creaked and bent as the men, eyes blazing, leaned forward, hands cut-stretched.

"Once more! and the woman to the highest. Evens now! Once more! Once again!"

The Wolf threw a five and laughed. Sa-t'ong looked up at Lotah, looked down, and threw a six.

He leaped, the victor, to his feet.

"Mine," he shouted. "Mine!" just as Rex ripped back the curtains wide with a mad, triumphant cry.

CHAPTER XX

"LOTAH! Beloved!"

"Rex! Oh, Rex!"

The crashing report of Rex's revolver drowned the voices, as Chang-ku turned instinctively and sprang, hunting knife in hand; followed a shout, a thud, and a roar from hundreds of throats when the Gray Wolf pitched forward on his face, and Rex raced towards the platform on which Lotah stood, hands outstretched, looking down.

One moment of utter silence in which, amazed, stupefied, every one stood dumb and motionless, then, as Sa-t'ong ran to intercept his enemy, the men, like a wolf-pack, rushed the barrier.

But Yi, the old nurse, was first, was in front of them.

Wizened, bent, she ducked under the iron bar, and, crazed with fear for the man she loved, caught him by the ermine cloak and pulled him back, flinging herself forward, clasping him by the knees. She loved him, she held him, she would not let him go, no, not to his death! And she bent her old head as he bent down upon her hands, and clasped his fingers and gripped the hem of his coat between her teeth, when Rex, with a shout, leaped to the platform and took Lotah in his arms.

Rex saw nothing of the howling mob of men fighting and jamming under the iron bar; heard nothing of their screams and oaths, and cries of pain and hate; he stood with his back to them, Lotah in his arms, whispering to her, laughing, touching her hair, her cheeks, her lips.

Then he turned, his arm about her, and looked for Trevor in this, his great moment, and frowned. John Trevor was nowhere to be seen. He pulled off his sheepskin coat and looked about the hall, and laughed, and whispered to Lotah, who looked towards the curtains.

Trevor stood outside saving his ammunition, watching, waiting for the moment when the great fight, the unequal fight which had not yet begun, might hang in the balance.

The moment, the critical, decisive moment? Surely it was this, in which the men fought to break down the barrier and Sa-t'ong to loosen the arms of the old woman which clasped him.

He loosened them brutally and swung her above his head.

One old woman who loved him, one woman, old or young, the more the less, what difference did she make to the Bengal Tiger, who loved Lotah, the White Rose?

To throw the old woman back into the crowd of yelling men he swung her behind his head.

"Ah! Ah! No! Stop him!" screamed Lotah, as Rex fired and missed, and Sa-t'ong, swinging sideways, flung the old woman through the curtains of the door, out into the night.

A thud, a whimper of pain, the pain of a broken heart, which hurt so much more than the broken, dragging limb, then Lotah screamed again, mad with rage, and stood pointing down at Sa-t'ong, who stood looking up at her. He looked at her, then at the slender figure at her side, the man she had married and who had appeared so swiftly, so unaccountably out of the night, and back again to her, whilst Dong, against the wall, held Chang-ku across his knee and stroked the blood-stained hair.

Trevor, hidden, drew one curtain back; the men stopped fighting at the barrier as Lotah laughed, and, lifting the diamond crown, the Tibetan marriage crown, held it above her head.

Her eyes blazed beneath the flashing diadem; her arms were bare; wrapped in something white and glistening, the triple row of pearls touching her jeweled girdle, she held the men breathless in her beauty and her wrath.

"Ah!" she cried, speaking in the language of Sikkim. "You coward! you brute! to treat a woman so. So would you have treated me! You, who thought me drugged, who thought I did not hear your words of love, your——"

"Nay, nay, White Rose! I love thee, White Rose! I love thee." Sa-t'ong stepped back almost to the barrier. The men who loved him touched his sleeve, his coat, his boots as he made one last, desperate, vain effort to triumph over the man who stood by Lotah's side, looking down at him, laughing, not in mockery nor in contempt, but in utter, bitter hate. "Lotah! White Rose! I have won thee, I have won thee as my wife, I love thee."

He stepped right back against the barrier as Lotah flung the marriage crown straight down to his feet, then turned and held out her arms to Rex, who caught and held her close. Rex laughed, laughed at the man who had failed, even with his great beauty; failed in love, in gentleness, just as he would fail with fear and force and death behind him. He laughed again when the barrier bent and gave as those in front, pushed by those behind, broke through it, falling to the floor, fighting, cursing as they struggled to their feet.

"Leave him to us, O Tiger——"

"Leave her to us to get for thee, master——"

"We are ready to die for thee——"

"What are his bullets but little gates to paradise? We are unarmed, save for our knives; say but the word and we tear him limb from limb——"

"And the woman too, unless thou desirest her as she stands——"

Quick and terrible came the prayers, the suggestions, the supplications, then a knife, two, six, a score whistled over the heads of the two who stood in each other's arms, looking down. Thrown in sport, thrown in an endeavor to frighten before death, they buried themselves in the door which the old nurse had locked behind the girl her master loved.

Rex drew Lotah closer still.

He made no other movement. He took no notice of the knives quivering in the wood behind him, nor of the men in front, kept from leaping to the platform and tearing him limb from limb by Sa-t'ong, who held them quiet by the mere lifting of his hand.

Sa-t'ong waited; Rex waited; the men in front fell back upon the men behind; John Trevor pushed the curtains clear from about his feet, and Chang-ku smiled evilly as he watched, unseen, through the tangled thatch of his blood-stained hair.

"Mine!" said Rex suddenly, derisively.

The storm, he knew, must break; they, the men, held in check by the gigantic man in white, were only playing with him as he held Lotah close, as the tiger plays before it deals the fatal blow, breaking its victim's back or neck; nothing could keep them long from storming the platform and tearing Lotah from him as they smote him dead.

"Ready, sweetheart?" he said, leaning his cheek against hers as he looked to where John Trevor stood watching. "They'll be on us in a moment. It won't hurt, beloved, and I shall be with you in a moment. Trevor, I think, if he wants to, will be able to get away. He'll have to, he has Cecily waiting for him. Those beastly pearls, sweetheart," he whispered as he lifted them above her head and flung them at Sa-t'ong's feet, then pulled the necklace of blue beads from his shirt pocket and held it out. "Ha! Sa-t'ong," he cried, slipping it over Lotah's head. "She wears these above her heart as she holds me in it!" He laughed. "There is no room there for you, and I take her with me."

A roar came from the men as he drew his revolver.

They had no firearms. Daggers, hunting knives with razor-edge, yes, but on the night of gambling, of love and laughter, firearms were left at home. The gods' curse upon the man, the boy, who stood above them, mocking them, a weapon of certain death in his hand. Certain death for some, but not for all! At him! Down with him! What held them back? Why did they wait? Ha! the Tiger laughed. The Tiger spoke!

"Whelp!" he shouted up to Rex, white to the lips with rage, white as the ermine cloak he tore from him and flung upon the ground. "Come down and fight, unarmed, for your woman! Come down, little boy, come down!"

"Come down!" yelled the men. "Come down to be smashed to pulp before your woman's eyes, come down!"

The storm was nigh to breaking, heralded by the booming of the great gong hanging in the tower. It crashed suddenly above their heads. Yi, faithful unto death, beat upon it, calling for aid. Some one had fired at her beloved master! He was not armed. Rifles, revolvers were left at home on the Night of Gambling! Let the women come! Let them answer the summons, bringing the firearms with them! A broken leg? What matter a broken leg when danger threatened her beloved! She crawled along the verandah up the stairs, up to the niche in the wall, high up, where hung the hammer with which to beat upon the gong. She was old, so old; she could not stand, her leg was broken, yes, her leg was broken; her arm would soon be tired, she was old, so old, but she would beat upon the gong until help came or until she dropped down dead.

The booming of the gong filled the Hall, the town, the great spaces of the Himalayas with its mighty sound, drowning that of feet running down the Street of Many Arches. The Birds of Paradise peered from the upper windows, the Laughing Thrushes sat silent, listening, watching three women running, running down the street.

The great gong boomed, knives flashed in the Hall, the air was rent with cries as Rex rolled back his sleeves.

"I come," he cried. "I come to——"

He stopped.

With a yell of terror, born of superstition, the men near
the door fought each other back.   They touched their
amulets as they fought, and turned and fought with fists
and knives to clear a way for the ghost, the spirit, the figure
clothed from head to foot in white which came running from
the night, with a woman, eyes flaming, mouth wide open,
calling upon the gods, a knife in hand, close upon her heels.

"A ghost!" they yelled as they fought back.   "The ghost
of a woman, a *purdah* woman!   Back!   Let her not touch
us lest we break her caste.   Back, in the name of the gods!
Back!   Back!"

Up the path cleared for her by love and superstition ran
Cecily, Ka-lok close upon her heels; ran without a plan in
her head, led by her love and her fear for those two standing
at the end of the Hall, facing death—alone.

John Trevor?   Where was he?   Somewhere!   He was not
dead!   No, he was not dead.   Rex would not be standing
scatheless if he were dead.

That great figure in white there, facing her, who was he?
Who pulled at her covering?   Who pushed her on one side?
right to the side empty of the men who had turned, and,
blind with superstition, had forced their brothers back.
No one noticed her, no one saw John Trevor pull her behind
the curtain or saw them as they crept along the wall and
scrambled to the platform.

Ka-lok had passed her, running like a deer; the men were
watching her, were intent on her as she ran, her flaming eyes
fixed on Sa-t'ong Nyko-Gung.

Sa-t'ong was there, standing like a god!   The Bengal
Tiger who had loved her, had made her his in the evil
Limehouse street.

He had been hers, if only for a little time, and hers he
should be for all Eternity!

He watched her coming, thinking her a friend!

He made no sound, gave no sign, when the dagger flashed
up, and down into his breast.   He walked forward, slowly,

steadily, a patch of crimson spreading above his heart, then turned and looked up at Lotah, the White Rose.

"Lotah!" he called, and spread wide his arms. "Lotah, *chung!* I love thee!" and spun round and fell, face downward, dead, his mutilated hand upon the diamond marriage crown.

Ka-lok stood above him, love-madness in her eyes, the dagger in her lifted hand.

"Mine!" she cried. "All mine!" and drove the dagger down, and fell, face downward, dead, her hand upon her one-time lover's hair.

The storm broke!

The Tiger of Bengal lay dead; the Gray Wolf lay dead across his servant's knees.

Ha! restraint was gone, swept away by the stroke of the dead girl's hand.

Now for the whelp who had defied the Tiger, the stripling who stood above them, with the girl who showed no sign of fear in her beautiful face nor in her laughing, opalescent eyes.

At them! Tear them down! Tear them limb from limb! Bury the knives, hilt-deep, in their hearts! At them! Pull them down!

A deafening shout went up!

In the name of the gods! who had multiplied the man and the girl so that four stood where had been two? Who was the big man, standing like a rock, a revolver in his hand, with a woman, a fair, a foreign woman at his side, a revolver in her hand?

Where was the ghost—the *purdah* woman? Demons fought for these people from a strange land!

Witchcraft! By the gods, witchcraft! On such a night! On such a night! Yet only humans carried firearms, mere men, mere women.

"Pull them down," yelled a youth, and fell dead as Trevor fired and shot him between the eyes, as a roar of laughter and shouts of joy and bitter curses rent the air.

Chang-ku, the Wolf, was not dead, he stood against the wall laughing, pointing at Lotah, the White Rose.

"Mine!" he cried, pushing the black hair from his evil, slanting eyes. "Mine, now that the Tiger of Bengal is dead. I fight thee for her, thou pup! I fight thee for this thing over whom might dogs fight as . . ."

The shouts of laughter which greeted the appalling insult hurled at Lotah sent Rex Power mad.

He pushed Lotah back against the wall, throwing his revolver at her feet.

"Come up, you mongrel!" he cried. "Come up, you thing of mixed breeding, half jackal, half pariah dog." He turned and laughed and pointed to his friends. "They will not fire, they will not waste the bullets on your mongrel body. I will kill you with my bare hands, and then they will spit upon you when you are dead,—you half-caste!" He laughed and mocked, and laughed again, watching the giant as he walked up to the platform and swung to the top. He shouted in the language of Sikkim, caring naught for his halting, limping words, then ran back and kissed Lotah on the mouth as she stood against the wall, her eyes alight with love. Chang-ku, as quick as a gray wolf upon his feet, rushed him as he stood beside Lotah; he ducked and turned and hit the giant full upon the mouth, breaking his teeth, then followed with a right to the chin, which stopped the huge man, and sent him reeling back, shaken to his feet.

Only for a moment!

Chang-ku watched Rex out of cunning, evil eyes, then rushed at Lotah, and, as the men roared, turned and swept Rex with his left arm clean off his feet and flung him across the platform to crash at Trevor's side.

"My fight!" yelled Rex, leaping to his feet, as Cecily ran to Lotah and Trevor shouted to him to be on his guard. "My fight! Only mine! Only—mine!"

He sprang clear off the ground straight at Chang-ku's throat as the huge man rushed at him; leapt straight at him, caught him by the neck with slender hands and round the middle, pinning the Wolf's arms with his knees, clinging to him, hunched upon his chest, so that Chang-ku's arms could get no hold about his ribs to crush them in, to bend him back and back until his spine snapped.

No, Chang-ku's arms could get no hold upon the slender body, tough as whipcord, but they were long enough and strong enough to reach under Rex's knees and lift them until his huge hands gripped the arms to drag them down, wrenching apart the long fingers, strong as steel, which held his throat in such a suffocating grip.

Quick! He must be quick! The boy clung to him like a leech, pressing, pressing on the great vein beneath his ear.

Ah! quick! Blood from the wound where the bullet had ripped his scalp trickled in his eyes! It was that that made them dim, that only, and made his heart beat heavily as something, a stone, no, the booming of the gong, beat upon his head like some gigantic hammer.

He must break the boy's legs, his arms, then his neck. Curses upon him! He clung like a leech, his mad eyes shining like great fires. He laughed! He laughed! Great gods! Would nothing stop the sound and the shouting from the Hall?

"To thy knees, O Wolf! To thy knees and upon him then! Shake him off! Throw him! To thy knees! To thy knees! To thy knees!"

Cecily pulled Lotah to her, hiding her eyes against her shoulder. Trevor stood still, quite still, his revolver in his hand, watching, waiting, whilst the Hall rang with the shouts of men, and the great gong crashed above their heads, drowning the sound of feet running, running down the Street of Many Arches.

"John, can't you, can't we help? Oh, John!"

"It's his fight, Cecily, it's his fight!"

Cecily hid her eyes. John Trevor cursed as Chang-ku fell suddenly to his knees. Rex laughed. Exhausted, nigh to fainting with the agony of his breaking knees, his breaking arms, he laughed as he swung sideways. Chang-ku swayed and fell upon his back, and Rex shouted as the giant loosed his hold for just one moment, and, pressing his hands hard upon the ground, sprang straight upon his feet, swaying from side to side, as Rex shifted his knees until they gripped his enemy about the ribs.

"Give in!" yelled Rex, sweat pouring down his face, his eyes blazing, his mouth wide open as he laughed in the madness of his hour. "Give in!"

"Throw him!" screamed the men. "Throw him! Fall forward! Crush him!"

The men stood packed close at the edge of the platform, a sea of terrible faces, of flashing, dreadful eyes.

"He fails! He faints! He dies!"

"A lie! A lie!" Lotah tore herself from Cecily's arms and ran up close to the fighting men.

"Rex!" she cried. "Rex! Rex!" and laughed and smiled as his eyes, blazing in his haggard, death-white face, locked straight into hers.

He was almost done, a little more and his hold would slacken. Chang-ku beat upon his back with clenched fists, pounded on it just below the waist; he could not stand the agony much longer.

"I love you, Rex! Rex! Rex!"

Something glittered on Lotah's breast, something blue, flashing like little streaks of fire.

Rex laughed suddenly and shifted his right hand.

"The blue beads!" he shouted. "The blue beads!" and with one last mighty effort, pressing his thumb upon the great vein and forcing back the Wolf's neck with long, slender fingers, strong as steel, gripped the chin with the other hand, bending the head back, and still farther back, until with a little click, Chang-ku, the Gray Wolf, dropped dead.

"Mine!" yelled Rex. "Mine!" and slung Lotah backwards as a long arm shot out, missing her robe by the breadth of a hair.

"They're on us! Get the women back!" yelled Trevor as he emptied his revolver into the seething mass of men who fought each other to get to the top of the platform, fell back and fought each other as they stood and sprang again, jammed too tight even to use their knives.

"To the back!" screamed some one in the crowd. "To the back! Trap them! Trap them!"

"My God!" shouted Trevor as he reloaded just as a knife ripped Cecily's shoulder. "Bravo!" he shouted again as she shot the man straight through the heart, then emptied her revolver into the faces of the men who, aided by others, were scrambling to the top.

"Look out!" yelled Rex. "They're at the door. Stand back, Lotah! Ha! Would you?" He flung Lotah back as the middle panel splintered and a bullet whistled past him. "They've got guns! This is the end. Lotah! Lotah! Let's die fighting."

A scream came from behind the door as he fired, a scream drowned in the yelling of the men in the hall.

"Trapped!" they shouted. "They're trapped! To the death! To the death!"

They rushed forward until they stood pressed against the platform, the broken iron bar, the walls. They used their knives, their fists; they fell and lay where they had fallen, trodden to death under their brothers' feet.

What matter? They had won!

The four devils on the platform were caught between two stones. But a space of time and they would have them down in their midst, and what then?

The door was almost down. Ha! the woman devil had fired and killed, and——

A scream of horror rose from the back of the hall where, to the crashing report of revolvers, men fell like trees.

What was it? What was it? Who were those two men in the doorway?

"At 'em!" yelled Gerald Banks as he emptied his revolver into the fighting mass and smashed a face in with the butt end. "Hang on, up there! We're coming!"

"Whoop!" yelled Ian Gascoigne. "They're going! They're running! Tally-ho! Tally-ho! Gone away! Gone away!"

He was most completely mad. He laughed, he shouted as a knife grazed his cheek and backed against the wall, and pulled the knife out and flung it with an over-twist, and yelled as it struck home. "Let's charge, sir! Come on! They're off, they're——"

He yelled and fired, and missed and cursed.

"They've got her! They've got her!"

Unnoticed in the appalling uproar, Dong, the servant of the dead Gray Wolf, had crept up to the platform, his eyes upon Lotah, who stood quite close reloading the revolver of the man who had killed his master.

He made a sudden grab and caught her by the robes and pulled her down and sideways.

Neither Rex nor Trevor dared fire; as she lay she sheltered the monstrous brute who pulled her slowly over the edge as Rex pulled her back.

"Her arm, her arm!" cried Rex.

"Hold me! Pull me!" Lotah raised her free arm as she cried and drove Pya's dagger down, then swung up and back as Dong dropped, wounded, to the ground.

"They're gone from the back, they're gone."

"They're stampeding! They've panicked!" yelled the boy as, side by side with Gerald Banks, he ran up the Hall firing, and stopping to reload as Gerald Banks fired.

Rex and Trevor sprang from the platform and lifted the women down.

Ian Gascoigne, out of sheer excitement, fired right and left through the side doors, by which the men, using their knives, their fists as they fought, had run, out into the safety of the night.

"Come on! We've got to get clear of this. Reload, pack 'em full, we may have to fight our way through the street. Ah! Sa-t'ong Nyko-Gung." Gerald Banks looked down at the Bengal Tiger, who lay with Ka-lok's hand upon his hair. "Who murdered Graham Trevor and Mrs. Trevor and——"

"Not the baby! This is Lucy Trexor, Lotah, my wife, for whom those two men were gambling."

"My God! And t'other, I forget his name?"

"Chang-ku, up there." Rex jerked his head as he filled his clip. "Dead."

"Come along, then, come along, we've got to get you out of this. You two men first, the women next, we two bringing up the rear, firing as we go!"

"Just a little more, you top-holers," shouted Ian Gascoigne, "and you'll be safe. No time for rest, don't look at the floor, it's none too nice a sight. Won't that gong *ever* stop?"

"It's that that's worrying me," said Gerald Banks. "It's like a drum in the jungle, it's maddening, it'll bring the men out to kill!"

"Just to let 'em know we're coming," the boy cried as he fired on the top step. "Isn't it quiet?"

It was quiet. Quiet with the knowledge of disaster and death.

The news had spread like wildfire through the town of Nyko-Gung. Servants were clustered on the roof of the Great House, the women and children on the roofs of their houses, the men in the stables and up the mountainside.

The sound of lamentation filled the air.

Their masters were dead! Of what avail to fight—to die?

Their masters were dead!   The House of Nyko-Gung was
ended!   Their masters were dead!

The Birds of Paradise ran hither-thither, hiding their
jewels in the holes and corners of their houses; the Laughing Thrushes sat silent, listening to the gong which boomed
and stopped and boomed again as though struck by some
feeble hand.

The Mongolian eunuch ran from arch to arch, hiding in
the shadows.   Now was his time to gather the spoil of his
harvest of insult and bitterness, sown by the Birds of
Paradise in the heyday of their beauty.

The Star of Dawn!   Ha! the Star of Dawn with her
pearls and her diamonds and her bags of gold and precious
stones.   She ran from her scented chamber clutching a bag
of jewels to her breast, ran to outstrip the great shape
which followed behind her in the shadows.

In and out of the shadows, in and out of the arches, a
dance of death to the booming of the gong.

Two huge figures loomed out of the shadows as she ran.
She screamed and dropped her bag of jewels and turned and
sped, screaming, under an arch, out into the shadows.

"Ah—ah!" sighed Zo-p'o as he slipped the knife, hilt-
deep, between the eunuch's shoulders as he passed.   Dzo,
the cross-bred yak, beckoned her brother as she stuffed the
bag of precious stones into the capacious bosom of her
gown and ran with him towards the party of four white
men and two white women as they walked slowly down the
Street of Many Arches, firing as they walked.

*   *   *

There was no sign of life, no sound, excepting the reports
of the revolvers as the men, with Lotah and Cecily, walked
slowly through the totally deserted street.

The gong had stopped.   No, once more, feebly, faintly,

then again, stronger, stronger as the first sunbeam struck like a pointing finger up from behind the Himalayas, across the lightening sky.

At the end of the street they stopped and looked back.

Evil, desolate, abandoned, it lay; a white hand at a window, a white face; the tinkling of a thousand silver and golden bells swinging in the wind of fear; the necklace of ruby lamps flickering out in the breeze of the coming dawn.

They moved slowly on, to the beginning of the zigzag path leading to life and love and freedom.

And there they stood quite still, silent, watching the snow of the Everlasting Hills change from gray to white, to saffron, rose and gold, as the eagles soared up and up to greet the sun.

There was no sound as Lotah stood crushed to Rex's heart, Cecily with John Trevor's arm across her shoulders. They said no word, they could not, they dared not! Perils, death, seemed so little, so very little before the wonder of the dawn. They watched the figures on the roof of the dread House of Nyko-Gung and upon the roofs of the houses built against and up the base of the range of mountains at the back of the broad ledge.

The boy stood with his hands in his pockets, his mouth set, his eyes lit with a strange, dull fire.

Life! Death! Love!

The booming of the gong. Once—twice—again—and Yi joined her dead master.

" 'Twere wise to be gone!"

Zo-p'o whispered the words, and Ian Gascoigne, the instrument of Fate, stretched out his hand.

"Just to let them know that we have gone, that we leave them in peace."

He fired twice, and, as though in answer, with a mighty crack the peak of the "Little Finger of the Great Spirit" seemed to split from top to base as, with a thundering roar, the snows, the ice, the glaciers swept down, shaking the great mountains behind the ledge, so that their ice and glaciers and snows broke and rushed downward, burying for ever the houses and the people of the village of Nyko-Gung.

A tumult like the voices of the gods of battle; like a storm sweeping the mighty ocean; like the thunder of artillery!

Then peace!

Mountains of snow piled high where it had been flat, the "Little Finger of the Great Spirit" pointing, bleak and black, up to the blazing heavens as, stricken dumb with awe, Rex, with Lotah in his arms, left the shelter of a great rock and beckoned the others.

" 'Twere wise to be gone!"

The whispered words fell gently on the peaceful, sunlit air.

Lotah pointed back to where, under a pall of snow, Sa-t'ong and Chang-ku Nyko-Gung lay dead.

Something moved on the mountainside; something came running, running over the blocks of ice, a black speck, running at full speed.

"Sona!" whispered Lotah. "Sa-t'ong's bear!"

The bear had come to find her master.

Buried under a mountain of snow and ice? Ah! but not so deep that love could not find him, not so deep that she could not make a way to his heart.

They turned away, leaving her as she widened the path down, deep down, to where the Bengal Tiger lay asleep with Ka-lok's hand upon his hair.

The rim of the sun showed like a crimson thread above the shoulder of the far mountain, banners of gold swept up and across the sky, night fled.

"A new day," said John Trevor quietly.

"It is!" Cecily smiled. "Our new day."

Rex bent and kissed Lotah and whispered for her alone to hear.

She touched the beads shining like blue flames above her heart.

"Yes," she whispered.   "It is the Dawn!"

www.ingramcontent.com/pod-product-compliance
Lightning Source LLC
Chambersburg PA
CBHW030340020726
47493CB00004B/1348